GRAVE OF THE LAWGIVER

Also by Peter Tremayne

The Sister Fidelma mysteries

SMOKE IN THE WIND
THE HAUNTED ABBOT
BADGER'S MOON
THE LEPER'S BELL
WHISPERS OF THE DEAD
MASTER OF SOULS
A PRAYER FOR THE DAMNED
DANCING WITH DEMONS
THE COUNCIL OF THE CURSED
THE DOVE OF DEATH
THE CHALICE OF BLOOD
BEHOLD A PALE HORSE
THE SEVENTH TRUMPET
ATONEMENT OF BLOOD
THE DEVIL'S SEAL
THE SECOND DEATH
PENANCE OF THE DAMNED
NIGHT OF THE LIGHTBRINGER *
BLOODMOON *
BLOOD IN EDEN *
THE SHAPESHIFTER'S LAIR *
THE HOUSE OF DEATH *
DEATH OF A HERETIC *
REVENGE OF THE STORMBRINGER *
PROPHET OF BLOOD *

* available from Severn House

GRAVE OF THE LAWGIVER

Peter Tremayne

SEVERN
HOUSE

First US edition published in the USA in 2025
by Severn House, an imprint of Canongate Books Ltd,
14 High Street, Edinburgh EH1 1TE.

severnhouse.com

Copyright © Peter Tremayne, 2025

Cover and jacket design by Nick May at bluegecko22.com

All rights reserved including the right of reproduction in whole or in part in any form. The right of Peter Tremayne to be identified as the author of this work has been asserted in accordance with the Copyright, Designs & Patents Act 1988.

British Library Cataloguing-in-Publication Data
A CIP catalogue record for this title is available from the British Library.

ISBN-13: 978-1-4483-1510-9 (cased)
ISBN-13: 978-1-4483-1852-0 (paper)
ISBN-13: 978-1-4483-1511-6 (e-book)

This is a work of fiction. Names, characters, places and incidents are either the product of the author's imagination or are used fictitiously. Except where actual historical events and characters are being described for the storyline of this novel, all situations in this publication are fictitious and any resemblance to actual persons, living or dead, business establishments, events or locales is purely coincidental.

No part of this book may be used or reproduced in any manner for the purpose of training artificial intelligence technologies or systems. This work is reserved from text and data mining (Article 4(3) Directive (EU) 2019/790).

All Severn House titles are printed on acid-free paper.

Typeset in Times New Roman PS Std by Six Red Marbles UK,
Thetford, Norfolk.
Printed and bound in Great Britain by TJ Books, Padstow, Cornwall.

The manufacturer's authorised representative in the EU for product safety is Authorised Rep Compliance Ltd, 71 Lower Baggot Street, Dublin D02 P593 Ireland (arccompliance.com)

Praise for the Sister Fidelma mysteries

"Fascinating legends and mores of ancient Eire meld seamlessly with a complex mystery"
Kirkus Reviews on *Revenge of the Stormbringer*

"[A] multilayered, complex, atmospheric, locked-room mystery"
Booklist on *Revenge of the Stormbringer*

"An impressive achievement"
Publishers Weekly Starred Review of *Death of a Heretic*

"Tremayne plays fair with the readers while evoking the period in vivid detail. This long-running series remains as fresh and inventive as ever"
Publishers Weekly on *The House of Death*

"Tremayne expertly incorporates historical and legal details of the time into the suspenseful plot. This impressive volume bodes well for future series entries"
Publishers Weekly Starred Review of *The Shapeshifter's Lair*

About the author

Peter Tremayne is the fiction pseudonym of Peter Berresford Ellis, a well-known authority on the ancient Celts, who has utilised his knowledge of the Brehon law system and seventh-century Irish society to create a unique concept in detective fiction.

www.sisterfidelma.com

In warm memory of David Peppiatt (1940–2010),
headmaster at Kelsale Church of England VC
Primary School near Saxmundham (1975–1978),
who first suggested Brother Eadulf's origins
should be at Saxmundham, Suffolk, East Anglia

Infernus et perditio non replentur similiter et oculi hominum insatiabiles.

Hell and destruction are never full; so the eyes of man are never satisfied.
              Proverbs 27:20
    Vulgate Latin translation of Jerome, fourth century

pRINCIpAL ChARACTERS

Sister Fidelma of Cashel, a *dálaigh* or advocate of the law courts of seventh-century Ireland
Brother Eadulf, of Seaxmund's Ham, in the land of the South Folk of the kingdom of the East Angles, her companion

At Domnoc-wic
'Mad' Mul, a trader
Thuri, a tavernkeeper
Mildrith, his wife

At Seaxmund's Ham
Athelnoth, a *gerefa* (lawgiver), Eadulf's uncle
Osric, his servant
Wulfrun, Eadulf's young sister
Beornwulf, Thane of Seaxmund's Ham
Ardith, stewardess of his house
Crída, Beornwulf's *druhting* or chief retainer
Stuf, a *geburas* or thrall
Widow Eadgifu, an elderly woman
Mother Elfrida, a wise woman
Wiglaf, a farmer

Osred, a fellow farmer
Afenid, a fisherman's wife
Werferth, commander of the bodyguard of King Ealdwulf of the East Angles, and a friend of Beornwulf

At Ceol's Halh
Mother Notgide
Scead, her husband
Brother Boso, a religieux
Brother Ator, his disciple

At the Abbey of Domnoc-wic
Abbot Aecci
Brother Titill
Brother Osbald
Brother Bedwin

At Toft Monachorum
'Brother' Mede
Brother Wermund, the 'hermit'
Sledda, the friend of Wermund
Braggi, a herdsman

At Cnobheres Burg
Abbot Brecán
Brother Siadhal, his steward
Brother Indulf

The Kingdom of the East Angles AD 673

Seventh-Century Place Names	Modern Place Names	Meaning
Beoderic's Worth	Bury St Edmunds	Beorderic's enclosure
Ceol's Halh	Kelsale	Ceol's enclosure
Cnobheres Burg	Burgh Castle	Cnobheres Fort
Deor Ham	Dereham	Deer enclosure
Domnoc-wic	Dunwich	Deep water port
Eige	Ely	Island of Eels
Elmen Ham	North Elmham	Village of elm trees
Flegg-sig	Flegg Island	Island of yellow iris (flags)
Geoc-ford	Yoxford	Oxen Ford
Gipeswic	Ipswich	Gap or opening
Gyrwas	The Fens	Marshland or wetlands
Gyrwenigas	Exning	Place of Gyrwe's people
Heortes Ford	Hartford	The Stag's Ford
Ica	Iken	Ica's place
Mede Ham Stede	Peterborough	Mede's Homestead
Randle's Ham	Rendelsham	Town on shore edge
Saegham	Soham	Village by lake

Seaxmund's Ham	Saxmundham	Seaxmund's township
Suth Tun Hoo	Sutton Hoo	South Fort on land spur
Toft Monachorum	Toft Monks	Monk's enclosure

Seventh-Century River Names	Modern River Names	Meaning
Alde	Alde	Serenity
Blide	Blythe	Calmness
Cam	Cam	Crooked
Frome	Frome	Brisk river
Mennesmer	Minsmere	River mouth and marsh
Use	Ouse	Water
Sture	River Stour	Powerful river
Wahenhe	Waveney	Twisting back and forth
Eár	Yare	Gravel river

It has been difficult to map rivers of this period due to altering courses, de-bogging marshlands and coastal erosions and changes. The Sture (Stour) remains the borderland between the East Angles and East Saxons.

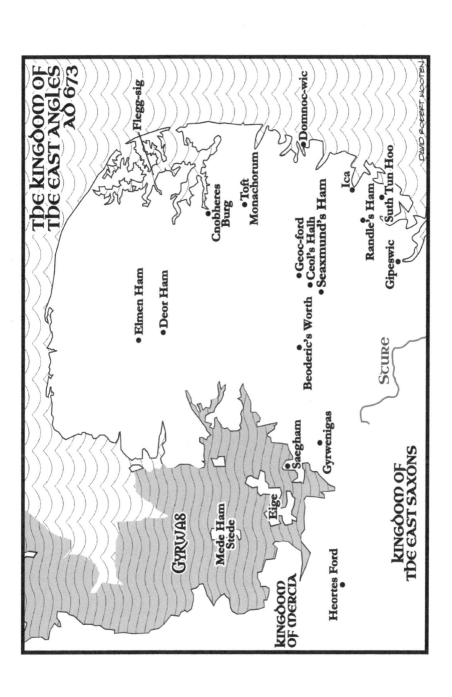

AUTHOR'S NOTE

This story is set in AD 673, during the harvest month that the Angles and Saxons called *Gerstmonath*, the month of the barley harvest, now known as September. Christianity had arrived in the Kingdom of the East Angles only seventy years before, and the Old Faith, with its ancient pagan deities and rituals, was still strong. *Gerstmonath* was the month when sacrifices were made to the *ése*, ancient deities, for a bountiful harvest.

Fidelma of Cashel has fulfilled her promise to accompany Brother Eadulf to visit the place of his birth and upbringing. This is Seaxmund's Ham, a township in the territory of the South Folk of the kingdom of the East Angles. Today it remains as Saxmundham, Suffolk, East Anglia.

Readers may remember that Fidelma paid her first visit here with Eadulf in AD 666, as recounted in *The Haunted Abbot*, set during the period of *Geolamonath*, equivalent to December/January, the time of the pagan festivals for the mid-winter solstice. From the Anglo-Saxon name *geola* derives the modern English word 'Yule', initially indicating a time of joking or playing games, which was later merged with the new Christmas festivities.

The council at The Stag's Ford (Heortes Ford), referred to in this story, was the first general council of the bishops of all the Anglo-Saxon Christian churches and their kings. The Venerable Bede records that this event took place in AD 673. The modern location of The Stag's Ford is Hartford, on the north bank of the Great Ouse river, now in Cambridgeshire. Importantly, it stood on the borders of the kingdoms of the East Angles and Mercia. The council was presided over by King Ealdwulf (AD 663–713) of the East Angles, and his bishop, Bisi of Dunwich (AD 609–c. 673/4). It was called on the authority of Theodoros, a Greek from Tarsus, Cilicia, who had been appointed by Rome as Archbishop of Cantwara-Burg (Canterbury), serving in office from AD 668–690.

I would like to express my appreciation to David Robert Wooten, Director of The International Sister Fidelma Society, for creating the sketch map of The Kingdom of the East Angles as it was in AD 673.

chapter one

The shouting had been growing louder until it became a resounding cacophony of voices at the gates of the Great Hall of Beornwulf, Thane of Seaxmund's Ham. Then a harsh voice rose above the noise and ordered silence.

Inside the main room of the Hall, a man, seated at a table before a blazing log fire, had been disturbed by the crescendo and sudden silence. He paused, his cut of cheese, balanced on his knife, halfway to his lips.

'By Thunor's Hammer!' he growled. 'What is this unmelodiousness that disturbs the breaking of my fast so early in the morning? It is barely beyond first light.'

His question, to the woman standing nearby with hands clasped nervously in front of her, was a snarl of anger.

'It sounds as if Crída has control of them, whatever they want,' she replied calmly.

'Go and see what this means, Ardith. If there is no good reason for this disturbance, then I promise that the culprits will be taught a sharp lesson in respect for their thane.'

Ardith, with hands still clasped in front of her, turned and hurried towards the main door of the Hall. Just before she reached it there was a thunderous knocking, suggesting an urgency of purpose. She opened the door to a weather-beaten-looking man, short and heavily built, with an authoritative air. From behind him came the sound of several people still with anxious voices raised, but more subdued than before.

The woman returned to the thane, accompanied by the man, and Beornwulf abandoned his breakfast and rose to meet him. He was a tall man whose tousled fair hair matched the colour of his large, shaggy beard. He was broad shouldered and muscular, bearing the carriage of a warrior. Beneath the shaggy hair was the face of a young man, no more than three decades old. His facial features were drawn together, half in anger, half in concern. His hand had automatically gone to the knife handle protruding from the sheath at his belt.

'What is this?' Beornwulf demanded of the visitor. 'Speak, Crída!'

'My lord, I have to report there is a house burning at the top end of the township,' the man responded. 'It is almost destroyed. The people are anxious and sent to alert us.'

'A house burning?' Beornwulf was surprised. 'Why am I vexed with this news? Is it so unusual?'

'It is a house up by the Gull's Stream,' confirmed the bringer of the news. 'The flames were fought, but to little avail.'

'Are the flames now contained?' Beornwulf demanded. 'Is there any danger of the fire spreading to other houses in the township?'

'The flames are isolated, my lord,' confirmed the man. 'There is no threat to other houses.'

Beornwulf exhaled noisily, letting his irritation show.

'Then why is there all this tumult, as if the entire township is threatened by some conflagration? Why am I pestered by this news? Are the Northumbrians raiding across our borders or have the Mercians threatened to march against us? What is all the commotion about? I have seen enough peasant houses burn down because these folk do not know how to tend their hearths properly.'

Crída shifted his weight uneasily from one leg to the other.

'My lord, those who brought the message say that the burnt house belonged to Athelnoth.'

At the name, Beornwulf's eyes widened.

'Athelnoth's house? The house of my *gerefa*?' he echoed in surprise.

'My lord, the word is that the lawgiver has perished in the conflagration, together with his servant Osric.'

The thane stared aghast at Crída, who was his *druhting*, his chief retainer, in charge of overseeing his estate.

'How can such a thing be?'

'It was Wiglaf the farmer who brought the news, accompanied by some concerned townsfolk. Rumours are already spreading about Northumbrian raids.'

'We must put a stop to that,' Beornwulf grunted. 'Panic is more destructive than reality.'

'Wiglaf was among the first to notice the fire and try to extinguish it, but the flames were strong,' Crída explained. 'By the time they intervened it was too late to do anything more than dampen the inferno. But Wiglaf felt he should report the alarming news to you. He told me that there was some mystery and malice in this deed.'

Beornwulf stood silently for a few moments. Then he ordered that Crída fetch his horse from the stable while he turned to the woman, Ardith, who, guessing his intention, handed him the signs of his rank: his sword and buckler, a small round shield carried on the forearm. The thane was conscious of his rank and privileges, and he knew that those he governed expected to see him attired befittingly. A sharp eye might notice there was something of an intimacy with the way Ardith helped Beornwulf adjust his appearance. As she was Beornwulf's stewardess, in control of his household servants, this was accepted.

'Mystery and malice?' she softly echoed Crída, clearly disturbed.

'Don't worry,' Beornwulf assured her. 'I have to be back shortly for I must ride to the King's Southern Fort this afternoon. Don't forget I am commanded by the king to attend his Witan, his personal council.'

Although Athelnoth's house was situated in the north of the township, just by the Gull's Stream, a small tributary of the river Frome, on whose banks the township was built, it was no great distance from the centre, where Beornwulf's own courtly Hall stood.

Beornwulf mounted his warhorse and, followed by Crída, he turned to the uneasy group that had gathered about the gates and, without pausing, assured them that all would be fine. Then he nudged the animal into a faster walking pace along the north track leading to the house of the *gerefa*.

It did not take Beornwulf and Crída long to reach the smouldering blackened ruins of the lawgiver's house, which had been built on its own plot of land. Several people were gathered there: men, women and children. They fell into respectful silence as Beornwulf and Crída halted their horses. Crída dismounted to inspect the smoking, acrid-smelling remains. The thane sat surveying the scene in the dawn's early light.

There was little to be done. The flames had almost completely levelled the wooden building, leaving only a few strong upright posts, and some beams that the fire had not been strong enough to demolish. Only by these supports could the outline of the once tall building be recognised.

'You say Athelnoth was unable to escape death by the flames?' Beornwulf addressed Crída while he looked around for a body.

'Athelnoth was overcome by the flames, my lord, as was his servant Osric. You would get clearer evidence from the witnesses,' Crída replied.

'Where are these witnesses?' Beornwulf demanded as he dismounted, and turned to the crowd that had gathered.

'Two men were leaders of those who tried to douse the flames,' replied Crída. 'There was Wiglaf the farmer, and Stuf the *geburas*.'

'Where are they?'

'Wiglaf came to the Hall to inform us of the news and he has been following us back on foot. He has not caught up with us as yet, but Stuf is here.' Crída turned to the group of people. 'Stuf, come forward and tell your lord what you know.'

There was a nervous silence and then a lean, emaciated-looking individual, dressed more like a beggar than any of his neighbours, came forward, bowing almost in a cringing attitude to mark his gesture of deference to his master.

A *geburas* was a position that was hardly more than a slave. In order to retain a degree of freedom, the *geburas* had to work for a number of days on his thane's estate for no remuneration. After working the appointed days, the *geburas* was allowed to do other work for pay. Stuf made an income from fishing and actually owned and lived on a small river craft.

'So, speak, man!' Beornwulf urged, as the man couldn't seem to find the courage to address him. Beornwulf knew the man well and had little liking for him.

'I was asleep in my boat, my lord. I meant to make an early start fishing today. I was going down to the Alde to fish for—'

'Get to the story of the fire!' Beornwulf snapped impatiently.

Stuf hesitated nervously before continuing. 'I was awakened in the darkness in my little boat, just before dawn. There were flickering lights and it was some time before I realised they were flames. The flames were from Athelnoth's house. I immediately crossed the river to moor on this side before I went to help.'

He paused as if inviting a question, but Beornwulf merely grunted in irritation, which Stuf took as encouragement to continue.

'By the time I reached here, several people had formed a line to the stream to fill buckets of water, but it was of little use. Wiglaf the farmer had already organised them. I later found out that Athelnoth and his manservant were both dead.'

'I was told that there was mystery and malice about this fire. What is meant by that?' Beornwulf glanced sharply at Crída.

'Wiglaf has just arrived back. He was the one who said that,' Crída replied, seemingly with relief. 'Come forward, Wiglaf. What did you mean by "mystery and malice"?'

A stockily built, muscular, dark-brown-haired countryman came forward. He stood uncomfortably before the thane, head bowed in obeisance.

'My cabin is nearby, as you may know, lord. I was awakened by my wife, who heard the crackle of burning wood and, seeing the flames, aroused me. We summoned neighbours and did our best to douse the fire.'

'You have not answered the question. "Mystery and malice"? Is that what you said?' Beornwulf demanded.

'Athelnoth, the lawgiver, was dead, but not by the flames,' the farmer declared.

'What do you mean?' the thane pressed.

'He was dead before the inferno,' the man replied quietly.

'Tell your lord what you found that gives you cause to make this deduction,' Crída said impatiently.

Wiglaf hesitated before explaining, 'We found the lawgiver with a dagger in his back. It was as if the body had been pushed back into the fiery building after that. The flames were not strong enough to incinerate him beyond recognition, as they had been with Osric. We could see that Athelnoth had been stabbed to death and thus, clearly, he did not die in the fire.'

Beornwulf was staring thoughtfully at the man. 'Are you telling me that an assassin came here, slew our lawgiver and his servant, then set fire to the house so that the bodies would be consumed in the flames?'

'It is not my place to decipher the meaning of such matters, lord,' Wiglaf replied. 'I am only a freeman and a farmer. I am just recounting what we found. If you go to the back of what was the lawgiver's house, you will find his body and see the dagger still protruding from it. The other body is unrecognisable because of the flames. But I suspect that Osric suffered the same death as his master.'

Beornwulf tightened his mouth in a grimace for a moment and then relaxed. He turned to his *druhting*. 'Crída, go and extract that dagger and bring it to me.'

Crída was back in a moment holding a dagger, which he handed to the thane.

Beornwulf took the blade between finger and thumb with a distasteful expression. There was still blood on it.

'This is not a warrior's weapon,' he observed immediately. Although thin and sharp, it was the sort of knife ladies might carry to the feasting table to enable them to cut their portion of meat or other offerings. He turned it over a few times. 'Good quality, a metal in one piece – the handle of wood, carved with a symbol on it,' he said quietly. Then he held it up to eye level. 'Curious. It is a fish symbol. What would that mean?'

Crída had the answer. 'Our priest, Brother Boso, once told me the fish symbol is used by members of the New Faith,' he offered. 'It is a secret sign of their allegiance.'

Beornwulf relapsed into thought for a moment before answering. 'So, what we know thus far is that Athelnoth's house was set on fire some time before dawn. That he was stabbed to death – and possibly his manservant was too – beforehand rather than that he perished in the flames. The fire was not noticed until Wiglaf's wife saw it and raised her husband and the neighbours. They helped douse the flames but were too late to save the building. Do I have the gist of the story so far?'

'That would seem to be what happened, lord,' Crída acknowledged.

Beornwulf had been peering about and his features became moulded with concern.

'What of Wulfrun? Where is Athelnoth's young niece, who lived with him?'

The crowd around him fell silent, some shuffling their feet and looking awkward.

Beornwulf's features hardened. 'Why has no one mentioned her before? Did anyone remember seeing her? Shame! As soon as the ashes cool, I need volunteers to search the ruins to find her body.'

'You expect the body to be found inside the ruins, lord?' Crída asked sceptically. 'Only the bodies of Athelnoth and his servant were found. Maybe she was away from the house when this happened? She would often carry messages for her uncle.'

'Have a search organised and make sure the bodies are clearly identified. If her body is not in the ruins, then inquiries must be made so that she is found. Someone killed Athelnoth and his servant. Therefore it is logical that they would kill his niece as well. Find her.'

They all knew that Wulfrun was the sixteen-year-old ward of Athelnoth. She was the younger sister of his nephew, who had left Seaxmund's Ham years before to follow the New Faith in other lands.

Beornwulf turned back to his horse with Crída at his heels.

'I am due to attend the king's Witan this afternoon,' he said. 'I have to leave before the sun reaches its zenith. I shall appoint you in charge while I am gone. I shall take a couple of estate workers who can serve as my personal bodyguard. Probably I shall not return until tomorrow about nightfall.'

He was about to remount his horse when there was a small disturbance in the crowd. A man came forward, almost propelling a woman.

'My lord, begging your pardon, here is the Widow Eadgifu. She has something to say.'

Beornwulf turned to examine the woman. He vaguely recognised her. He recalled that her husband had once been a good bowman who had marched with the late King Athelhere's army against Oswy of Northumbria. He had been killed in battle alongside King Athelhere. Widow Eadgifu was elderly now and the thane had heard it said that her mind was lacking its former vigour.

Now he noticed that the old woman had a vacant look about her, and he tried to sound gentle and encouraging. 'Have you something to say about this matter?'

'It's not time for the dancing,' she mumbled, looking about her in bewilderment.

Another woman appeared alongside her.

'Forgive her, my lord. I am taking care of her. She is elderly and often her mind wanders.'

Beornwulf knew this woman, Mother Elfrida, as a wise healer in the township.

'I thank you, Mother Elfrida. Do you think she has anything that she can relate that is helpful in identifying the culprits?'

'Impossible to say, lord. From disjointed thoughts sometimes truths may emerge.'

Just then Widow Eadgifu started moaning softly, almost to herself, her pale eyes raised and fixed on the thane.

'My mind is not lost among the nine worlds, young lord. Not lost yet. I will speak. When the sun lay below the eastern horizon, there were signs of the lamentations of Tiw, who throws the symbols of the *ése*, the sacred ones, across the canopy of our sky in order to warn us of grief to come.' Her quavering voice rose in a spellbinding rhythm.

Mother Elfrida turned and whispered an apology to the thane.

'She is one who does not abandon the Old Faith, lord. I must look after her. You will understand, lord.'

Beornwulf looked kindly on the old woman and bent down to her, his voice encouraging.

'Tell me, old one, after seeing these signs of Tiw, the sky goddess, which offered foreboding . . . what then? What did you see?'

'I saw the warning that the Nicors, the water spirits, would be needed before the morning grew older. I was up to look after my chickens when I saw the flames of Athelnoth's house. I was hurrying towards it then I saw two strangers coming down the lane on horses. They came from Athelnoth's house. The flames were behind them. Something made me take shelter behind a tree because I feared strangers on that night.'

'You saw that they were strangers? Why did you fear them?'

'They were of the religious, the New Faith. Worse than that, they rode black warhorses.'

'Religious of the New Faith on horseback? On warhorses?' Beornwulf was surprised. Apart from the bishops, the *episcopus* of the religion, as they called them, most religious of the New Faith, did not travel by horse, let alone own such breeds as could be described as warhorses. The bishops often made it a point of walking or riding on asses.

'They were on horseback like mounted demons,' confirmed the woman.

'But you recognised them as religious? How did you know that?'

'One had his cowl off, but I saw his robes, and the symbol hanging from his neck was such as worn by those foreign folk.'

'Foreign folk?'

'Those of Ierne.'

'She means Hibernians, lord,' Crída explained. 'I am told that they still dwell in a religious house in the old, ruined fortress by the sea just north of here.'

'You mean that they were of those who came here and were the first to start preaching the New Faith in this kingdom?' Beornwulf frowned. 'They came from Hibernia in my father's time. It was old King Sigeberht who gave them the ruins of the Roman fortress on the banks of the gravel river. That was thirty years ago or more.'

The old woman shuddered and gave a sigh. 'I was a young woman then. I saw them when they came to talk about this new god who had been killed by men. They had funny names and spoke in strange tongues with curious manners.'

'Are you sure they were Hibernians? It was not yet fully light when you saw them.'

'It was light enough, my lord. I saw them as they passed. Neither of them saw me. They were heading north along the river. Then I heard the alarm cries as my neighbours awoke and realised there was a fire at the *gerefa*'s house. I went to see what was amiss. They were trying to douse the flames but the fire was too strong.'

Beornwulf's eyes were narrowed. 'Hibernian religious, mounted on warhorses and riding north, you say? That could take them to Cnobheres Burg, the community where they live. Widow Eadgifu, you have our thanks. This is most helpful information.'

He turned to Mother Elfrida, who was standing by her companion. 'Guard her well, Mother Elfrida, my faithful *weofodthegn*. Ensure no harm comes to her.'

He turned his horse and mounted, looking down at his *druhting*.

'You have your orders, Crída. If you discover word of the whereabouts of Athelnoth's niece, let me know before I ride south to the Witan at midday.'

'I will endeavour to come with news, either good or bad, before you depart, my lord,' his *druhting* replied.

Beornwulf returned to his Hall with grim thoughts. Now he had no lawgiver to guide him. He uttered a silent curse as he recalled that he should have told Crída to send word to the hamlet of Ceol's Halh, where Brother Boso had his chapel. Custom dictated that the bodies should be buried immediately, usually at midnight on the day of death. Brother Boso was the Christian religieux who had authority to conduct such rites.

Beornwulf was uneasy. If he had not been summoned to King Ealdwulf's Witan, he would probably have raised his *fyrd,* or local bodyguard, to descend on the Hibernian religious house at Cnobheres Burg to seek answers and retribution. He had no doubt that the old woman spoke the truth. There was much suspicion about the Hibernians in the kingdom these days, especially since their defeat at the great council debate at Abbess Hilda's abbey in Streoneshalh in Northumbria. Yet he did not want to act without the authority of the local *ealdorman* – a leading noble – or some senior member of the Witan.

At the Hall Beornwulf found Ardith was waiting with mead to wash the taste of the acrid smoke from his mouth. He sprawled moodily in front of the fire. He did not need to interpret the question on her face.

'Athelnoth has been murdered, along with his servant Osric. His house was burnt down and there is no sign of his niece Wulfrun. Old Widow Eadgifu claims that she saw two Hibernian religious riding away on warhorses at the time of the fire.'

Ardith raised her brows. 'Hibernian religious riding warhorses? That doesn't sound right. They don't usually travel by ponies, let alone warhorses.'

'Maybe not, but curious things happen these days, especially with the rumours about the council at The Stag's Ford,' Beornwulf muttered.

'When do you depart for the king's Witan?'

'At midday. You had best let the master of the stables know to have horses for me and two of my men as we ride forth for Suth Tun Hoo.'

The southern fort on a spur of land towards the southern border to the kingdom was King Ealdwulf's favourite residence.

Beornwulf was beginning to fret at the swift passage of the

sun, showing the approaching zenith, when Crída returned to the Hall and was shown straight to his impatient lord.

'Well?' Beornwulf demanded before Crída could form a preamble. 'Speak plainly, man.'

'There is no sign of the girl's body in the ruins,' Crída replied. 'Nor has anyone seen her since just before the fire was noticed.'

'No sign?' repeated the thane grimly.

'We went through the burnt ruins carefully. I will swear by the light of Bealdor that she was not in the house when it was set ablaze.'

The thane sniffed disparagingly. 'Better these days to take oath by a stronger deity than one who was banished for ever to take his mystic light to rule in the dark vaults of *Hélham*,' he reflected.

'I have already sent to Brother Boso, at his chapel in Ceol's Halh,' continued Crída. 'I've asked him to come and say whatever words are necessary for the burial of Athelnoth and his servant. That should be done tonight or by the morning light tomorrow. I know that you say that you will not return until nightfall tomorrow. But the condition of the bodies is such . . .'

He did not have to explain further.

'That is good,' Beornwulf sighed. 'When our former kings converted to the New Faith, they declared that we must all convert. Such changes are taking a time. King Ealdwulf seems to support the new rules from Rome, brought to us by the Greek Theodoros.'

'Leave it in my hands, my lord. We will not offend the new High Bishop.'

Beornwulf rose suddenly from his chair. For some moments he stood, hands on hips, gazing down at the flickering wood fire.

'This day has not started well,' he mused softly. 'I like not such mysteries. Perhaps old Widow Eadgifu was right. It is not a day blessed by our gods.' He hesitated and smiled grimly at Crída. 'Nor is it blessed by any god.'

He dismissed Crída with a gesture of his hand before calling to Ardith. When she appeared, he instructed her to send for his master of the stables.

'My escort and I will ride at once.' Beornwulf sounded tired. He paused and added: 'I wonder why I have been summoned to the king's Witan.'

'Perhaps to learn of the decisions from The Stag's Ford,' Ardith suggested, but she was not happy either. 'Perhaps it is to learn what further evils can now afflict us.'

CHAPTER TWO

Fidelma felt a curious mixture of anxiety and sadness as she watched the changing expression on the face of her husband Eadulf as he moved to the ship's rail to stare at the approaching shoreline. The harbour, with its stone quayside and several wooden jetties, was now clearly visible through the sea mist. She could see large sea-going vessels were moored. Watching Eadulf's face, she saw it was animated with something other than normal excitement. It seemed that he was almost on the verge of tears. His lips appeared to quiver slightly and yet there was no denying that the overall expression was one of happy anticipation. It was an expression of pleasure that he was trying hard to restrain. His forward-leaning stance reminded her of a dog that had recognised its master in the distance. It occurred to her that he wanted to leap across the bow of the slow-manoeuvring vessel and fly over the waves towards the land.

Then Eadulf glanced round, met Fidelma's gaze and smiled broadly.

'Home!' he shouted. 'Home, after seven years!'

Fidelma was thankful that he immediately turned back to look at the approaching harbour, so that he missed what she knew must be apparent on her face: a mask of irritation dissolving into sadness.

Home? She had always thought that home was not the place where one had been born but where one was happy. Her home was in the fortress of her brother Colgú, king of Muman, the largest and most south-westerly of the five kingdoms of Éireann. Yet, in spite of the long years that Eadulf had spent happily married to her, in her homeland he always seemed to regard himself as a foreigner.

Although King Colgú had made him a *fine thacair*, one adopted under law into the Eóghanacht family, which extended the rights and protection of the royal dynasty to him, Eadulf was not happy. He often referred to himself as a *murchairde*, one thrown up by the sea upon a strange shore. He had taken to long periods of brooding. In his mind he remained Eadulf of Seaxmund's Ham, in the country of the South Folk of the Kingdom of the East Angles. He was the son of a *gerefa*, or lawgiver, and of no princely rank.

Home, after seven years! Fidelma felt a strange foreboding at his words. What did they imply for their relationship, and their young son Alchú? It was during the winter months, seven years ago, when Fidelma had last accompanied Eadulf to this kingdom in answer to a request for help from his friend Brother Botulf of Aldred's abbey, that she had told Eadulf that she wanted to return to Cashel so their baby could be born there. Now she was glad that they had left Alchú behind in Cashel in the hands of his nurse Muirgen, and under the caring eye of her brother Colgú. She had had many doubts and forebodings before she had agreed to accompany Eadulf on this journey back to his place of birth; to the land and culture that he had been raised in. Yet she knew it had to be done otherwise the future of their relationship would be darkened by clouds of remorse and unhappiness. She no longer wanted to live with an 'if' dominating their thoughts.

Now, as they neared the shore, she realised that soon their positions would be reversed. She would be the foreigner cast upon a strange shore and stripped of her rights and status. She had first been sent to these strange kingdoms as a legal delegate to the council at Streoneshalh, at Hilda's abbey, where the Northumbrian King Oswy had decided his kingdom should follow the rules and rites of the Roman Church. It was at that council of Streoneshalh that she had met Eadulf, who had then been advising the opposite side in the great debate.

After King Oswy's decision to follow Rome, she had heard that many had not embraced the reforms as advocated by Bishop Wilfrid. Many Hibernian missionaries and teachers were no longer welcome in Northumbria. They had left to seek converts in the other kingdoms of the Angles and Saxons. She had even heard that many of her countrymen had been badly treated in spite of entering these kingdoms years before to teach the New Faith, as well as literacy and learning. Some Angles and Saxons had left to follow the New Faith to Hibernia rather than remain among their own people. Now she felt nervous, wondering how she would be treated. She had long ago left the religious to become her brother's *dálaigh*, or legal adviser. Did that allow her legal status to be recognised among her husband's people? Her mind swam with questions but, above all, she was faced with a sense of foreboding.

She realised that she had to shake off this feeling, if only to be able to survive this visit to Eadulf's homeland.

'So this port is where your home is?' she asked, trying to force her thoughts to conversation. She had not travelled this coast before because on the last visit the journey had been overland from Dyfed.

Eadulf turned again with an expression of pride.

'This is the closer to my home of two deep-water harbours in our kingdom. It is called Domnoc-wic, which means "the harbour of deep water". The other is called Gipeswic, just south of here.'

'There seem to be many merchant vessels in this harbour,' Fidelma observed, glancing round and trying to ignore his reference to 'our' kingdom. 'I presume a lot of trade is done here.'

'It has become a busy port since my almost namesake, Ealdwulf, became king,' Eadulf agreed.

'Then is your birthplace, Seaxmund's Ham, near?'

'Once ashore it will be a short ride, mainly to the south-east of here.'

'Remind me, who is this Seaxmund and what is his ham?' She tried to remember.

It was Eadulf's turn to hide his irritation because he had explained the background of his township to Fidelma several times.

'A *ham* is an enclosure usually by a river, or a meadow, which has grown into a settlement and permanent township. We are told that Seaxmund was our ancestor, a warrior, who settled at the place with his followers. The name means "hand of victory", what we call a "protector". It is just a simple inland township with nothing of significance to mark it.'

'But you still have family there?'

'My mother was dead before I grew into youth and my father died not long after I joined the religious. But I have a young sister there and she has been raised by my uncle. I was still a youth when I decided to follow the teachers from your country. They were led by Fursa and his brothers, who spread the New Faith and demonstrated your methods of healing. I was so enamoured by their teachings that I went to Tuam Drecain, in your land, to study them. It was then your most famous school of medicine . . .'

'That much of your story you have told me a hundred times, but you say that you have a sister?'

'My mother died from a bee sting while giving her birth. She was young when I left to follow the New Faith.'

'We did not see her seven years ago,' Fidelma pointed out.

'That was because she was absent getting schooling here in Domnoc-wic.'

'What of your relatives in this Seaxmund's township? I don't recall seeing much of them when we visited, apart from your uncle.'

'I am sure we did,' Eadulf frowned, trying to remember. 'As you know, my uncle became the hereditary *gerefa*, the lawgiver, when my father died.'

'Apart from that visit, seven years ago, you have not been in touch with your family since coming to Éireann? I thought this role of lawgiver, or *gerefa,* was passed from father to son. How were you not called back here to fulfil this role?'

'It is only partially hereditary. One has to study as well as be born to it,' Eadulf admitted.

'I am still unsure what a *gerefa* is. One who composes the laws of your people?'

'The laws are made by the king and his Witan, his council of wise men. They are advisers based on our ancient traditions. The *gerefa* merely recites the law from his oral knowledge of it, in the manner of a judge.'

'You don't have a written law text?' Fidelma was surprised.

'Now that our people are abandoning oral traditions and adopting writing and literacy, some kingdoms are writing down the laws,' Eadulf explained. 'Aethelberht, who was king of the Cantwara fifty or more years ago, was the first to have the laws of his kingdom written down. He was the first to embrace the New Faith.'

'Aethelberht of the Cantwara . . .' Fidelma was thoughtful. 'I have heard of him. Didn't his son reject his father's New Faith and revert to the ancient gods, slaughtering everyone who did not revert back again?'

'A complicated story. As you know, there are many who remain steadfast to the old religion. All our kings can trace their descent from one or other of the sons of the great god Woden.'

'Including your own king?'

'Our kings claim descent from Woden's fourth son, and from

him descends Wuffa, son of Wehha. So our kings are known as the Wuffingus . . .'

A sudden shouting distracted them. It was the captain of the vessel. His crew were using ropes and poles to slip the vessel sideways towards the quayside and preparing to make fast alongside. Lines of hemp rope were thrown and secured to bring the vessel closer and then secured to the bollards before there was a further flurry of activity as passengers were helped to disembark and others of the crew prepared to unload cargo to the waiting wagons already pulled up to receive it.

It seemed only a moment later that Fidelma and Eadulf had left the quayside and found themselves in the main square of the township, with its many stone and wooden buildings. On a hill overlooking the port Fidelma could see what looked like a Roman fortress. Around the port were buildings that seemed mainly to be warehouses. The crowds of people surprised Fidelma, although they generally ignored the visitors. Fidelma had insisted on wearing the simple robes of a religieuse. There was nothing to indicate her rank or status except the cross that hung around her neck. She carried a satchel containing domestic items as she and Eadulf had decided it was pointless trying to persuade any servant or bodyguard to accompany them on this trip. Eadulf carried only one extra bag and his *lés*, his medical bag, which he had been in the habit of carrying since his studies at Tuam Drecain. Other than that, there was nothing to distinguish either of them from the milling throng in the town.

They had paused to take in the sights and sounds of the busy sea port.

'It has certainly grown wealthy since we were last here,' Eadulf said with pride in his voice.

'I am afraid "we" were never here,' Fidelma pointed out acidly. 'When I accompanied you to see your friend Brother Botulf, we went to his abbey at a place on a river called the Alde, near the coast. After that we had a brief visit to your Seaxmund's Ham.'

Eadulf hesitated, pressing his lips together. He was realising that his attempt to include Fidelma in his world was meeting with resistance.

'Well, this place has doubled in size, I am sure,' he went on hurriedly. 'The abbey didn't exist so prominently then. See the building on that rise that looks like a Roman fortress? One of the sailors on our ship said that was where a Frankish religieux called Felix was allowed by Sigeberht to form a community and become abbot.'

'Who was Sigeberht?' Fidelma asked patiently after a moment.

'He was our king when I was a boy. He had become a devout follower of the New Faith. So devout that he gave up the kingship to his brother Egric and went into that abbey to contemplate the Faith. Then the Mercians, who adhered to the old gods and goddesses, invaded, destroying the churches, abbeys, and even Fursa's abbey at Cnobheres Burg. So Sigeberht left his community and joined his brother to repel the invaders. They say that he advanced on his enemies with only the staff of his Faith to protect him.'

'And was he protected?' Fidelma asked cynically, expecting some miraculous story.

Eadulf shrugged. 'No, he was cut down. King Egric was also slain in the battle. This was about twenty years ago. The result was that we found ourselves paying tribute to Penda, the pagan king of the Mercians.'

Fidelma was not surprised. 'Something stronger than a symbol is often needed to protect one.' There was irony in her tone. 'I suppose a lot of Christians were killed then? What of Felix, whom you mentioned?'

'He survived by taking refuse among the Gyrwas, the Fen people. He built another abbey at Saegham. That means a town by the lake. That is where he died and is buried.'

'Fen people?' Fidelma frowned.

'The Gyrwas dwell in the eastern marshlands. Like the bog land in your country,' Eadulf replied. 'A low, flat and swampy land. The Gyrwas have their own princes to govern them. These now pay tribute to our king. They do not have a good reputation.'

Fidelma heaved a deep sigh. 'I am sure there is much for me to learn about this country. However, I will not learn while standing here in this market square and trying to take in all this new information. It's hard enough trying to absorb your language.'

She immediately regretted the remark, but something about Eadulf's enthusiasm for being back in his homeland made her nervous and depressed. He was such a different person in Muman. She shook her head to clear her thoughts.

'If you say that Seaxmund's town, or *ham*, as you call it, is some distance from here, had we not better start finding out where we can obtain horses?' she inquired pointedly. 'Or perhaps we can find a carter, a merchant, who might be travelling in that direction. We could ask for a ride on his vehicle.'

Eadulf was hesitant. In his boyhood and youth, his family had not owned more than a few goats and a cow for milking. He had been used to walking everywhere and perhaps that was why he had never been a good horseman. In contrast, Fidelma seemed to have been born in the saddle. If he were honest, he had not even considered the idea of obtaining horses. As in his youth, he had not thought beyond walking, or seeing what boats would be heading westward along the rivers that would join up with the Frome, the brisk river that ran south through Seaxmund's Ham. He felt momentarily awkward at his lack of consideration. He glanced around at the people walking by and hailed one.

'Is there a hostelry, a stable, where ponies might be engaged or purchased?' he asked.

The man barely halted his stride.

'Who do you think is trading up at the market?' was the terse response.

Fidelma and Eadulf looked to where a great commotion could be heard and saw people with animals all heading in one direction. Eadulf decided to follow them. It was a right decision, for when he and Fidelma came to the corner of the last building they saw the land opened into an even larger square packed with stalls, carts and a myriad animals in pens: pigs, goats, mules and all manner of poultry. Immediately they were assailed by a roar of human voices and animal protests. The business of the market was in full swing.

'Well, this seems to be the likely place to find horses,' Fidelma commented, trying not to sound overly sarcastic.

Eadulf was peering around to see if he could spot a likely horse trader.

'There's a small crowd at the far end with some ponies,' he said pointing. 'Even if they don't have anything to suit us, they probably know someone who does.'

Fidelma followed him through the crowds, forcing a smile but shaking her head when enthusiastic traders tried to push items in front of her and let forth a flood of vocabulary she had little hope of following. Eventually, Eadulf led her to an area where cages of ducks, chicken and pheasants were being carried to wooden wagons. The odour drifting in the air changed abruptly and unpleasantly as they passed by pig enclosures and one containing a disgruntled pair of boars. Further on they saw several horses tethered and, before them, a group of men arguing. Fidelma hoped that Eadulf understood the shouted arguments as he approached them and tried to call for their attention.

One of the men turned towards him and he suddenly froze. His eyes widened as they wandered beyond Eadulf to examine Fidelma.

'By the sacred Cats of Freyja!' the man exploded in a sudden bellow. 'It is the wandering Christians who resolve mysteries! May we be preserved from all evil dwellers of Aelfheim!'

His voice was a roar almost of challenge, turning the heads of people not only in his group but also passers-by.

He was a coarse, ruddy-faced man with a bushy beard; middle aged, broad shouldered, with flaxen hair and a skin tanned by the elements. His thick-set shoulders and arms gave him the build of a farmer or a smith. His eyes were piercing and bright above a beak-like nose. There was something familiar about him.

'You don't remember me? Didn't I take care of your ponies when you were last wandering this land? And didn't I tell you that there is always a warm bed in my farmhouse when you need it? A warm bed, sweet cider and a wholesome meal.'

It was Fidelma who recognised the man first. 'You are Mad Mul,' she exclaimed. 'Mul the trader.'

The man gave another great yell of laughter. 'Once seen, I am never forgotten!' he roared. 'But perhaps less "mad" than I once was.'

'Mul of Frig's Tun,' Eadulf confirmed more quietly, although with a broadening look of pleasure. 'What are you doing here?'

'The same that I was doing seven years ago – selling my wares. How else can one keep a farm sustainable and feed a wife and family? And what of you both? Are you still chasing mysteries in the service to your new gods?'

'Not exactly. I have come to visit my birthplace at Seaxmund's Ham and see my family.'

'I saw a foreign merchant ship coming into the port. Were you off that?' Mul asked.

'We were,' Fidelma confirmed. 'And now we are looking for a means to get us to Eadulf's township, which I am told is a ride from here . . . if we had horses.'

Mul nodded. 'Right enough. I can probably help you. But not yet.'

Fidelma's brows drew together. 'Why not?'

'Because, dear lady, it is seven years since you were last here and now we must drink, feast and speak of these changing years.'

Inwardly, Fidelma groaned, but logically she knew that the hospitality of one who had helped them in the past should be something to honour, as it was in her culture, especially when Mul had half promised to help them get transport to Seaxmund's Ham.

'Come,' Mul announced. 'If you have just stepped off that merchant ship you will want sustenance and liquid refreshment. These will be provided as you will be my guests. Then we will talk about how I can help you in your travels.' He pointed to the far end of the marketplace. 'There is a tavern there, where I am staying. The food is good and the mead is even better.'

It was Eadulf who hesitated, but Fidelma was already nodding in agreement.

'A good idea, Mul. Lead on and I am sure you will be able to answer Eadulf's many questions as to how this port has grown in importance and why there seems so much trade about since he last saw it.'

Mul chuckled as he gestured for them to follow him.

'The kingdom has had much good luck in recent years,' he told them as he led the way to the tavern. 'So much prosperity has come to the kingdom that King Ealdwulf has started to mint his own gold coinage this very year. Now we can contend against other kingdoms like the Cantwara.'

'But a sailor told me that we still have to pay tribute to Mercia,' Eadulf pointed out. 'Doesn't that keep the kingdom subservient and in poverty?'

Mul sniffed deprecatingly. 'Then the sailor knew nothing. We thought all would be better when Oswy, king of the Northumbrians, defeated Penda of Mercia at Winwaed. That was in a battle in which our own King Athelhere fell. We did not realise how bad things would become when Oswy's son Ecgfrith became their king.'

Fidelma closed her eyes in exasperation for a moment.

'It seems you have a confusion of kings, all of whom have names unpronounceable to my ears.'

Eadulf flushed in annoyance. 'I suppose the same may be said of the kings and rulers of the Hibernians to our ears. Let Mul continue his story for I would hear how my country has changed.'

Mul did not appear to hear anything antagonistic in the exchange and he continued happily.

'It was when Penda's son Wulfhere rose to power in Mercia and became a convert of the New Faith that those things altered,' he went on, enthusiastically. 'Wulfhere felt the Northumbrians had dominated the kingdoms for far too long. He started to take back what the Northumbrians had annexed. When Ealdwulf became king of the East Angles, he and Wulfhere formed an alliance that successfully prevented Northumbria from expanding. On the contrary, in losing their previous conquests Northumbria became weakened. Three years ago, Wulfhere even became overlord of the East Saxons. So now we are also protected on our southern border. With Wulfhere as a powerful ally to the north and to the east, Northumbria would not try to invade us again. There is also talk that Wulfhere has made the Mercian armies so strong that he will eventually take over all the other kingdoms to the west and establish himself as the *Bretwalda*, ruler of the Britons, as well as of the Angles and Saxons. For us, it has meant nearly ten years of peace – a peace only glimpsed when you were last here, friend Eadulf.'

Fidelma made no comment, observing how this continual warfare seemed to be a matter of pride, a way of life, to these people, and not a means to achieve any specific end except power and dominance.

'Doesn't it mean King Ealdwulf has to pay tribute to Wulfhere?' Eadulf asked.

'Only in use of our ports or to supply warriors in case of war. Needless to say, that works as well for us. If ever Northumbria attacks us, Mercia will come to our aid.'

They reached the doors of the large log-built tavern and Mul pushed them open. The place was not busy, and Mul and his guests were soon comfortably seated. The owner of the tavern, an elderly, thick-set man named Thuri, greeted Mul like a long-lost brother. Having been told by Fidelma that she would find mead too heavy, Mul ordered cider, and they were soon relaxing as he pointed out that, being near the sea, the choice of fish and seafood was of a quality that was impossible to over-praise.

'If we have a long ride before us, it might not be wise to eat much,' Fidelma pointed out.

'It might also be wise to think further ahead,' Mul smiled.

Eadulf frowned. 'I don't understand.'

'Ah, my friend Eadulf,' Mul replied with a shake of his head, 'you were a country lad here once. Just go to the door and look eastward for we are on the east coast here.'

Eadulf was still frowning but before he could make a move to obey, Fidelma smiled faintly.

'You mean that at this time of year, dusk is descending and will soon overtake us. That will mean, providing we get suitable horses or other means of transport, we would be riding in darkness and certainly arriving at our destination in blackness. Perhaps it is not a good time to arrive in a strange place.'

Mul inclined his head in an affirmative gesture. 'It is not a good idea anyway to be travelling in the darkness of night, and especially in these times. There are many about who would prey on those coming or going to the markets of this port.'

'You mean some who would not shrink from robbery?' Eadulf asked.

Fidelma caught Mul's meaning 'So you suggest that we try to find a room and do not proceed until after sun-up tomorrow?'

'Precisely, lady, but you do not have to try to find a room. As you are my guests, I will have a word with old Thuri there and secure you a room for the night. In the meantime, let us make a choice of food.' He signalled to the elderly landlord, who came across. 'And now to food, good Thuri. What can you provide?'

'We have a popular dish of lump crab dressed in butter and wild garlic with shelled shrimp. It goes well with a dish of codling, also made with garlic and burdock. There are the usual dishes of parsnips, carrots and I think we still have mushrooms.'

'Lump crab I know,' Fidelma replied. 'The large muscles of the crab connected to the swimming fins? Yes, an excellent dish. But what is a codling?'

It was Eadulf who tried to translate it. 'A small, immature codfish, a young *trosc*, as you call it in Hibernia. It is fished in the shallow waters off the coast here.'

'That sounds fine.' Fidelma was impressed. 'It appears as though you are a good cook, Thuri.'

'Ah, no, lady.' The man spread his hands in self-deprecation. 'It is my wife Mildrith who prepares all the meals.'

Having made their decision, they sat back with more cider and with Mul smiling at his former friends in adventure.

'So, after several years, Brother Eadulf, you have returned to the township of your youth?'

'As I said,' Eadulf confirmed.

'You are not here for the council meeting?'

'No, my friend. What council meeting would this be?'

'The word is that there is a great council of the kings and bishops of all the kingdoms of the Angles and the Saxons. The council has been meeting at a place called Heortes Ford, The Stag's Ford, which is on the border between our kingdom and that of Mercia. They say that a Greek has been appointed by Vitalian, the Bishop of Rome, to be the chief bishop of the Cantwara, and, as such, Rome's representative of all the bishops here. At least he is determined to unite all the kingdoms in obedience to Rome.'

Fidelma was interested.

'For what purpose? I have heard nothing of this, although someone is always calling a council to discuss what is correct and not correct in the New Faith.'

Mul sighed. 'I know what you mean. The rumour that we hear is this Greek, who has been sent to us from Rome, proposes that our King Ealdwulf and his bishop Bisi be the prime instigators of this council. The cynics say that if the council fails to agree then our kingdom will be held responsible for the failure.'

'Well, we did not know about this,' Eadulf admitted. 'Who is this Greek?'

'Theodoros of Tarsus,' replied Mul. 'He has been a few years among the Cantwara and now he hopes to extend his authority.'

'We are certainly not here to attend any such council,' Fidelma said firmly, before Eadulf could speak. 'I would have to be given authority by my king and his bishop Cuán of Imleach to witness the thoughts of such a council, but not to participate.'

Eadulf was shaking his head. 'Ten years ago, the council of Streoneshalh decided on these things for Northumbria. What is the difference now?'

Fidelma smiled cynically as she explained. 'That was when Oswy called everyone to debate the Faith in Northumbria. It was decided that his kingdom would follow Rome in their reform of the rites and philosophies of the Faith. They did not want those who continued the original teachings, like the Hibernians. Everyone was allowed to argue which rites and philosophies the religious should follow. Of course, only Oswy had the power to decide, and he decided to follow Rome. His leading advocate was Wilfrid of Northumbria.'

'Wilfrid of Northumbria?' Mul mused. 'I have heard of him. Gossip has it that he is not well liked by the current king of Northumbria and so is currently in exile as bishop to the South Saxons, where the Old Faith is still strong.'

Fidelma was not surprised. 'Oswy's decisions were only for

the Churches in Northumbria so that let the other kingdoms follow their own path.'

'This Theodoros will have a hard job on his hands to make everyone believe the same thing,' Eadulf said with a shrug. 'There is no way that you can unite people in belief, for men's minds are always so diverse and argumentative. Even when a group of people agree on something at one moment, the next moment they are developing different interpretations of what they have already agreed.'

Mul did not seem interested. 'Anyway,' he said, 'you say that you are not here to attend any such council as called by the Greek?'

'I no longer take part in such matters,' Fidelma assured him. 'When I was young I trained and qualified in the law of my people. I joined an abbey only to advise them on law. I became disillusioned with the people I encountered as they were not interested in law, in truth or justice. So I left the religious – although not the religion – and when my brother became king of Muman, I accepted the position of his legal adviser. So I am not emotionally involved in religion and such councils where old men argue endlessly about what should or should not be believed.'

'When you left, I was so impressed by your ability to solve mysteries that I took myself into the abbey at Alde, where your friend Botulf had been, and I sought an education,' Mul admitted, surprisingly. 'I endured it for four years: how to spell and how to write. That was long enough for me to see that mankind does not always need to change the name of their philosophy or religion. People in their hearts always remain the same as when they started. I left and went back to my farm to work with animals, which are more consistent in their nature.'

Eadulf regarded him with deep interest. 'I thought there was something different about you, Mul. The book learning seems to sit well on you. You never thought to use it as a means of improving your station?'

'Improve?' Mul seemed astonished. 'What better station in life is there but to be a good farmer? To live in fields and woods and raise animals or wrest food from plants you set in the ground or from the trees you nurture. I would not exchange that for any fortress and the slaves of an *ealdorman*. No, not even for the finest hall of a rich *aetheling*.'

Seeing Fidelma's puzzled frown, Eadulf quickly explained: 'An *aetheling* is a prince and an *ealdorman* is a leading noble.'

Mul agreed with a smile. 'We have a young *aetheling* named Alfwald, the youngest son of King Ealdwulf. Fidelma, your knowledge of our language is much improved with Eadulf's teaching. Personally, I would rather be taken to *Hélham*, the home of the dead, than lose my farm and freedom in the countryside.'

'*Hélham*? But don't you believe in another world, which only the virtuous are privileged to go to when they die?' Fidelma asked.

'*Éormensyll*, the World Tree, supports nine worlds,' Mul replied solemnly. 'We are taught that above the World Tree is *Heofon*, the bright and shining place. Me? I prefer to dwell forever in *Middangeard*, the Middle Earth.'

'Then your years in Aldred's abbey did not make you into a Christian?' Eadulf sounded almost disapproving.

'It taught me about the New Faith until I came to know those who practised it,' Mul conceded. 'I found that I admired the teachings of this Christ, but of those who claimed him as their deity . . .? They seemed to have no relationship at all with him. So I would rather be sent to *Aelthéf* or *Éttenhám* – the worlds of the elves or the giants,' he replied gravely.

'Isn't it difficult to be of the Old Faith in this kingdom these days?' Fidelma pressed him, out of genuine interest.

Mul laughed shortly. 'Even though it is claimed that our former mighty King Redwald was converted at the court of Aethelberht of the Cantwara, he also had temples built to the old gods and goddess at the same time as those dedicated to Christ. Until Sigeberht became king and encouraged the preachers from your country, Fursa, Foillan and Ultan, and gave them Cnobheres Burg in which to set up their abbey, Christians were not always welcome here, begging your pardon, Sister Fidelma. But it was Anna, our king twenty years ago, who made Christianity almost compulsory. He thought it would make the kingdom stronger against Northumbria and against Mercia. Both those kingdoms, larger than ours, wanted to reduce our land to keep us in obeisance to them. So now we find our King Ealdwulf has to form alliances with Mercia to prevent our being attacked by Northumbria.'

'Politics and religion,' Fidelma sighed. 'Why don't the kings and their religious leaders stop insisting their people believe what *they* believe? Religion becomes another tribal banner to entice people into war.'

Eadulf smiled sadly. 'Did not Syrus write that those who claim that politics and religion do not mix understand neither?' He knew that Fidelma was often fond of quoting Syrus, a Greek slave taken to Rome whose writings bought him his freedom.

'If he didn't write it then he should have,' Fidelma replied sarcastically. 'And another thing Syrus should have remarked upon is that without sleep one should abandon logic.'

They had not realised that the evening had passed so quickly and they should be rested for the journey the following morning.

chapter three

It was the aroma of freshly baked bread that awoke Fidelma. It had been late when they had finally left Mul and retired to the room that Thuri's wife Mildrith had prepared for them. It had been some time before Fidelma fell asleep, for the evening had provided her with much information to try to absorb. Thankfully, Eadulf was able to interpret most difficult phrases that Mul had used. Even resorting to Latin, a *lingua franca* of the religious, was not helpful because although Mul had spent time at Aldred's abbey, he was not conversationally fluent in that language. However, Fidelma was always enthusiastic when it came to learning about different cultures, although she was not in the best of spirits, due to her preoccupation with the changes in Eadulf.

She went to the bowl in the corner of the room and poured some water from a jug into it, splashing her face and hands in the custom of her people. In her culture, a full body wash was only taken at night before the evening meal. She picked up her comb bag, took out a comb and mirror and tidied her hair. When she had finished she heard Eadulf coming out of his slumber, groaning a little in protest at the amount of cider or mead he had imbibed the previous evening.

'I am going to break my fast,' she told him. 'The smell of

freshly baked bread is too alluring for me to want to delay longer. Follow me down when you are ready.'

She interpreted the unintelligible grunt he replied with as affirmative.

She made her way down the short flight of wooden stairs into the almost deserted main room of the inn. It seemed most guests had already breakfasted and departed. She looked around and chose a table. As she was making her way across to it, Thuri the innkeeper emerged and wished her a pleasant morning.

She realised the sun was already streaming its light from a cloudless sky.

'A good day for seafaring folk,' she remarked.

'That it is,' agreed the innkeeper. 'And a good day for the market. We rely on the market and its merchants for our trade.'

'You have a busy port here and so your business must be a good one.'

'We are second largest next to that of Gipeswic, which is to the south of here,' Thuri confirmed. 'It is not far from the great Southern Fort where our king dwells.'

'The Southern Fort? The Suth Tun Hoo? What does the "hoo" signify?'

'It means a spur of land. Are you interested in the meanings of names?'

'I am.' She paused and looked around. 'Where is Mul?' she inquired.

The innkeeper shrugged. 'He has the constitution of an ox, that one. He was up at cock-crow and heading home to his farmstead at Frig's Tun.'

Seeing her dismayed expression, he incorrectly interpreted it and added: 'Don't concern yourself. He paid for the food and the room before he left. He assured me that you were his guests.'

'It is not that,' Fidelma said quickly, not wishing to seem ungrateful. 'I was just surprised he left without a farewell.'

'That is Mul for you. He is always acting on the spur of the moment. But now, what will you break your fast with? It is all paid for.'

Fidelma had just ordered a mug of goat's milk and fresh baked bread, butter and some fruit when Eadulf came to join her. He saw her scowl and demanded to know what the matter was.

'Our friend Mul,' she responded shortly. 'He has already left for his farmstead while we slept.'

Eadulf was indifferent. 'We were due to leave him this morning and be on the road to Seaxmund's Ham. We would have parted from him anyway.'

'You fail to see the point,' she replied irritably. 'He promised to find us some ponies to make that journey.'

Eadulf chuckled sardonically. 'You have a suspicious mind. He promised to loan us the use of ponies and, if you ask the innkeeper, you will be told that Mul has left two ponies for our use. They are in his stable. I just asked Mildrith as I came down. We can have them for as long as we need them. When we have done with them, we can return them to his farm or send a message to him to say where we have left them.'

Fidelma was surprised, and more than embarrassed at her ungenerous thoughts.

'I misjudged the man entirely,' she acknowledged contritely.

'You must not judge people too quickly,' Eadulf advised. 'Above all people, you should know about hasty conclusions.'

While she agreed with his comment, it made her feel petulant. A short time ago she would have made some humorous riposte. She could not understand the shortness of temper that she had developed since . . . since when? She must spend more time in contemplation of her irascible mood and new-gained intolerance.

She was still fretting about her feelings when, a short time later, she and Eadulf left the tavern and the busy port on the two dappled-grey ponies that Mul had left them. They were sturdy and good-natured animals, and she approved of Mul's choice.

Eadulf led the way southward from the port, following a main track until they came to a small estuary and turned inland, where it was clear many merchants had used the route through marshland alongside a broad river. Eadulf told her its name was Mennesmer. It was a curious landscape, without hills or mountains. There was hardly a ripple on the surface of the river to denote currents. Fidelma had an impression of the countryside as a great flat wetland and endless sky. What dry land there was, was barely higher than the marshland and was intersected by many streams, crisscrossing and feeding one another. She picked out the numerous sedges and rushes along its borders. The blossoms were all withering in accordance with the season. Along this river route were groups of trees familiar to Fidelma: mainly clumps of willow and alder but also, here and there, gnarled and twisted oaks.

Eadulf seemed in good humour and turned more than once to her with his old, amused smile to break the silence.

'If it is good to believe in Fate, we must have been destined to meet Mul after all these years, otherwise a search for ponies for the journey might have taken some time.'

Fidelma's face was immobile. She had realised that he would raise the matter eventually to criticise her misjudgement of Mul.

'Mistakes in judgement can happen when one is not in full possession of the facts,' she replied irritably. 'Mul had not said anything to me about loaning us his ponies. You should have told me.'

'Was it not a rush to judgement instead of waiting to be put in full possession of the facts?' Eadulf countered.

'I was told that he had left and no more was said. So I thought there was no more to be said.' There was an icy defence in her voice. 'How was I to suspect that Mul had left these two ponies at that tavern with instructions for Thuri and Mildrith to give them to us and say we could use them for as long as we needed the use of them? I was not told.'

'Mul is a generous man,' Eadulf replied quietly. 'Moral men still exist, even among the people here.'

Fidelma felt increasingly annoyed at what she perceived was his sarcasm. 'I would not doubt it. Unfortunately, Saxons have garnered a reputation as raiders whose intentions seem to centre on looting, pillaging and raiding. Ask the Britons who, until a few centuries ago, lived happily on the whole of this land. Now they are driven in their droves westward or to seek sanctuary in the land of the Gauls or in Hibernia to escape annihilation after the confiscation of their lands.'

Eadulf was regretting bringing up the point. 'Anyway, we are Angles here.'

'As you know, my language has no separate word for Angles,' she replied frostily. 'For us there is no difference between the sounds of the Angles and Saxons. You are all *Sasanach*. I remember, years ago, that you did not correct people when they called you Saxon.'

'The reason was as you just said. You had no separate word for Angle. Anyway, Mul is an Angle and of high principles.'

'Indeed, he is,' Fidelma said, exasperated by now. Then, changing her tone, she asked: 'Can you remember where his farm is?'

'Frig's Tun? As I recall it was near Aldred's abbey, where we went to see Brother Botulf. It is where the Alde river empties out into the eastern sea. It is a little place by Ica's stream, which feeds the river. Why?'

'We must ensure the return of these beasts to him. He must have brought them to Domnoc-wic, to the market, to sell, and now he has let us have use of them for no fee at all. As you said – a generous man. What he had to say about the coming of the New Faith to your people was fascinating. I had not realised that when your king converted to the New Faith he ordered everyone to be converted.'

'It might be thought so, but the old beliefs run deep.'

'I try to understand why people act as they do,' she replied thoughtfully. 'You always told me that you were raised in the old beliefs before you were converted to the New Faith.'

'I was only a youth when the teachers from your country arrived in our kingdom. Fursa and his brothers came from the kingdom of Connacht, as I recall.'

'From what Mul has said, religious of the Hibernian Churches are not as welcome in these lands as they were before. The decision at Streoneshalh, in favour of the new reforms of Rome, as advocated by Bishop Wilfrid, has had a profound influence, and not just in Northumbria but in these other kingdoms.'

'I can understand it.' Eadulf shrugged. 'The people of your island don't seem to have had sympathy with the Angles or Saxons because of our wars against the Britons. I have been told there is hard fighting against the Dumnonians in the southwest. The kingdom of the West Saxons is threatened daily by the warriors of the Dumnonian king, Judhael ap Erbin.'

'Where did you hear this?' Fidelma was interested.

'On the boat bringing us here. I also hear there is great danger now from the north, from the Picts, or Cruithne, as you call them. Also from the Dál Riada clans. The Hibernian missionaries and teachers seem to support them all.'

Fidelma was without sympathy.

'I think we, Hibernians, are sympathetic with anyone who suddenly finds their country and homeland being invaded and colonised by others who are alien in culture and language. They are driven from their lands, which are being taken over. Don't forget, it is only two centuries since your people landed here, where the Britons lived in their own kingdoms, many emerging after centuries of Roman rule. Now they are being pushed west or are even having to flee the island. Why is it that your people are not content with what they have but want more and more of the land? They have even invented a title showing their intentions: *Bretwalda* – overlord of the Britons. Each king wants to earn that title.'

Eadulf stirred uncomfortably. He had never heard Fidelma so condemning before. He had noticed that since they had left Port Lairge and the shores of her brother's kingdom of Muman, there seemed to have been a change in her attitude, which he could not comprehend.

'I can understand what you say,' he eventually acknowledged. 'I hope you will not let your views run free while you are here. Ask yourself whether everyone should be responsible for the ambitions of their rulers.'

Fidelma's mouth tightened. 'I am a king's daughter and sister to a king. Have no worries I shall not be looking for conflict. However, as well you know, among our people we do have laws that show the path to take to curtail an unjust ruler, especially one who exceeds the power he is given.'

She looked up at the blue sky and noticed the position of the sun. They had made a slow start and it was already approaching midday. She glanced at Eadulf and saw the excitement on his features as he peered ahead.

'You will be finally at your birthplace,' she commented softly, almost sadly. 'I always found it curious that you did not follow your father as a hereditary judge of the law of your people. I know you encountered the teachers of the New Faith from my land and that you went to Tuam Drecain to study the healing arts. Even then, you abandoned those studies before qualifying, and instead went to Rome to learn their ways in the New Faith before coming to Streoneshalh to support Bishop Wilfrid and his pro-Roman faction.'

Eadulf was silent for a while.

'I suppose as a youth I was a restless soul,' he replied eventually. 'Perhaps that is why we formed our bonds. You were often travelling to resolve mysteries and give judgements. I was fascinated that a woman could do this in your culture. Even recently, we were travelling to all parts of your brother's kingdom, and even beyond, to investigate some mystery or other on his behalf.'

'Now we have come here to the place of your boyhood,' Fidelma said with a soft inflection. 'What is it you hope to find here? Your lost youth?'

Eadulf was disconcerted by the question.

'I am not sure what I expect to find. Perhaps I merely seek an assurance.'

'An assurance?'

'That I made the right choice in choosing the New Faith; an assurance that I did the right thing in going to your country to study and then in going on to Rome before returning.'

'So you are not sure that you have made the right decisions in life?'

'Perhaps everyone reaches an age when they question if they have made the right decisions. I hope to find a resolution.' Eadulf, in concentrating his mind on the unease that had grown within him over the years, was missing the fact that he was appearing to reject his very relationship with Fidelma.

'So the uncertainty starts in the fact that you did not complete your studies at Tuam Drecain?' Fidelma inquired coldly, but not pointing this out. 'Yet you were not uncertain when you left this place, which meant leaving your father and all you had known. Did nothing along the path away from this township give you any fulfilment? You seem to have completed no undertaking. You left before finishing your studies in the healing arts and went to Rome to see how their interpretations of the New Faith differed from those you were originally taught.'

'I did absorb enough of Rome's philosophies to go to Northumbria to attend the council at Abbess Hilda's abbey as an adviser to Bishop Wilfrid, who led the arguments against the Hibernians. That is where we met. Then I went back to Rome and happened to meet you again when we joined to investigate the murder of Archbishop Wighard. I suppose such travels gave me less time to think about consequences.'

'I left you in Rome and went back to Cashel,' Fidelma reflected.

'It was not my choice that you later arrived in my country. Seven years ago I persuaded myself to come with you to this kingdom. I knew it was not the country I would settle in.'

'I followed you back to your country, when you became pregnant.'

Fidelma's features dissolved into a mask of repressed anger.

'Out of guilt or because you wanted to make a genuine life with me in Cashel?'

Eadulf blinked. His lips tightened.

'That is a shallow thought,' he replied.

'Even on the eve of our wedding you were expressing doubts.'

Eadulf could not restrain his look of surprise.

'You believe that I did not know?' Fidelma continue grimly before he could speak. 'I was told you had expressed such sentiments.'

Eadulf found himself realising that he was in a sea of mixed emotions that he thought he had mastered years before.

'I have been a good father to our son Alchú,' he began, seeking justification in himself.

Fidelma shook her head. 'You are searching for certainties, so do not settle for excuses. You have returned to this land of your birth and upbringing. Do you think that you will find what you are searching for?'

For a moment, Eadulf's jaw rose belligerently. Then he relaxed and shrugged.

'Perhaps. Perhaps not. I won't know if I don't try.'

'If you find what you want here, then what?'

Eadulf was hesitant. 'I am not sure what you mean?'

'Will our son Alchú have a place in your future existence or, indeed, will I? Has that thought ever raised itself?'

Eadulf had opened his mouth to respond when the reality of the words struck home to him. It was as if he was suddenly devoid of breath, opening and closing his mouth as if trying to swallow air.

Fidelma's expression hardened again at his hesitation.

'I have no plans beyond returning to my son and my home as soon as it can be arranged.' Her statement was delivered coldly and devoid of any emotional rise in tone.

Eadulf stared at her for a moment but he felt he could make no reply. There was a sudden recognition of a curious remoteness. He found himself staring at her as if she had suddenly become a stranger. A series of self-justifications burst through his mind, but he was a prisoner of his tongue. He could not articulate into sentences the words that jumped into his thoughts; words that were too inadequate or too banal. For the first time since he had first encountered Fidelma at the council at Streoneshalh he was experiencing a feeling of unfamiliarity between them. The silence was almost threatening. The words and images raced through Eadulf's mind but there seemed nothing he could articulate to ease the tension.

They had ridden barely a few minutes more in silence when an unexpected event forced a return to rationality. A large black shadow seemed to sweep at Fidelma, causing her to tense and her pony to miss a step and almost stumble. It recovered and Fidelma glanced around to catch sight of her assailant. A large dark shadow was rising into the sky from almost ground level a short distance away.

'What was that?' she demanded in alarm. 'A kestrel? It couldn't have been an eagle.'

'It was what we call a marsh harrier,' Eadulf found himself replying. 'You will see plenty of those about. It's a large bird of prey in these parts.'

'Why did it attack me?'

'It was not attacking you,' Eadulf assured her. 'It is a hunting bird that lives on small mammals or weaker birds. I think it was in the middle of a dive for some animal and your pony stepped into its path. This is its territory – low-lying marsh country – and it likes to nest in the reeds and marshes here.'

Fidelma sniffed in annoyance. 'It could have driven straight into me.'

'I think you are misjudging how quick and agile these birds are.'

'Are there any other animals that I should beware of?' she inquired, unconvinced.

'Most creatures are afraid of man,' Eadulf replied, easing back into a more comfortable mood with a silent expression of thanks that a confrontation had been avoided. 'Even the most poisonous of our snakes will shy away once aware of the approach of humans. Why, when I was a boy, my friend and I used to play in a place deep in the marsh woodlands that was famous for these poisonous snakes but they did not bother us. We built a camp there. Well, a tree house, anyway.'

'Did you say a poisonous snake?'

'There is only one kind, which rarely attacks unless confronted. We call it a *naedre*. It can even cause death when it bites. But we knew the places it likes, and so kept safe.'

Fidelma shivered. She had a dislike of reptiles, for she had grown up in a land that harboured no snakes.

'Thank God I dwell in a country without such creatures,' she muttered.

Eadulf grimaced in acknowledgment. 'So I am told. The religious claim that the Blessed Patricius drove them out.'

'There are more ancient and better legends than that as to why there are no poisonous snakes in the land of the goddess Éire,' Fidelma replied dryly.

'What better stories?' Eadulf demanded.

'Have I not told you of Golamh, a warrior, who took service with the Egyptian pharaoh called Nectanebus? He served the pharaoh so well that he was allowed to marry his daughter, who was named Scota. Because Golamh had once saved someone from the bite of a deadly snake called an asp, it was prophesised that Golamh would take his two sons, Eber Fionn and Eremon, and go to a land where there would be no poisonous snakes and that they and their descendants would rule it. While Golamh did not reach the island, Scota his widow and their sons did. Scota was killed fighting in the subsequent conquest.'

'Why does that cause a memory to stir?' Eadulf frowned, puzzled.

'Because you have been west of Sliabh Luachra, in my brother's kingdom, in the territory of Uaman, the ill-fated lord of the Pass of Sliabh Mis. In that area is Scota's Glen. That was where Scota, daughter of the pharaoh and widow to Golamh, was killed and buried. That is why it is still so named.'

Eadulf was cynically amused again. 'I suppose that story is spread to claim your ancient gods sent the snakes to this country to antagonise the Saxons instead?'

'I doubt it,' she replied in a dour tone, not rising to his humour. 'Your ancestors were not even here then. Your people did not invade the land of the Britons until after the Romans left.'

At least the story had broken the growing tension, as Fidelma had intended. But she could not help thinking that at some future point there would be questions to be answered that might inevitably lead to conflict. She was not looking forward to it.

Fidelma suddenly halted her pony and stared ahead.

'We are coming to a bend in the river,' she pointed. 'There is a tributary that goes due south. Do we continue straight on or proceed south?'

'This point is called Geoc-ford, the Oxen Ford. The lesser river going south is the Frome, which means a brisk river. We will take the track along this eastern side. The river runs through Seaxmund's Ham. So we turn south along it,' he replied confidently. 'Beyond this ford, westward, Mennesmer is called the river of oxen.'

'There is a building ahead,' she called abruptly. 'Is that the outskirts of Seaxmund's Ham?'

She could not remember much about her one brief visit with Eadulf seven years before. Then, of course, they had been mainly south of this place, down at what Mul had called Suth Tun Hoo, the South Fort where the king dwelt.

'We are still a distance north of it. Those buildings by the river are marking a ford where a yoke of oxen has room to pass over the river in safety.'

'A yoke?' she frowned.

'What you called *cuinge*, and in the tongue of the Angles is called *geoc* or yoke. This is the ford of the yoked oxen.'

'The names of all places are given for a meaning,' Fidelma acknowledged. 'It is an absorbing study. But does it bring us nearer to our destination?'

'We are almost there,' Eadulf assured her. 'It is only a short track south along this bank, following this river into Seaxmund's Ham. Ah, look! There are some people on the other side of the river there.'

She followed the indication of his hand. There was a small stationary group on horseback apparently discussing something. They appeared from their positon quite animated, for one of them was waving his arms as if to emphasise his statements. She realised there were three riders, all clad in the brown homespun robes affected by a growing number of religious to denote their calling.

Yet there was something different about them. One was bare headed, and when he turned his head the thick black hair carried no tonsure, which seemed unusual for a religious. The other two mounted figures had cowls over their heads.

'Religious,' Eadulf muttered unnecessarily to Fidelma. He leant forward on his pony and raised his voice in greeting. *'Whis thú hál!'* To Fidelma it sounded like a curse but it took a moment for her memory to realise Eadulf was greeting them in his language: 'Be you in health!' Whatever they took as the meaning, the three riders looked startled and reacted as if Eadulf really had cursed them. They kicked their horses into a canter and headed into the western trees on the far side of the river, where they were quickly lost to sight.

Eadulf's astonishment was obvious as he halted his pony.

'Your religious folk don't seem to be friendly to strangers.' Fidelma pursed her lips cynically.

'I don't understand, unless they were foreigners,' Eadulf replied in bewilderment. Then he added hurriedly in case Fidelma interpreted it as an insult: 'I mean, travelling religious from Rome who do not speak the language of the country. Perhaps I should have greeted them in Latin.'

Fidelma did not bother to reply and motioned they should move on.

They passed through a small copse of red dogwood, which she knew indicated growth in a wet marshy soil, even if she had not been aware of the nature of the country still bestrewn with sedges, moss and ferns.

They were coming to another group of wooden cabins and buildings on the western side of the river. Eadulf indicated them with a nod of his head.

'Those few cabins and the farmstead ahead are named Ceol's Halh. *Halh* means a place or land belonging to Ceol. He was one of the first who settled in this area.'

'But how far to Seaxmund's Ham?' Fidelma repeated, suppressing an exasperated groan. The buildings he indicated were, to her eyes, more a collection of hovels, huts around a larger wooden building. She wanted to tell Eadulf that he did not have to explain every place name even though he had come to know that she was more than interested in such things. However, by now she was feeling tired and irritable, and wondering how she might deal with the inevitable discussion on their future.

'Well, we don't need to enter that hamlet,' he said. 'We follow the river a short distance before we come to my township. My uncle's house is on the north side of the township and I am sure we will want for nothing once we get to his door.'

'I hope your uncle is more friendly than those three religious.' She motioned back to the place Eadulf called the Oxen Ford. 'Did I meet your uncle seven years ago?'

'We saw him only once and briefly.'

'He is now your only relative apart from your young sister?'

Eadulf was almost dismissive. 'Practically. My uncle looks after my younger sister. Most of my family perished during the Yellow Plague and others were killed in the various raids from Northumbria and the pagans from Mercia. As far as I know, apart from my uncle, my young sister is my only other close relative. She would be about sixteen years old now.'

'Until we arrived here, you've never before mentioned a younger sister,' Fidelma observed.

'She probably has a family of her own by now. That is no reason why I should not acknowledge her. She was raised by my uncle after my father's death.'

'Odd that you never mentioned her in the years we have been together,' Fidelma repeated with emphasis.

'There did not seem any necessity.' Eadulf sounded curiously indifferent. 'Nor was there an appropriate moment to raise it.'

'So we did not meet her when we were here seven years ago?'

At that moment he halted. 'Here we are.' He pointed to a cluster of houses. 'That small stream that flows into the river ahead is one that runs in front of our . . . of my home. It is called the Gull's Stream. My uncle's house is just along the lane here. I am surprised that we did not see its roof because it is two storeys in height . . .'

He suddenly grew quiet.

Riding slightly behind him, Fidelma frowned. 'What is it?' she asked.

'I don't know . . .' he began hesitantly. 'Something is wrong. Come on, the river is not deep and we can ford it here.'

She followed him as he walked his pony across the fast-flowing but shallow waters to a track on the far side. Beyond a few sturdy wooden buildings she could see a blackened area. From the charred remains she was able to see that a building of some substance had once stood there. Eadulf let out a muffled cry as he halted and slid off his horse. He stood staring at burnt debris in disbelief.

'The house!' he gasped. 'The house of my father . . . my uncle's house . . . it's gone.'

chapter four

Fidelma drew her pony alongside Eadulf and was dismounting before she saw the extent of the blackened ruins about which he had exclaimed in horror.

'It can't have happened long ago, judging by the condition,' she said slowly. 'I can still smell the acrid, choking smell of burnt timbers.' She paused, realising that she was being insensitive, then turned to Eadulf. 'Are you sure that this was your uncle's house?'

Eadulf stared at the building, his face full of emotion.

'I was born here. My mother and father died here. When I left, my uncle became the lawgiver and took over the house. He lived here with my young sister and a servant.'

He took a few steps towards the charred remains of the building. His hands clenched and unclenched spasmodically. 'What can have happened?'

He stood looking at the burnt timbers as if seeking an answer. Only the strong upright piles that had supported the walls and roof, all blackened and scorched, were discernible. It was clear that the fire had not spread far into the grounds surrounding the house because the animal sheds there were all untouched by the flames. These were now empty. Obviously, there had been an attempt to remove items from the burning building. A jumble of broken ornaments and possessions lay strewn across the scorched grass and remaining patches of planted garden. Abandoned buckets showed that there had been an attempt to put out the flames.

'I was born here,' Eadulf repeated in a dull, shocked tone as he stared around.

'We had better find someone who will be able to tell us what happened and where we might find your uncle,' Fidelma prompted.

She had to repeat it twice before Eadulf turned his head.

'What did you say?'

She repeated herself a third time since she had his attention.

'Oh, yes. Yes, there are a few houses further along the stream here,' Eadulf mumbled, still in shock at the sight.

He grabbed the reins of his pony but did not remount. The next house was on a bend only a short distance away.

An elderly woman was standing just outside the door and beating a rug on a wood rail with a stick.

She heard their approach, and looked round with surprise, taking in the appearance of her visitors and their ponies. She was quite elderly, with white, wispy hair, her eyes pale in a fleshy shrunken face.

'Tell me,' Eadulf called anxiously as they approached, 'what happened to the building that was here?' He indicated the blackened ruins.

The woman glanced at him and then at Fidelma, returning to him with a scowl.

'Who are you?' she countered.

'I am Eadulf, son of Wulfric. I have come back to see my uncle Athelnoth and my young sister Wulfrun.'

Just then a second elderly woman emerged from the house, limping forward, back arched and supported with the aid of a stick. She, too, had straggling white hair in a pale face, and her eyes were so pale that it was almost impossible to tell if they had pupils.

Eadulf recognised her.

'Widow Eadgifu! It is me, Eadulf. Don't you know me?'

She crooked her head to one side as if it enabled her to hear better.

'Why should I?' she muttered, her watery eyes narrowing suspiciously. 'Who are you claiming to be?'

'Eadulf, son of Wulfric,' he repeated loudly. 'I came to see my uncle Athelnoth.'

The woman who had been beating the rug shook her head.

'You look like an outlander to me. What do you want here?'

'Come, Widow Eadgifu,' Eadulf said, ignoring the other woman, 'you surely remember the young man who left here to join the religious? I am Eadulf, son of Wulfric.'

The bent woman still stared at him without recognition. Then she raised her voice, summoning up a pugnacious tone. 'He's gone. Be off with you, stranger. My husband will be here soon.'

'I know your man is long dead,' Eadulf replied with exasperation. 'Come, woman. Think well. I am Eadulf and have come to find my uncle Athelnoth. What has happened here? His house is burnt down. Where is he? Where is my sister Wulfrun?'

The woman blinked but there was no recognition in the pale, watery eyes.

'The priest left him just now,' she suddenly said.

'The priest? Where is he? What happened? Is my uncle hurt? Tell me!'

Eadulf raised his voice in a flurry of questions. The old woman seemed to be strangely detached, standing muttering to herself. His raised voice had started to attract a few people. They had emerged from the surrounding buildings to discover what was amiss and were closing around the visitors before Eadulf realised it.

The woman who had been beating the rug moved closer to the other elderly woman as if to protect her.

'Do not fear, Widow Eadgifu,' she said. 'I will not let these foreigners threaten you.'

Eadulf turned to the spectators as if in appeal.

'I am Eadulf, son of Wulfric. I came to see my uncle. His house has been burnt down, and recently. I want to know what happened. Where is he and—'

'Wulfric is long dead,' interrupted another man. 'Who does the stranger claim to be?'

'He was talking about the lawgiver,' the old woman, Widow Eadgifu, muttered absently.

The other woman pointed to Fidelma with suspicion.

'That woman is one of those foreigners; one of those who inhabit Cnobheres Burg. Wasn't it witnessed that such people were seen riding off from the direction of Athelnoth's house even when the flames were devouring it? These might be the culprits!'

Eadulf was still trying to make himself heard.

'Someone must know me. I am Eadulf—'

'I don't recognise him,' proclaimed another man who had joined the circle.

'They are probably those who burnt Athelnoth's place and now return to see if there is any loot that they had overlooked,' another voice accused from the crowd.

The growing crowd around them now seemed menacing.

'Here's Wiglaf the farmer,' someone called. 'He was speaking with lord Beornwulf yesterday, just after the fire. He'll know what to do.'

A broad-shouldered, bearded man pushed forward through the crowd.

'Strangers, Wiglaf,' cried the old woman who had been beating the rug. 'We think they were involved in setting the fire at Athelnoth's house. What shall we do with them?'

'We should do nothing with them, Mother Elfrida, but act

according to the law,' the burly man replied. 'Has Beornwulf been sent for?'

'He left to attend the king's Witan yesterday,' replied the woman, who seemed to be the companion of Widow Eadgifu.

The man called Wiglaf examined Fidelma with suspicion before he looked at Eadulf.

'Your woman is a Hibernian.' It was a statement of fact. 'We will have to send for the thane's *druhting*. As Beornwulf is at Suth Tun Hoo, his *druhting* will be in charge.'

Eadulf knew this was the senior retainer of a thane.

'But he has gone hunting,' another voice countered.

'He was here to arrange the funeral rites this morning. But perhaps Brother Boso is still here. He might advise us.'

'Brother Boso has returned to his chapel at Ceol's Halh. Should someone chase after him? You should take charge, Wiglaf.'

The farmer shook his head. 'I have more important things to do, Mother Elfrida,' he told the companion of Widow Eadgifu. 'Osred and I are in the middle of erecting a new barn. We have to attend to that immediately or the work will be set at naught. I can't waste time escorting prisoners to lord Beornwulf's Hall.'

'You and Osred are the only ones with authority to take the strangers to lord Beornwulf,' replied another person in the crowd. 'It seems that Wyrd, the goddess of the Fates, has allowed you no choice today.'

Mother Elfrida grimaced in amusement. 'By Gefion's sacred ploughshare, it was obvious you should be chosen for the task, Wiglaf.'

This raised some mirth as Wiglaf's name meant 'a ploughman'.

'I have work to attend to,' the big man said defensively. 'It does not need one of rank to take prisoners to lord Beornwulf.'

'If that is so,' came another voice, 'here comes Stuf. He has rank enough to escort the strangers. He helped douse the flames and found the bodies. He went to Ceol's Halh with Crída to bring Brother Boso back here to conduct the funeral rites this morning. He will take charge of the strangers.'

Another man pushed forward through the crowd. He was emaciated and poorly clothed, and he was holding a short-handled axe. Eadulf did not take much confidence from his appearance, but turned in exasperation to him.

'I am trying to tell these people that I am—'

'You can tell what you want to my lord Beornwulf,' he snapped, regarding Eadulf and Fidelma with narrowed eyes. 'In the meantime, stranger, you and your foreign woman will be searched for weapons.'

'I tell you—' Eadulf began to protest.

The man Stuf interrupted sharply. 'Do you see this wood axe? It is a powerful weapon and has despatched many a Northumbrian who tried to raid our township. Raise your hands, stranger; the foreign woman as well. I will search you for I have heard the tricks played by you sneak thieves of Ecgfrith.'

'Ecgfrith?' Eadulf was bewildered. He vaguely remembered the name of the king of Northumbria. 'This is ridiculous. I am nephew to Athelnoth. Does no one recognise me? Anyway, you have no right—'

Stuf ignored him, turning to the man called Wiglaf. 'You may leave it to me to escort them to the thane's Hall.' Then he faced the crowd and raised his voice. 'Does anyone claim to know them? Do you know him, Osred?'

Another thickset man, almost the image of the man called Wiglaf, pushed forward and examined Eadulf with a shake of his head.

'I heard a story of a boy who betrayed his father's gods and went off with the foreigners to Cnobheres Burg,' he said, regarding Eadulf suspiciously. 'His father was Wulfric, our lawgiver before Athelnoth. It will do you no good in our eyes if you are the one who betrayed your father. You could have returned to kill your uncle and then claim his wealth.'

'Kill him?' Eadulf was shocked. 'Are you saying that Athelnoth is dead?'

Stuf regarded him with cynicism. 'You see the blackened ruins? What do you think happened here? You say that you don't know what this means?'

'You have it all wrong. You have no right—'

'This axe gives me all the right I need,' the thin man interrupted with a sneer. 'As Osred says, even if you were, as you claim, Wulfric's son, it gives you no status and the axe is enough right for me to use it unless you obey.'

Eadulf tried to gather his thoughts. He realised that he had to deal with this for Fidelma's sake. He knew that her knowledge of the language was competent, but certainly not fluent enough to persuade this mob of his good intentions. The crowd had already identified her as a foreigner, a Hibernian, and this seemed to arouse some hatred.

'We have just arrived here,' Eadulf tried to explain again, raising his voice. 'We saw the ruins and were looking for an explanation. That is why I tried to ask Widow Eadgifu what has happened to my uncle and my sister, and—'

At the moment something hit Eadulf at the side of the head, sending him stumbling sideways. It was a clod of hard soil thrown by someone in the crowd.

'Away with the foreigners!' came a shout from the crowd.

The man Stuf turned round to the threatening mob.

'No violence against them!' he cried as they started to gather stones and sticks. 'If our thane returns and finds that we have taken it on ourselves to punish these outsiders before he has a chance to examine them, then he will flog us. We must take them as prisoners to the Great Hall and hand them to the thane's *druhting* to await our lord Beornwulf's pleasure.'

'Wait, Stuf!' came another voice. 'Here comes that religieux that Brother Boso sent to check that all had been done correctly after the burial. He will advise us.'

The people made a passage for a tall, bearded man, wearing dark robes and with a silver cross hanging from his neck, just discernible under his beard. He had sallow skin, sunken cheeks, and stubble as if he had shaved badly. His hair was long and unkempt. He pushed his way through the people with a surprising arrogance of manner.

'Clear my path,' he called haughtily. 'I must get to my horse. My duty here is done, so be about your work or proceed to your homes.'

Fidelma's eyes widened and she glanced at Eadulf, wondering if he also recognised the man as she did. It was only a short time before that he had been one of the three religieux that had ignored Eadulf's greeting at the river crossing.

Stuf moved forward. His very demeanour indicated that he was of a low rank for he bent almost double before addressing the man.

'Your forgiveness, your honour,' he greeted. 'We need guidance. We have accosted two strangers who are acting suspiciously. We think they might be involved in the killing and destruction of the lawgiver and his servant, whom your fellow religieux Brother Boso has just laid in the grave with all due ritual. It is good that he sent you back to check the grave was well completed. So we wish to ask a question of you.'

The man was forced to halt because he could not push through the people. He turned, albeit reluctantly, to Stuf before he spoke to Eadulf.

'You are dressed as a member of the religious. Who are you?'

'I am Eadulf, son of Wulfric, and I came to visit my uncle Athelnoth.'

The man's eyes took in Fidelma and scowled.

'You came with one of the Hibernian women? Yet you claim to be kin to Athelnoth, who was lawgiver here.'

'It is true,' Eadulf confirmed. 'The lady Fidelma is my wife. I have just returned from Hibernia.'

The religieux sniffed and looked round. 'So what is the complaint?'

'That's just it,' Stuff replied immediately. 'No one here recognises him.'

It was then that Fidelma spoke in Latin, presuming this would be a language the religieux would speak.

'It is seven years since we were last in your country and it seems there have been changes. Eadulf was born and raised here before he converted to the Faith. He has represented the Faith in Rome, at Streoneshalh, Autun and many other councils. Now when he comes to his home town, as nephew of Athelnoth, it seems no one is prepared to recognise him.'

The religieux did not appear to regard her in friendship.

'We are not having good relationships with your kind,' he replied dourly in a very broken Latin. 'The sooner you of Hibernia recant your heresy and accept the rules of Rome, the better. So it was decided by King Oswy, so should it be done.'

'Oswy decided his own kingdom should follow Rome,' Fidelma pointed out. 'This is the kingdom of the East Angles. This is not the time for such discussion.'

The religieux was clearly in a bad mood.

'Your argument is with these local people and not with me. Find someone who identifies you or be asked to be taken before the thane of this place to state your case.'

'We need to know what has happened here,' protested Fidelma. 'What has happened and what are we being charged with?'

The man named Stuf cut in, ignoring her and speaking to the priest.

'We were taking them to lord Beornwulf's Hall to await his return from attending the king's Witan.'

'It is nothing to do with me,' returned the religieux. 'Take them to your master's Hall – there must be someone there who acts for your thane. If you suspect them of what you say, you can hold them until your thane returns.'

With that, even with Eadulf's protests ringing out, the religieux pushed through the surrounding group of people and disappeared. Stuf, waving his axe handle, called for quiet.

'You all heard that? We shall take the strangers to my lord Beornwulf's Hall, to be held for his examination when he returns. There will be no harm inflicted upon them unless it is his decision. We might benefit from his largesse by so doing, but if we do not, and he is displeased, then we can be certain that we will feel that displeasure.'

There was a reluctant murmur of assent from the people.

Then Mother Elfrida came forward, propelling her elderly companion, the Widow Eadgifu.

'What do you say, Mother Elfrida?' Stuf asked. 'You are wise. Does the old one whom you take care of insist she does not know the stranger?'

Mother Elfrida helped the old one draw close, facing Eadulf. Widow Eadgifu stared at him with her watery blue eyes. Her face was so close that he felt nauseated by the reek of her bad breath.

She was mumbling but some sense seemed to come out of her words.

'I sense bad blood,' she muttered.

'Can't you remember when Wulfric was alive?' Eadulf appealed to her. 'He was my father. Can you remember the young boy...?'

Abruptly, the old woman's voice rose, drowning him out.

'There was a boy. He ran off with the foreign folk. He went to a strange land where the sun dies. It is a land even beyond that of

GRAVE OF THE LAWGIVER

the Britons and their mountain vastness. That's where the foreigners dwell. Strange mystic folk with a curious ritual – they eat flesh and drink blood, and claimed it was the blood and flesh of their god.' Widow Eadgifu screwed up her features and spat. 'So the boy was influenced away and no more was heard of him.'

'I was here seven years ago,' Eadulf almost cried in frustration. 'Someone must know me. Athelnoth was my uncle.'

'He's a liar!' someone yelled from the crowd.

Stuf raised his hand. 'All we know is that Athelnoth's house was burnt down and he and his servant were slain in the process,' he said. 'We know that someone saw some foreign religieux, like those foreigners at Cnobheres Burg, riding away from the scene when the fire started. Here you are, a stranger dressed as a religieux, with a woman of Hibernia, poking around the ruins of Athelnoth's house. For what? Loot?'

'This is madness!' Eadulf was exasperated. 'Surely someone in this township must know me. I was born and raised here. I was here as little as seven years ago. My uncle . . .'

He paused as a thought came to his mind, a question he should have thought about a long time before. He stared into the vacant eyes of the old woman.

'Where is Wulfrun? Where is my young sister? When I last saw Athelnoth, seven years ago, my sister was being raised by him. Where is my sister? She will calm your fears as to who I am.'

His question seemed to cause more angry murmurings among the assembly.

'On the night that Athelnoth was killed, young Wulfrun was not found,' Stuf told him. 'We have searched. There was no trace of her in the cinders of this building. It seems that those who did this have taken her hostage or for a slave.'

Mother Elfrida said, 'If they have, then I pity them, for they will have taken more than they bargained for when they try to tame that hell-cat.'

Before Eadulf could ask her meaning, Widow Eadgifu drew herself up. Her voice was almost a screech.

'Wulfrun, the vixen. She judges no more, for her last judgement must be in error. She went to watch the snakes dancing and they will welcome her to the dance.'

She ended with a curious croaking cackle. The other woman took Widow Eadgifu's arm to calm her.

Stuf grinned, tapping his temple with a forefinger. 'The old one is back in the world of the Aelthâf . . . the world of the elves and their mischief.'

'Don't you torment the old one!' Mother Elfrida told him angrily.

'Calm now, Mother Elfrida. The old one is all right,' Stuf replied indifferently. 'She has not been harmed.'

'If I find out that you have been making sport of her, I shall tell lord Beornwulf and you will taste the sting of his whip.'

'Calm down, Mother Elfrida. Would we harm her when we know you are our thane's *weofodthegn*.'

'Indeed, calm down,' added another of Stuf's supporters. 'You have lived in our township long enough to know our ways. We do no harm and our intention is only to have fun.'

'Then see to it that your fun does not hurt another!' Mother Elfrida replied sharply.

The crowd was growing impatient for a resolution to the situation.

'Let us settle this, Stuf!' yelled one of the crowd. 'Even if the stranger is who he says, then he is still a foreigner to us. For he left us to follow the foreigner mystics. He comes back to us with a foreign woman, which shows his evil intention.'

During this time, Fidelma had tried to remain silent, trying her best to follow the conversation, but feeling that any intervention from her would only exacerbate the mood of the crowd. There was no recourse to anything other than to let Eadulf do the arguing. She gathered that none of these townsfolk would know Latin, which was what she most relied on when in foreign places. Even the brief exchange with the gaunt religieux had not been satisfactory, for he was clearly biased against strangers. She would have to wait until such time as someone appeared who might have more intelligence. One thing she had understood was the words of dislike against her countrymen. She could also plainly interpret the scowls and grimaces given to her, and she reasoned that if she started to give Eadulf words of advice in their shared language that might be seen as provoking these people. However, she could not help asking: 'What is it that they called this woman just now . . . a *weofodthegn*?'

She whispered the question to Eadulf who responded briefly, 'It's nothing. It just means that she was one of the witnesses at a wedding. I think the implication of her status was the important point.'

Eadulf was looking grim as he tried to get an answer to the question that was worrying him.

'Are you saying that Wulfrun was here until the fire? That she disappeared and, while the bodies of Athelnoth and his servant were found, she—'

'The girl vanished at that time. Whoever slaughtered our *gerefa* and took the girl will pay heavily,' uttered someone darkly.

Stuf turned to Eadulf.

'You will both be handed into the care of the *druhting*. That is the senior retainer of the thane. He manages our thane's estate. He will keep you safe until our lord returns.'

Eadulf looked reassuringly at Fidelma. 'At least Cynehelm will know what is logic and law. He was a friend of my father and uncle.'

Stuf gave him a puzzled glance. 'Cynehelm?' he queried.

'I refer to the thane of Seaxmund's Ham,' Eadulf replied hesitantly, puzzled by the response. 'Who did you think I meant?'

Stuf smiled, an almost sadistic look of triumph.

'That shows you are a stranger. Beornwulf is our thane. Cynehelm was killed in a Northumbrian raid several years ago.'

For the first time Eadulf experienced a feeling of helplessness, as if he was drowning in a sea of black emotion. He now realised that the name Beornwulf had been mentioned several times. Cynehelm would have known him well for he had been a close friend of his father Wulfric, but Cynehelm was dead.

The emaciated-looking man, Stuf, was still grinning.

'It seems that Wyrd, the goddess of the Fates, has allowed you no luck today,' Mother Elfrida chuckled, and those nearby broke into jeering laughter.

'Enough!' Stuf called firmly. 'We shall take you to Beornwulf's Hall.'

Eadulf glanced across to Fidelma with a gesture of resignation.

Stuf, with an axe-wielding motion, indicated for Eadulf and Fidelma to follow him and leave their ponies to one of the crowd. The more interested among the spectators gathered around them as they walked after Stuf.

They crossed over the strip of water, which Eadulf had called the Gull's Stream, and followed a track down the hill towards the main square of the township. Eadulf appreciated the reason for Fidelma's silence. She was usually more verbal in confrontations such as this, but her decision to be quiet was a wise strategy to provoke no further arguments until they were able to speak without further feeding the suspicions of this antagonistic crowd.

Eadulf glanced about at the people who had gathered to watch their progress, peering hopefully in case there was anyone he had known in the past who could support his claim of identity. Yet he recognised no one. Most of those they passed were unfriendly, having heard that the strangers were the suspects for the attack on the lawgiver. Some of the crowd were young. Others bore signs of having passed through some debilitating illness, such as the terrible Yellow Plague or, indeed, having recovered from some severe wounds inflicted in the raids and conflicts of recent years.

They finally reached a group of large buildings on the south side of the square next to the main river. These had an impressive entrance with two large upright carved oak supports, which rose some fifteen feet and were connected at the top by similar carved wood, in the centre of which was a large polished wooden shield with an emblem carved on it. Fidelma looked at it and then at the curious wolf-headed figures carved into the wood supports. Gates barred the way, but a man had come forward, obviously drawn by the noise of the approaching crowd. He wore an ivory-handled hunting knife in his belt, but no body armament except a stout leather jerkin. Fidelma presumed this place was the Hall of the thane, the ruling noble of the township.

Stuf went forward and she could not hear the words that were exchanged. A small jangling bell was heard. Then the gates were unlatched and swung open to allow them to pass through, the crowd following with the ponies. Fidelma saw workers tending patches of land, and there were several sheds, which obviously housed animals. She and Eadulf were led through these towards a large building with a high, pointed thatched roof, its entrance raised on a broad-planked loggia accessed by steps.

A young woman of pleasant-looking disposition had come out to stand at the top of these steps. She watched their approach with an expression of slight concern on her features. She did not appear to welcome their guide.

'What do you wish here, Stuf?' she called. 'What manner of cavalcade are you leading and for what purpose?'

'Greetings to you, Mistress Ardith,' Stuf replied, moving forward. His features assumed a false smile. It was clear from his body language and tone that his attitude bore all the respect of one addressing someone of higher status. 'Do I presume my lord

Beornwulf has not yet returned from the meeting of the king's Witan?'

'You may presume it,' she replied, brusquely. It was clear that she did not like Stuf.

'And is his *druhting* still absent?'

At this the woman frowned suspiciously. 'What makes you think Crída is absent?'

Stuf assumed a humorous smile of knowledge. 'I saw him at the interment of Athelnoth this forenoon. He mentioned that he was going hunting after.'

'If he said so, why do you ask?'

'I would not like to venture presumption for fact. He might have returned,' replied the emaciated man smoothly.

'What is it you want, Stuf? Why bring a crowd here? Are those two prisoners you escort, with the crowd holding their ponies? Why have you brought them hither?'

'I have brought two prisoners to await lord Beornwulf's return from the Witan so that he may judge them.'

The woman addressed as Ardith glanced at Eadulf and Fidelma with interest.

'Why are they to be judged?'

Stuf looked coy, almost simpering.

'I'm a plain man, mistress, so I don't know anything about high law words and charges. The woman is a foreigner, one of the Hibernians, and the man claims to be of this township, but no one recognises him. They were both found at the burnt-out remains of Athelnoth's house.'

One man in the company escorting Stuf called: 'The man claims that he is the nephew of Athelnoth and just arrived here. Widow Eadgifu didn't recognise him and we found no one else who could positively do so. In view of what happened to Athelnoth, and no one knowing who these people are, we decided to bring them here to await lord Beornwulf's pleasure.'

Ardith turned her gaze to Fidelma and Eadulf. Her expression was one of curiosity and not antagonism.

'You do not answer the accusations,' she observed, as neither had spoken.

At that Eadulf spoke angrily. 'I have been doing nothing else but answering, and that is getting us nowhere. What is the point of speaking when no one is prepared to listen?'

The woman looked concerned. 'You claim to be the nephew of the late lawgiver Athelnoth?'

'I will say this just one more time. I am Eadulf, son of Wulfric. I am nephew to Athelnoth, and elder brother to Wulfrun. I arrived with my wife, the lady Fidelma of Cashel, disembarking at Domnoc-wic. We arrived at my birthplace today; the place that I was born and raised, only to be seized by these people who, led by this man, has brought us here and made false claims against us.'

At this, the woman turned to the man who had let them through the gates.

'Take their horses to the stable and instruct that they should be well cared for. See if there is any word of the *druhting*. If Crída is around, tell him to come here immediately.'

Eadulf seemed to straighten in recognition of the name.

'Is that the Crída who was son of Burgred that you speak of?' he asked.

Ardith's turned back to him with interest. 'You know Crída?'

'We played together as children, when we weren't helping with herding Cynehelm's cattle. At least Crída will tell you who I am. We used to play on a secret hill in the marshes nearby.' Eadulf turned to Fidelma with a grin. 'Finally, we should get some sense into this stupidity.'

Perhaps it was good that he spoke automatically and in his own tongue before he turned back to the woman. At least she appeared at ease.

'Come, Eadulf, you and the lady Fidelma follow me inside where I can offer you hospitality and apologies for the unintentional insults that you have suffered. I am Ardith, house stewardess to Thane Beornwulf.'

She was about to lead the way inside when a puzzled murmuring arose from the crowd that had accompanied them. She turned back to where Stuf was standing defiantly.

'Dismiss this crowd, Stuf, and you will wait by the stables for the return of the *druhting*, for you may have things to answer for.'

There were more mutterings of protest from the crowd that had accompanied Stuf in the hope of seeing some excitement. Stuf's hesitation to obey caused Ardith to turn on them in annoyance.

'You will return to your homesteads and back to your labours. If you do not do so, then, mark me, you will not like it if I call on the thane's *fyrd*, who will be more than willing to help guide you home.'

Seeing Fidelma's puzzled look, Eadulf explained: 'A *fyrd* is a small bodyguard.'

The muttering subsided and, with reluctance, the crowd began dispersing slowly. A moment or so later Ardith led the strangers through a main hall into a side room, close to the cooking area. She motioned Eadulf and Fidelma inside to take seats before a fire. She called to a servant for drinks to be brought to them. It was clear that the thane was someone of wealth, for this kitchen was spacious and well equipped.

'Those people outside told me that Cynehelm is dead,' Eadulf opened at once. 'I am sorry to hear it. He was a great friend of my father Wulfric. Who is this new thane, Beornwulf? I don't seem to recall him.'

Ardith hesitated a moment.

'Beornwulf is my . . . is the new Thane of Seaxmund's Ham. And you, Fidelma, you are . . .?'

Fidelma smiled ruefully. 'I am wife to Eadulf. I have a poor

GRAVE OF THE LAWGIVER

facility in your Saxon tongue, as we call it. I have picked it up from Eadulf over the years. I have fluency in Latin, if it is easier to converse in?'

Ardith sighed. 'There is not much use for Latin outside of the few religious here. I know little beyond the language of my people, although I am sure my lord Beornwulf has good knowledge of that tongue. But I understand you well.' She turned to Eadulf. 'You claim to be Eadulf, son of Wulfric and therefore nephew to our *gerefa*, Athelnoth?'

'Not a claim but a fact,' Eadulf assured her.

'Do not worry, for I have heard Athelnoth speak of you and your wife . . .?'

'My wife is Fidelma of Cashel in the kingdom of Muman.'

'I know enough by the formula of words that you imply she is a noble of that country? Where is Muman located?'

'It is one of the five kingdoms on the island called Hibernia in Latin. Her brother is King Colgú,' confirmed Eadulf.

The woman's eyes widened slightly. 'Then I am sure that I have heard stories of you spoken by Athelnoth and Wulfrun. Athelnoth spoke of a young nephew who followed the foreigners back to their country where he became a great judge and solver of mysteries.'

Eadulf glanced, embarrassed, at Fidelma.

'I think the stories are a little exaggerated.'

'Nevertheless, that is what Athelnoth spoke of.'

'Yet no one now recognises me here and I am even accused of setting fire to my own uncle's house. This is hardly a welcome home.'

Ardith shrugged apologetically. 'A lot of people in the township have died in recent years. First the raids from Mercia when Penda was king there. Then came the terrible Yellow Plague before the final peace with Mercia, when Wulfhere became a Christian king. That sparked off a conflict with Ecgfrith of Northumbria. Yes, death has constantly depleted our people. So this may explain the treatment that you have suffered. People are simply frightened. They are scared of anything they do not understand.'

'Is it known why and how my uncle was killed?'

'At the moment, there is no explanation and no real suspects. This is why the fear is so discernible. The people are inclined to panic. His house, as you have seen, was set afire but he and his servant were killed before it was set ablaze.'

'So my young sister Wulfrun . . .?'

'That is more puzzling. There was no sign of her. She was living in your uncle's household and he was training her in law. According to Crída, her body has not been recovered in spite of intensive searches. There has been no sign of it. The concern is that she has been abducted.'

'Who is the deputy *gerefa*, who will take over from Athelnoth?'

'With Wulfrun's disappearance, there is none here that is qualified,' sighed the woman.

'Someone must have been in charge of a legal investigation?'

'My lord Beornwulf will take charge when he returns from attending the Witan, the council of our king. He should be back soon.'

'You were about to tell me what happened to Cynehelm,' Eadulf pointed out.

'He was killed in a Northumbrian raid.' Ardith was reflective. 'A few years ago, that was. Beornwulf was deemed to be thane when Cynehelm was killed. Beornwulf was a cousin of Cynehelm. They were raised together and lived at Beoderic's Worth, not far to the west of here. That is where I come from as well.'

'Cynehelm would be a great loss,' Eadulf reflected. 'I last saw him seven years ago when I was visiting. I never knew Beornwulf, nor you, for that matter. So when Cynehelm was killed, you both came from Beoderic's Worth? I never went there and did not know Cynehelm had family connections there.'

'At least you knew Crída,' Ardith pointed out with a smile. 'I am sorry for the discourtesy that you are receiving. I am afraid Stuf was exceeding his status. For that I apologise, Lady . . .?'

'Fidelma is an ample title,' Fidelma replied gravely. 'It was, however, something of a strange encounter.'

Small tankards of chilled cider had been served when Stuf suddenly appeared in the doorway.

'I have taken the horses to the stable, Ardith,' he began petulantly.

'Has Crída arrived back?' she demanded.

Stuf was silent but there was still something venomous in his expression.

'He is still out hunting,' the emaciated man exclaimed. 'The ponies are safely looked after. I have examined the strangers' bags, which they were carrying on their ponies.'

Eadulf's cheeks reddened in anger. 'You dared search our belongings?'

'Especially when one of the stable boys recognised the brand mark on the ponies. The horses belong to Mul of Frig's Tun. These people stole them, there is no doubt.'

'Mul is a friend who met us at Domnoc-wic,' Eadulf explained at once to Ardith. 'He gave us the use of the ponies while we are here.'

'Of course,' Stuf sneered. 'You would say that. Mistress Ardith, call the *fyrd*. These are definitely those who slaughtered Athelnoth and his household. This one,' he pointed at Eadulf, 'this one carries a bag with all sorts of strange things in it that look like the tools of a torturer. Curious knives and other such things.'

'The bag is called a *lés*, you idiot,' Eadulf explained through clenched teeth. 'It's a medical bag and it shows that I studied for some time at a school of the healing arts.'

'Studied the art of torture, you mean, stranger,' the man replied with a cynical laugh. 'And the other one, the foreign woman – she may be wearing the robes of the poor, but her bags contain more wealthy clothes and even some of those strange things that people of rank often wear. It is obvious the clothes do not belong to the person she claims to be. And inside her bag was a smaller bag in which were jars of perfume and the like. There were even some jewels. A golden circlet. Now, tell me that these are innocent travellers.'

His voice rose to a high, accusatory note. His expression was one of self-satisfaction. 'I demand you send for your bodyguards for our protection! Have them bound.'

The stewardess's voice was brittle. 'Are you giving me orders, Stuf? If I send for Beornwulf's *fyrd,* the bodyguard, you will be the one who is bound and you will not enjoy where they take you.'

The emaciated man looked shocked.

'What do you mean? Have they threatened you, that you make so rash a statement?' He was peering about as if looking for help at the same time as his hand went to the large knife he carried in his belt.

'Stay that weapon,' Ardith admonished coldly, 'or I will call the guard. When you have calmed down and listened without fear disabling your thoughts, then you will realise Eadulf and the lady Fidelma are guests under my protection. They have every right to be visiting this township.'

'I tell you, no one knows him in the township. Why are you accepting them? I demand you call your *fyrd,* so that we may be protected. We must bind them before they escape.'

Ardith's eyes narrowed. She rose up, seeming to tower over the angry little man.

'You demand, Stuf? Since when have you obtained the status to demand anything? You are not even a *ceorl.*'

At that moment they heard a blast from a distant hunting horn.

Stuf straightened up, his expression changing to self-confidence.

'Whether I am little more than a slave, I shall be heard. That is the sound of my lord Beornwulf's return. So now we will have the truth. Beornwulf will recognise that I speak and act in his loyal service. We will soon have the truth out of these foreigners.'

CbAPTER FIVE

The sound of several horses arriving through the main gates seemed to broaden the self-assured smirk on the face of Stuf. A moment later footsteps echoed on the boards of the wooden loggia. Doors opened into the main reception hall and a strong male voice was calling, 'Ardith! I've brought a friend back . . .'

The woman rose with a smile of relief and apparent pleasure as she called in reply, 'We are here, Beornwulf.'

The door swung open to the area where they were sitting.

'We are in need of mead, Ardith, for we have ridden—' The burly figure of a young warrior appeared in the doorway and halted abruptly. His fair tousled hair and shaggy beard did not disguise his regular, handsome features. He was broad of shoulder, muscular and clearly one used to action. He fell silent as his eyes fell first on Fidelma, sitting by the fireplace, and then took in Eadulf standing next to her.

'Who are . . .?' began the thane.

Before he could finish, Stuf stepped forward. His tone when addressing the young thane had become almost a cringing simper.

'I have taken prisoner those who burnt down Athelnoth's homestead, lord.' Stuf bowed low. 'I bring them as prisoners for your examination and punishment.'

Behind Beornwulf a figure appeared at his shoulder. He was

also tall, his head crowned in a silvery steel and bronze war helmet. His eyes were ice blue and were a prominent feature within the war bonnet. He paused and took in the group confronting the thane. Then the newcomer pushed past Beornwulf and strode across the room towards Fidelma. Both hands were held out in greeting.

'By the Hammer of Thunor, it is the lady Fidelma! Of all people to find . . .' Then the man glanced at Eadulf. 'Brother Eadulf . . . of course. I should have known you would be together. Well . . . the goddess Wyrd's hand must be involved in this meeting!'

Fidelma merely extended her right hand to the newcomer who bowed low over it before turning to Eadulf and enveloping him in a bearlike hug. Eadulf disengaged himself from the man's embrace, taking a few breaths to recover. As the warrior backed away, his hand went up, he removed his war helmet with an easy motion and dropped it to the floor before standing back, hands on hips, and chuckling as he regarded them.

He was a young man, almost the image of Beornwulf, the thane.

'It is good to see you well, Werferth,' Fidelma greeted him solemnly. 'Seven years have passed and yet you still recognise us. I think, whatever deity you ascribe it to, your arrival is most timely.'

'Wyrd is the arbiter of our Fate and a guide to our Destiny, lady,' he replied, ruffling his hair, which had been flattened by his helmet. 'Wyrd has impressed memories of our last meeting forever in my mind: the time we spent resolving that mystery seven years ago, down at Suth Tun Hoo. If Lord Sigeric had known that Wyrd had planned our paths to cross again . . .!'

'I presume the Wita Sigeric is still high steward to the king?' Eadulf asked.

'We have only just come from a meeting of the Witan. Lord

Sigeric is still the leading adviser. I am still the commander of the king's bodyguard.'

He suddenly swung round to his companion, Beornwulf.

'Forgive me. Such is my excitement at seeing my old friends, that I am forgetting my manners. You may not know my friends since you became thane of Seaxmund's Ham only after Eadulf and the lady Fidelma left us to return to Hibernia.' He indicated Eadulf and Fidelma. 'This is Eadulf, son of Wulfric, who was the hereditary *gerefa* of this place. And this is his wife, the lady Fidelma, sister to the king of Muman, one of the kingdoms on the island of Hibernia. My friends, I present Beornwulf, Thane of Seaxmund's Ham.'

The young thane greeted each of them with a smile and proffered hand.

'I have heard stories of you both from the *gerefa* Athelnoth . . .' An expression of sadness suddenly changed his features. 'I suppose that you have heard the news? You have learnt the sadness that we now suffer?'

'We have heard,' Eadulf acknowledged.

'My absence from the burial this morning was meant as no discourtesy. Yesterday, on the very day of the murders, I was summoned to the king's Witan, otherwise I would have led the obsequies and the investigation into the deaths in person.'

'There is also the pressing matter of the disappearance of my young sister Wulfrun,' Eadulf agreed shortly. 'We were trying to discover some facts about it when this man,' he pointed to the now bewildered Stuf, 'led a mob to almost attack us. He then insisted on bringing us here as prisoners.'

Beornwulf looked grim. 'And your loss is our sorrow. As we have no *gerefa* now, I have authority to investigate and judge. But it is good my lord Werferth took the opportunity to return with me. He has other matters to attend to later, but he will be . . .'

He hesitated with a frown and glanced to where Stuf was

standing uncomfortably, almost crouching, with a disconcerted expression as he tried to understand the meaning of the unexpected scene that had developed.

'Didn't you say that you have found people you suspect of burning down Athelnoth's house?' There was a sarcastic note as Beornwulf now addressed him.

It was then Ardith interrupted with almost cynical laughter.

'Stuf came with a crowd, which he had persuaded to follow him. He had forced Eadulf and Fidelma to come with him as prisoners. He accuses them of being the ones who burnt down Athelnoth's house.'

'Explain yourself,' the thane demanded.

Stuf almost let out a whine as he hunched before the infuriated gaze of Beornwulf.

'Lord, they were acting suspiciously and no one knew who they were. The woman was clearly a foreigner, a Hibernian, and the other claimed to be related to Athelnoth. The folk did not know him; no one knew or recognised him. Not even old Widow Eadgifu, who should have known, if anyone did. A decision had to be taken for the safety of the township. I took it on myself to take them as prisoners and bring them here for your interrogation.'

'Old Widow Eadgifu?' Beornwulf sighed in exasperation. 'She is passing the stage where she would not recognise her own father if he returned from the flames of Hélham. But, more importantly, do you think that you have the authority over such folk as these?' He nodded to Eadulf and Fidelma. 'You actually made them your prisoners?'

Now that he had been recognised, Eadulf felt that he could be conciliatory. 'This man might have been more than enthusiastic in his actions but there is now little harm done. It seems it was just ill luck that we arrived when we did. Seven years have passed since I visited here and no one seems to remember or know me.'

'Even so,' Ardith said grimly, 'Stuf forgot his position. Eadulf explained clearly to me who he was, and I recalled the stories Athelnoth used to tell of Eadulf and his wife, the lady Fidelma. I see no justification for Stuf to have acted so hastily, nor so far above his station.'

Beornwulf was nodding with a grim expression.

'I take it that you started giving orders, Stuf?' His voice had controlled anger in it. 'Where was my *druhting* or any other of my household that you could not have expressed your suspicions to? You are no more than a *geburas* . . . you have no right to take any decision upon yourself. In doing so you are insolent and such insolence will be punished. A good thrashing will teach you to respect your betters.'

Ardith saw Fidelma's frown as she tried to follow what was going on.

'A *geburas* is one of the lowest ranks in our society,' she explained quickly. 'They are basically slaves with certain freedoms for which they have to work as tribute to the local thane for two days a week; more days in the time of sowing and harvest. Sometimes, if they are clever and frugal, they can save enough to get a piece of land to the value of a quarter of a hide, and use it to grow food and thus obtain an income.'

'But this poor man is to be thrashed because he thought he was doing right? Isn't that unjust?' Eadulf turned and repeated as much to Beornwulf. The thane did not seem impressed. Then, after a moment's thought, he grimaced.

'I have had trouble with this one before, Eadulf. I doubt he acted from any moral thoughts. He probably thought it was a way of seeking a reward. I shall decide his reward.' He turned back to the emaciated man, standing nervously and hanging his head. His lips were quivering as he awaited the decision of his lord. He was a totally different person from the overbearing and conceited man who had paraded them through the township.

GRAVE OF THE LAWGIVER

'Where is Crída?' Beornwulf demanded. 'My *druhting* was in charge during my absence.'

Stuf stirred apprehensively. 'After the burial of the victims this morning, lord, he went out hunting. He has not yet returned to the township.'

'So you took much on yourself? Was there no *ceorl*, no one of higher rank than you, who had authority?' demanded Beornwulf.

'Wiglaf had no time, so I brought them here, lord,' protested Stuf.

'But you assumed to take them as prisoners. I don't doubt that Ardith reminded you that you are hardly more than a thrall.' He glanced at the woman, who nodded in agreement. 'I shall give you plenty of time to think about your position in life. You will go to my master of pigs and tell him that you are to be given work immediately cleaning the pig pens. You will work until I say otherwise. Go! I will send for you when I want you, and woe betide you if you expect it to be soon.'

Stuf, bending almost double, left them.

Beornwulf then turned to the others and resumed a broad smile.

'Do not be concerned for him. He is an idle scoundrel and I have encountered him several times before. Numerous times he came near to being found in the act of illegally acquiring chickens or rabbits. He is a thief if he can get away with it. He has no morals. Anyway, in this matter, he should have known his place and not tried to take on authority that he could never aspire to.'

Werferth, who had been quiet for a while, turned to Ardith.

'I swear that I and my friend Beonwulf will perish of thirst if we have to wait much longer for a drink. We have ridden hard to get here. After we have eased our parched throats, hopefully we shall sit down with a good meal to welcome our unexpected, honoured guests.'

Beornwulf was nodding in agreement.

'I presume accommodation can be arranged for them?' Without waiting for an answer, he turned to Fidelma and Eadulf, adding: 'Our house is yours. Since your uncle's house is no more than ashes you may be my guests for as long as you wish.'

Ardith had hurried off to instruct the household servants to start making the new arrangements.

Eadulf began to thank the thane for his hospitality, but Werferth interrupted him.

'Don't concern yourself, my friend. If you feel indebted, I suspect my friend Beornwulf might well expect some service in return.'

'What service do you expect?' Eadulf asked, trying not to make his immediate suspicion obvious.

'Quite simple,' Beornwulf replied seriously. 'We need to resolve this mysterious death of your uncle, not to mention the mystery of your missing sister. Werferth is right. Who better than you and the lady Fidelma to be involved in this matter? I am sure the stories that Athelnoth used to tell us about your adventures were not all fantasies.'

Eadulf glanced to Fidelma with a question in his eyes. The question was not returned.

'Of course,' Eadulf replied after a moment's hesitation. 'It is also something I was going to suggest. I undertake it as a matter of family honour. The finding of my sister is my priority.'

'Then my house is yours,' Beornwulf smiled.

Ardith rejoined them with a servant bearing jugs of mead, although she handed Fidelma a tankard of cider, realising that Fidelma would have no stomach for the heavy, bitter mead that the men shared.

Eadulf was reflective, as something was concerning him.

'If I may ask a question, Beornwulf, when you left here to attend the Witan, I presume it was not to report the death of my uncle, your *gerefa*?'

'You thought the matter of the *gerefa* would be important to the king's council?' Beornwulf smiled sadly. 'Important as it is, there are other matters of concern to the kingdom.'

'Ah, I was just wondering if this matter might concern Sigeric and the Witan,' Eadulf replied. 'I wondered why, Thane Beornwulf, you returned in the company of the commander of the king's bodyguard. The murder of a *gerefa* is not to be lightly dismissed but I have no delusions of grandeur and I am sure my family are not important enough to warrant the concern of the king or his high steward.'

There was a silence in the room. Eadulf could sense some atmosphere of nervousness between Beornwulf and Werferth.

'We will talk more of this after we have rested and feasted,' Beornwulf declared abruptly, not answering the query. 'I left instructions that a search should be made for Wulfrun and any news of her whereabouts should immediately be relayed to my household. From my *druhting*'s lack of appearance, I have deduced that there has been no further word during our absence?'

The question was addressed to Ardith, who shook her head: 'None. The situation is exactly as when you left.'

'But—' Eadulf had scarcely begun when a voice shouted from beyond the doorway.

'Hello, inside! It is I, Crída!'

The thane's *druhting* – his senior retainer – appeared at the threshold with a brace of hares in one hand and his bow in the other. He halted and his eyes widened as they fell on Eadulf. Immediately a grin spread over his features.

'Is that you, Eadulf son of Wulfric? Do you still live?' He came forward, dropping his burden from both hands on to the floor and reaching out to embrace him.

'I still live, my friend,' Eadulf replied solemnly as he disengaged himself.

'It looks as though the god Helith, the preserver of health, has not neglected you, old friend,' rejoined the other with a playful punch at Eadulf, who dodged and returned a similar punch at Crída. It appeared to be part of an ancient childhood ritual between them.

Crída pulled away and suddenly remembered his whereabouts. He turned apologetically, but still grinning, to Beornwulf.

'Forgive me, my lord, but Eadulf was my boyhood companion. We grew up together; we hunted as boys, and planned imaginary battles together until he converted to the New Faith. Then he went off to join those Hibernians at Cnobheres Burg. I heard he travelled to many outlandish places. He was here seven years ago when our friend Botulf was in trouble, but—' He suddenly halted and seemed embarrassed. 'Have you been told about your uncle?'

'I have, Crída.'

Ardith glanced at Beornwulf with an ironic grimace. 'It was a pity Crída was not around earlier to put paid to Stuf's nonsense.'

Crída frowned inquisitively. 'Stuf's nonsense? What has that rogue been up to?'

'Stuf claimed that Eadulf was responsible for Athelnoth's death and the burning of his homestead,' replied Beornwulf. 'He even brought him and Fidelma here as prisoners. Don't worry, I shall make him work for a week in the pig pens until he learns his rightful place.'

Crída looked shocked. 'But to accuse Eadulf, of all people . . .?' he began.

'He could not find anyone to identify me,' Eadulf explained, 'therefore he is not entirely to blame.'

'But that one of his rank should even dare . . . it is hard to believe. Even if people thought you were strangers, they would have heard about you from Athelnoth, who never neglected stories about you.'

'More of that later.' Eadulf now felt embarrassed. 'Let me introduce you to my wife. This is Fidelma of Cashel.'

GRAVE OF THE LAWGIVER

Crída turned with an awkward attempt at a bow.

'My service, lady. I am yours to command. Athelnoth spoke of your marriage, Eadulf, and your reputation among the Hibernians.'

'It is good to meet you, Crída, and to know one person at least who knew Eadulf when he was but a boy,' Fidelma replied distantly. She was growing irritated at being overlooked. 'I shall look forward to hearing stories from you of those times.'

A female servant had entered and whispered to Ardith, who then stood and clapped her hands to attract their attention.

'The meal is ready and served in the main hall,' she announced.

It was Crída who suddenly appeared embarrassed now, and he retrieved the string of hares and his bow and arrows that he had dropped while greeting Eadulf.

'I was out hunting, lord,' he explained unnecessarily to Beornwulf. 'I was bringing these to Ardith. Then I shall—'

'Then you shall join us in this feasting, Crída,' declared the thane enthusiastically. 'We must celebrate the arrival of your old friend and his wife. Sad circumstances, but their presence may be to our good fortune. They will certainly be able to contribute much when we discuss the vexed problem of Athelnoth's death and the disappearance of young Wulfrun.'

The contents of the table surprised Fidelma, with cuts of roasted lamb, dishes of small, purple-red carrots, mushrooms, turnips, parsnips and beetroots, sauces of garlic and burdock. Fidelma remembered the young stalks of burdock were eaten in salads, but the juice of the plant had often been used to soothe burns and sores. There was also an abundance of apples, plums, even a mixture of sloes and edible berries. Beornwulf himself rose from the table to go to the kitchen and returned with a jug.

'Red wine from Frankia,' he announced, pouring from the jug. 'What's the point of being close to a thriving port like Domnocwic, and not take advantage of the merchandise that the ships bring in?'

'It was different when we were boys, eh, Eadulf?' Crída remarked, savouring the contents of his tankard. 'The Old Wolf has brought prosperity to this kingdom since he formed the alliance against Northumbria.'

Fidelma was puzzled. 'The Old Wolf?'

'Ealdwulf is our king. Ealdwulf and Eadulf – they both mean "Old Wolf",' laughed Crída. 'Do you remember our young days when we played in the marshes? I wonder if the tree house we built together is still there?'

'A tree house in the marshes?' Fidelma commented. 'Not a very healthy place to play.'

'It was quite comfortable,' Crída replied. 'Once you reached it, along a track through the swamp, it was a fair-sized mound, a piece of ground that did not itself rise above the height of the trees. There are many trees that like the wetlands, and they were magical jungles to young boys, as we were then.'

'But there was an old tree, an oak, where we built our fortress, our tree house, as I recall,' Eadulf confirmed. 'We vowed to defend it against all comers. No need. For it became our secret place and no other boys from the township would venture into the marsh to reach it.'

'We had a name for that little island,' Crída smiled. 'What was it?'

Eadulf thought for a moment and then shook his head.

Crída chuckled. 'We called it—'

Werferth interrupted with a sound indicating impatience. 'Shouldn't we get down to the business of discussing Athelnoth's death? There should be time for childhood memories later.'

'Where should we start?' Beornwulf asked in agreement.

'But all stories have to start somewhere,' Eadulf suggested. 'Beornwulf was alerted about the fire and went straight away to see what was happening. How was Beornwulf alerted?'

'I told him,' Crída explained. 'Neighbours saw the flames and went to try to extinguish them. One of them, Wiglaf, came down here to inform me. I then told Beornwulf. We went to Athelnoth's house immediately. The timbers were so dry that the building had almost vanished into cinders by the time we reached there.'

'No one seemed to witness anything before the flames?' Eadulf frowned.

'I seemed to recall that Stuf, in his claim that we might be responsible for the burning of Athelnoth's house, said something about Hibernians being responsible,' Fidelma said quietly.

Eadulf was startled. He had forgotten.

'It was pointed out that I was Hibernian and that some who might have been Hibernian religieux had been seen riding from that direction when the flames were rising,' Fidelma went on.

'Who was it that said that?'

'We shall find out from Stuf,' Eadulf agreed. 'We will go through all the witnesses' evidence. Now I recall, there was a distinct feeling of antagonism against Hibernians.'

'There are still members of the Hibernian religieux at Cnobheres Burg,' Beornwulf confirmed, 'so it is possible there is a link.'

'Then there are still some of the old community that Fursa and his brothers established there many years ago?' Eadulf asked. 'I thought they had all fled after the decision made at Streoneshalh.'

'There was a lot of movement of people after that decision,' Werferth agreed. 'But the Hibernians were never persecuted here in this kingdom. Of course, the Britons, who practise similar religious rituals as the Hibernians, were certainly made unwelcome here.'

'Things might change soon,' Beornwulf said, and then his mouth clamped shut as if he had not meant the words to come out.

Fidelma frowned. 'There is an implication in your voice, Thane of Seaxmund's Ham.'

'It is just that there are rumours that the new Greek bishop, who was sent by Bishop Vitalian of Rome to be the Archbishop of the Cantwara, has plans to try to unite the separate Churches in the kingdoms of the Angles and Saxons. To unite them under his rule.'

'I want to know more of that,' Fidelma said, trying to hide her heightened interest. 'But let us not be distracted from the matter of Athelnoth.'

'We need to talk to all those who were near Athelnoth's house on the night it was burnt,' Eadulf pointed out.

'That is a good plan,' Beornwulf agreed wearily. He glanced at Crída as if inviting him to speak.

'I know my friend Eadulf likes facts,' Crída answered. 'The homestead was on fire. Athelnoth's body was burnt but not badly enough to deny recognition. A servant was also dead. Both the servant and the *gerefa* had been stabbed in the back with a thin-bladed dagger. Only one dagger was recovered, being buried in the body of Athelnoth.'

'Was that dagger kept?' Eadulf asked.

'I still have it,' Beornwulf confirmed.

'The only bodies were Athelnoth and his servant?' Fidelma pressed.

'We searched and there was no one else in the building. No other bodies. There was no sign of young Wulfrun.'

'I am interested in the fact that a witness saw two riders leaving the town from the direction of the house when the flames took hold. More particularly, that these two riders were identified, as I recall, wearing the robes of the religieux of Hibernia,' Fidelma said thoughtfully.

'A lot of the Britons and Hibernians continue to wear the robes and tonsure associated with the insular Churches rather than the tonsure of Rome and the eastern Churches,' pointed out Werferth.

'That is true,' Fidelma agreed. 'But we have two riders seen leaving Seaxmund's Ham as the flames took hold. Two riders at a suspiciously specific time. Were they positively identified to the point where one of them could not have been Wulfrun?'

'If it was Wulfrun, I doubt whether she would flee in such a manner from the *gerefa*'s burning homestead,' Beornwulf pointed out. 'I thought she was very close to her uncle and the only way she could have left would have been by force.'

Eadulf sighed. 'The witnesses have given no word that Wulfrun was seen being forcibly removed?'

'None, so far as we know. It is another point to make certain of.'

'Tell me more about my sister,' Eadulf pressed.

'An attractive and intelligent girl. You could say she was very self-willed. She lived with your uncle and he instructed her in law. She would often help him and, perhaps, fulfil his office.'

'Would her role, helping my uncle with law, give rise to ill feeling towards her?'

'Why do you ask that?' Beornwulf frowned.

'I remember someone expressing some ill feeling.'

'Not everyone looks on a lawgiver as their friend,' Ardith intervened.

'Do you think this event has some connection with Athelnoth's status as lawgiver?' Eadulf asked.

'It is one logical suspicion,' the thane replied easily. 'Lawgivers and judges make enemies easily by the very fact of their judgements. Once a decision is made, many feel themselves unjust victims. They seek revenge.'

'That is why I raised my question. Has there been any judgement that has especially upset those against whom it was given?'

Beornwulf and Werferth were looking perplexed.

'Is there some legal matter that required Werferth to come here?' Eadulf asked impatiently.

'I was passing through here for another reason. I am a warrior, not someone qualified to investigate such matters,' Werferth smiled. 'Now that I am here, I hope you both will regard me as a blessing from the hand of Wyrd, the goddess of destiny. I will do my best to help. If there is some connection perhaps it will arise when we make an investigation. I am at your service.'

'So why are you here?' Eadulf asked dryly. 'What is the reason? Beornwulf seemed to imply there was an important one.'

'Perhaps you are trying to progress too quickly,' Fidelma cautioned quietly.

Ardith regarded her thoughtfully. 'Too quickly?'

'We must confine ourselves to facts at this stage,' Fidelma replied. 'Apart from that ploughman Wiglaf, and the old woman Widow Eadgifu, and her companion Mother Elfrida, who were the other witnesses? Who saw the two religieux leaving the scene? We should make careful note of their accounts.'

'It was only Widow Eadgifu who saw the religieux. That's what she also told us on the night of the fire,' Crída offered.

'Widow Eadgifu?' Eadulf exclaimed in frustration. 'She couldn't even recognise me. Yet she nursed me when I was a baby.'

'I am told the old woman has good days and bad days,' Beornwulf said. 'She certainly seemed in possession of her faculties when I spoke with her before I left to attend the Witan.'

'Was she the only one to witness Hibernians close by?' Fidelma asked.

Crída grimaced. 'I think there were others. We should probably gather all the witnesses together and question them more thoroughly.'

'That would do no harm,' Fidelma agreed. 'So we can start first thing tomorrow. In the meantime, it has been a long and stressful day and I feel it is time for me to repair to rest.'

Ardith immediately rose to her feet apologising.

'I had forgotten your long and arduous journey here and the stress your unexpected greeting must have caused.' She shook her head at Beornwulf. 'Shame on you, keeping your guests up. You must all have fresh minds to deal with the problem tomorrow. So now we shall all retire to our beds.'

Eadulf was late joining Fidelma in the room that had been provided. Fidelma had been unable to sleep earlier. She had allowed Eadulf more time with Crída to talk about their boyhood and youth; about families and old friends. While she tried to concentrate on the problem of the death of Eadulf's uncle and missing sister, she found it almost impossible. She reasoned that a lot of her irritation was due to the life changes that she was now forced to endure. She had forgotten how different was the lifestyle of Eadulf's people compared to her own culture. Even in simple things. She was so used to having a full body wash in the evening before the last meal of the day. The washing of only hands and face was customary in the morning in her culture.

The Angles and Saxons apparently liked to spring out of bed in the early morning for a cold dip in a river or lake. Only the nobles in society, such as thanes, ealdormen and princes indulged in occasional heated baths. Even thanes were not so assiduous in the practice. Now all she could do was wait to see what the morning wash would provide. However, she was determined not to go plunging into some cold river.

When Eadulf came to bed he was surprised to find Fidelma still awake. He was somewhat disconcerted as he felt her gaze on him in the flickering candlelight.

'Is there a problem?' he asked hesitantly.

'There seem to be several,' she responded in a distant tone. 'I am not fully convinced that we have a proper understanding.'

Eadulf had started to ready himself for the night but halted and sat on the end of the bed.

'In what way?' he declared in surprise. 'I would have said that we had more than enough information to investigate.'

She hesitated a moment. 'Oh, this murder? I feel that Beornwulf and Werferth know more than they are sharing with you. Werferth suggests he came here by coincidence. He is the commander of the king's bodyguard. Does it make sense that he is here?'

'Werferth might be telling us the truth. It is a coincidence.'

'The Witan is the council of your king, is it not?' Fidelma asked.

'A Witan means the council of the wise. It consists of the nobles, like ealdormen, thanes and the senior clergy. Now, with the New Faith, the kings allow bishops and abbots to take a place when invited,' explained Eadulf.

'And the function of the Witan?' Fidelma pressed.

Eadulf shrugged, puzzled by the question. 'It is just like the function of your brother's council. They meet to advise, to make judicial judgement to promulgate the laws and give opinion in all matters affecting the running and wellbeing of the kingdom.'

'So there could be more than a few people on it who give opinion about legal cases?'

'I suppose there could be . . .' Then he saw where Fidelma's points were leading.

'But Werferth has no judicial role on the Witan?'

'He advises on matters concerning the defence of the kingdom. Not necessarily resolving legal matters.' Eadulf sighed. 'You don't really think that Athelnoth was assassinated due to some political conflict?'

'It is an itch that I cannot properly scratch,' Fidelma assured him.

'So you consider that Werferth has some ulterior motive for being sent here over the matter of Athelnoth's murder?'

'I admit there is not enough information to speculate. Just more questions.'

'So what you are saying,' Eadulf said, 'is that the killing of my uncle and the disappearance of my sister may go deeper than what we are being told?'

'It puts things into perspective. What does your friend Crída say?'

'Not much, for we merely caught up about old friends and some relatives. Alas, many we knew are now perished. There have been the Yellow Plague, various illnesses, and others have died in wars and conflicts. We did not speak much of the attack.'

'Of course, he offers the depletion in population by plague and wars as a logical reason why no one recognised you?'

'It is a reason.'

'But there must have been many who have died since you left this place. If he was your companion as a child, he must have known your uncle and your sister as well. Even the servant who was murdered.'

'Oh, of course. He knew my sister and was like an older brother to her.'

'Yet he does not seem overcome with grief.'

'We are a people hardened by life. We are the Wuffingas, scions of warrior gods. Six of our kings have died in battle defending the kingdom, even in the time we know of.'

'I can't say that is something to boast about,' Fidelma replied with a dismissive sniff. 'Better to live long and serve the people than to die leading them into a graveyard.'

Eadulf was exasperated. 'You do not understand the philosophy of my people. We believe it no greater honour than dying for justice.'

'But not living for justice?'

'When I was a boy, I was told to raise my sword and shield and shout the name of Woden, the chief of our gods, to secure my place in the other world . . .'

Fidelma was staring at him in concern. All her anxieties and doubts, all her uncertainties and qualms about the future, came back with a dark force.

'This homecoming, the talking with your childhood friend, has brought out some strange thoughts in you that you have never expressed before. Or, at least, I thought they had been entirely eliminated when you converted to the New Faith.'

'What do you mean?' he demanded.

'During these years you would never have called on your ancient gods and goddesses. Was your conversion not that sincere?'

Her reply was sharp and stunned Eadulf to silence. He was troubled as he realised, in the heat of youthful memories, that he seemed to have been transported back in time and place to going hunting with Crída, when the two pretended to be hunters chasing wild bears to bring home a trophy to prove their prowess. He swallowed nervously.

'I was just trying to explain the culture; explain the beliefs that you will find here. Of course, it has nothing to do with me now. We will talk of it more tomorrow.'

He turned on his side with a troubled mind, leaving her to extinguish the candle.

Chapter Six

'So where shall we start this investigation?' Werferth inquired after they had finished breakfast the next morning.

Eadulf was hesitant, glancing to Fidelma. It was difficult to overcome his habit of seeking approval from Fidelma before announcing any decision in an investigation. He was not used to leading an inquiry without her guidance.

'As we said last night, we should see those people who helped extinguish the fire and who found the bodies at my uncle's hall,' he replied. 'The more witnesses, the better, especially anyone who saw and can describe the figures that Widow Eadgifu claimed to be Hibernians leaving the area.'

'I would be interested to know who the religieux was who appeared among the crowd and who made no effort to correct Stuf when he seized us,' Fidelma pointed out.

Crída, who was with them, looked surprised.

'There was a religieux there after the burial? Did Brother Boso return after he had gone back to Ceol's Halh? He left after the ceremony and I thought all was finished. That's why I left to go hunting.'

'Yes, a religieux appeared when Stuf was trying to take us as prisoners,' confirmed Eadulf.

Crída was puzzled. 'It must have been Brother Boso. Beornwulf had instructed me to arrange the burial while he was attending the Witan. Brother Boso came to conduct the funeral rites yesterday morning and then said he was returning to his chapel at Ceol's Halh. But he did not say that he would return later.'

'So we must go and question him,' Eadulf said, 'and see why he did not intervene with Stuf.'

'Is it usual to bury people here in the morning?' Fidelma asked. In her culture, burials were usually held at midnight on the day after death, after a day's ceremonial watching over the corpse.

Crída shrugged. 'Usually it is good to put a corpse in the ground within a short space of time. This time it was essential, due to the fact that the corpses had been partially incinerated. So Brother Boso felt the morning was appropriate. The rituals and sacraments were concluded well before midday.'

'Yet Brother Boso, if it were him, was still there during the afternoon when we arrived, or else he had returned.' Eadulf was thoughtful. 'I did not like him. I saw him as a brusque sort of man, with little sympathy to listen or understand what was being said.'

'Yet that sounds so unlike Brother Boso,' Beornwulf commented.

'Perhaps it was a stressful time for him. We can take a ride to Ceol's Halh, where he has his chapel, and see what was in his mind that might justify his behaviour,' Crída suggested. 'After all, he was a good friend of Athelnoth.'

'Yet it is strange that he made no interference in what was clearly an illegal act by one of Stuf's class,' Beornwulf commented.

'He would certainly know that a *geburas* would not have such freedom to act,' Crída pointed out. 'A *geburas* cannot give orders to free men.'

'I am beginning to think I was too lenient in just giving him extra work to do on my estate as punishment,' Beornwulf reflected. 'Perhaps a good whipping . . .?'

GRAVE OF THE LAWGIVER

'You have pronounced his punishment, my lord Beornwulf,' Fidelma interceded. 'Let it end there. Your word is the judgement and you have declared it. It is not wise to show people that you initially have made a wrong judgement by amending it.'

Beornwulf thought for a moment. 'As your husband will tell you, lady, our laws and manner of judging do not always mirror your own. But it is true; a whipping may not render encouragement to any future obedience and service to his lord. So be it. His punishment to labour for me this week will be enough.'

'You said Brother Boso knew Athelnoth well?' Eadulf asked Crída. 'So do you have any explanation why this Brother Boso behaved discourteously?'

'None. In fact, young Wulfrun often went to his chapel at Ceol's Halh.'

'It just does not sound like him. He was a close friend of Athelnoth, as Crída said. He knew the law and should have intervened to exert his authority. He could have saved you much embarrassment and potential injury,' Beornwulf said.

'If Stuf is still on your estate then we will start the questioning with him,' Eadulf decided.

While Beornwulf and Werferth were called to look at the welfare of the horses by the stable master, Eadulf and Fidelma went to find Stuf, working in the pig pens. It was not hard to find them as the odours were a ready guide. Fidelma could not help feeling sympathy for the emaciated semi-slave, bending over a shovel and bucket. She could not quite interpret the concept of his position in her own mind although she guessed it was something like the *daer-fuidhir* of her own culture: someone who did not have full rights in the community. When called to talk to them, he approached almost shaking with nerves as he stood before them. His lips trembled so much that he could hardly speak.

Eadulf opened the questions.

'You now realise that you acted above your station yesterday?'

I did not know your status otherwise I would have warned you. Your behaviour might have ended with the lady Fidelma and me being injured or killed by the false accusations.'

The man was unable to say anything, but stood with head hung, not meeting their eyes.

Fidelma whispered something to Eadulf. He nodded and addressed the man again.

'I am reminded that your lord has set your punishment for this infraction of custom and law. So be it. I will abide by it. Therefore you will now tell us, slowly and carefully, your role when my uncle's house was burnt down.'

The man finally managed to mumble an answer, with a great deal of nervous hesitation. 'It is as I told my lord Beornwulf.'

'Then repeat it, slowly and carefully.'

When he had finished, Eadulf remarked: 'It seems just as Beornwulf recounted it. He has added nothing new.' He examined the man carefully. 'How long have you lived in this township, Stuf?'

The man clearly did not expect the question and hesitated before answering.

'I was brought in service to folk at a farm at Geoc-ford. I was there many seasons before they perished of the plague and I was claimed to the partial service of lord Beornwulf.'

'Geoc-ford? The Oxen Ford? Yet you say you did not know of me or my family?'

'I knew lord Athelnoth, the *gerefa*, but only by sight; also Wulfrun, who was often on errands for her uncle.'

'So where did you originally come from?'

'I was one of the Gyrwas – the people of the Fens. I was taken in a raid by the farmer at Geoc-ford,' Stuf replied.

'So you did not know me. But others should have known me.'

The man spread his arms. 'I now understand you have been many years away from this place.'

'Why did you not realise that you had no rights to challenge us? That farmer, Wiglaf, had no right to allow you to take charge. Why is it that you thought you could level suspicions at my wife because she is a Hibernian?'

'There was talk about Hibernians, and old Widow Eadgifu says she saw them at the time of the fire. So I thought that was evidence enough that you should be made prisoners.'

'Is this question relevant, Eadulf?' Fidelma asked softly. 'We seem to have entered this path before.'

'I was just interested why no one seemed to recognise me yesterday when Stuf was forcing us through the township. Was there no one who lived nearby who was in the township at the time to know me?'

'I think it has already been said,' Fidelma insisted gently.

Beornwulf and Werferth approached.

'Have you found out anything new?' the thane asked.

'I just cannot accept that one is born and raised in a township where everyone who knew you has suddenly vanished. It is just not logical.'

Fidelma felt she knew the reason for Eadulf's dwelling on the subject. She realised how, after boasting over the years of his township and his family position as lawgivers of the town, that not being recognised and then accused of being a belligerent stranger, he took it as an insult.

'Well, they did find out who you were,' Werferth observed dryly. 'I suspect on closer questioning you will find many others who knew you, if it matters. At least Crída knew you as a young man in the township and, by Thunor, I know you both enough to support you against such idiots who tried to deny you. So all is well, surely?'

Eadulf looked as though he was not convinced.

'We are straying from the point, Eadulf,' Fidelma said quietly. 'The point now is to find out what has happened to your young sister, and who was responsible for the murder of your uncle and his servant. Your identity is now established by those who matter, so we can move on.'

Eadulf swallowed to disguise his irritation. The fact that he had not been immediately acknowledged had cut deeply into his ego, just as Fidelma suspected.

Fidelma felt she should try to bring the questions round to the subject of the fire. 'So, Stuf, you have a boat on the River Frome? Did you always moor it at the top end of the township?'

'Frequently, but not always.'

'You said that you knew Athelnoth by sight?'

'I would recognise him. I knew his servant Osric, for he would occasionally give me jobs to do when I was not summoned to serve my lord Beornwulf. Also, as I said, I often saw Wulfrun going on errands for the *gerefa*.'

'Cast your mind back to the day before the fire. What prompted you to moor where you did?'

'During the day I was at Geoc-ford. I moored my boat at Ceol's Halh. When darkness fell, I then moored it further down river, meaning to join the Alde later the next morning. There can be some good fishing along the Alde where the Frome joins it.'

'So you must have known Brother Boso?' Eadulf asked Stuf.

'I have seen the priest from a distance in my travels, for the river rises beyond Ceol's Halh. I often return to fish there. But I do not know him as such. This new religion is not for the likes of me, although I have spoken to the young brother that dwells in Ceol's Halh.'

'A young religieux?'

'A young fair-haired boy. Wulfrun often spoke with him. They were friendly.'

'Then you must have known that the religieux who allowed you to take us prisoners was not Brother Boso?' Fidelma said sharply. 'Who was he?'

Stuf shrugged. 'I thought he was one of those from Domnocwic who sometimes helps Brother Boso.'

'Brother Boso was the priest I asked to carry out the rituals,' Crída intervened. 'His disciple, as he calls him, did not come to the burial services. Wulfrun was often in Ceol's Halh with legal matters on behalf of Athelnoth. I am not sure how long the young one has been in that place as Brother Boso's disciple.'

'How long has Brother Boso been a priest here?' Eadulf asked.

'At least three or four winters,' Crída replied. 'But your description sounds a bit strange, for he was always a friendly sort – a jovial person.'

'Well, there was little of friendship yesterday with the person we saw.' Eadulf turned back to Stuf. 'On that day that you came and moored not far from Athelnoth's hall – did you see anyone in the vicinity?'

'I did not arrive until the evening. I saw the Widow Eadgifu. She was always about. She often gave me a slice of cheese or a sausage. It is hard being a *geburas*. One often has no settled place and has to fend as best one can, but still be ready to answer the demands of the thane. However, Widow Eadgifu always remembered me, even when she became distracted. That was when she was living in the good times.'

'The good times?'

'In her mind, of course, she thought she was still in those times; the times before the nobles started to demand that we worship the new God and reject our own.'

Beornwulf smiled thinly. 'He means back three decades or more, when there was one overall god, Woden. Old Widow Eadgifu will always worship the Wise Ones, as the old gods are called.'

'You saw no one else that night?' Eadulf went on.

Stuf was shaking his head, but then he hesitated, remembering something. 'I saw Wiglaf and others, but that was when they were fighting the fire. They turned out to help douse it. Wiglaf's hut is nearby and he is a *ceorl*, a free tenant, who owns his patch of land.'

'Very well,' Eadulf sighed. 'I suppose we should go up to my uncle's house . . . the remains of my uncle's house,' he corrected. 'We'll speak with everyone who lives close by or who were gathered that night to fight the flames.' He turned to look questioningly to the others. 'Is there anything else to ask at this stage?'

'You have covered all you can, Eadulf,' Fidelma replied, and then turned apologetically to Beornwulf. 'Can we ask to be accompanied there? That is, in case we are met with the same suspicion as before?'

'Most certainly,' Beornwulf declared at once. 'This mystery is as much our concern as it is that of your husband.' He turned to his *druhting*. 'Crída, make sure our horses are ready. And you had better come along as well, as it turns out you are a central witness to some of these events.'

'I am coming too,' Werferth added. 'I said that any help I can give is yours to command.'

In just a short time, Crída was leading the way through the township, north along the river, with Eadulf and Fidelma following and Beornwulf and Werfreth behind them. It had been Beornwulf's decision to dispense with the services of any bodyguard, seeing they were confining themselves to the township. The group of riders were followed with curious looks by the inhabitants, who paused in their business to examine their thane and his companions as they passed by. By now, the news, or rather rumours, of what had transpired, had spread through the small population. At least this time there was no animosity towards the visitors, just curiosity. Now those along the route bowed to the thane as social ritual demanded, but they also noticed the presence of Werferth, noting his clothing and insignia and realising that here was one of *ealdorman* rank.

When they arrived at the northern outskirts of Seaxmund's Ham, at the small group of buildings that surrounded the now blackened pile of what had been Athelnoth's house, the area was deserted. If anyone had been apprised of their coming, they had taken themselves behind closed doors.

The party dismounted in front of the blackened ruins and secured their horses to some saplings by the Gull's Stream.

'Let us proceed along to Widow Eadgifu's cabin,' Beornwulf suggested. 'We should talk to her first, as it was she who saw the Hibernians riding away.'

'I am not sure that is going to help us much if her mind is wandering,' Eadulf replied doubtfully.

'We can try, at least,' Beornwulf replied enthusiastically. 'I knew her in her good days as well as bad days.'

He turned and led the way along the dirt track towards the wooden cabin where the old woman lived.

'Was it not said that she was looked after by someone?' Fidelma queried. 'Or does she live entirely alone in this place?'

'The community does not let her go hungry,' Beornwulf assured Fidelma, 'but Mother Elfrida looks after her. She was once our servant in Beoderic's Worth and came with us when we settled here. Widow Eadgifu is her own healer. When Eadulf was a boy, she was the wise woman of the township and people came to her for charms and cures.'

Eadulf sighed. 'As you say, she once was that. Now she is aged and needs someone else to take care of her. She could not even recognise me.'

'While you speak with the old woman, I will see if I can find Wiglaf or anyone else who was witness to the events,' Crída suggested.

Werferth signalled that he would accompany him. Beornwulf led Eadulf and Fidelma along to where the old woman was sitting on a stool just outside her wooden shack. She seemed to be staring into the middle distance and humming to herself. As they approached she did not make any effort to greet them, not even by a glance, but remained head down, crooning softly to herself. Eadulf realised that, in spite of this, she was aware of their approach.

'A good day to you, Widow Eadgifu,' Beornwulf greeted, standing almost over her.

She did not even look up.

'What do the omens of the sacred Tiw tell you today?' The thane raised his voice to ensure she heard him.

The old woman suddenly stretched out her hands upwards but with palms downwards and sniffed as if in deprecation.

'The leaves are yellowing,' came her quavering voice.

'Come now, the summer is still warming the land. Autumn is a long way off,' Beornwulf chided in amusement.

'Yet the leaves are yellow, even when the seasons do not agree. Flames do not die only in fires but in the hearts and minds.'

'I don't understand. Tell us what this is a sign of?' Beornwulf frowned.

'The dark clouds are coming, that is all.'

The thane sighed in exasperation and bent forward a little, speaking deliberately and slowly: 'Do you remember what happened here yesterday? Do you recall the fire at Athelnoth's house?'

'It is blackened,' she replied gravely. 'The flames have died but the blackness continues. Blackness on the ground. Blackness in the heart.'

Beornwulf tried again to speak slowly and loudly. He motioned Eadulf to come closer.

'Do you remember Athelnoth's nephew?'

Eadulf bent in front of the old woman so that his face was close to her watery eyes.

'You must remember me as a young boy growing into manhood

GRAVE OF THE LAWGIVER

here? I was son of the *gerefa* Wulfric. The other day you were probably distracted by the noise and shouting of the crowd gathering around my uncle's hall after it was burnt down. So, think back now, Widow Eadgifu. Do you remember what happened yesterday?'

There was a silence but her watery blue eyes did not focus on him.

'Yesterday is another country,' the old woman finally responded.

'Substances disappear,' Eadulf agreed, 'but images are constant in the mind. We still have memories. You must remember what happened to Athelnoth, and to his young niece Wulfrun? Wulfrun was my sister.'

'Wulfrun has gone. She was once a comfort to my ageing eyes.'

'But where has she gone?' Eadulf demanded.

'A flame burns brightly for a while. It shines brightest before there is a breath of wind and then the flame starts to flicker.' It was as though the old woman was talking to herself. She was not looking at anyone but her voice came as from some deep thought.

'Are you saying that she is dead?' Eadulf's voice was unsteady.

The old woman did not appear to hear him and made no reply.

Eadulf stood back as a familiar figure was coming along the track.

'Here is Mother Elfrida,' Beornwulf announced. 'We should be able to get a little sense now.'

Mother Elfrida greeted the thane with due deference.

'That is a suitable name for one who uses their powers in the service of the old,' Eadulf remarked in an attempt to encourage a good relationship. He had registered that her name implied a magical healing being – literally 'elf strength'. Tell us, Mother Elfrida, I suppose you knew Athelnoth the lawgiver very well?'

With Beornwulf indicating his approval that she should answer, Mother Elfrida replied reluctantly.

'I have lived here long enough. Likewise, I knew Wulfrun his niece. I do not remember her brother, who you claim to be. I heard that Athelnoth had a nephew who was a great disappointment to his father. Many years ago, he deserted his family and people and went off with the Hibernians to follow their new religion. I would not recognise him.'

Eadulf was clearly embarrassed at the response.

'I came back and visited the family seven years ago,' he protested. 'It was a short visit and I did not spend much time here for . . .'

'Like my lord Beornwulf, I was not then in Seaxmund's Ham.'

'I am sure there were reasons why you did not meet then,' Beornwulf agreed. He had already pointed out that Mother Elfrida had first come to the township with him when he became thane.

'It is not whether you remembered my husband that is important,' Fidelma suggested, once more trying to turn the questions to the evidence. 'We just wanted to ask you what your attitude to the *gerefa* Athelnoth was?'

'My attitude?' Mother Elfrida sounded as if it were an insult.

'Did you consider Athelnoth to be a fair judge? Was he considerate of his neighbours? Were you happy being of this community?'

'There is no reason why I should not consider him fair,' she countered belligerently. 'I do not understand what you are accusing me of.'

'We are not accusing you of anything,' Fidelma assured her, trying to calm her. 'We are merely wondering whether there was anyone you knew of who disliked him enough to provide a motive for this attack?'

Mother Elfrida was still antagonistic to her.

'He treated everyone according to the traditions of our people, including his niece. Athelnoth had to raise and educate her after her brother deserted his family and joined the Hibernians. That was what brought about the death of the old *gerefa* Wulfric, who died after his son left.'

Eadulf reddened and stumbled over his words before forming a question.

'By what right and knowledge do you claim I deserted my family?' he finally said, trying to modulate his anger.

Mother Elfrida was not perturbed by his tone.

'Everyone knows that the family were saddened when you converted to this new religion and went off to follow the Hibernian teachers. They knew you spent a time in study at Cnobheres Burg and then went off to the western island, Hibernia, and were lost to your family and friends. I was told these stories when I came to live here.'

'A pity, then, you did not speak of them last night, when people claimed I was unknown to them. When I was here seven years ago there was no animosity.'

'I think the past should remain the past,' Beornwulf said hastily. 'I think Eadulf wants to know how his uncle was regarded among us; not just as a *gerefa* but as a person. It is good to know whether Athelnoth had any personal enemies here because of his role as a lawgiver.'

Mother Elfrida sniffed deprecatingly. 'As a *gerefa* he would have made enemies of all he gave judgement against. However, as a man he was well respected in the community.'

'And his house servant Osric – did he have enemies?' Fidelma asked.

'Osric had no enemies and, like Athelnoth, treated all people with respect.'

'And Wulfrun his niece? How did Athelnoth treat her?'

'She wanted for nothing. Athelnoth was hoping he could arrange a good marriage for her.'

'She would be of marriage age? She was dutiful and respectful to Athelnoth's wishes?' Fidelma pressed.

'She was no different from other girls of her age. She was not a shining example of virtue and obedience. But she knew her duty as a daughter.'

'Was Athelnoth hoping for a good marriage for her? I thought he was training her to follow him in law? Was there anyone he had in mind for marriage with her?' Fidelma asked.

Mother Elfrida stared at her a moment and then uttered a cynical chuckle.

'By the sacred foresight of the Wyrd! There were a couple of prospects, but neither would be suitable for Athelnoth. The *gerefa* wanted his niece to have a marriage that elevated the family among the people here. There was some talk and arrangements with an *ealdorman* at Elmen Ham but young Wulfrun was not happy about it. He was an old man. She and Athelnoth had a fierce argument about it.'

'An argument?' Fidelma pressed.

'My opinion was that she wanted no marriage at all, if the truth be known. She once confessed that she wanted to go to a small community that was set on land owned by Ica, on the coast. It's just near the mudflats, at the estuary of the Alde. She wanted to go there and become the abbess and not to marry.'

Beornwulf raised his brows with a smile. 'So her ambition was not to marry anyone? But she certainly had ambition.'

'Ambition, but little patience to achieve it,' the woman affirmed.

'Would you say that she was more concerned in achieving the role of abbess than in the long path that leads to becoming one?' Fidelma asked thoughtfully. 'She wanted the result but not the years of study; all the learning, philosophy and duties to the New Faith that it entails?'

'I suppose so. But when we are of that age we tend to dream of achieving unobtainable objectives.'

'What prevented her from joining a community and starting to study towards that role?' Eadulf asked. 'She was surely of an age to do so?'

Mother Elfrida shrugged. 'Her uncle's will was the stronger one. He was fixed on her making a good match, and while he was happy that she learnt the art of law, he felt religious education was worthless. I think he was biased by what happened to you.'

'What you are saying is that Wulfrun had no reason to run away? So her disappearance was definitely something to do with the burning of Athelnoth's house,' Eadulf pressed. He turned to Widow Eadgifu. 'Do you wish to add anything?'

'You will not get any more out of her,' Fidelma advised him softly. 'Even I can understand that her mind is in another place and I can recognise the cadences of her responses even though they are in Saxon. Best leave her alone now.'

Beornwulf was in agreement. 'We do not need to press the old one further.'

Eadulf looked at him with an angry scowl. Before he could protest, Fidelma, judging his expression, intervened. 'Beornwulf is right. We will not learn anything more positive here about what happened.' She realised what was really troubling him. 'We already know that the fellow Stuf was trying to make a name for himself by leading that mob into some silly hysterical fashion. You have now been identified without the blessing of this poor old woman.'

Eadulf compressed his lips angrily. Before he had a chance to speak, Crída rejoined them with Werferth. They were followed by two other men. Eadulf recognised both from the crowd who had been so unfriendly the day before.

His voice was bitter as he turned to one of them. 'You were the one who knew me, but claimed that I was a traitor to my family!'

The two men were both muscular-looking farming types. They stood nervously, glancing at Thane Beornwulf. He scowled at them.

'I recognise you,' he said. 'You are both freemen with full rights. Why, then, did you let a mere *geburas* like Stuf take charge of the crowd to whip up hostility, which might have resulted in an assault on Eadulf here and his lady?'

'Lord,' Wiglaf spread his arms in helpless fashion. It seemed he had elected himself as spokesman for both of them, 'Everyone was upset. We were angry that Athelnoth and his servant were killed and his house was burnt down. Mother Eadgifu said Hibernians had been seen on the night of the fire. The next day the strangers came and were not recognised, and one was a Hibernian woman.'

'You recognised me,' Eadulf contradicted, looking at Osred. 'You were the one who used the word "traitor" to describe me.'

The man was nervous.

'I . . . I, well . . . I vaguely remembered that Athelnoth talked about a nephew who had left here and gone off with the foreigners to follow the New Faith. I cannot say I recognised you specifically at the time.'

'That is not the same as naming me as a traitor to my family,' Eadulf replied sourly.

'Maybe my interpretation of what your uncle and young Wulfrun said about you was misdirected? I was only repeating gossip.'

'You say Wulfrun also spoke about me?' Eadulf asked.

'She had a harsh opinion that you had abandoned her,' Wiglaf replied when Osred hesitated before Eadulf's scowl.

'Tell me more of how Wulfrun felt.' Eadulf's voice was tight.

'You went off with the Hibernians and left your family. She felt that was a betrayal.' It was clear Wiglaf was trying to think of a way to make the words less sharp.

'On what grounds was it a betrayal?' Eadulf asked sharply.

'There was some decision at Streoneshalh . . .' Wiglaf began. 'I suppose Wulfrun heard all that from that the young man she visited at Ceol's Halh.'

'What young man?' Eadulf demanded.

'Brother Ator. He was the disciple of Brother Boso. He had strong views on many things and often disagreed with Brother Boso.'

'Did Brother Ator have views on the Hibernian teachers?' Fidelma queried.

'He often quoted the decision at Streoneshalh.'

'Which applied only to Northumbria,' Fidelma said tightly. 'It was a decision made long after Eadulf here converted to the New Faith and had gone to Hibernia. In fact, he and I were at that council and advised during the debate that took place.'

Beornwulf was slightly embarrassed when he said: 'Yet Wiglaf has a point.'

'How do you mean?' Eadulf asked.

'Bishop Wilfrid of Northumbria has been telling his followers to spread the decision to other kingdoms. He even went in person to the kingdom of the South Saxons to convert their king Athelwealth,' the farmer offered. It was clear he was the more intelligent of the two. 'The bishop says that we must all follow Rome and ignore the heresy of the Hibernians and the Britons, who both follow other ways. Only Rome upholds the true Faith, he says.' He stopped, realising his voice sounded too enthusiastic. Then he added in a low tone, 'So it is argued, anyway.'

'I remembered Bishop Wilfrid at Streoneshalh,' Fidelma said grimly. 'Did Wulfrun follow those arguments?'

'She was certainly influenced by Brother Boso's disciple. When it was claimed that Hibernians might have done this terrible deed, it seemed plausible to me.' Wiglaf seemed to grab at the justification as to why he had not intervened when they had been accused.

'You felt that it was an excuse to stand by and let the mob have their way?' Eadulf almost sneered as he made the point. 'A mob led by a half-slave.'

'I was not alone,' Wiglaf protested. 'That religieux who was here from Ceol's Halh agreed that you should be taken as prisoners to the thane to await his judgement.'

'It is said that he was not Brother Boso. Who was he?' Fidelma asked. 'He was too old to be this young Brother Ator.'

'Brother Boso had returned to Ceol's Halh after the rituals,' Wiglaf agreed. 'I did not know the other religieux who was in the crowd. I presumed he was a companion of Brother Boso or Brother Ator.'

'We shall deal with that later,' Eadulf dismissed. 'But, at least, you now admit that you have heard my uncle and sister speak of me?'

Wiglaf's gesture was one of admittance.

'Yet you stood by and allowed one to take charge who had no right to do?' Beornwulf was clearly angry. 'You are both freemen and yet you submitted to the hysterical cries of one who was a half-slave without rights? This is truly a matter that is punishable. For a slave not to know his place is one thing. Those who are not slaves, but allow a half-slave to dictate, are culpable of great offence.'

'Lord, we were confused by the things that the New Faith teaches,' Wiglaf protested. 'When we were young we knew what the wise ones taught. We knew our place; everyone from the *theow*, the slaves, from the *ceorl* up to the *ealdorman* even to the *cyning*. Now we have these so-called Brothers with the new god who teaches that we are all His children? They say that it is ordained that even slaves have a right to rule us. Are they the new ealdormen who rule over all ranks of men?'

Beornwulf glanced at Werferth and shrugged slightly, as if to admit he could not answer.

'It is a matter that should soon be settled,' Werferth announced quietly.

Fidelma glanced at him in surprise, but the commander of the king's bodyguard did not amplify further.

'Go back to your ploughshare, Wiglaf,' Beornwulf finally said. 'You as well, Osred. I shall send for you both later. You are both culpable of ignoring our laws of rank and privilege.'

The men exchanged glances and left reluctantly.

'So what have we learnt, Eadulf?' Werferth asked. 'I admit, I am more confused than ever. This does not appear to getting us near to the reason for this attack on the lawgiver.'

'The only path seems to lead to Ceol's Halh,' Fidelma pointed out. 'There are two leads there. One is Brother Boso. The other is that, on the night of the fire, two riders were seen riding away from here. They appeared to be Hibernian religieux.'

Beornwulf was in agreement.

'We also learn that young Wulfrun was a frequent visitor to Ceol's Halh. According to Crída here, she was an emissary about legal matters between Athelnoth and Brother Boso and we are told she was friendly with Brother Boso's disciple, Brother Ator.'

'Another point,' Fidelma added. 'That morning, after the fire, Eadulf and I were coming here from Domnoc-wic. We saw a group of religieux on horses near a place called the Oxen Ford. Eadulf hailed them. They wanted to avoid us. I can tell you now that I think the mysterious religieux who was among the crowd, who could not be identified, was one of them.'

'So we should go to Ceol's Halh and see what we can discover there?' Eadulf asked.

'That is the natural next step,' Fidelma confirmed quietly.

CHAPTER SEVEN

Ceol's Halh was a short ride north along the River Frome. Fidelma remembered it from passing the place two days before. It was a small group of buildings surrounding a wooden chapel, marked as such by a carved wooden cross above the lintel. Fidelma doubted whether more than six people could squeeze into such a construction. She had not even noticed it when they had ridden by previously. The buildings rose on some elevated land on the western side of the river. Further west of the hamlet was a thick forest area. That landscape contrasted with the open wetlands to the east, although there were areas that encompassed some crops as well as pasture land on which various roaming, wild animals – deer, cattle, even goats – appeared in small groups. None of the grazing animals seemed to react either with one another or with the occasional movement of the human inhabitants.

'This is my territory as well,' Beornwulf informed Fidelma as they approached the outskirts of the hamlet. 'There are half a dozen free tenants here and all pay me tribute; they are what we call *geneatas*, landowning *ceorls*. That is, apart from Brother Boso, who is the leader of the New Faith in Seaxmund's Ham. He is in charge of that chapel here with his young assistant . . .' He hesitated as if trying to conjure the name.

'Brother Ator,' Crída supplied immediately.

'It is interesting to have the religious of the New Faith outside of the township,' Fidelma observed, thinking of the situation in her own society. 'Usually one would expect to find them inside the township and at the centre of it.'

'Things are different here,' replied the thane. 'As well you know, it is not long since we encountered the Christian religion – only sixty years since your teachers and those from Rome started to preach seriously here. The people felt that outside of the townships was the proper place for these newcomers. People were still finding the changes of gods difficult. No more than a generation or two have passed since our kings adopted Christianity. We spent some time under the overlordship of Penda of Mercia and he was a fierce adherent to the old religion. Kings change and religions change, and so confused did the people become that they decided the new religious should live outside the communities. They thought it was a better protection, as what was acceptable one day was not accepted the next.'

'So this is where your religieux teacher, Brother Boso, lives?' Fidelma clarified.

'As I say, Brother Boso and his disciple Brother Ator live here.'

'But they are not native to your township?'

'Brother Boso arrived here from the abbey at Domnoc-wic about five years ago.'

'You said that he was a jovial person and not at all like our description of the man that we saw at Athelnoth's house, who refused to intervene with the crowd?'

'Brother Boso is highly intelligent and knows the law.'

As they came near the cabins around the chapel, some women and a few young children emerged to watch the newcomers. One woman in particular stood, hands on hips, waiting as they rode up and dismounted before her house. There was a chorus of respectful greetings to Thane Beornwulf.

'I seek Brother Boso,' Beornwulf called, looking round as several people began to gather around them. They were obviously the wives and daughters of workers who were in the fields. One of them, a large, moon-faced woman, came forward.

'If it please, my lord, I am Mother Notgide. I and my man Scead are the elders of this settlement.'

'Where is Scead?'

'In the fields, as usual, my lord. I will speak for him.'

'So where is Brother Boso? I see the chapel is shut up.'

'He left early this morning.'

'Left to go where?' Beornwulf asked impatiently.

'He said he was riding to Domnoc-wic, lord. If you want confirmation, young Brother Ator is down by the river. There is a pool beyond that outcrop of rocks where he has a hut. He is probably there, fishing.' The woman pointed to indicate the direction.

'It seems a strange time for Brother Boso to have gone to the abbey at Domnoc-wic,' Beornwulf said. 'Did Brother Boso ride off alone? Did anyone accompany him?'

'Such as who?' the woman frowned.

'Was he with another religieux? There was a strange religieux who seems to have attended the funeral of Athelnoth and his servant Osric.'

'We don't know any other religious person accept Brother Ator, lord. He is still here.'

'Is it possible that Brother Boso might be escorting the *gerefa*'s daughter there to a place of safety after her uncle's place was burnt?' Crída asked. 'You may know that she has disappeared since that night.'

Mother Notgide actually chuckled. It was a sour sound. 'He rode alone. Had young Wulfrun gone to Domnoc-wic, then Brother Ator would not be sitting here fishing. Yes, we heard that she had disappeared. She frequently came here. She was here on the evening of the attack on Athelnoth's house.'

'What was she doing here?' Eadulf asked immediately.

'Visiting Brother Ator, who else?' The woman gave a knowing smile. 'But she returned home well before midnight. Before the fire.'

Fidelma decided to interrupt. 'Did anyone see any riders yesterday, or on the day of the fire, who looked like Hibernian religieux on horseback? They might even have been meeting with this Brother Boso or someone else.'

The woman examined Fidelma suspiciously.

'Are you from that Hibernian group at Cnobheres Burg?' she demanded slightly belligerently.

'Answer the question,' Beornwulf interceded with an exhalation of impatient breath.

The woman hesitated. 'What was the question?' she evaded.

'It was simple enough,' Fidelma pressed. 'Were there riders around dressed in religious robes during the last three days? They were seen at the Oxen Ford yesterday and some saw them earlier near Athelnoth's house when it was set alight. Did they ever come here to meet Brother Boso?'

'There was talk that such people were seen on the road to the Oxen Ford,' Mother Notgide admitted. 'Whether they had connection with Brother Boso, I know not, nor would it be any concern of mine.' She turned to Beornwulf. 'My man Scead and I run the small farm here and pay tribute to you, my lord. Should I answer such questions?'

'You are a respected tenant,' Beornwulf agreed gravely, noting her reluctance to give information to Fidelma. 'So it will help if you can answer all questions to the best of your knowledge. This lady is under my protection and is wife to Eadulf, son of Wulfric, the former *gerefa*, and nephew to Athelnoth.'

The woman showed some surprise and examined Fidelma closely.

'There are certainly less of your kind to be seen about in these times. These are changing times.'

'Who saw such people?' Fidelma pressed, although wondering what the woman's words implied.

'Scead saw those on horseback, but only from a distance. He was working in the fields nearby. I really cannot say whether they came to visit Brother Boso or not. My man says he saw two of them a few days ago up by the Oxen Ford while he was working on the barley crop above here.'

'Was this before or after you heard the news of the *gerefa*'s death?' Eadulf asked.

'Scead mentioned he had spoken to Wiglaf the farmer some days before he had seen them. We had the news of Athelnoth's death only when Brother Boso had been asked by Crída to conduct the funeral rituals yesterday morning. That was when we learnt that Wulfrun was missing.'

'There was no further sign of these strangers? More importantly, there was no sign of Wulfrun being with them?' Eadulf asked.

'I know that Brother Boso came back yesterday from Seaxmund's Ham. He spoke with young Brother Ator and then at dawn this morning he departed by himself for Domnoc-wic. I can say no more.'

'Brother Boso did not explain why he was riding for the abbey at Domnoc-wic?'

The woman said shortly, with a curious grimace, which was not lost on Fidelma, 'I knew Athelnoth was a great friend of Brother Boso, but neither followed the teachings of the Hibernians about this New Faith.'

'There seems a lot of resentment against the Hibernians,' Eadulf observed.

'A lot of folk have been hearing the teachings of the Greek,' the woman shrugged. 'He has great influence now, so Brother Boso said.'

'The Greek?' Fidelma was puzzled.

'Brother Boso was talking a lot about the Greek. Saying that he had come from Rome to be the head of the New Faith among our people. The Greek says that all the Hibernians were teaching lies and we should obey the rules of the New Faith, as dictated from Rome, ignoring what others, like the Hibernians, teach.'

It was Werferth who explained. 'The woman refers to Theodoros of Tarsus, lady, who was recently sent by Rome to be Archbishop of the Cantwara.'

'And chief bishop over all the peoples of this island,' Crída added, not hiding his lack of enthusiasm for the subject.

'Are you saying that this Theodoros of Tarsus is creating dissension and animosity against the Hibernians?' Fidelma asked in surprise.

'Only that he is preaching that Rome alone should be obeyed in all matters of the New Faith,' Werferth confirmed.

Fidelma was opening her mouth to comment when Eadulf intervened: 'Let us speak with this Brother Ator. He will surely know more, as he is Brother Boso's assistant and he knew my sister. Where did you say we can find him? By the river?'

The woman again indicated the rocks by the river by inclining her head.

'He'll be fishing there as usual,' she said, disapprovingly.

They began to move in that direction, but Fidelma paused a moment and turned back to Mother Notgide. The elderly woman had noticed her hesitation and so remained watching her suspiciously.

'From the tone of your voice I gather that you disapproved of my husband's sister Wulfrun?'

Mother Notgide made a negative gesture, letting one shoulder rise and fall.

'It is not up to the likes of me to criticise the family of the *gerefa*. I remembered your husband's father Wulfric. He was unhappy that his only son had rejected his family and the old gods to follow the Hibernians. It is said Wulfric died of disappointment. He died before he could be disappointed in Wulfrun.'

'In what way would he be disappointed in Wulfrun?'

The woman was silent.

'Do not tell me that it is not your place to express your own opinion,' Fidelma was disapproving. 'You are not . . .' She was about to say *dáer-fuidir* – a non-freeman – in her own language, but she could not think of the equivalent in this culture. 'You are surely free to express yourself? What you tell me will not go beyond the two of us.'

The woman hesitated a moment. 'I felt sorry for Athelnoth. He was given the responsibility of raising her after Wulfric died,' she replied. 'He was a good man and he did not tolerate those whose behaviour was contemptuous of others.'

'Contemptuous of others? Are you saying that Wulfrun was disparaging towards others?'

Mother Notgide grimaced. 'Wulfrun disapproved of anything that she could not understand nor control,' she said. 'I am sorry for what has happened to Athelnoth and Osric his servant. Sorry also if something has happened to Wulfrun. Yet my sorrow is mixed, for she was not a likeable person.'

'Can you explain more?'

'Your companions will be missing you,' the woman countered.

'So tell me quickly,' Fidelma insisted.

'Wulfrun often passed through here, supposedly on errands for her uncle, the *gerefa*. She was always arrogant to everyone except those she considered her equals, which were few, I have heard.'

Fidelma heard Eadulf calling.

'Continue . . .' urged Fidelma. 'What have you heard?'

'Perhaps you should speak to Brother Boso,' advised the woman. 'As you will hear nothing but praise from Brother Ator.'

'Brother Boso is not here. I am asking your opinion.'

'I know she argued with her uncle about a suitable marriage partner.'

Fidelma smiled. 'It's a regular occurrence between a daughter and her parents. But I presume you mean, from what you say, that she had an infatuation with the young religieux here?'

'That is for you to find out,' the woman sniffed. 'If anyone challenged her wishes, she had a temper that made the gatherers of souls, the choosers of the slain, seem like peacemakers.'

'But she is just a young girl, is she not? Sometimes youths cannot articulate their thoughts rationally and often lose their tempers while trying to do so.'

'Your talk sounds like old Mother Elfrida,' the woman said, dismissing the subject with a shrug. 'You best go after your companions or I shall be reprehended by the thane for gossiping and delaying him.'

Fidelma offered a word of thanks and hurried away.

'What was that woman saying?' Eadulf asked curiously as she joined them. They were walking through a group of trees towards the rocky area that bordered the river.

'I was trying to get some more details of this Brother Boso.'

A small hut stood nearby the river bank on a rocky promontory. Outside of it was a glowing fire under a cooking pot. A little further on, sitting on one of the rocks, was a slim, fair-haired youth, with a rod and line in hand, staring at the rippling waters. He was dressed in simple robes, which immediately identified him as a religieux. A wooden cross, on a strip of hide, hung around his neck. He could not have been much more than a score of years in age, with deep blue eyes, a pleasant mouth and a firm jaw. In spite of his slim build, he did not seem to fit his role well. He had more of an indolent attitude to life, an enjoyment of living, than one devoting his life to the contemplation of obedience and service to others and a strict deity.

'Brother Ator!' Beornwulf called as they approached.

The young man must have been deep in thought for he jerked suddenly at the sound of the voice, nearly dropped his rod, and turned. He saw the group and scrambled to his feet.

'My lord?' He staggered a moment, regained his balance, put aside his rod and then came forward a few steps. 'How may I serve you, my lord?'

'You usually help Brother Boso at services?'

'I do, my lord.'

'You were not helping at the interment of Athelnoth and Osric,' Crída intervened sharply.

Eadulf frowned. His old friend seemed almost to be insinuating something.

'Brother Boso wanted me to remain here.' The young man did not seem perturbed.

'Did you know the religieux that Brother Boso sent to Seaxmund's Ham after he had returned from the funeral?' Beornwulf questioned.

The young man's reaction was one of bewilderment.

'He sent no one else. He conducted the rituals himself. He was waiting for a message, which is why he wanted me to remain here. Then he returned here quickly afterwards.'

'I don't suppose you know who Brother Boso was waiting for?'

The young man shook his head. 'All I know is what he told me,' he replied. 'As I say, I was told I was not needed to attend the rituals but should remain here in case of a message.'

'What do you know about the fire and deaths at Athelnoth's house?' Beornwulf asked.

'Nothing except what Brother Boso told me. I was told that Athelnoth had been killed, along with his servant Osric. I was told Wulfrun was missing.' The young man blinked in passing emotion for a moment. The expression was not lost on Fidelma.

'So you remained here. Did anyone show up with a message?' It was Beornwulf who put the question.

'After Brother Boso returned from the burial and no message had come, he had waited awhile and then took his horse and rode off. He returned later and then this morning he took his horse again, telling me he was going to the abbey at Domnoc-wic.'

'So Brother Boso has a horse?' Fidelma mused, thinking once more that it was rare that ordinary religious travelled on, or even owned, horses.

'Not all those of the New Faith are committed to vows of poverty,' replied Brother Ator with a tight, disapproving tone.

'Can we make this clear?' Eadulf asked. 'Brother Boso returned from the funeral at Seaxmund's Ham and then rode off to see someone. He came back and then this morning went to the abbey at Domnoc-wic. So who did he ride off to see after the funeral?'

'He did not tell me. I think he went up to the Oxen Ford. He was gone there but a short while and then returned here. When he told me he was going to Domnoc-wic, he mentioned that he thought Wulfrun's disappearance could be that she had gone on some errand for her uncle and that is why she was not at the *gerefa*'s house when the attack came.'

Fidelma examined the young man thoughtfully. 'Mother Notgide has just said that Wulfrun frequently visited Ceol's Halh. She was here on the evening of the conflagration in Athelnoth's house,' she pointed out.

'She returned to Seaxmund's Ham long before midnight.' Brother Ator's tone was defensive.

'So she would have been at his house when it was attacked?'

'She told me she had to go back to her uncle as there was another errand that he wanted her to complete before midnight.'

'She was going back to her uncle to pick up a message to take somewhere?' Eadulf asked, in surprise. 'She did not tell you what that was?'

Brother Ator shrugged. 'If I knew, then I would have told Brother Boso.'

Eadulf was looking unhappy. 'Wulfrun is my sister,' he told the youth. 'This is the first time we have heard of a possible reason why she was not in the *gerefa*'s house when it was burnt down. Did she often take messages for her uncle at such late hours?'

The young man seemed uncomfortable and paused before finally responding.

'It was not usual, but not unknown. Wulfrun was being trained by Athelnoth in the matter of laws.'

'Did she take messages between Athelnoth and Brother Boso?'

'That is so.'

'Are we saying that Wulfrun went home that evening but expected to be sent out with another message? So the odds are that she did not witness the killing of her uncle and his servant, nor the burning of his house? Why did she not return after the attack?' Fidelma asked.

The young man shrugged awkwardly. 'I have asked that question myself. Maybe she was abducted by the attackers.'

'It does not sound very reasonable,' Fidelma observed.

'What about these messages between Athelnoth and Brother Boso?' Werferth intervened. He rarely spoke, but when he did so, it was to the point. 'What were they about? Was Brother Boso expecting a message from Athelnoth that night?'

'I do not know,' Brother Ator replied.

'Wulfrun never mentioned what messages she carried?'

'She never told me.'

Crída, who had been silent most of the time, suddenly chuckled acridly. 'The boy is a liar!'

They were surprised at the unexpected intervention, and Eadulf turned to him in disapproval.

'Crída, this is a legal investigation. We must follow protocol. You must allow me to follow my questions.'

Crída clenched his jaw and said nothing further.

Eadulf turned back to Brother Ator, who was now staring in anger at Crída.

'Tell me, Brother Ator, would you recognise a short, stocky man, with heavy jowls and thick lips?' he asked. 'Little hair of wheat colour, with heavy brows and pale eyes. He does not have a pleasing manner. Rather one of curtness and aggression.'

Brother Ator looked bewildered and then shook his head.

'He was a religieux who claimed he was sent by Brother Boso,' Eadulf went on. 'Could it be that he was the same person that Brother Boso went to meet at the Oxen Ford after the interment? You don't recognise his description?'

The young man shook his head. Then he seemed to have an idea. 'It is strange you should ask.'

'Why so?' Beornwulf demanded.

'Because someone passed through here this morning. I nearly forgot. A trader came along the river, taking some rabbit furs to sell in Domnoc-wic. He asked me the name of Brother Boso's assistant. When I said that I was the assistant, he said I could not be as Brother Boso had sent an assistant who was older than I was, to ensure that he had not left a saddle bag at the site where he had performed the funeral rites. I have just remembered. Brother Boso had not told me of any such a thing. I had no idea what the man could be referring to. Perhaps this was the strange man of whom you refer?'

'So this strange religieux was not anyone you knew?'

'The man with the rabbits had been at the funeral. He was the son of Osred.'

'You remember that at this moment? Convenient, isn't it?' Crída sneered.

'I don't understand.' Brother Ator was bewildered.

'He probably understands a great deal,' Crída said, turning to the others. 'You have been told that Wulfrun came here a lot. Obviously she brought messages from Athelnoth. My lord, force the boy to tell the truth. What was that all about? Wulfrun must have told him.'

Beornwulf seemed surprised at Crída. But he turned to the young religieux.

'Brother Ator, it sounds as though you and Wulfrun were good friends. Are you sure she did not mention to you anything that might help us?'

Brother Ator flushed. Fidelma knew guilt when she saw it on a youth's features.

'It will do you no good to hide the truth,' Crída prompted, almost triumphant.

'It would be best if you told the truth, Brother Ator,' Fidelma agreed quietly.

There was a long silence and it was thought that Brother Ator was not going to respond, but then he said in a reluctant tone: 'It is true that messages from Athelnoth were delivered to Brother Boso. I was not privy to them, although I was shown some by Wulfrun.'

'How is that?' Fidelma asked immediately.

'They were written on parchment. Wulfrun asked me if I knew what they meant. I did not.'

'And you, a religieux, claim to have no knowledge of writing?' Crída was a little triumphant. 'Don't all the New Religious learn letters?'

'I learnt how to form letters in Latin and in Greek when I studied at the abbey in Domnoc-wic and I was complimented on my knowledge,' protested Brother Ator. 'But these were letters in forms I did not know.'

Fidelma turned to Eadulf. 'What languages did your uncle know that he was able to understand such written characters other than those we use with Latin?'

Eadulf was perplexed. 'It is a long time since I saw him . . .' he said thoughtfully. 'I know he knew some Latin and Greek, for he

GRAVE OF THE LAWGIVER

studied under the Burgundian Felix, who dwelt at Domnoc-wic many years ago.'

It was Beornwulf who surprised them. 'Your uncle once told me that he had learnt to write in our own language; the language of the Angles. He once told me that he wanted to do what Aethelberht, king of the Cantwara, did years ago. You must know the story, Eadulf. Aethelberht had a law code written down in the language of the Jutes some seventy years ago. That's what Athelnoth wanted to do for the Angles.'

'I did not know that my uncle was interested in such things. Few people have any idea of writing in their own language. But surely,' Eadulf turned to Brother Ator, 'the characters would be in the Latin forms, which the Hibernian missionaries brought to our people. By using the sounds of those characters you might have picked up what was being written in your own language?'

'I said that I did not recognise the characters,' Brother Ator maintained.

Brother Eadulf frowned for a moment. Then he took a nearby twig, bent to an area of mud and drew some symbols.

'Were they like that?'

The young brother shrugged. Fidelma glanced over Eadulf's shoulder and could make nothing of them. Beornwulf, Werferth and Crída stood puzzled for a moment, staring down, and then Werferth started to chuckle.

'Athelnoth and Brother Boso corresponded in *futhorc*?'

The others looked blank.

'*Futhorc*.' Eadulf searched his memory. 'Of course! That is the ancient runes, which the Jutes began to use as a means of writing down their own languages. It is the art of writing that is still used among some people who speak similar tongues to us, like the Franks, Jutes, Angles, Saxons . . .'

Fidelma was curious.

'I have not heard of this *futhorc*, as you call it. Do you use it?' she demanded of Eadulf, who shook his head.

'It is not used much,' Werferth intervened in agreement. 'It is archaic and those of the New Faith do not approve of it.'

'I have seen some form of it, so I recognise its outlines and some symbols, but I do not know it,' Eadulf admitted.

'Can you show me some more symbols, Werferth?' Fidelma asked.

After some hesitation Werferth took the twig from Eadulf and drew some more symbols on the flat mud.

Brother Ator was nodding. 'I do not understand it, but I can see that they are of the same type of symbols used in the messages Wulfrun showed me. But they are not exactly the same.'

'So it seems your uncle was writing to Brother Boso in some native form of your language,' Fidelma said to Eadulf. 'The only way of taking that further is to find Brother Boso.'

'Brother Boso has gone to Domnoc-wic,' Eadulf pointed out.

'Which is where we must go now,' Fidelma added, 'if we are to search for the truth.'

'We are overlooking something,' Werferth said. 'What was the point that Crída brought up?'

Crída reminded him enthusiastically.

'If Athelnoth was exchanging messages with Brother Boso, which Brother Ator had no understanding of, why was Wulfrun coming here, except not just to pass on the message, but to spend time in Brother Ator's company?'

Fidelma's eyes widened slightly at the point.

'You did not make that point so precisely before, Crída. How do you know that Wulfrun was spending time with Brother Ator as something extra to bringing messages from her uncle to the religieux?'

Crída returned her inquisitive gaze defensively. A slight colour came to his cheeks.

GRAVE OF THE LAWGIVER

'I happened to pass this way several times. My lord Beornwulf will tell you that one of my duties is to keep a watch on the wild deer to the east of the river here. They are his to demand tribute on and I am sent to see they have not been stolen.'

'So you come this way often and have seen Wulfrun in the company of Brother Ator? What is your point?' prompted Eadulf, frowning.

The young religieux was red faced and seemed angry.

'It is no secret,' he protested in a tight voice. 'Wulfrun and I were in love. What harm?'

'What harm, indeed?' Crída sneered.

'We were going to be married!' Brother Ator added coldly.

Beornwulf looked startled. 'Did Athelnoth know of this? Did he approve?'

'He knew our decision,' Brother Ator confessed.

'*Our decision!*' Crída's tone was raised in sarcasm. 'Aren't you religieux supposed to live without women?'

Fidelma felt she should correct the man.

'There is a small group in the New Faith who believe that celibacy brings them closer to their deity. The group is not many, and even few bishops would advocate it. So there is nothing surprising if Wulfrun and Brother Ator were planning this. So what was Athelnoth's reply when, as you said, you and Wulfrun went to tell her uncle?'

'He approved,' Brother Ator replied at once.

'And Wulfrun agreed?' Eadulf asked.

'She did.'

Crída gave a sardonic bark that was more malignant than humorous.

'There is something amiss, my lord,' he said, turning to Beornwulf. 'No one knows of this alleged approval. It is not something that Athelnoth would refrain from announcing.'

'It was only decided the day before the fire,' Brother Ator declared.

'There is an obvious question to be resolved,' Crída intervened belligerently. 'This permission was asked the day before the fire. Then Athelnoth and his servant are murdered. Wulfrun disappears and the house of the *gerefa* is burnt down.'

Fidelma was regarding Crída and Brother Ator thoughtfully.

'Wulfrun had come to see you on the evening before the fire, before the attack. When did you see Wulfrun next?'

'I have not seen her after that.' Brother Ator's voice was bitter. 'She did not come back after she left that evening. The next thing I heard was when Crída brought the news to Brother Boso that Athelnoth and his servant had been murdered and his house had been burnt down. Because of the state of the corpses, he requested Brother Boso to go and conduct the burial services immediately.'

'Weren't you anxious about Wulfrun?'

'She had disappeared, so I felt I should remain here in case she came to find me. Had I not been here, where would she turn?'

'You suspected that she had survived the fire and would come to tell you about it first?'

Brother Ator hesitated and then shrugged. 'I suppose I felt that,' he confessed.

'But she never came and you have not seen her since? You have been waiting here, hoping that she would just turn up?'

'That is so. Though . . . it is not the way it now sounds.'

'I believe Athelnoth refused permission for her to marry you.' Crída's voice was bitter in accusation. 'There might have been an argument in which the *gerefa* was killed and, in a rage at his refusal, the fire was set as revenge.'

'Are you accusing me? Or Wulfrun?' cried the young man. 'You better have more than lies to support your accusations.'

Eadulf had turned to Fidelma with a protective expression.

'I have not known my sister since she was a child, but I do feel that this is beyond her character.'

'Rage is in everyone's character when provoked. However, I do not see that this would engender such a rage,' she assured him. 'Also, it seems that there are other questions that negate accepting this one as the solution to this mystery.'

'It would be best if Crída withdrew the accusation,' Eadulf said.

'I was merely making a suggestion,' Crída replied.

'Suggestions are not made without facts to support them,' Eadulf said, still angry.

Crída was about to say something when Beornwulf spoke.

'I think you are right, lady. Wulfrun must first be found and questioned. Brother Ator, you have absolutely no idea where she would go if she was free to do so?'

'I have waited two days here. Had she been free I am sure she would have found a way to let me know. Your arrival here has only confirmed my fears. She is not free, and what happened at Athelnoth's hall is nothing to do with what she and I felt for each other.'

Crída made a sound like a bark of laughter. It was clear to Fidelma that the *druhting* and the young priest entertained no amicable thoughts of each other.

'Apart from yourselves – apart from Wulfrun and yourself – did anyone else know of your serious intent to marry?' Fidelma asked.

'Only one other. That was because I felt, as a young member of the religious, I needed advice about my future intention. I could not go back to the community at Domnoc-wic. I needed advice as to whether I should leave the religious to follow the path in my heart. It was felt that we should marry and join a mixed community, of which there are many.'

'And this person who you told?' Beornwulf asked.

'Was my mentor Brother Boso.'

'And he's vanished as well,' Crída muttered cynically.

'Not exactly,' Eadulf pointed out. 'He's gone to the abbey at Domnoc-wic.' He looked at Fidelma. 'That is the next place we should ride to.'

'It is the logical thing,' she agreed.

Beornwulf sighed. 'I would suggest that we do not all have to undertake that quest. I have much to do in the governance of my township. Also, I need my *druhting* at my side.'

Crída seemed disappointed. He made as if he would protest, but there was a determined look in the thane's eye.

Brother Ator looked from Beornwulf to Eadulf.

'Whoever is leading this investigation, I would like to make a request. I would like to accompany you to the abbey at Domnoc-wic, for not only can Brother Boso support my statement, but he can make suggestions of how best we might find a reason for Wulfrun's disappearance.'

'He made that unexplained journey after he came back from the burial services. He knows, then, that she had disappeared,' Crída pointed put. 'He might have learnt something new or have new ideas on the subject.'

'I see no impediment to you coming with us,' Eadulf said.

'Except that you'll need a horse,' objected Crída.

'I can borrow a horse from Mother Notgide's husband Scead. That is, if you speak up for me, my lord,' the young man said immediately.

Werferth was the only one who seemed satisfied with things.

'There are no problems. I agree with my friend Beornwulf that we do not all of us have to go. I shall accompany Eadulf and Fidelma myself because it so happens that I have a message from the Witan to deliver to Abbot Aecci at the abbey at Domnoc-wic. Young Brother Ator may come along if he wishes. Therefore, Eadulf and Fidelma can continue the investigation under my authority.'

CHAPTER EIGHT

It was with mixed feelings that Fidelma rode alongside Eadulf. Werferth and Brother Ator were leading the way north along the road on which she had recently journeyed from Domnoc-wic. She tried to consider the curious changes that had occurred in such a short time. Whatever anticipated concerns and fears she had been projecting during the ride from the port of Domnoc-wic, she could never have conjured the reality of the past day or two. Now she could sympathise with the impact on Eadulf. This trip was to have been a crossroads in Eadulf's life, but the crossroads had suddenly turned into a black chasm. While he had been preparing finally to come to terms with the problems he had developed about his family, his culture and his life among the East Angles, he was now dealing with ramifications that he could never have expected.

Fidelma realised that she must keep some sort of logical balance when it came to this growing mystery. It was essential for Eadulf to find out why his uncle had been murdered and why his young sister had disappeared. There were questions to be put and answered. One thing she felt sure of was that Brother Ator was hiding something. He claimed he was in love with Wulfrun, and this seemed to be the cause of the animosity shown to him by Crída.

There were other matters to consider, such as the new hostility she was encountering towards the religious of her countrymen and -women, whereas they had once been welcomed among the Angles and Saxons. Was it due to this new bishop, the Greek sent from Rome by Pope Vitalian, to be senior bishop among the Angles and Saxons? Although that was not as important as the murder investigation, it had to be considered none the less.

Another thing concerned her. Why had the commander of the king's bodyguard been sent to Seaxmund's Ham with Beornwulf? Werferth had admitted that he was carrying a message to Abbot Aecci at Domnoc-wic, but he had made no further reference to it.

This time Fidelma could not distract herself by viewing the flat marshy countryside. Now and then, among the sedge-covered marshlands, grew patches of small purple reeds, more colourful than the brown sedges. The four riders crossed some dry rises, strengthened with boulder clay. Upon these areas, alder and willow trees grew in clumps. A few animals were seen in the distance, obviously wary of these tracks, where there might be hunters with bows and arrows. Nothing that caught Fidelma's eye was of interest, except a wading bird with a black-capped head, up-turned bill, black and white body and blue-grey legs, which was feeding among the rushes. It was a species she could not identify and it looked so curious.

They were coming to a crossroads where wooden bridges spanned the Frome, flowing south, but coming from a larger river flowing west to east. Fidelma remembered this was the Oxen Ford. Werferth was guiding them to turn due east along it. She remembered that Eadulf had identified this as the Mennesmer, flowing through flat marshland into a great sea beyond.

'Do you object if Eadulf comes to ride alongside me for a while?' Werferth suddenly called after they made the turn to the east. 'Brother Ator can take his place alongside you. Do you mind?'

There was no reason to object. Fidelma suspected that Werferth had become bored with the young man's company. As Eadulf nudged his pony forward alongside Werferth, Brother Ator halted his pony until Fidelma came abreast of him. Ahead of them Werferth engaged Eadulf immediately in their shared language. Fidelma could barely make out more than a few words, due to the rapidity of their speech. She shrugged and turned to the young man now alongside her.

'So you are adept in Latin?' she opened, trying to think of a means to engage with the young religieux.

Brother Ator nodded. 'And a little Greek, a little Hebrew and, of course, the language of my own people.'

'That is no mean achievement. I think you said you studied in the community in the abbey of Domnoc-wic before you joined Brother Boso?'

'Brother Boso was one of the teachers there at the time. When he was sent to Ceol's Halh I went with him as his disciple. He had taken the Latin classes at the abbey so it was from him that I learnt much of the language.'

'I compliment you on your Latin.' The conversation had been exchanged in that language because Fidelma still found difficulties speaking the language of the Angles. 'Your Latin is such a good standard. Was Brother Boso your only teacher helping your diction, or did you learn the pronunciation elsewhere?'

'I can tell you, as you are a Hibernian . . . I believe Brother Boso was born a Briton. His real name was Cadimedd. He claimed that he had an ancestral knowledge of this land when it was a province of Rome.'

Fidelma's eyes widened. 'Brother Boso was a Briton who taught at Domnoc-wic?'

Brother Ator smiled cynically. 'We do not all hate the Britons.'

'But how did it come about, if he was a Briton, that he was accepted here in this community?'

'The story goes that he was found on a battlefield when young and adopted by one of our warriors because he made that warrior laugh. He could recite poems and had an uncanny gift for languages. He said he had initially survived wandering the land, troubling no one but teaching many things. No one wanted to hurt him. He exchanged poems and knowledge for his sustenance, was converted to the New Faith and so joined the community at Domnoc-wic.'

'This Brother Boso sounds an exceptional man,' Fidelma commented. 'Apparently, he even learned your ancient runes, *futhorc*, to exchange messages in it with Athelnoth. Yet you Angles and Saxons have been in a state of constant war with the Britons ever since you started to settle on their lands and drive them west. You even call them foreigners in their own land. Your word for foreigner is *Welisc*, is it not?'

'I learnt many things from Brother Boso,' the young man agreed. 'Some things I am not proud of. He had a forbidden book in Latin called *De Excidio Britanniae* . . .'

'*On the Ruin of Britain*,' Fidelma translated. 'I know it. It was written by the Blessed Gildas, who was a great scholar of the Britons at the time your people first came to this island. He was one of those who had to flee for his life to Armorica. I once saw a copy of that very manuscript in an abbey set up by Gildas in Armorica when I was wrecked there travelling back from the Council of Autun. I find it amazing that Brother Boso has survived in this kingdom.'

Brother Ator smiled broadly. 'That is because he can now pass as an Angle. People don't bother him and he does not refer to his past.'

'But he told you his story, so he must trust you very much.'

'He survived because of the knowledge he was able to give us acolytes,' Brother Ator replied gravely. 'Knowledge is survival, for without knowledge there is no understanding.'

Fidelma smiled thinly. 'You are very perceptive in your youth, Brother Ator. Tell me more of the things this Brother Boso spoke of.'

The youth was thoughtful. 'We are riding for Domnoc-wic, aren't we?'

'That is our intention,' she agreed solemnly.

'Brother Boso once told me that before my people came here, two centuries ago, it was a big Roman port called Silomagus and they built a large fortress here with several roads leading to it. That is why it became a great trading port.'

'So it has always been a trading port since the days when the Romans occupied Britain? How did the name Silomagus become Domnoc-wic?'

'He said they both meant a deep-water port. He also said that even before the Romans came and conquered this area as part of their empire, there was a kingdom of Britons here. It was a small kingdom, just like ours. The Britons were called the Trinovantes – the vigorous people – and they had kings that were very powerful. Their kings even issued coins of gold, silver and copper for people to use. Some people still use them to this day, especially the gold and silver. These ancient Britons made their own coins here centuries before the Romans arrived.'

Fidelma was intrigued by what she was learning.

'We think that we have learnt something new, only to find that people had learnt it long before,' she said.

'It shows that nothing is stable in our lives,' the young man remarked. 'What people believe one day is changed the next. It is a curious world.'

'Why does Thane Beornwulf's chief retainer – his *druhting*, you call it – dislike you?' she asked abruptly.

The young man blinked in surprise at the unexpected change of subject.

'You mean Crída? He had aspirations to marry Wulfrun

himself,' he admitted. 'But, as I told you, Wulfrun and I have an agreement. In accordance with custom, I had spoken with Athelnoth.'

Fidelma reflected on what Mother Elfrida had said about Wulfrun's ambition to become an abbess rather than to marry.

'You said Athelnoth agreed?'

'He gave permission.'

Fidelma thought for a moment. 'Did Crída also go to Athelnoth with his offer of marriage?'

'It is the custom. Athelnoth refused his offer. This much did Wulfrun tell me.'

'You think that Athelnoth's refusal explains Crída's ill feeling towards you? Would Crída have told anyone among the townsfolk?'

'Crída would know better than to tell people about it, for he would be shamed. Isn't he a boyhood friend of your husband? Eadulf would know that traditions are closely kept in Seaxmund's Ham.'

'You are not from these parts? Where do you come from?' Fidelma had caught his inflexion.

'My parents had a farmstead in a place east of here. Saegham, the township by the lake. They were converted to the New Faith by the Burgundian Felix, who formed a community there. He founded the abbey there and that's where he died. As I grew older I made the journey to Domnoc-wic and commenced my studies there when I was but twelve years old.'

'So Athelnoth had agreed to your marriage with his niece Wulfrun? She was happy with this plan?'

Fidelma was genuinely interested. She found it intriguing to be observing this society in the midst of the flux and change between one religion and another, almost between one culture and another. Not that she felt the philosophical arguments among the religious in her own culture were stable, but there, there was a blend of the

Old Faith and New that did not seem to create as many frictions as were here. The New Faith had been accepted in the Five Kingdoms some two or three hundred years before, compared to the fifty years or so since its introduction to these Angles and Saxons, and was now far more stabilised.

She felt sorry that the confusion of ideas about the New Faith was beginning to spread. Each missionary and teacher seemed to preach different ideas. Adoptions, Apollinarism, Arianism, Maniaechism, Nestorianism . . . the choice of what to believe in was like different beliefs instead of a simple faith. When people were asked what they believed, the philosophies were almost endless. She didn't want to confuse the young man by asking him further. However, it seemed that Brother Ator had been thinking about her last question and now, finally, answered.

'We discussed joining a *conhospitae*, a double house, where we could live raising our children. There is such a place in the fortress by the River Blide, where the bodies of our King Anna and his son, the Atheling Jurmin, were taken for burial. They both fell in battle against the pagan Penda, when he invaded us. At the same time we could devote ourselves to study and teaching.'

Fidelma thought again what Mother Elfrida had told her. There were clearly two contradictory views of Wulfrun's ambitions, but she reflected it was better to garner opinions than present a challenge. 'It sounds a good idea, for I think your mind has the ability to absorb matters,' Fidelma observed. 'You would make a good teacher. Are there many *conhospitae* near here?'

'All our abbeys are mainly mixed houses. Princess Athelthryth's was built recently on the Island of Eels,' the youth pointed out.

A *conhospitae* was a mixed community where male and female followers of the Faith dwelt together, raising their children in the New Faith. They were fairly common in many countries. At

Streoneshalh, Fidelma remembered that Hilda's abbey, called 'The White House', was a leading mixed community. It turned out that hardly any of the communities were not mixed, although there were a few places inhabited by hermits.

They could smell the sea strongly now as they turned from the river road and headed slightly north-west, where they could see some slightly higher elevations on which the buildings proclaimed the outskirts of the large port of Dumnoc-wic. Ahead, Fidelma caught sight of the gathering of houses of stone and wood and, above them, on elevated land, one or two larger buildings with round corner towers made of stone, flints and red brick in the style that the Romans constructed.

'Some of the old Roman buildings have been taken over and are used by our people,' Brother Ator pointed out, catching her gaze.

'Used only for the New Faith and not for defences?' Fidelma queried. When she and Eadulf had arrived in the port, she had not particularly noticed such buildings, which were on the north side of the town on a small hill.

'That building there,' the young man pointed, 'that is now the abbey. It was where Felix, the Burgundian teacher, was given permission to form his community. So King Sigeberht named him bishop of this town. Bishop Bisi was abbot here before he became bishop to the current King Ealdwulf.'

'Who is the abbot of this community now?'

'Abbot Aecci. I don't know him. I think the entire community was replaced when most of the original religious were wiped out by the Yellow Plague. Brother Boso and Bishop Bisi were survivors of that.'

'So the community who live there now is mainly new?'

'They mostly come from a community at Deor Ham, the deer enclosure.'

They fell silent as they moved into the township and could

see the marketplace still functioning and as busy as ever. There were ships at anchor and wagons moving around, especially where ships were setting down their cargoes, to be picked up by carters and taken to be sold and distributed among the market traders. The four of them rode through the square where there were many traders' carts and barrows, carrying all manner of edibles: cheeses and other goods, especially bags of dried seeds, and baskets of fresh harvest crops and herbs. There was livestock aplenty, and Fidelma had no difficulty identifying the spot where they had met Mad Mul, and the tavern where they had spent their first night.

Moving quickly through the township, they joined a road leading upward towards the abbey building, which Eadulf had pointed out to Fidelma. As they approached the square-walled building, she realised how austere it looked. The young man had been accurate about it being more a fortress in the Roman style than some of the more friendly buildings that were recently erected to house the new religious communities. Its walls were of stone, pebbles and brick packed together with clay, and the main entrance had ancient oak wood gates strengthened with bars and hinges of iron. They were tall enough that riders on horseback could pass between them under an arch of curved stone with carvings similar to those Fidelma had seen during her visit to Rome.

The visitors' approach had been noted, for a burly religieux had come to the open gates, standing between them. His arms were folded in the sleeves of his robe and his cowl was drawn over his head so that they could barely see his features.

'*Bene vobis*,' called the man in ritual greeting, although there was no welcome in the tone.

Eadulf was replying, '*Bene vobiscum*,' when Werferth interrupted.

'I am Werferth, commander of the king's bodyguard. I am here to see Abbot Aecci.'

Obviously the name and rank had an immediate effect.

The religieux bowed deferentially. 'Enter with your party, my lord.'

He stood aside, having signalled to someone behind the great doors. A bell started to ring immediately. Fidelma realised it was rung in a curious way, like a signal, and it stopped shortly.

They rode into a large courtyard. The entrance to the religious buildings was on the far side of the courtyard, while other buildings around the interior were stables and outbuildings used to house all manner of works, including a smithy. Some members of the community had come out to take charge and attend to their horses as they halted and dismounted.

A young religieux was hurrying from the main building to greet them. It became obvious that he had been summoned by the bell.

'*Bene*—' Eadulf began, but again Werferth interrupted in sharp authority.

'I am Werferth, commander of the king's bodyguard,' he interjected. 'Abbot Aecci should be expecting me.'

The young man bowed. 'You are welcome to this place, my lord. I am Brother Titill, scribe to my lord Aecci.'

'Then you will take me to him at once,' the warrior commanded. He paused a moment before turning to his companions and forcing a smile. 'You will forgive me if I leave you for a short period while I deliver my message to the abbot, for it must be handed to him personally. You may ask to see Brother Boso and put your questions to him while I am engaged.'

Werferth was striding away towards the main buildings. Brother Titill issued rapid orders to a young man who stood close by before hurrying after the tall warrior.

Fidelma was surprised at being so dismissed by Werferth. Even Eadulf seemed nonplussed. Fidelma was about to comment when the young brother turned to them.

'I am Brother Osbald,' he announced. 'We have a small chapel where you may wait in contemplation while lord Werferth speaks with the abbot.'

Fidelma looked at Eadulf and grimaced, making her disapproval known. They said nothing, but followed the young man into what was obviously a chapel and took seats on some wooden benches by the wall.

'Can I get you anything?' inquired their guide. 'A mug of cider, perhaps? We have some freshly baked bannocks. Please do not hesitate with your requests. If you want to know anything about this chapel, feel free to ask. I can tell you that this little chapel was a favourite place for the Blessed Felix, the Burgundian, to come and contemplate the Faith. We were surely blessed when Felix of Burgundia arrived at our great port of Domnoc-wic.'

'We wish to see Brother Boso from Ceol's Halh,' Fidelma interrupted, as she had no wish for more information on such matters. She did have a passing thought that no one appeared to have recognised Brother Ator, although this had been where he had spent much time educating himself. Then she remembered how communities had changed since the raids from the pagan Penda and, above all, the devastations of the Yellow Plague.

Soon Brother Osbald returned bearing their refreshment. With him came a more senior figure, who introduced himself as Brother Bedwin.

'It is good to welcome you here to this holy place, where the blessed Felix first brought light to this kingdom,' he greeted. Fidelma felt his smile was somewhat false. She wondered whether Eadulf would point out that Fursa and his brothers and the Hibernian religious community at Cnobheres Burg had equal claim to being the first to bring the New Faith to the kingdom. It was actually Brother Ator who seemed to take the contradictory view.

'Isn't it said that Felix went to preach among the Gyrwas?' he asked innocently.

'The Fen people?' Brother Bedwin almost sneered at the mention. 'They are sometimes known as Babba's people. Mean, cruel and thieves, one and all; only fit to be slaves.'

'Surely not all of them?' Brother Ator queried innocently. 'And the Blessed Felix went to Saegham, to take them the message of the New Faith?'

Clearly Brother Bedwin was not happy, for he sniffed noisily. 'There are many different stories about the blessed Burgundian who saved us from the evils of the old ways. But he thought it was a duty to help the Gyrwas.'

'Like the fact that he did not die here, but at the abbey that he built at Saegham, where his remains are buried.' Brother Ator smiled triumphantly.

Brother Bedwin was now angry.

'You are youthful to claim such scholarship, brother,' he said harshly. 'May I suggest that you are the one who should be careful in your learning. Perhaps you did not go to a good scholastic school?'

Brother Ator regarded him with a smile of malignancy. 'I spent many years studying in this very abbey, and much is the time I sat with my books in this very chapel.'

The effect on Brother Bedwin was one of mortification, quickly followed by a look of intense hatred at being bested.

Eadulf felt he should attempt to dispel the angry atmosphere.

'Was it not the blessed Burgundian who was the one who asked Sigeberht to establish a school here where boys might be taught their letters?'

'Just boys?' Fidelma queried softly.

Their would-be guide still had anger on his features.

'*Ignosce, amici mei. Habeo munta praestare.*' The words were sarcastically spoken as he excused himself, for he had much to do.

Fidelma felt his superior tone was dislikeable.

'*Opus tuum morari nolumus,*' she replied, equally sarcastically, emphasising that they did not want to delay Brother Bedwin's work.

The religieux hesitated a moment and then turned sharply and hurried off.

Brother Osbald then offered to refill their tankards.

'You have upset Brother Bedwin,' he remarked, but he did not seem particularly concerned. 'Brother Bedwin is proud of his prowess in history and in languages, especially in Latin.'

'Did he think that recourse in Latin might impress us?' Fidelma asked. 'Or exclude us?'

'He also likes to boast knowledge,' Brother Osbald returned. 'He joined the community from the abbey at Deor Ham.'

'His is no way to impart knowledge,' Fidelma disapproved. 'So what is happening to our request to see Brother Boso?'

'I gave your request to Brother Bedwin. I will go after him and find out. He must have forgotten.'

Fidelma turned to Eadulf, who had been morosely silent since they parted company with Werferth.

'You are suspecting that I was right?' she prompted.

'About what?' Then Eadulf caught himself. 'Oh, you mean your remarks concerning Werferth last night?'

'I felt there was another reason why someone of his standing came to Seaxmund's Ham with Beornwulf straight from the meeting of your Witan. It was nothing to do with the investigation of Athelnoth's murder, which he could not have known about. I would like to know what message he had to pass on to this Abbot Aecci.'

'It is probably nothing to do with Athelnoth's murder,' Eadulf reflected. 'Anyway, are we to be allowed to see Brother Boso? Are we to get an answer to our demand to see him?'

Brother Osbald returned at that moment.

'I reminded Brother Bedwin that you wished to see Brother Boso.'

'It is why we came here – to see him,' Eadulf said.

Brother Bedwin re-entered the chapel then.

'I apologise for my ill temper. I dislike to hear our great teacher, Felix, criticised in any way.'

'There was no criticism but a matter of geography,' Brother Ator replied, not backing down.

'Your apology is accepted,' Eadulf said hurriedly. 'Can we repeat our request to see Brother Boso . . .?'

'I have been sent to bring you to Abbot Aecci and the lord Werferth,' Brother Bedwin interrupted him. 'I understand that lord Werferth has conducted his business with the abbot, but there are some other matters you need to discuss.'

They exchanged puzzled looks before Eadulf rose with Fidelma, and Brother Ator followed.

As he led them from the chapel, Brother Bedwin turned to Fidelma. 'I wondered at the fact that you were of the Hibernians. I suppose that you have been delegates to the council at Heortes Ford? It is going to be very exciting to hear of the decisions made there.'

Fidelma and Eadulf again exchanged quick, puzzled looks. Fidelma hoped that the youthful Brother Ator would not make any comment to distract him.

'These are very exciting days,' Fidelma pretended to agree solemnly. 'I suppose you know all about this council?'

'Now that the lord Werferth has come to instruct Abbot Aecci, we presume there might be news for us. I am allowed to know only the minimum of facts. But come, let us not keep the abbot waiting.'

'Why did they choose this place, The Stag's Ford?' Fidelma enquired innocently.

'Sadly, politics must prevail,' Brother Bedwin replied. 'You will realise that. That is why Heortes Ford is an ideal location, being on the border between our kingdom and the kingdom of Mercia.'

GRAVE OF THE LAWGIVER

'It is in Fen Country, on the north bank of the Great Ouse, not far south from Saegham,' Brother Ator pointed out.

No one said anything further. There was something about this council that Werferth had not wanted them to know. Fidelma was trying to remember what Mul had told them about it when they had met him.

Brother Bedwin led them through the dark brick and flint building that had been a Roman fort centuries before. The high chambers all seemed damp and the odours were the dampness mixed with a curious flower scent that combined into a pungent atmosphere. They were led to the abbot's chamber where Werferth awaited them. He immediately came forward to introduce them to the elderly and stern-looking man who rose to greet them. His features were sharp as he examined them with dark inquiring eyes. He was a thin man whose sallow features gave emphasis to his sharp jaw and aquiline nose. His dark eyebrows almost met across the bridge of his nose. The thin red lips were set in a grim line.

'Werferth has told me of the reason for your visit to this land of your birth, Eadulf. It is my sadness to hear of the death of your uncle Athelnoth. The *gerefa* was a good man. My condolences. My greetings to you, lady Fidelma. I am told you are on a short visit to our kingdom.'

Was there some relief in that comment? Fidelma did not answer verbally but simply inclined her head in acknowledgment. The abbot then dismissed Brother Bedwin.

'We came here seeking to speak with Brother Boso,' Eadulf announced. 'Perhaps Werferth has already told you?'

'Only that you hoped that Brother Boso might provide you with information as to the motive for your uncle's murder and give some clue as to the whereabouts of your sister,' confirmed Abbot Aecci.

'We understood that Brother Boso seemed to be a particular

friend of my uncle and that they often exchanged communications. We were told that he set out to come to your abbey this morning. Therefore, we would like to see him.'

Abbot Aecci moved his hands in a curious, negative gesture in front of him.

'As I have just told lord Werferth, such a thing is beyond my powers.'

Eadulf thrust out his jaw belligerently. 'Beyond your powers?' he demanded coldly.

'Due to the fact that Brother Boso is not here,' the abbot replied.

Werferth leant forward with an apologetic expression at their surprise.

'Abbot Aecci told me that Brother Boso arrived here but barely stayed to have his horse watered and he himself took only a mug of cider before he was riding off again.'

'He has already left here?' Eadulf was bewildered.

'Exactly so,' Abbot Aecci acknowledged.

'What did he say of what had transpired at Seaxmund's Ham?' Eadulf pressed.

'He mentioned only that he was in a hurry. It was lord Werferth who has told me of the sad details of the incident at Seaxmund's Ham.'

'Then it was not your abbey that was his destination? He told people that he was coming here. So where was he going?' Fidelma asked. She saw that Brother Ator was looking astounded. It was clear that this was a revelation to him.

'I don't suppose that you have any idea of what Athelnoth's relationship with Brother Boso was?' It was Eadulf who intervened with the question.

'Relationship?' Abbot Aecci sounded disapproving. 'I can only say what I know.'

'We found that Brother Boso and Athelnoth frequently exchanged messages and in some ancient hieroglyphics of our people,' Eadulf amplified.

'He means the *futhorc* or runes,' Werferth added. 'Would you have any idea of the meaning of such exchanges?'

'I would not,' Abbot Aecci replied firmly, without hesitation. 'Nor can I understand why you should think I could provide you with any. I know nothing about such heathen practices.'

'Heathen . . .? began Eadulf.

Fidelma intervened. 'It seemed a matter of urgency that we should follow Brother Boso. Having learnt of Athelnoth's murder, we need to know why Brother Boso would immediately ride for this abbey as though there was some matter of importance to be conducted here. As you say that there was not, we must find out where he has gone.'

'I am as confused on this matter as you are.' The abbot's voice was still cold. 'He spent only a few moments here and rode on. I have neither knowledge of why he came nor why he left. I should also point out that I teach my brethren that I do not approve of the attempts to adopt the pagan language of the runes to write our laws.'

'Ah,' Eadulf mused. 'Then you acknowledge that it was the intention of Athelnoth to transcribe the oral laws of the Angles in our ancient written form?'

Abbot Aecci scowled, realising he had made a slip.

'Let me put it this way, Brother Eadulf, we are aware that some among us have been greatly influenced by Aethelberht of Cantwara, who died sixty years ago. Some in other kingdoms disapprove of these ideas and think any writing should be done in the hieroglyphs of Rome . . .'

'You mean writing should only be done in Latin?' Fidelma smiled. 'So you disapproved of Brother Boso attempting to shape these Saxon hieroglyphs?'

'I knew and disapproved,' Abbot Aecci affirmed. 'Your uncle

Athelnoth, as a *gerefa,* had an interest in this matter and that interest brought him many enemies.'

Fidelma hoped Eadulf would control his reaction to this statement because it could open the way to asking many other questions.

'Then why would Brother Boso come here?' Eadulf asked. 'He would know you disapproved of the use of these *futhorc.*'

It was Werferth who replied. 'As the abbot said, perhaps we were wrong and this was not his main destination. He merely said as much to distract any pursuers.'

Eadulf turned to him, bewildered. 'But you said . . .?' he began.

'That Brother Boso had set out for this abbey. That does not mean that this was his ultimate destination,' Werferth emphasised.

Abbot Aecci exhaled in irritation. It was obvious he now wanted to get rid of his guests. He reached for a small hand bell on his table and rang it. 'You will forgive me, for I have much to do.'

Werferth bowed his head in agreement as Brother Bedwin emerged at the door and bowed to the abbot's dismissive gesture, motioning them to follow him. Moments later they were leading their horses to the gates. No further words were exchanged between them. It was as if they had reached an agreement to remain silent. At the gates of the abbey, they were about to mount their horses when Brother Bedwin leant forward to Werferth.

'According to one of our brethren, a stable lad, he overheard Brother Boso mention he wanted to reach Cnobheres Burg before dark.'

'Cnobheres Burg?' Overhearing, Eadulf could not hide the surprise in his voice.

'It's a place at the confluence on the gravel river, where the Eár meets the Wahenhe. It is the—' began Brother Bedwin.

'I know it,' Eadulf interrupted him. 'It is there that I came to an understanding of the new religion. It was where the Hibernian missionaries and teachers, Fursa and brothers, were given permission to set up their community.'

'Does the Hibernian religious community still dwell there?' Fidelma asked.

'As far as I know, there remains a small community,' said Werferth. 'They survive there in spite of the fact that most Hibernians left after the decision made by Oswy in Northumbria. Most of your missionaries and teachers, lady, felt their interpretation of the Faith excluded them from trying to teach among the people.'

'Why would Brother Boso go there?' Fidelma asked thoughtfully. She glanced at Brother Ator as if asking him the question. The boy shook his head.

It was not until they had descended the hill into the main street of the port that Werferth called: 'Shall we pause for a meal before we head south again?'

Eadulf replied sharply, 'Who said that we should head south?'

The warrior tried not to show emotion, but he asked: 'Not south?'

Fidelma had already picked up on what was passing in Eadulf's mind.

'Our intention was to find Brother Boso, and if he has ridden to Cnobheres Burg, then that is where we should follow. Rather than return, I agree we should follow Brother Boso, as was our original intention.'

Werferth was hesitant, but when he saw the others were determined he said, 'I shall join you, of course.'

'You must have further demands on your time, having delivered your special message to Abbot Aecci?' Fidelma said, with a curious probing emphasis.

'My business here is done,' Werferth confirmed flatly.

'Which business was only to do with this council at The Stag's Ford?' she smiled thinly.

Werferth's features showed Fidelma's deduction was accurate.

'I underestimate you, lady,' he said slowly. 'After we have eaten and left this town, we will find a place where we may not be heard. There I shall tell you something of this council, which may affect all our lives in the future.'

Chapter Nine

A short distance north of Domnoc-wic they found a copse of elders by a small brook. It appeared a good, isolated place to halt and discuss plans. They could take their ease on seats provided by fallen timber, while the horses were hitched to bushes with grass and water within reach. Once seated, Fidelma, Eadulf and Ator regarded Werferth expectantly.

'This is supposed to be a matter of secrecy,' Werferth announced. 'I tell you as friends, and I hope Brother Ator will agree to it.'

'It is hard to give such a promise before the facts are known,' Brother Ator immediately protested.

'If it has nothing to do with the murder of my uncle then you can count on my discretion,' Eadulf added.

'I can assure you that it bears no significance to the happenings at Seaxmund's Ham,' promised the warrior solemnly.

'Then tell us about it,' Fidelma invited. 'If it is as you say, it is of no concern to us, and there is no problem.'

Werferth stretched himself with his back against a tree trunk. He still looked serious.

'There might be an indirect effect. I came from the king's Witan with a message for Abbot Aecci, as you discovered. As my path led through Seaxmund's Ham, I naturally rode with Beornwulf. There I found you and it made sense to proceed with you.'

'I thought that might be the case,' Fidelma said softly.

'You might have already heard stories about The Stag's Ford. Vitalian, Bishop of Rome, sent a Greek from Tarsus, to become chief bishop of the Cantwara. He is the seventh such bishop of the Cantwara acknowledged by Rome since Rome sent Augustine to lead the New Faith there seventy years ago.'

'We know that,' Eadulf agreed irritably. 'We heard of this Greek from Mul when we landed at Domnoc-wic.'

'Like his predecessor, this Greek, Theodoros, was given the Latin title of *arch*, or chief, *episcopus*,' Werferth went on, ignoring him. 'As Archbishop of the Cantwara, he claims that he is chief bishop over all the bishops in the kingdoms of the Angles and Saxons, as well as the Jutes. He even extends that claim over the Britons and their kingdoms.'

'I think the Britons will soon correct him over that,' Fidelma muttered. 'There was even word that he claimed the same authority to the kingdoms in my country.'

'Many will not tolerate this arbitrary claim,' Brother Ator added. 'I heard that from Brother Boso.'

Werferth paused awkwardly for a moment before continuing.

'A short time after Theodoros arrived from Rome, Vitalian sent another bishop from Africa – from one of the Berber nations – named Adrianus. It was rumoured that this Berber had actually refused to take the title of Archbishop of the Cantwara, which Theodoros had then accepted.'

'So are the two of them at war?' Fidelma asked.

'The reverse; they are united in their philosophies. The Berber has become abbot of a community in the chief township of the Cantwara, of which Theodoros, as I say, is high bishop.'

'I presume, Werferth, this has some relevance to your main theme?' Eadulf asked. 'I don't see where it is leading.'

'Patience, Eadulf,' Werferth replied calmly. 'In the short time that Theodoros has been here he has been quiet, trying to understand the politics of the several kingdoms that he has been sent to assert religious control over. He found a friend in Wilfrid of Northumbria.'

'Wilfrid was the advocate who persuaded King Oswy to decide in favour of Rome during the great debate at Streoneshalh,' Fidelma acknowledged.

'The same,' Werferth agreed. 'In fact, Wilfrid has had a falling-out with the new Northumbrian king, Ecgfrith, who is Oswy's son. But Theodoros has insisted Wilfrid be reinstated as bishop in Northumbria.'

'Church politics are so much more vicious than disputes between kings,' Fidelma sighed.

'The kingdoms are not united by the New Faith but, on the contrary, divided by their different versions of the New Faith,' Werferth continued. 'That is why my message from the king's Witan was meant to be a secret. It appointed Abbot Aecci as the new King's bishop instead of Bishop Bisi.'

Still bewildered, Eadulf and Fidelma looked at Werferth.

'My task was to inform Abbot Aecci of his new appointment and to tell him that our king, Ealdwulf, is considering supporting the proposals to unite the Churches of the kingdoms under Rome.'

'So this council is an important one?' Fidelma reflected. 'I would like to have witnessed it.'

'Neither Hibernians nor Britons were invited,' Werferth said. 'Only the kings and bishops of the Angles and Saxons were ordered to attend by Theodoros.'

Fidelma was censuring. 'Ordered? So the conflict there goes on?'

'The final decisions have yet to be decided. The council is still meeting. The point of it is to stop the conflicts between the Angles and the Saxons and unite them,' Werferth replied.

'Some among the kingdoms maintain the original teachings of the Hibernian missionaries and teachers,' Brother Ator explained. 'But it is true others have followed the decision made in Northumbria. The kingdoms of the Angles and Saxons continue to fight each other to claim the title of Bretwalda, overlord of the Britons, which really means the overlord of all the kingdoms of the Angles and Saxons.'

Werferth hesitated for a moment and then grimaced. 'I see no obstacle in telling you now. Theodoros has, as you know, called this council. He has declared that all the kings and bishops of the Angles and Saxons must agree to accept union under the Bishop of Rome, being the supreme head of the New Faith.'

Fidelma shook her head in disbelief. 'It has been an ambition that has been attempted for centuries and always failed,' she declared. 'Even the leaders of the New Faith in Rome, in Alexandria, in Constantinople and many other lands, have never been able to come together and accept one leader.'

Brother Ator raised his head with an expression of amazement as a thought occurred.

'The council called by Theodoros is currently being held at The Stag's Ford, on the borders of this kingdom and that of Mercia. But how can this Greek from the Cantwara have authority to hold it there?'

Werferth was hesitant. Then he said: 'You should also know that Theodoros persuaded King Ealdwulf and Bishop Bisi to accept his authority from Rome. The call to attend this council was issued in the name of our king and our bishop. They preside over it, but with the attendance of Theodoros, exerting the will of Rome.'

'But you say Bishop Bisi is now replaced by Abbot Aecci.'

'Because Bishop Bisi already disagrees with the concept.'

'The basic point of this council is . . .?' Fidelma asked, wanting to be sure.

'The kings of the seven major kingdoms of the Angles and Saxons, and their chief bishops, were invited to participate in a debate that will approve that all the Churches of the New Faith

GRAVE OF THE LAWGIVER

will be united under Rome, and Theodoros, as the chief bishop, will be obeyed.'

Fidelma was cynical. 'I cannot believe this will happen. When is the council to agree its final resolutions?'

'Before the end of this month of *Gerstmonath*,' Werferth declared.

'That is the month of barley, when that crop is harvested,' Eadulf explained to Fidelma.

'I should like to be a witness to that council,' Fidelma said, not for the first time.

'I have more urgent things to attend to,' Eadulf snapped. 'I must first find my sister Wulfrun and discover the murderer of Athelnoth. As Werferth said, this council has nothing to do with the murders.'

'I agree,' Brother Ator declared firmly. 'Wulfrun means more to me than the politics of the New Faith.'

'So we must continue on to find Brother Boso,' Fidelma declared.

Werferth looked from one to another in resignation. 'I have carried out my instructions from King Ealdwulf's Witan,' he said. 'I am now free to help you, my friends. I shall continue with you.'

'It is agreed that we go to Cnobheres Burg together?' Eadulf asked, looking at the others.

'It is agreed.'

'Then the sooner we start north the better,' Werferth said, rising. 'We have delayed awhile and I doubt whether we shall make it before sundown.'

Dusk was spreading with a deep chill as they were passing through what seemed to be a thick forest area. Werferth had been right. It was clear they would not reach their goal before the blackness of night closed around them. Even the sporadic birdsong had gradually faded. Eadulf wore a worried expression as he confessed he did not recognise the route, pointing out that, when he was a young man, he had travelled to Cnobheres Burg along the rivers by boat. It was the common way of travel among the people who dwelt along the countless rivers, lakes and marshes of this kingdom.

'Didn't you point out that the river we crossed some time ago was called the Wahenhe?' Fidelma asked, puzzled at the confusion when Werferth pointed to an approaching river and named it. 'Now you say that this old Roman fortress is on the banks of that river. I thought we had already crossed north of it?'

It was Brother Ator who answered her.

'The river that rises in the west twists and turns almost back on itself, which is why it is called by the name Wahenhe.'

'It means a river like a dog's wagging tail,' Eadulf explained. 'It moves this way and that.' He made a descriptive motion of his hand.

'After we cross it to the north-west, it twists and turns along to our east, and after a while it will turn again almost west, crossing our path before pushing north. It heads north-east to join the great River Eár, which flows eastwards into the sea,' Brother Ator said, seeking to clarify the situation but confusing Fidelma even more.

'What you are telling me is that we are going to have to spend a cold night camping in these woods?' ToFidelma, that thought was not a happy one.

'For which we will have to be careful,' Werferth affirmed, glancing around. 'To the east, which is on our right, is very low, marshy land that abuts the sea. To our left, on the west, are lots of woods, but in even more difficult marshland. It would be better to find shelter at the side of this track, which is slightly elevated and therefore dry.'

'I have a suggestion,' Eadulf suddenly announced. 'It was told to me by a fellow student when I was at Cnobheres Burg.'

'That was some time ago,' Werferth interrupted with scepticism.

'Yet I can remember he said that along this track here, on the western side, is a hermit's dwelling. If we could find that place, at least we might gain shelter for the night. Even a hermit will afford us hospitality.'

'A hermit?' Brother Ator said enthusiastically. 'I remember that Brother Boso often spoke of him.'

'That's all very well, but unless we know where the hermit's dwelling is, it doesn't help,' Fidelma remarked cynically, pointing to the thick, impenetrable-looking woods.

'Brother Boso said that there were two gnarled and ancient oaks standing to the west of the track: strange-looking growths, which were so thick that six men holding hands might encircle one of them. They were of similar height, and the upper limbs entwined so that they formed an arch. If one could pick out the small track that went under the arch of the trees and follow it – although you had to keep careful watch because the track twists through marshlands – it would not be long before you came to where the hermit lived. Brother Boso called the place Toft Monachorum – the enclosure of the monk.'

'If the track leads through marshland, it sounds dangerous.' Fidelma was not excited at the prospect.

'Nevertheless, if we were to find Toft Monachorum, then it would be better than sleeping out in this area with wild animals to worry about,' Werferth pointed out. 'There are wolves that often scavenge along the highways at night, not to mention other creatures that we had best avoid.'

'What if we have passed these oaks already, without noticing them?' Eadulf asked pessimistically.

'I don't think that is so,' Brother Ator replied, sounding cheerful. 'I would have noticed such a strange collective growth. I remind you that I am of the Gyrwas, the Fen people, and was raised with knowledge of woodcraft and tracking in the marshlands. Let us press on, alert for the signs that point the way to this monk's enclosure.'

'What is the best way to do that?' Eadulf asked.

'If it is on the west side of the path, I suggest Brother Ator ride that side and look out for these strange tree growths,' Werferth suggested.

'Agreed,' Eadulf returned at once. 'Werferth, if you ride behind Brother Ator then we will have two pairs of eyes on that side. I will ride on the east side and Fidelma can ride after me. If we miss the oaks, the only other impediment to our path will be the twisting river, and I doubt we shall reach that before tomorrow after dawn. We have to find the curious trees before nightfall.'

Feeling a little more invigorated, in spite of the growing chill and darkening skies, they set off once more along the track due north.

Two incidents caused them some apprehension and led them to halt with unease. Some distance before them, a group of half a dozen low dark creatures suddenly leapt across their path and scampered into the western woodland. These creatures had short powerful legs, thick barrel-shaped bodies and short flat tails.

'Badgers,' Werferth explained, identifying them. 'At night they move to their feeding grounds. They have strong jaws and sharp claws, so do not take them for granted even though they don't hunt for anything more than voles, mice, frogs and such like.'

The second incident was when strange screams caused the travellers to halt their ponies. At once several black shapes appeared on their path ahead of them, visible, then vanishing at a speed that seemed impossible to Fidelma. The shapes were far longer and fatter than those Werferth had identified as badgers.

'These ones you do have to watch out for,' the warrior advised. 'Wild cats. They attack rabbits, hares and even rodents, but do not think they bear any relationship to the creatures folk take as domesticated pets that sometimes go wild. These are ancient animals that dwell throughout the woodlands.'

Fidelma did not bother to point out that so far there had been little animal life that she had not already seen in her own country.

However, it was not long before Brother Ator gave a cry and pointed ahead beyond Werferth.

'The trees! That is the sign!'

True enough, in the fading light they could see the dark shape of oaks, exactly as Brother Ator had described them.

Werferth dismounted and walked under the curious arch made by the branches of the ancient growths. He carefully tested the ground that formed the track through the archway of gnarled boughs. The others waited while the warrior bent to his woodcraft to ensure the safety of the path that spread between them. Eventually he came back to join them.

'The track is fairly solid but narrow. There is only room for one person to move along it at a time. Either side will lead you into the marsh. The path rises a bit so it will probably move to a more solid level above the marshland. We should have brought a lantern with us but hopefully there is still enough light for us to make it to this monk's enclosure.'

'If the enclosure still exists,' Eadulf added.

'Well, let us attempt it. No use waiting here,' Fidelma urged.

'Very well,' Werferth said. 'I will lead the way. I suggest we dismount and each lead his or her horse in single file. Keep close to the rear of the pony ahead of you, but not close enough to distract it in case it kicks out. Try to follow the steps exactly to avoid slipping into the marsh on either side.'

Fidelma volunteered, being an expert horsewoman, to be last. Thus they would have someone experienced at the front and at the back of the line. Eadulf was to follow Werferth and then Brother Ator was to be third in line.

They dismounted and set off in the agreed order. The surroundings darkened more rapidly as soon as the travellers passed between the two ancient, gnarled oaks, due to the thickly growing marsh woods. Lakes or ponds could be seen here and there in the wetlands. The level of the track certainly did not seem high or dry enough to allow for any misjudgement of the path. Fidelma began to wonder what sort of place this monk's enclosure could be.

'I see a light up ahead,' Werferth called. 'There seems to be a group of buildings on rising ground and even fencework not far through the trees.'

'It doesn't look like a hermitage to me.' Fidelma peered into the gloom. 'Looks more like a farmstead of sorts. I can smell pigs and chickens.'

'Who says that a hermit must dwell in a hole in the ground without the comforts of life?' Eadulf asked, jubilant that he could abandon the idea of sleeping on the track with the prowling wildlife. It was meant as a joke yet it clearly irritated Fidelma.

Before she could reply, Werferth called softly, 'The path goes to a gate and, beyond, the ground rises up to that main building where the light is.'

'There are several outbuildings. It certainly looks more like a farmstead to me than a hermitage,' Fidelma commented.

'Well, at least the hermit is at home,' Brother Ator said positively.

'It would be unusual if a hermit was not at his hermitage, otherwise he would not be a hermit,' Eadulf replied with a touch of his old humour.

'We'll need someone to light the path, in case he has let out the hounds,' Brother Ator pointed out nervously. It was a reminder that in the countryside, apparently here as well as in Fidelma's own land, dusk was a time when many countryfolk let loose their hounds to prevent visitations from wolves, foxes or bears, where such predators were plentiful. Even here, where the Roman legions had been in occupation for centuries, they had set about trying to diminish the wolf population, but so far had not been successful. It occurred to Fidelma that hounds had acute hearing and would be aware of the approach of strangers, yet all was strangely quiet as they gathered before the gate leading to the farmstead.

Werferth put his hunting horn to his lips and blew an experimental blast. There was immediately some movement in the darkness, but these were the restless movements of domestic animals, as evidenced by the nervous bellow of a heifer and gentle protest of cows, the annoyed screech of a rooster, and the protest of chickens. There was nothing more sinister – no howling of wolves or barking of stray dogs.

A light appeared as the door of the main building opened and closed. There was a pause, then the door opened and closed again as a lantern was brought out. A tall man was standing on the wooden step holding the lantern in one hand. He was too far away for them to discern him in any detail other than that he appeared youthful and wore a robe. He was certainly not what they expected a hermit to look like.

'Who are you?' came a sharp male voice. It seemed to Fidelma that it was a voice given to command.

'We are travellers seeking hospitality,' Werferth called back.

There was a pause and Fidelma thought she heard the man mutter something in a low tone to someone behind the door. The door opened slightly behind him and then closed swiftly again, leaving him still illuminated by the light he held.

'What makes you believe that this is a tavern or a place for providing hospitality?' came the harsh tone. 'It is neither. So I suggest that you return to the main track with your companions.'

'Wait!' Fidelma called as the man started to turn away. He hesitated and turned back, perhaps surprised to hear a woman's voice. 'We came seeking no tavern but the hermitage of a brother in Christ. In accordance with law and tradition we demand a shelter for this night.'

The lantern was lifted higher but it was obvious the man could see them no more distinctly than they could see him.

'Who are you?' came the demand.

'We are four travellers – Brother Ator from Ceol's Halh,

Brother Eadulf from Seaxmund's Ham, while I am Fidelma of Cashel, wife to Eadulf. We are escorted by Werferth, commander of the bodyguard of King Ealdwulf.'

She had saved Werferth's name until last because she had a feeling that it would have more effect. She was right: she heard the intake of breath even from this distance. There was a pause and then the man said in a lower tone: 'What exactly do you seek here?'

'A cover over our heads: a place to lie in the warmth until the cold and darkness of the night has passed,' she replied.

'And it would not go amiss if some beverage and something edible could be offered,' Werferth added.

'One moment,' the man called. Then the door behind him was opened and shut again as he went back inside.

'A strange welcome, even from a hermit,' Werferth commented.

'If we have to make our way back to the main track it will not be good,' Eadulf pointed out.

'There is something curious here,' Fidelma said softly. 'Did you see what was by that fenced area in the darkness? I saw the shadows of three horses in an enclosure there. So the hermit has company.'

At that moment, the tall man returned, still with the lantern in his hand, and walked down from the main building towards them. They could now see he was clad in religious robes and was swarthy looking with long dark hair and a bushy beard. The eyes, reflecting the light of his lamp, were constantly moving, as if by some nervous affliction. He halted and held up his lamp as if he were inspecting them. He examined Werferth very carefully.

'You say you are the commander of King Ealdwulf's bodyguard – why are you escorting religious? One of your party is an Hibernian woman, by the sound of her voice.'

Fidelma again detected that curious note of command in the man's voice.

'I bear the king's seal, if you doubt me,' Werferth replied, his own tone matching the haughty attitude of the other.

'I don't doubt it,' the man replied with what Fidelma felt was an irritated grimace behind his beard. 'It is odd to see a warrior of senior rank escorting religious. We would not refuse you hospitality, so bring your horses through the gate and put them in that enclosure.'

So saying, he unlatched the gate and swung it open to allow them through before he turned to open another gate to a paddock where there were already three horses.

'There is plenty of food and water for your ponies there. Bring your saddle bags and follow me to the house.'

Fidelma was again bemused by the man's authoritative manner. They removed their horses' saddles and reins and placed them by the fence, taking their saddle bags and then turning to their host.

'You neglected to tell us, to whom we should be thankful for this courtesy,' Fidelma prompted.

The man appeared confused for a moment.

'I am Brother Mede.'

'Do you dwell here alone, Brother Mede?' she asked innocently. 'We have heard that this was a hermitage.'

'You would be right.'

'But you seem to have more visitors than us tonight,' she indicated.

Brother Mede latched the gate of the paddock and motioned them to follow him.

'You can bed down for the night in the main room,' he said without responding to her implied question about other visitors. 'There is food and drink available for you to help yourselves. I regret that I must leave you to your own devices for the night.'

Fidelma was wondering what was going on.

It was Werferth who said: 'You have pressing matters to attend to, Brother Mede?'

The man entered the main building and set down the lantern on a central table, looking uncomfortable. Fidelma was expecting someone else to be in the room but it was empty and she saw signs of a hurried departure.

'There are other visitors to attend to . . . this night especially,' Brother Mede replied hesitantly.

'Why especially this night?' Eadulf asked.

'Our group spend this night in a ritual in the small chapel at the back of this building. We had just started when you arrived at the gate.'

'So you are not exactly a hermit?' Fidelma asked softly.

'I am usually here alone, but on this day a few of the Brothers of Mount Tabor gather here to commemorate the miracle of the Transfiguration.'

'The Transfiguration?' Brother Ator's eyes widened. 'But it is not held usually until the fourteenth Lord's Day after the Passover. Today is not that day.'

'It depends what calendar you follow,' came the quick, belligerent response of Brother Mede.

Werferth was looking a little out of his depth. 'I thought you lived in isolation,' he said. 'Who are the Brothers of Mount Tabor and what is this Transfiguration?'

'I live in isolation until this day, when my Brothers of the Order come and join me for the night of vigil.'

Werferth still looked bewildered.

Brother Ator decided to intervene. 'Mount Tabor is where Christ was transformed from man into godhead and from where he ascended from the earth into Heaven,' he explained. 'As Matthew wrote – *et transfiguratus est ante eos. Et resplenduit facies . . .*'

Brother Mede interrupted dismissively. 'I am sure you all know the story of Christ's ascent to the Heaven after his death.'

'This is what you are celebrating?' Fidelma pressed. 'We would like to witness and participate in this ceremony.'

GRAVE OF THE LAWGIVER

Brother Mede shook his head. 'It is only for the eyes and ears of the Brotherhood, the Brothers of Mount Tabor. That is why I must leave you here. You will see there are places where you may lie down and find sleep. You will see on those shelves items of food from which you may make a meal. The bread was baked fresh this morning. There are jugs of mead and cider there.'

'Your hospitality is warmly appreciated,' Eadulf said gravely. 'But is there anything we can do in repayment? We would like to contribute, especially as you are neglecting your night's vigil and rituals for us.'

Brother Mede shook his head firmly. 'There is nothing you can do. Now I must rejoin my brethren. You may rest as you desire, but ignore everything outside these walls.'

'You mention that you have a chapel at the back of this building,' Fidelma observed encouragingly. 'That is where you celebrate this vigil? It would still be nice to see the chapel and say a prayer before midnight.'

'Did I not say that only the Brothers may attend the rituals?' Brother Mede's tone was adamant and there was impatience, which he tried to control. 'You will remain in these rooms away from the chapel while the vigil continues, for it is sacrilege to intrude.'

'My apologies,' Fidelma calmed him. 'I was forgetting that your ceremonies must have already started.' She had not forgotten at all, but wanted to see how far she could press this curious Brother Mede, who was certainly, in her mind, no hermit.

'I expect you to remain here until I come, with my brethren, at first light. Our ceremonies will be over then. I would advise that you do not attempt to leave here until the sun comes up. In such a place there are many animals wandering at night, so it is quite dangerous.'

'What of our horses? Aren't they in more danger than us?' Fidelma pressed, trying to sound sincere.

'My final duty will be to make them all secure.'

'Then we can help,' Eadulf offered. 'You should have hounds guarding the place.'

'Even hounds are no guarantee,' Brother Mede muttered, still trying to disguise his irritation but not succeeding. 'Now I am afraid that you have delayed me long enough. So I bid you good night. Heed my advice and do not stir outside until I come at first light.'

Fidelma inclined her head to him.

'Dominus et angeli ejus te protegant ab omni hac nocte,' she intoned solemnly.

Brother Mede frowned a moment.

'I will be here at first light.' He turned and left, closing the door behind him.

'A curious man,' Werferth sighed. 'What do we think?'

'He has no knowledge of Latin,' Fidelma replied. 'I thought he didn't when Brother Ator was quoting the very passage in Holy Scripture on which his so-called Brotherhood of Mount Tabor is based. So when I simply wished him a good night, he looked confused and made an inappropriate response.'

'Then you don't think he is the hermit who is supposed to dwell here?' Eadulf asked.

'He is certainly like no hermit of the New Faith that I have ever encountered,' she responded.

'What shall we do?' Brother Ator asked.

'We can't do much, being exhausted,' she confessed. 'We have shelter and there is food and drink here. I suggest our first duty is to attend to our hunger and thirst and then we take the time for a sleep. One of us should remain awake in case of anything unexpected. But we cannot do much until first light when we can see the situation better and find out what these so-called Brothers of Mount Tabor are up to.'

'For a start, it looks like they are running a small lucrative

GRAVE OF THE LAWGIVER

farmstead, which Abbot Aecci would not approve of,' Brother Ator smiled thinly. 'Perhaps they are avoiding paying tribute on this farmstead to the local thane?'

Fidelma turned towards the shelves of food.

'If the bread is too stale, I believe that there are oatcakes – the cheese is from a goat. There are beetroots, small purple carrots and onions, also some cold goat meat. That should stave off any hunger for the time being. As Brother Mede said, there are even jugs of cider and mead.'

It was an intriguing end to the evening as they sat around nibbling at the array of dishes they had put together and sipping now and then on the mead and cider without really relishing it. It was strange how an exhaustive sleep crept up on them – even on Fidelma, who admitted she was so suspicious of their absent host that she was determined to spend the entire night awake. But her last memory was as if she were descending into a deep, dark cavern.

Suddenly there was a tremendous crack like thunder, as if the very building had been struck in a storm. She jerked to a sitting position with the vibration in her ears. She looked wildly around in alarm, trying to identify the source of the noise.

CHAPTER TEN

Fidelma realised it was daylight. She was in the hermit's cabin, where she had been when sleep had caught her unawares. From the tone of light seeping in she knew that it was not long after dawn. Eadulf was pushing himself up uneasily from where he lay. Then she saw Brother Ator standing nearby and staring and her eyes followed the direction of his gaze to the doorway, where Werferth stood. Werferth's heavy breathing, making his shoulders heave, and the position of his body, told her that he had just impacted on something. The shattered remains of the door lay before Werferth. It had not been thunder that had awoken her.

Fidelma was on her feet. She asked the obvious question.

'We were locked in sometime during the night,' Werferth replied grimly, still breathing hard. 'I came awake to hear horses moving. I found the door locked. I peered through the crack in the planking. I could see to the paddocked gate. It was open and our horses were being stolen, so I kicked the door down. But it was too late to do anything. They were gone before I could get out.'

Fidelma rose and crossed to join him at the opening. The paddock was, indeed, empty. The conclusion was obvious.

'So, Brother Mede and his companions have ridden off and taken our mounts as well as their own?'

'I saw the tall man leading them,' Werferth muttered, almost grinding his teeth.

Brother Ator was red faced and looking guilty as he joined them. 'It's my fault,' he said. 'I thought I heard the shifting of a bolt in the night. I was half awake. It must have been when one of the so-called Brothers was putting a bar across the door from the outside. Had I awoken properly we would never have been locked in.'

Werferth made an amused grimace. 'And possibly we would all have been dead. It's all right, Brother Ator. We are free now anyway although we have lost our horses.'

'Let us have a quick look around,' Fidelma suggested.

It was Eadulf who made the first discovery, pointing to the side of the inner gate.

'Well, this explains why there were no guard dogs when we arrived. We missed spotting them.'

The corpses of two hounds were now obvious in the daylight.

They gathered at the open paddock gate and saw the hoof marks of the departing horses.

'They seem to have taken all the horses with their bridles and reins,' Eadulf pointed out unnecessarily. 'But they have left our saddles.'

'We will have a long walk to the Wahenhe,' Werferth said with clenched teeth. 'That river would probably be the nearest habitation where we could pick up mounts.'

Fidelma was looking sadly at the slaughtered hounds.

'I'd say these poor beasts were killed when Mede and his companions gained entrance. They were killed by sword or spear point, if the wounds do not lie.'

'Which means that those men came here as looters or thieves. When we arrived they probably thought our horses would bring them a better price than some of the average stock in this place.' Werferth was looking around moodily, almost unable to believe that he was the victim of such a trick.

'Three riders?' Eadulf mused. 'Could they possibly be the three we saw at the Oxen Ford, those seen to be leaving from the direction of Athelnoth's house when it was fired?'

'You forget one thing,' Fidelma replied firmly. 'If this is the hermit's place, and they were thieves, killed the guard dogs and came to rob, what has happened to the hermit?'

Eadulf's jaw tightened as he considered the implication. 'I suggest we search the place immediately.'

'Now we are searching for a body?' Brother Ator was not enthusiastic.

'What else?' Eadulf replied dryly. 'I suggest that Werferth and I search the back of the main building. The so-called Brother Mede told us there was a chapel there. It seems that he and his comrades were hiding there until they were ready to leave, so that is an obvious place. Fidelma, would you and Brother Ator search these animal sheds in the front?'

It was agreed, each pair going quietly to the areas indicated.

Mede had not lied about one thing. There was a small wooden building at the back of the main house. The emblem carved on it, the sign of a fish, indicated it had some Christian use. Eadulf opened the door and looked around the interior. It was fairly dark as there were no windows, but the morning light showed that it was strewn with debris, which indicated some people had used it overnight, and not for any religious ritual. There were empty jugs and a few animal furs on which people had sat or lain, and other debris that indicated the remains of a meal.

'Nothing,' Werferth muttered, peering over Eadulf's shoulder. 'We'll have to look elsewhere for the body of the hermit.'

They were turning away when sounds caught their attention. There was a groan, and a faint banging like someone kicking at dirt. They halted and listened intently. There was a silence, but then the thumping came again.

Eadulf realised where it might be coming from.

'There must be a *fotoll talman* in here,' he declared. If he had known the native word for a souterrain he had forgotten it, and only the term in Fidelma's language came to his mind. Seeing Werferth looking puzzled, he added: 'It's an underground chamber where sometimes food is stored against the harshness of winter.'

He was already peering round and then bending to pull away a pile of furs that had covered a corner of the floor. The trapdoor was obvious. Wooden batons, in the form of two bars, prevented anyone below from opening it. It needed Werferth, with the aid of a lump of wood, to hammer the blocks away from their holdings. Then he pulled open the trap. A curious sight met their eyes.

A man was staring up at them, eyes wide. There was a gag in his mouth and his hands were tied behind him. His feet, they discovered, were also tied. Werferth bent down and managed to haul the bound man bodily out of the hole. The first thing Eadulf observed, as this was happening, was the man did not look like a religieux, hermit or otherwise. He looked more like a farmer, in spite of being covered in mud and dust from his imprisonment in the hole. When Eadulf removed the piece of cloth that had been tied as a gag, the man started coughing, and it took some time for him to start breathing normally. Werferth went to the door and called loudly for Fidelma and Brother Ator, instructing them to bring water.

The man was clearly agitated. He tried several times to articulate his words, jerking his head to the hole.

'Down there,' he finally gasped. 'Brother Wermund. Help him!'

Werferth summed up the situation quickly and climbed into the underground chamber. It did not take him long to drag forth the body of an elderly man, similarly bound and gagged, by which time Fidelma and Brother Ator had arrived, with Brother Ator carrying a jug of water. He knelt by the first man, who gulped at the water while Fidelma had to warn him to imbibe it more slowly.

The elderly man was now sitting with his back against the wall. He was unconscious. Eadulf moved to examine him. He discerned shallow breathing, although it was difficult to tell, for he had a thick, bushy beard that almost covered his chest.

'He is still alive,' Eadulf said, reaching for the jug of water.

The other man was sitting up, rubbing his wrists and neck. He was of short muscular build.

'Who are you?' Fidelma asked.

The man did not pause in his efforts to restore his circulation. 'I am Sledda. This is my farmstead.'

'Your farmstead?' Fidelma's eyes widened a little. 'I thought this was supposed to be the retreat of a hermit?'

Sledda was now massaging the calves of his legs.

'So it is.' He nodded to the unconscious man. 'That is my friend and companion here, Brother Wermund. It is as much his home as mine.' He paused and seemed to examine them closely for the first time. 'And you are – a warrior, two religieux and a Hibernian woman. What are you doing here? Are you connected with those sons of whores . . .?'

'If you mean the man who called himself Mede and claimed to be a religieux when we arrived, no; we are not connected. We are just travellers who were seeking hospitality and were then misled by Mede and his companions. They left this morning, having stolen our horses.'

There was a sound of retching and Eadulf called: 'The old one is coming to. More water.'

The farmer Sledda started up. 'Is he going to be all right?' he demanded.

'I hope so,' Eadulf responded. 'We will try to get him, and you, to the main house as I am sure there are things there that will help treat your ailments.'

'Were you locked in that hole all night?' Werferth asked.

'One can't tell the passing of days in a black hole.' There was irony in Sledda's tone. 'But when the creatures of Hobb appeared, seeking hospitality, the moment they entered we were bound and thrown into the hole.'

Fidelma looked at Eadulf for an explanation.

'Hobb, Grim or Succa . . . they are all expressions of the evil spirits,' Eadulf explained in an offhand tone. 'Not nice beings. Evil spectres.'

'Now are you going to tell me who you are?' Sledda was becoming more in control of himself. 'You, foreign woman, who speaks our tongue, will you tell me what you are doing here? You say you are not related to those thieves but are also victims?'

Fidelma quickly explained, and the reason for coming to the hermitage, if that is what it was, ending with how they had been locked in and their horses stolen.

'Brother Boso mentioned this sanctuary to me,' Brother Ator explained. 'I was his acolyte.'

Sledda recognised Brother Boso's name at once. 'He sometimes stayed here on his journeys.'

It did not take long for Werferth, with his warrior strength, to carry the elderly man to the main building and get him seated in a chair while Eadulf searched for some alcoholic spirits to revive him. Sledda did not seem physically affected by his experience at all. He explained that both he and his companion had lain for a long time in the darkness, bound and gagged. Now he began moving around, checking on items in the building while Eadulf continued to attend to his companion.

'It is strange that items of value have not been taken,' Sledda remarked, puzzled, looking around the contents of his house.

'Maybe it was our arrival that prevented that,' Fidelma suggested. 'Or maybe they thought the price they would get for our horses would adequately compensate them for the night.'

'Perhaps.' Sledda was sceptical. 'But they were armed, like warriors. Why did they not simply take you as prisoners or even kill you, instead of the curious subterfuge of locking you in the building, waiting for you to sleep, before making off with your horses? They had their own horses anyway, so why steal yours? If they were thieves, why leave valuable items behind when they could be carried off so easily? It is curious.'

'Perhaps they were those men Widow Eadgifu saw in Seaxmund's Ham?' Eadulf repeated his earlier thought.

Sledda glanced at Fidelma, bemused. 'And who do you think those sons of evil were?'

'We can deduce that by their actions. They killed your hounds, so they were prepared to take something without disturbance.'

The news made Sledda explode with curses that Fidelma had not heard before.

'I did not know my hounds were slain,' he called over his shoulder as he hurried to the door. 'I must check the livestock. Maybe they have stolen or killed other animals.'

Fidelma turned to Werferth. 'Is there anything we should do? Who can we report this to?'

The warrior sighed. 'We should find the local thane or *ealdorman*, for this is an affront to the king's peace. We will have to ask this farmer – what's his name – Sledda? However, we are now on foot, lady. There is not much we can do until we can reach a township. As I said before, we are quite a walk from the River Wahenhe. That is the only place that there are habitations. It is there we might find the local thane, and maybe get a horse or even a boat.'

'The old man is coming to now,' Brother Ator called.

They turned back to where Brother Ator was allowing the elderly man to sip some strong spirit that he had found. Colour was returning to the pale cheeks. He was blinking as his senses returned to him. His eyes opened, pale and fearful, as he peered at the strangers before him.

'Have no fear, we are friends,' Fidelma assured him. 'We found you in the . . . the underground chamber where you had been imprisoned. Your friend Sledda is looking round the animal pens to see if your attackers have taken anything of value.'

The elderly man nodded, motioned for another sip of the liquor, coughed and seemed to relax.

'You are not connected with them?' he finally asked.

'By no means. We were their prisoners overnight as well as you,' Eadulf assured him.

'They stole our horses,' Werferth added.

'Then who are you?'

When Eadulf introduced them, the old man only reacted slightly at Werferth's identity.

'Were you chasing those men?' he asked the warrior.

Werferth shook his head, puzzled. 'Why would I be chasing them?'

'You are the commander of the king's bodyguard,' replied the old man as if this was an answer.

'I still don't understand,' Werferth replied. 'But first, we presume you are the religieux hermit who is supposed to dwell here.'

This drew a wan smile from the old man.

'Hermit? A good word. Yet I dwell here with Sledda. It is his farmstead. He rescued me when I was caught in the marshes hereabouts. I had fallen into a boggy patch and was being drawn under when he came by and dragged me out. He nursed me for a while and we became friends. So he allowed me to live here and we have worked this farmstead for two decades or more. We dwelt here in comfort, sometimes visited by a few friends without interference until last night.'

'So your name is?' Fidelma prompted.

'I am Brother Wermund.'

'Is your isolation known to many travellers? Brother Ator here knew of your location from Brother Boso . . .'

'Brother Boso? He is a good friend. We do not hide ourselves, if that is what you mean,' the old man replied. 'How did you come here? Did Brother Boso send you?'

'We were trying to join him. We were travelling along the main track to the river when night overtook us and our young friend remembered what Brother Boso had said about a hermit dwelling here and had heard of a turning off to where it was thought he lives. We found this place and were welcomed to it by someone calling himself Brother Mede.'

Brother Wermund exhaled deeply. 'Mede? He was no religieux. Mede is Thane of Mede Ham Stede.'

Fidelma glanced to Werferth, who had reacted to the name.

'Mede Ham Stede? It is an island on the north-eastern side of the Fen country. It is claimed by King Ecgfrith of Northumbria. He was formerly King of Deira, the son of Oswy. Elfwine, Ecgfrith's brother, now rules in Deira. So you recognised this man?'

Brother Wermund shook his head. 'I did not recognise him, but I heard one of his men speak his name. I kept quiet. If he knew I had identified him, then I would probably have been a dead man.'

'Then tell me what his name means to you,' Werferth pressed. 'Tell me why I should be chasing him.'

'He is a Northumbrian raider in our kingdom. I will tell you more detail after I have rested,' the elderly man assured him. 'Natural sleep is what I need immediately.'

Sledda had reappeared at the door. He was relieved at seeing his old friend almost recovered from the ordeal of the night. After an exchange, the old man retired to get some rest.

Sledda then helped himself to a tankard of mead and sat down.

'It is strange,' he opened. 'I cannot understand why they have not taken anything but your horses. Apart from the loss of two good hounds, only bruised feelings and anger over our imprisonment remain with us. All is well with our livestock and goods.

They have slaughtered the hounds for no reason other than to keep them quiet. Were your horses of value?'

'To be honest, the only horse they took of high value was my warhorse,' Werferth claimed without modesty.

'But one warrior's warhorse is hardly worth their raid,' Sledda observed. 'Besides, they were here with ill intent before you turned up.'

'It was not the value of the horses that made this Mede, whoever he was, take them,' Fidelma corrected. 'I believe it was simply to prevent us following them if we managed to release ourselves. It was to deny us access to transport.'

'Why should you follow them?' Sledda demanded in surprise.

'Brother Wermund says they were Northumbrian raiders. We will wait until we hear his reasoning. It might have something to do with our search for Brother Boso.'

'Brother Boso?' Sledda was surprised. 'He is our friend and often stays here.'

'So we told Brother Wermund,' Brother Ator said. 'I am his disciple.'

'Then while you wait,' Sledda said, rising suddenly, as if reanimated, 'I will go to my neighbours. It's best to ensure that they have not been raided, and maybe they would have news about these thieves. Travelling after first light, the raiders might have been seen and the direction of their travel noted. It is best to know if they have cleared the district. Three riders leading four unseated mounts would attract attention. It will take me a while but I know the marshes like the back of my hand.'

Brother Ator offered to go with him but was turned down.

'Knowing the marshes as I do, I can travel more quickly and safely than you,' Sledda told him with a smile.

'Very well,' Werferth said, approving the plan. 'Go with luck.'

Half a day passed before the elderly Brother Wermund stirred from his sleep, and by that time Fidelma had prepared a meal for all of them. The time had been spent not merely going over events of the preceding few days. Attempts to coax Werferth to share his thoughts, before Brother Wermund awoke, were unsuccessful, but that he had something serious on his mind was obvious.

It was Fidelma who raised the subject that was concerning her. She had been thinking of the consequences of any decision reached at the council called at The Stag's Ford by Archbishop Theodoros of the Cantwara. If it was successful in uniting all the Churches of the kingdoms of the Angles and Saxons into one body, that would surely lead to a new unity of their kingdoms. Werferth was unconvinced that such an ambition of Theodoros could be achieved and the religious ambition could then be transferred to a political one shared by the kings.

'At the moment, the Mercian king is in the ascendancy in the kingdoms and that's why King Ealdwulf of the East Angles has made an alliance with him,' Werferth explained. 'But the Northumbrians have not forgotten their defeat and are waiting to reclaim their position and influence over the other kingdoms. I do not think, in spite of the message I was told to carry from my king's Witan to Abbot Aecci, that all the bishops and kings will ever agree to such a proposal as Theodoros puts to the council at The Stag's Ford.'

Only Fidelma seemed cautious about the possible result of the decision of the council. She did not say much. She realised that the warring kingdoms were the only obstacle preventing the Britons from being completely overrun. Once that happened, these warlike settlers from the northern lands would probably turn their aggressive might on the Five Kingdoms of Éireann. There had already been a few opportunist raids. She felt that she had to learn as much as she could about the council in order to report to her brother King Colgú. He could advise the High King so they would be ready for such an eventuality. On the other hand, like Werferth, she was sceptical of such an agreement. Could the insular Churches be united under Rome? All her life she knew that Rome's reforms and authority were always challenged in the west, while in the east the Christian Churches, even in Egypt, had firmly established their own chief bishops and patriarchs, who governed independently of the Bishop of Rome and did not recognise him as the Papa or Father of the Church.

It was quite a relief when Brother Wermund finally rejoined them, feeling refreshed from his natural sleep. He was disappointed to hear that Sledda had not yet returned from his mission to get more information about the raiders.

'I was hoping we could learn something of your stolen horses,' the old man said. 'I do not think Mede wanted to be encumbered with them. It was not as thieves they came.'

'We hear from Werferth that you say the leader was a thane of the island of Mede Ham Stede, hence his name Mede,' Eadulf said. 'We thought . . . I thought, that they maybe have some involvement in the murder of my uncle – who was the *gerefa* at Seaxmund's Ham – and the possible abduction of my sister.'

'I think this man and his comrades took your horses simply to stop you following them,' Brother Wermund said. 'It came to mind that there might be another purpose to their behaviour.'

'Another purpose?' Werferth frowned.

'Assuredly so,' Brother Wermund replied solemnly. 'They are not simple thieves or murderers. At worst, I fear they are bounty hunters or mercenaries in the service of King Ecgfrith of Northumbria.'

A silence greeted this.

Fidelma didn't know the term 'bounty hunter' until Eadulf explained in her language. 'He means Mede is an *amsach* – a mercenary warrior.'

'Didn't you say this Mede Ham Stede was an island in the Fens?' she asked.

'It is in the Gyrwas, but close to the western area that owes allegiance to the king of Northumbria,' Werferth confirmed. 'So what is your thought, Brother Wermund? Why would I be chasing these mercenaries, as you said?'

'Mede supported King Ecgfrith's illegitimate brother Aldfrith in his attempt to become king of Northumbria. As a penance, he has to serve in the position of a mercenary until he has paid recompense in kind.'

'A curious custom,' Fidelma muttered.

'So you are saying that these men are Northumbrian mercenaries raiding into the kingdom of the East Angles,' Eadulf summed up. 'Why? To stir up the war? But if they attack the kingdoms, even as mercenaries, they would not only have to answer to this kingdom but also to Wulfhere and Mercia.'

'They have a particular purpose,' Brother Wermund replied with a sad smile. 'I might be old but I was a long time in that hole they put me in last night and with nothing to do but use the God-given senses of my ears. I heard many things discussed before I was overcome by the black shade.'

'So enlighten us,' Eadulf requested.

Brother Wermund helped himself to another tankard of mead and smiled.

'It is, perhaps, a tale of which Werferth might have more details to recount. They are hunting the Princess Athelthryth.'

While Fidelma did not recognise the name, the others expressed surprise.

'I know the story vaguely, but I was never closely involved,' Brother Ator said. 'You say, Brother Wermund, that you heard them talking about this while you were imprisoned in that hole?'

The old man gave an affirmative grimace. 'I heard a word here and there. It came about when Mede told his comrades that you were commander of the king's bodyguard. He suspected that you might be pursuing them. That's why he decided to accede to your request to stay the night and then imprison you rather than kill you.

GRAVE OF THE LAWGIVER

If he killed you, he knew that the entire kingdom would rise against him, seeking retribution. That might lead to the East Angles and the Mercians marching into Northumbria, set on revenge.'

'Are you sure that they were in search for Princess Athelthryth?' Werferth insisted.

'Of that I am more than sure,' Brother Wermund confirmed.

'Who is this princess?' Fidelma asked.

'She was one of the three daughters of our late King Anna. Our current king is the brother of Anna, therefore Princess Athelthryth is his niece,' Werferth replied.

Brother Ator seemed eager to tell the story.

'She is a great heroine,' he told Fidelma, excitedly. 'When she was sixteen she married Tonberht, who was the prince of the South Gyrwas.'

'The South Gyrwas are what you call the Fen people who dwell in the great marshes?' she remembered.

'The south-east half of the Fens,' Brother Ator added. 'I was born and grew up there.'

'Prince Tonberht died six or seven years ago,' went on Brother Wermund. 'Apparently, the death of the prince had a great effect on Princess Athelthryth. With the support of the people of the Fens, those who had converted to the New Faith, she took possession of an island – they called it the Island of Eels – in the Fenland. On that island, she settled a community of the New Faith and ordered an abbey to be built there. She dedicated it to the memory of Tonberht and declared herself as abbess.'

'The Island of Eels can be seen from Saegham, my village,' interposed Brother Ator.

'Your explanation leaves me more confused than ever,' Fidelma confessed. 'Why would this princess, a daughter of a king of the East Angles, be pursued by these . . .' she hesitated, trying to remember the description '. . . these mercenaries from Northumbria?'

'Athelthryth was still very young and she had much to learn about the Faith, indeed, about life,' Brother Ator replied piously. 'She decided to make a journey to a relative called Princess Aebbe, who was actually a sister to late King Oswy of Northumbria. Aebbe became abbess of a *conhospitae*, a mixed house, on the coast of Northumbria.'

'I remember dealing with Oswy when Eadulf and I attended the famous council at Streoneshalh,' recalled Fidelma. 'Oswy was not really a bad man, but he was ambitious and influenced by that pro-Roman Bishop Wilfrid.'

'And King Ecgfrith is the most ambitious of Oswy's sons,' Werferth pointed out bitterly.

'Abbess Aebbe had founded a community in the north of the kingdom,' Brother Ator continued his story. 'Athelthryth was with Aebbe when Ecgfrith visited his aunt. Athelthryth was regarded for her beauty. Ecgfrith declared his intention to marry her. Athelthryth, who was still mourning her husband Tonberht, refused. Ecgfrith had his warriors surround the abbey of his aunt. His warriors were to seize Athelthryth once she had left the sanctuary of the abbey. Curiously, Bishop Wilfrid defended her because he was a believer in celibacy among the religieuse.'

Brother Ator was clearly a good storyteller and knew when to make a dramatic pause, which he did now.

'Princess Athelthryth announced that she had taken vows of perpetual celibacy in honour of her late husband Tonberht, Prince of the Fen people. This only increased King Ecgfrith's ardour and he was angered when Bishop Wilfrid did not support him because he believed celibacy brought one closer to God. He was not concerned with love and integrity.'

'So want happened?' Fidelma asked.

'With his father dead and Wilfrid sent in exile, Ecgfrith ordered his clergy to announce that a proxy wedding would take place.'

'Proxy?' Fidelma was bemused.

'An alternative wedding in which vows were exchanged by substitutes in the name of the deputised representatives,' Eadulf explained. 'Her role was enacted by a stand-in. Athelthryth refused both to attend and to approve use of the stand-in who represented her.'

'Stand-in?' Fidelma was still not happy with the concept.

'You have the concept *léicid* – one who allows or permits a contract being entered into,' Eadulf pointed out. 'Except that it is said Ecgfrith was lying and the marriage was illegal. Bishop Wilfrid denounced it.'

'Wilfrid was our antagonist at the council of Streoneshalh and led the victorious side, swinging the decision of the delegates towards accepting Rome,' Fidelma reflected. 'I am surprised that he decided to stand against King Ecgfrith about this bizarre marriage, although this marriage is a travesty in any language. The marriage was illegal and Ecgfrith was a liar.'

'But a king's word is sacred in our land,' Eadulf pointed out. 'It is not limited by the various restrictions set forth in law as in your culture and law system.'

'But surely a marriage has to be shown to be legal under law?' She paused, frowned and then asked: 'Something must have happened, otherwise why would mercenaries be hunting her?'

Brother Wermund stirred restlessly.

'The simply reason, so I heard from travellers, was that rather than submit, Athelthryth managed to escape from Aebbe's abbey, where Ecgfrith thought she was safely imprisoned until he sent for her. Remember, he had surrounded it with his warriors. When her escape was discovered, Ecgfrith raised his men in pursuit.'

'I presume that she also escaped from Northumbria completely? How could the king of Northumbria threaten an abbey in his kingdom whose abbess was his own aunt?' Fidelma demanded. 'Don't tell me the laws are different?'

'It is said that Athelthryth is now somewhere in hiding in this kingdom,' Brother Wermund replied. 'Ecgfrith is cunning. He did not send his army to chase her. He has sent certain agents, or mercenaries, to abduct her and return her to his kingdom. Hence his use of Mede. He is Thane of Mede Ham Stede. I hear King Ecgfrith has even put pressure on Bishop Wilfrid to recant his decision to support the princess. Wilfrid has refused and has been sent into exile. Wilfrid has sought asylum with the South Saxon king, Athelwealth, and his wife Eafa. They have only just been converted to the New Faith so they are not fixed in their attitudes.'

Fidelma could not repress a desultory sniff. 'All this is happening when Archbishop Theodoros thinks he can unite these kingdoms?'

'You seemed to have heard a lot while you were locked in that underground chamber,' Eadulf remarked dryly.

'Athelthryth is said to have made it safely back to this kingdom but the fact is that there are Northumbrian spies and informers in pursuit,' Werferth reflected. 'So the story that this Mede is looking for her makes sense.'

'But you say she had an abbey on this island – the Island of Eels?' Fidelma was thoughtful. 'She would surely have fled there? She would be protected by the authority of her own abbey. Isn't that a place of safety?'

'Ely is an island in the marshlands. It's a difficult place to exist in,' Brother Ator explained. 'The great marshes can only be crossed by boat from Deira, on the Northumbrian coast, to the coast of East Anglia. Even so, raids on the islands in the Fens were not infrequent during the wars. To the southern area, it was also the border with Mercia and when we were at war with the pagan Penda, who was father of King Wulfhere, we were often subject to devastating raids there. The Fenland was both our fortification and our weakness, against both Mercia and Northumbria.'

'If Mede and his companions were searching for the princess, why would they be in this part of the kingdom?' Fidelma asked.

GRAVE OF THE LAWGIVER

'Unless this has something to do with the murder of my uncle and the disappearance of young Wulfrun,' Eadulf pointed out. 'I tend to believe Widow Eadgifu that she saw one or other of the raiders in Seaxmund's Ham. I believe they were the same we saw at the Oxen Ford. Could it be that this Princess Athelthryth had some connection with my uncle?'

Fidelma regarded the elderly Brother Wermund thoughtfully.

'You had a clear sight of these mercenaries when they first arrived here. How were they dressed – as warriors?'

Brother Wermund made a negative gesture. 'Not in warriors' clothing. They were dressed in religious clothing. The robes were like those used by the Hibernians. They must have greeted you in that way, too. You saw them when you asked for hospitality and when they let you in.'

'We only saw the one man – the one called Mede,' corrected Eadulf. 'The others were, I suppose, guarding you in the chapel building. Mede made the excuse they were holding some religious ritual.'

'The ritual was in tying us up and putting us in the underground chamber,' Brother Wermund replied cynically. 'Anyway, they were dressed as religious, which is why we let them in at first. Two were claiming to be Hibernians and the one called Mede was dressed in normal robes.'

'Well, they were no Hibernians,' Eadulf said firmly.

'I almost forgot,' Brother Wermund suddenly said. 'They initially said they were on their way to Cnobheres Burg.'

Chapter Eleven

There was a moment's silence at Brother Wermund's announcement. Fidelma resisted exchanging a glance with the others although it was Eadulf who said, dryly, 'Well, it seems everyone is heading for Cnobheres Burg in this matter.'

'But does this matter have a connection?' Werferth asked. He did not bother to explain to Brother Wermund.

'Mother Elfrida claimed two Hibernians were seen fleeing on horseback at the time Athelnoth's house was burnt down,' Fidelma reminded him. 'The day after the fire, Eadulf and I saw two religious, joined by a third, discussing something at the Oxen Ford. Now we find Mede and two companions here.'

'Well, Mede was no Hibernian. Why would they be going to Cnobheres Burg, which is given for the use of Hibernian religious?' Werferth asked. 'Even if there was a connection in their searching for Princess Athelthryth, why would they do that?'

'We do not have the information to speculate,' Fidelma pointed out.

'*Speculatio tempus vastatat*,' Brother Ator added piously, pointing out it was time wasted to speculate.

'Is there any reason why this princess should seek sanctuary with your uncle?' Fidelma asked Eadulf.

He was immediately dismissive. 'Sanctuary with Athelnoth?'

he asked. 'But why? He was a lawgiver. He was not one of the religious and neither was he one of the nobility. The princess would have found sanctuary with her own family or with some other abbey.'

'Yet you admit we saw those suspicious ones who fit the description given by Brother Wermund of Mede. Mede and his companions might also fit what witnesses described on the night of the fire. But can we be certain it was they?'

'If the princess came here for sanctuary,' Brother Ator said thoughtfully, 'then she would go to her uncle's palace and fortress at Suth Tun Hoo. There she would surely be safe under the protection of King Ealdwulf.'

'King Ealdwulf might not be able to give her protection, even though she is his niece,' Werferth said.

'But she is a princess of your people,' Fidelma pointed out in surprise at his comment.

'The matter of statecraft might enter into consideration,' Werferth grimaced uncomfortably.

Fidelma uttered an exhausted exclamation. 'It usually does,' she agreed. 'Religion is always one of the great weapons of statecraft.'

'But family is more powerful than that,' Eadulf protested.

'Ealdwulf has been our king since the time of the Streoneshalh decision,' Werferth responded. 'He has guided this kingdom into a time of peace and prosperity. He does this by playing Wulfhere of Mercia against Ecgfrith of Northumbria, but not antagonising either of them. He is related through family to both Wulfhere and Ecgfrith. Particularly he has not interfered officially by condemning the pursuit of Athelthryth by Ecgfrith. That is not to say that he turns a blind eye on matters. I am sure that he has his own agents looking out for her interests. But he does not want to confront Ecgfrith openly. By doing so, the balance of power could be upset. Ealdwulf wants to maintain the stability of the kingdom with its growing riches from the trade coming through the sea ports of Domnoc-wic and Gipeswic.'

'But Ealdwulf could call on Wulfhere for an alliance if Ecgfrith decided to confront him on the battlefield or attempt to invade?'

'It is like playing chess,' Werferth sighed. 'Each move must be calculated. Ealdwulf might find a sanctuary for his niece, but if he openly declared he supported that sanctuary then it would be a provocation. So any sanctuary is likely to go unmentioned.'

'But surely Ecgfrith would know that?' Fidelma observed.

'Knowing something and proclaiming are entirely different matters,' Werferth replied firmly.

'Would Eadulf's uncle have been a friend and helper to this Princess Athelthryth?' Fidelma asked again. 'Would he have been in such a position that he would be killed rather than betray her hiding place, if finding it was the intention of Mede and his warriors?'

'All things are open to interpretation, but I doubt a local law-giver would be in that position.'

'The politics of ruling people,' Brother Ator sneered. 'I learnt a lot from old Brother Boso.'

'Such as?' Fidelma asked.

'Brother Boso once told me that, if Theodoros has his way, and manages to unite all the kings and bishops of the kingdoms of the Angles and Saxons under one authority answerable to Rome, then there would be a great war. Brother Boso used to say that one day all the Britons would unite to retrieve all their lost lands. That is why the Britons call the kingdoms of the Angles and Saxons "*Lloegr*" – the lost lands.'

Fidelma was astounded. It seemed that Brother Boso shared her own fears for the future. Once more a pensive silence fell before Fidelma finally exhaled sadly.

'If Eadulf's uncle was killed by these Northumbrians, and they were also involved in the disappearance of his younger sister, and these acts were done in their pursuit of this Princess Athelthryth, it leads to another sad conclusion. The reason is because your King Ealdwulf does not want to challenge Ecgfrith of Northumbria over the matter because of expectation of a crucial decision: the reaction to Archbishop Theodoros' attempt to unite the kingdoms in a religion governed by Rome. In other words, your king would sacrifice this princess, and others, to keep the kingdoms from the possibility of war with each other.'

Eadulf was suddenly very bitter. 'It would also mean that the responsibility for the murder of my uncle and the disappearance of my sister Wulfrun is the responsibility of the king. She would be a sacrifice so that this kingdom can support Theodoros' plan.'

'Sledda seems to have been gone a long time,' Werferth said, seeking to change the subject.

Brother Wermund, who had been silent for some time, listening to their conversation, grimaced indifferently. 'We are some distance from the nearest habitation. My friend has doubtless not only sought news of the raiders but is looking to see if my theory is right and they have abandoned your horses. As I said, I suspect that they did not want to be encumbered by having them along. It was just to stop you following them. If they do so, then it might be easy repossessing them.'

'That would be an ideal situation,' Brother Ator replied brightly. 'I, for one, don't fancy wading through endless marshlands to the next village.'

'Sledda is a good tracker. If the horses have been abandoned, or sold, then he will discover where. However, I have to say there are only a few isolated farmsteads on the main track before you get to Wahenhe.'

Fidelma regarded Eadulf thoughtfully. 'With Brother Wermund's permission, we could take a stroll around,' she suggested.

'We could perhaps pick some vegetables and fruit so that we might help prepare a meal while we are waiting.'

Brother Wermund offered no objection and turned to answer a question from Brother Ator. Werferth was dozing in his chair. Eadulf knew that Fidelma wanted to speak to him alone, so he rose and followed her out into the grounds of the homestead. Fidelma had noticed before that Sledda and Brother Wermund kept a patch of ground that was well planted with vegetables. It also occurred to her that the livestock had not been fed. When they had searched the place earlier, she had noticed where some of the feed was kept so she turned to Eadulf.

'Come, we have the poultry to feed as well as the pigs and the goats. Poor Brother Wermund must have forgotten the daily chores of a farmstead after that experience. I don't suppose you know how to milk the does?'

'Does?' Eadulf frowned, his mind clearly elsewhere.

'The female goats need milking,' she reproved. 'So you should find a pail.'

Eadulf looked about helplessly.

'I suppose you think it is woman's work.' Fidelma exhaled irritably. 'I'll show you how to do it.'

'I thought you wanted to speak with me?' he protested.

'That does not mean that two things can't be done at the same time. Come on.'

She led the way to the pig pen first and found the feed and water, leaving it to Eadulf to place it in the troughs while she scattered the berries and nuts for the anxious poultry.

'So what now?' Eadulf demanded, as they entered an area where there was a variety of goats.

'First find a pail,' Fidelma instructed, looking round. There was a small shed nearby in which they found such an item and a small stool. 'So now you can get to work, while I keep the bucks fenced off and we can talk.'

'What do I do?'

'Thumbs and forefinger together, pinning the top of the teat where it meets the bulge of the udder.'

Eadulf looked at the animal helplessly. Fidelma was impatient.

'I know you were raised in a township, but your family must have had goats to sustain them? Come on, I'll show you how to do it. But you make sure the bucks are kept away.'

She promptly sat down and, as she had seen women do when she was small, she used two fingers to trap the milk, to prevent it being taken back into the udder when squeezed, letting her fingers maintain a soft rhythm with the milk of the goat spurting into the pail. Once she had achieved this measure, she turned seriously to Eadulf. She decided it was easier not to ask him to take over as she could continue and speak at the same time.

'This trip to your birthplace has turned out to have unexpected consequences.'

'Life is full of the unexpected,' he replied irritably. 'That I would find my uncle murdered and my sister missing was not something I would have anticipated.'

'In spite of what we learned about this man Mede and his companions, you still wish to follow Brother Boso to Cnobheres Burg?'

'Brother Boso is our only thread in this mystery, even if it is proved that the Northumbrians had nothing to do with the event. We need to find Boso.'

'Logical,' Fidelma agreed. Then she asked: 'Why did you never mention your young sister? Even when we came here seven years ago, she was not mentioned.'

'It did not seem relevant then. She was away being educated at the time.'

'Very well.' Fidelma did not feel it worthwhile to pursue this point. 'So what do you think about all the information we have received? Do all these facts we have been given make sense to you?'

'I don't understand. We have been in places before where we have been deluged with facts. Why do you ask this question?'

'Remember, I am a stranger to your culture, Eadulf, although you have taught me to understand and speak your tongue with some adequacy. But only you would feel whether it is possible that Athelnoth was really involved in this affair of the princess, and whether this is a matter worth pursuing.'

'There is the link of us having seen the people who fit the description given by Brother Wermund at that place – the Oxen Ford,' Eadulf pointed out. 'And people saw similar figures leaving Seaxmund's Ham when Athelnoth's house was incinerated.'

'You raise the point that your uncle was just a lawgiver and would generally have no connection with the noble families of your people. So why would these Northumbrian warriors descend on his house?'

'If that is what they did. Werferth says—'

'I think the commander of your king's guard knows more than he is saying,' Fidelma interrupted shortly. 'I think it *was* the Northumbrians that were seen at Seaxmund's Ham.'

'I cannot yet answer the questions about my uncle,' Eadulf said, shrugging.

'It seems that there are too many questions and no answers,' Fidelma replied.

'We've been over this before. You seemed to have something else on your mind,' he added softly, regarding her thoughtfully.

Fidelma realised she was not getting to the point of what was really in her mind. He was perceptive enough to realise that. She had agreed to accompany Eadulf back to the country and township of his birth because she knew that he had, in recent years, been feeling more and more of an outsider in her country. He was increasingly dwelling on the social distances between his upbringing and her own as a princess of her people. She knew that these misgivings had first occurred to him seven years before, and she had hoped that they would settle as she and Eadulf engaged in raising their son Alchú. But now his fears had come flooding back.

The unexpected events that had greeted them at Seaxmund's Ham would, she had hoped, distract him from his uncertainties, but the opposite had happened. Even the story of the pursuit of Princess Athelthryth had heightened his depression, especially when he had considered whether the hunt for her had been a motive for his uncle's murder. Fidelma shook her head as if the action would clear the thoughts from her mind.

'There is no need for me to say that I am here to support you,' she finally said. 'Even though I am not really competent enough in matters of your culture to help resolve this case, I will give you what support it is in my power to offer.'

Eadulf grimaced after a moment or two. 'It goes without saying that I am thankful, and I am sure our journey will bring us to a resolution.'

'What if there is no resolution?' she asked. 'How long will the pursuit of the resolution be?'

'It is not like you to ask such a question,' he replied with a frown. 'You always told me, in previous tasks, that it takes as long as it takes.'

'I admit it, but—'

He suddenly had a flash of intuition. 'You are worried about Alchú? But he is being well looked after by Muirgen and protected by your brother.'

'It is not just that . . .' Fidelma began.

'We have been away from Cashel many times before,' Eadulf went on, warming to his idea. 'Alchú has always been well looked after. We may have to be away some time and we can send for Alchú to be brought here to join us. I am sure Beornwulf will assist in having Athelnoth's house rebuilt and we can establish a good home there.'

Fidelma felt suddenly cold. She realised that she had to speak about her feelings and her growing disquiet, but as she was about to speak, a voice called out. It was Sledda returning. He came trotting up the path towards them with a wave of his hand.

'Is Brother Wermund well?' was his first question. His anxiety dissolved when Eadulf gave a positive answer. It was clear that Sledda and Wermund seemed to care much about each other.

'Did you have any success?' Fidelma asked Sledda.

'Some,' he admitted. 'Let us join the others and I can tell you all together.'

He turned and headed for the main building, followed by Eadulf. Fidelma followed with a frustrated tightening of her mouth. Once again, the opportunity to bring up her fears and concerns with Eadulf had been missed.

Brother Wermund embraced Sledda with a quick exchange of questions. Then Sledda helped himself to a mug of mead, took a swallow and exhaled in satisfaction. They all sat down.

'What news?' Werferth prompted immediately.

Sledda wiped the froth of his drink from his mouth.

'As was obvious,' he began, 'the raiders went back to the main trackway. They were mounted on their own animals and leading the horses of our friends here. They turned north towards the Wahenhe. I followed until just beyond Braggi's cabin.'

'Braggi tends the herds of fallow deer that graze the eastern lands,' explained Brother Wermund.

'Fallow deer?' Fidelma queried.

'The Romans brought them here when this was part of their empire,' Werferth explained. 'They are orange brown, with white spots, although they tend to lose the spots in winter. They are different from the native deer and considered of more value to the nobles, who claim ownership of such herds over the other species.'

'Braggi serves the local thane,' Sledda added. 'Braggi's cabin lies a good walk north along the main track.'

'So he watches these deer for this noble?' Fidelma tried to hide her exhaustion at dealing with the non-essential information. 'Why did you stop at his place?'

'Because, not far beyond, I spotted a disturbance on the track. I saw that the raiders had released the ponies and driven them into the eastern forest. Naturally, it would have been dangerous for me to follow. There are not only buck deer but feral goats in those woods.'

'What did you do?' Eadulf demanded.

'I checked the tracks and tried to see whether the ponies had kept together as they had moved into the forests. I did not go far in myself, but it seemed that they had, as far as I went. However, I returned to the main track and spent some time separating the hoof prints of the raiders' horses. Three distinct horses were indicated, then the four abandoned ones. The raiders moved on northwards towards the river.'

'There were three horses in the paddock when we put our beasts there, so that is logical. So our horses are abandoned in this forest?'

'I went to see Braggi,' Sledda replied. 'It was then midday and I was in need of a drink. I thought he probably would have a venison steak ready on his fire. Braggi is always a good source of information. Thankfully I found him not far from his cabin, which is on a cleft of a hill just emerging above the marsh forest.'

'So you had a drink and a meal? Fidelma prompted, not particularly interested.

'That I did,' Sledda replied complacently. 'Also, I gathered good information.'

'What information?' Werferth asked. He sounded as irritable as Fidelma felt.

'Early this morning, Braggi had seen the raiders moving north leading the horses. He even saw them halt and drive the horses they were leading into the forest. After that they moved off, continuing north. Braggi was intrigued so he had decided to go in search of the horses, but unfortunately he had matters to attend to, due to this time of year.'

'Then it was lucky that he returned to his hut in time for you to gather this information,' Brother Ator commented, missing the point Sledda was probably making about the upcoming rutting season.

'You did not have time to attempt to secure the horses and bring them back with you?' Fidelma asked.

'As I said, Braggi had other matters to attend to. You should understand that at this time bucks are getting aggressive. Anyway, I told him what had happened and assured him that he would be rewarded if he managed to secure the horses for you early tomorrow.'

'It seems as if our plans have already been prepared for us,' Fidelma observed, almost petulantly.

'At least, this way we have a good chance of regaining our mounts,' Eadulf pointed out.

'If we are able to reclaim our ponies, what then?' Brother Ator inquired. 'Are we still following Brother Boso? If so, I am in favour of it.'

'Brother Boso is certainly a person we must question,' Eadulf said.

'So far as we know, Brother Boso has some task at Cnobheres Burg,' Werferth agreed. 'Brother Wermund says that he heard Mede's raiders were also going there. Then I submit that there is no other destination for us.'

'If we regain our mounts,' Fidelma added dryly.

Eadulf examined her, puzzled. He had finally picked up on what appeared to be a continual resentment in her acrid comments, and he was baffled.

It was Brother Wermund who drew their attention back to what Sledda had been saying. 'If you heed my friend's advice, you will wait until tomorrow to start your journey to Braggi's place.'

'Why so?' Brother Ator seemed to have missed the previous point.

'Because Braggi said he will help you to get the horses in the morning,' Sledda answered. 'Also, if you start now, you will not reach his place until dusk. That's hardly the right time to find his cabin, which I shall show you how to locate. And it certainly isn't an appropriate time to search the forests to find the animals amidst all the feral wildlife.'

'We owe you for our lives. So the hospitality of our farmstead is yours,' Brother Wermund said.

'Tonight you will dine like nobles,' Sledda added. 'That is, if those unwelcome guests have not found the remaining side of pork that I have been hanging. We will raise the fire so that we may roast the pork. I can prepare a good apple sauce and Brother Wermund is a master at vegetable preparation.'

'That sounds excellent,' Werferth acknowledged. 'If there is anything we could do to make a contribution . . .?'

Fidelma closed her eyes for a moment. She would have preferred to start walking immediately to this place Sledda had described. She felt oddly trapped and her instinct was to head back to the port where they had landed and find a ship that would take her back to the kingdom of Muman. She wanted to be with her son, in familiar and less stressful surroundings . . .

She opened her eyes and found Eadulf looking at her across the room with a bewildered expression. She turned abruptly away from his gaze with a feeling of anger, and of guilt.

The sun was high in the sky although it was pale and there were plenty of white fluffy clouds. Fidelma's party set out under

Sledda's guidance along the single track from the homestead through the wetland forest towards the main track. Here, there was little warmth but a distinct feeling of dampness. The frustrating thing was they had to carry their saddles and bags. However, they were thankful that they had taken these into the house, otherwise the raiders would probably have taken them too. They trusted that the raiders had put the missing bridles and reins on the horses in order to lead them when they left. Sledda conducted them along the twisted path through the marshland to the main trackway, where, two days ago, they had emerged under the curious arch of the twisted, gnarled oak trees. Sledda pointed them northwards and directed them on their way towards Braggi's cabin. Along the track, he told them, they would see a particular clump of alder trees on the right-hand side, and a hillock rising among the surrounding woodlands and marshy meadows. They would probably see groups of fallow deer and frisking bucks.

They each thanked Brother Wermund and Sledda profusely, promising to give their respects when they met up with Brother Boso. Then they set off at a determined pace. For some reason no one wanted to speak as they strode along. The walking was not difficult and they fell into an easy pace together. At least the track was fairly dry, with only a few muddy areas, which they could easily avoid. It was not a land that Fidelma felt comfortable with. She longed for mountains, high hills and, near the coast as they were now, she always felt comfort with the rocky bastions against the threatening sea. Here, she feared that, with one threatening wave, the sea would engulf the entire land.

Contemplating how alien she felt, she drew her despondent thoughts back to her feelings about Eadulf. She knew she should understand why Eadulf was feeling a stranger in her land, yet she could not completely empathise with his attitude. Last night she had been about to open up to him to discuss their relationship and then the opportunity had passed. The time was not right. But when was the right time to approach the matter?

She glanced at her companions and stifled a sigh.

She felt sorrow for young Brother Ator. He was obviously in love with Wulfrun, Eadulf's young sister. He was facing the fact of her disappearance with suppressed emotional determination to resolve the mystery. His emotional conflict might be, Fidelma thought, the reason he was given to outbursts of rapid discourses about his knowledge. He was an intelligent and determined young man, although he seemed blind to the fact that Crída obviously resented him. In another context that quality could be interpreted as arrogant and boastful.

Beside him, striding easily, although she had the impression he could outpace them all if he wanted to, was Werferth, the commander of the king's bodyguard. He, too, was determined, but Fidelma felt the reason for his determination was not the same as theirs. Fidelma's suspicion of him was like an uneasy itch. When he had confessed that his accompanying Thane Beornwulf to Seaxmund's Ham was to deliver a message to Abbot Aecci at Domnoc-wic, she had not entirely accepted it. She wondered why, after he had delivered his message, he had decided to continue on to Cnobheres Burg with them.

Then Brother Wermund had raised the matter of the escaped Princess Athelthryth, and the chase after her by the warriors of Ecgfrith of Northumbria. Again, question after question tumbled through Fidelma's mind. What did Werferth know about the princess and the pursuit of her? Did it connect with the murder of Eadulf's uncle? All these thoughts added to Fidelma's feelings of alienation and almost helplessness at being in a world over which she had no control. This was compounded by her feelings of isolation from Eadulf. She had hoped his coming back to his homeland, after such a long absence, would strengthen their relationship but it seemed to be doing the opposite.

'That's it!' The shout from Werferth almost made her start. The group came to a ragged halt.

Werferth was pointing to a higher piece of ground to their right on which distinctive alder trees rose. Alders thrived in wet areas and were easily recognisable among the willows, which also loved wetlands. There was a narrow path from the main track rising through the thick growth and leading to the knoll. Peering closely, the others could see what Werferth's trained eye had spotted – the dark outlines of a hut. It was just as Sledda had described. Here was the cabin of Braggi the deer keeper.

'Let us go and find the man, and pray to Hreda that he has recovered our ponies, as Sledda said he would,' Werferth said.

His references to the Saxon goddess brought a look of disapproval from Brother Ator, but Werferth had already turned from the main track to follow the path up the hill.

They had not gone far before a strong voice called on them to halt.

'Identify yourselves!'

Werferth paused mid-step.

'If you are Braggi, then I am Werferth, commander of King Ealdwulf's bodyguard,' he announced in a belligerent tone.

'Impressive,' replied the voice with cynical humour. 'I was expecting friends of Sledda the farmer.'

'We come from Sledda,' Eadulf called in a softer tone.

'Then come ahead,' replied the voice.

Eadulf now led them the short distance through the trees, emerging into a little clearing before the wooden cabin. In front of it stood a stocky man who was just hanging up a bow and quiver on one of the support posts of the shack. He was clearly the deer keeper, his clothes denoting that he was someone used to working in the marshland environment. He wore a coarse woollen shirt, leather jerkin and tight trousers. At his leather belt he carried a large broad-bladed knife in a leather sheath. He had a thick rust-brown beard and brows of a similar colour, which almost met across the bridge of his nose. His hair had a reddish tint in which lights seemed to dance and play as the sun caught it. He stood, hands on hips, staring at them with an almost contemptuous humour. His eyes were wide and pale.

'So, how is old Brother Wermund? Has he recovered from the abuse of the Northumbrians?'

It was obvious that Sledda had told him the story.

'He is well and suffers no ill effects,' Eadulf replied, acting by mutual silent consent as their spokesman.

'That is good. It was an unusual happening. No one usually knows Sledda's place, apart from a few religious that pass this way. Sledda rarely emerges except to barter goods now and then. You could almost say that they are both hermits. Why these Northumbrians appeared and then, so soon after, you appeared, is coincidental.'

'It must be nothing more than coincidence,' Eadulf replied.

Brother Ator stepped forward with a frown. 'If you are curious, my mentor is Brother Boso. He mentioned the hermit's place to me several times. He called it Toft Monachorum, the monk's enclosure.'

Braggi's amusement at this was evident.

'Sledda might not appreciate that name. It is his farmstead. But he saved old Wermund from a death in the marsh and so they became friends and have lived there with one another ever since.'

'We were following Brother Boso and hoping to catch up with him. Darkness overtook us and we looked for hospitality in Toft . . . in the place where Sledda and Brother Wermund live,' Eadulf explained. 'The raiders were already there.'

'When they left they took our horses,' Fidelma added. 'It was not because they needed them, but probably just to stop us following them.'

'That would certainly explain why they turned them loose into the woodland below. Sledda was a good tracker and saw one or two of them in the woodlands. He could not help me then because he wanted to get back to old Wermund. He was worried about his old friend's health.'

'Are the ponies still there?' Fidelma pressed, trying to get back to the purpose of the conversation. 'Is there a possibility that they can be caught without difficulty?'

Braggi's eyes twinkled. 'Praise Woden, who makes all things possible, the ponies were as docile as lambs, even the black stallion, which I imagine is your warhorse, commander of the king's bodyguard?' He grinned at Werferth. 'Indeed, they have been caught and are in my paddock at the bottom of the hill below here.'

'How can we thank you?' Fidelma asked over the chorus of gratitude that arose.

Braggi turned to her. She was sure he was smiling again behind his beard.

'Be assured that Sledda has looked after things. You saved his and Wermund's lives. I have need of a new goat for milking and so my friend Sledda and I have agreed to make a bargain.'

'Why didn't he let us know?' Fidelma demanded in annoyance. 'We must find a way of repaying him.'

'That is not my affair,' the deer keeper dismissed.

Werferth lowered his voice. 'Have no concern, lady. We will compensate him.'

Braggi now waved a hand towards his hut. 'The sun is at its zenith. So let me invite you to share the hospitality of my poor house.'

'We should be on our way to reach Cnobheres Burg,' Brother Ator began. 'We should get there before dusk.'

'But a refreshing mug of cider and a barley cake would be welcome,' interrupted Werferth, reminding the young man of social custom.

'By all means,' Eadulf agreed immediately. 'Cider sounds good.'

Braggi indicated benches by a table, then disappeared through a side door before returning with a jug and mugs, which he placed before them.

'This is cooled in a stream that rises nearby,' he said, pouring the liquid into the mugs, at the same time indicating a platter of barley cakes.

They toasted Braggi enthusiastically for his recovery of their mounts, after which the deer keeper examined Eadulf with interest.

'Why do you ride with such an august person as Werferth?' he asked, still with a tone of mockery. He looked then at Fidelma. 'Sledda told me that you are from Hibernia. I've met with a few Hibernians, several of whom have a community at Cnobheres Burg.'

Eadulf immediately intervened to introduce himself and Fidelma. Braggi seemed astonished to be told Fidelma was a princess.

'Sledda seemed to think that these raiders were after a princess,' he observed.

'But a princess of this land,' Eadulf pointed out. 'According to Brother Wermund, they were in search of Princess Athelthryth.'

The deer keeper thought for a moment. 'I hear gossip when I go to the market up on the river. I don't take much note of it unless it directly affects me, and that is seldom. I suppose the only matter of contention these days is that our king now insists we all obey this Greek who has come among us. I seldom see old Brother Wermund, but if I decide to visit my friend Sledda, Wermund tries to explain this new religion to me. I have no understanding of such storytelling. Now, stories of the deeds of the Aesir, of Woden, Freya, Frigg and Thunor – these I can understand. I would die sword in hand to be reborn in Esegaard with Woden and Thunor than dwell on my knees in this life only to wind up in Múspelham, the world of fire.'

'Well, we are not here to change your ways,' Werferth smiled reassuringly. 'We are here only to collect our horses.'

'Mind you,' Fidelma said, 'you seemed to recognise Brother Boso's name when Brother Ator mentioned it, and know him. Did he not challenge the old gods?'

'As your young friend mentioned,' Braggi replied. 'Boso sometimes stayed at Sledda's place. I did meet him there. He tried to tell me these strange stories of a god who was killed by men by being nailed to a tree. Imagine, if we *ceorls* had tried to nail Woden or Thunor to a tree? Even the very thought would cause lightning to incinerate us.'

'So what stories did Brother Boso tell you?' Eadulf asked abruptly. 'Did he talk about this princess? And why was Brother Boso journeying on this route?'

'I know nothing of that, as I said. I last saw him some time ago. It was back when Eostre, goddess of fertility, commands the world.'

'Eostre's celebration is in the spring,' Eadulf explained to Fidelma.

'Did Brother Boso talk about anything in particular?' Fidelma asked.

'I suppose the only thing people talk about now is the New Religion. Nothing else.'

'So that was all?' Eadulf pressed. 'For example, he didn't talk about Athelnoth, the *gerefa* of Seaxmund's Ham?'

'Or his niece Wulfrun,' Brother Ator intervened quickly.

'Seaxmund's Ham?' Braggi seemed puzzled. 'I thought Sledda said this Brother Boso was from a place called Ceol's Halh.'

'That is very close by Seaxmund's Ham.'

'I do not know that territory,' confessed the deer keeper. 'I can't say that I have been as far south as Domnoc-wic, nor do

I want to. I have been told by travellers what a city like Domnocwic looks like. It sounds a fearful place.'

'Where is this market on the river you spoke of?' Eadulf asked.

'Oh, that's on the banks of the Wahenhe. If you continue on this track north, you will come to the river crossing. That is just a short ride from here.'

'It is time we set off because we have much further to go than the river crossing,' Eadulf pointed out.

CHAPTER TWELVE

As Baggi had said, their horses were in a paddock below the rise on which his hut was placed. The deer keeper pointed out that they had been found with bridles and reins still on them. Fidelma and her companions put on the saddles and bags, which they had carried from Sledda's farmstead, before leading the animals back to the main track. Then, repeating their thanks to Braggi, they set off.

'Well, there was not much to learn there except we have regained our horses,' Werferth remarked, trying to break the silence that had descended on the group as they headed northward along the track.

'There is always something to learn from talking to someone with local knowledge,' Fidelma replied, but trying not to sound as if it was a rebuke.

So far as Eadulf was concerned, the only thing he learnt was the shortness of the ride to the stretch of river where a ford could take them across to the northern bank. There were several wooden cabins on both banks. As Braggi had said, it was a place where local people gathered to exchange their produce or barter, mainly from passing river craft. The settlement appeared fairly prosperous, with owners of boats and merchantmen with wagons and horses engaged in trade. The ford was well marked although an old woman there offered her services to guide the way across. She put Fidelma in mind of the mythical 'Watcher at the Fords' and some of the strange magical stories associated with such a figure. Fidelma was more used to rivers that gushed from mountains with such force that they surged along. This twisting river, the Wahenhe, was so flat, and had so little current that it seemed it would never reach the sea of its own accord, if it was the sea that it was ultimately trying to reach.

Once across, it was Werferth who resumed charge of the group.

'If we follow along the eastern bank, as it turns north, we will find it meets with the great river called the Eár, the gravel river, as it flows out to the sea,' he said, having apparently listened carefully to Braggi's instructions.

Eadulf agreed. 'I remember it from when I was a youth here. The old Roman fortress is at the confluence of the two rivers. King Sigeberht gave it to Fursa and his Hibernian community to form their Christian mission at least twenty-five years ago. That is where I first learnt about the New Faith.'

Fidelma made no comment; she had heard this many times.

As they had broken their fast and subsequently been fortified with Braggi's cider and barley cakes, they decided to move on directly without pausing, in spite of the enticing smells from the various cooking fires. The track that ran parallel to the river was little different from the country that Fidelma had previously seen. She would never grow used to the low, flat vista with small humps of land barely rising here and there like islets. The entire territory that surrounded her was a strange marshland and she wondered how people could live in such a place. Once again, she missed the large hills and the inaccessible mountains, the feeling of the granite bastions facing the sea, and she felt once more unprotected from the hungry whisper of the seas a little way to the east.

Memories were coming back to Eadulf and he was recognising aspects of the countryside they were moving through, northwards along the river. After he had recognised yet another landmark, Fidelma asked him if that made them close to their objective.

'If we increase the pace, we should be at Cnobheres Burg well before dusk,' Eadulf assured her, not picking up on her irritation.

'In that case, we should proceed at a canter for a while,' Werferth suggested, overhearing the response. He urged his horse forward before Eadulf, who was a poor horseman, had time to object.

They progressed by cantering for a while, then walking the animals before cantering again. Eventually they heard the rush of two major rivers meeting. There were dark buildings rising ahead. It was almost dusk when Eadulf stretched out a hand with a shout of excitement.

'Cnobheres Burg.'

Ahead Fidelma could see the high walls of a large fortress. She felt impressed in spite of the feeling of isolation they inspired. The walls seemed entirely deserted, and as high as three or four tall men. There were round towers. Even in the gloom, she could see flints and dark red tiles. She knew from her travels that this was typical of Roman buildings, often built of stones and sand-coloured bricks. The height was probably made more impressive because the structure rose from flat ground, and with few trees about by which they could estimate its height. The south-west walls met at an acute angle, which, she learnt later, provided protection from winds and rains for those who sheltered within.

She would eventually realise that the inhabitants had built their huts using the walls as a break against the strong winds that swept the land. In fact, the Romans had built the structure on a tongue of land in an area often visited by harsh winds and weathering. The walls were in fine condition except the western wall, which was crumbling and disappearing due to the erosion of river, sea and weather. Fidelma wondered how the sea could do such damage on the western side. Later, Eadulf told her that much of the ruins that she saw were caused when the great pagan king of Mercia, Penda, had invaded and devastated Cnobheres Burg. Many of the Christians there had been able to flee into the marshes and returned only after Penda had suffered defeat and death.

'Brother Boso told me there is another fortress on an island to the north. Both forts had guarded the estuary where four rivers merged and emptied into the big eastern sea,' Brother Ator said.

'It is many years since I was here,' Eadulf said. 'I know the large River Eár rises in the west and pushes eastwards across the marshlands to the sea here.'

'We might get further information from the community here,' Fidelma suggested. 'When we see Brother Boso, we should get some answers to our questions.'

The main entrance was lit by burning braziers and lanterns. It was opposite the point where the rivers Wahenhe and Éar joined. Brother Ator was viewing the arched but ungated entrance of the fortress with open admiration.

'It is amazing to think of the Roman legions in this place. Brother Boso used to say that it was garrisoned by Roman cavalry. Their task was to defend these shores against the raids of the Angles and Saxons.'

'Even more amazing is to consider it being inhabited by missionaries and teachers from my own land,' Fidelma replied, softly sarcastic. 'Some of the first teachers of the New Faith, and showing the people how to read and write.'

They soon realised that the main gate was no more than the large arch into a vast deserted enclosure beyond. This had been the centre of the fortress. It was a rectangular level and bordered by the high stone walls, with the exception of the decaying western one. There had probably once been many buildings of all types in the central space but now there were just stone ruins and a few derelict wooden structures. In the south-west corner, clearly lit by several open fires and hanging lanterns, was a group of wooden structures that were newly erected. They used the high walls of the sharp right angle as a protection against the weather. The buildings were like a small farmstead, with enclosures for various animals and areas that had been planted and cultivated. Smoke was rising from some of the huts and there were religieux wandering about.

'This is where Fursa built his first community,' Eadulf said with some emotion in his voice.

'The first community of the New Faith in this kingdom,' Werferth agreed.

Fidelma was disappointed. She had imagined the historic community of Fursa, a prince of Connacht, would be impressive – a community dwelling in some imposing fortification, not a ramshackle group of wooden huts. Only a few people had apparently noticed them.

'I had not imagined what we called the abbey of Fursa would be so sparse and unimpressive,' Fidelma confessed, shaking her head. 'Fursa and his brothers were once princes, grandsons of the king of Connacht. This is no more than a campsite.'

'What did you expect in this wilderness . . .?' Eadulf tried to sound light hearted but he felt defensive as he realised that the wandering teachers of his youth had not survived well.

Werferth was sympathetic. 'Remember it was not long ago that Penda and his pagan hordes destroyed what was initially here. I am not sure who leads the community today. We best make ourselves known.'

A bell started to ring from one of the wooden buildings and there were movements as several people emerged in answer.

'We have been spotted,' Eadulf observed. 'Let us go across to them and introduce ourselves.'

'And find Brother Boso,' Brother Ator added.

A small group had assembled at the edge of the buildings, as if waiting for them to approach.

'If they are Hibernians, perhaps I should lead the way?' Fidelma suggested.

She did not wait for an answer, but swung down from her horse and began to lead it to the group. The others followed her example.

'*Salvete alieni, quid quaeritis?*' one of them shouted.

'*Benedictionis,*' Fidelma replied gravely.

'*Gratum in nomine dei,*' was the response.

Then she greeted them in her own language. '*Beir-si bennachtain*... I am Fidelma of Cashel. We are travellers and would welcome your hospitality.'

Eadulf joined her before they replied. 'I am Eadulf of Seaxmund's Ham and was taught the New Faith in this very place before I went to Hibernia to complete my studies. The lady Fidelma is my wife.'

One of the men stepped forward after a whispered reaction.

'You are twice blessed and welcome, travellers. I am Brother Siadhal, steward of our community. Come inside and sample our hospitality. Our brethren will take care of your ponies.' He waved two of the men with him to come forward to take the mounts as the other riders descended. Then he acknowledged the names of the companions of Fidelma and Eadulf before saying: 'Come with me. I am sure Abbot Brecán will want to greet you in person before you break bread with us.'

'Abbot Brecán?' Fidelma queried.

'He is the leader of our community,' the steward replied.

A moment later Brother Siadhal was guiding them into a large hut that was clearly designed as a dining room. It had a long table on which one or two members of the community were already placing jugs and dishes. There were chairs all along, and at the head of the table sat a tall, silver-haired man, sturdy and of elderly years, dressed in robes with a carved wooden cross hanging around his neck. His arms were folded across his lower chest so that his hands were hidden in his broad sleeves.

Brother Siadhal went forward and announced their names. At once the tall man rose and his eyes widened as he regarded Fidelma. 'You are all welcome to this place. I am Abbot Brecán.' Then he turned to Fidelma. 'You and Eadulf are especially welcome here, lady, for who has not heard of the remarkable judgements of the sister of Colgú, king of Muman?'

Fidelma smiled modestly. 'I would not have expected my name would be known outside of the borders of Muman.'

'That is where you are wrong, lady. The name of Fidelma, the *dálaigh*, is whispered in many places, even in Rome itself where I was a pilgrim once.' He turned to Eadulf. 'Inevitably linked with the name of Fidelma is that of Eadulf. I have heard many stories of you both for I was training at the abbey of Lios Mór. I volunteered to come on this mission to try to rebuild Fursa's devastated community and so took on the leadership. So you are both welcome and thrice welcome here.'

He then turned towards Werferth and his eyes narrowed slightly.

'I have heard of you, commander of the bodyguard of the king of the East Angles. We hope the rumours of your king forcibly expelling all Hibernian missionary teachers is not a reason for your presence?'

Fidelma was astounded at hearing her suspicion about Werferth's possible intentions abruptly stated by the abbot.

'Why should I not come in peace?' the warrior countered with a frown, clearly embarrassed. 'Have no fears. I might be commander of the king's bodyguard but I am a friend to the lady Fidelma and Eadulf.'

'If you come in peace then you also are welcome.' Abbot Brecán paused before finishing his examination of Werferth's face. Then he turned to Brother Ator. 'You are . . .?'

'I was disciple to Brother Boso of Ceol's Halh,' the young man replied at once. 'And we—'

The abbot interrupted him with a hand held up, palm outwards. 'You are the disciple of our good friend Brother Boso?'

'He is my mentor and, indeed, we have all come here in search of him.'

'He is here,' Abbot Brecán confirmed. 'He is resting at the moment, for his journey has been arduous. He will join us shortly. But first, be seated and at least taste a tankard of our cider to refresh yourselves after your journey.'

It was understood there were the conventions of behaviour to be gone through first.

'Did Brother Boso mention that he had come from Seaxmund's Ham? Did he mention what had happened there?' Eadulf asked immediately after they were seated and had taken the first sip of the cool drink.

To Eadulf's surprise and disappointment, Abbot Brecán shook his head.

'He mentioned little. His main concern was to come to warn us about a council that the new emissary of Rome has called: the Greek called Theodoros, who is now claiming to be the senior bishop in the kingdom of the Cantwara.'

'We had thought that Brother Boso was a supporter of Archbishop Theodoros,' Werferth frowned suspiciously. 'Why would he travel here, to your Hibernian community, to discuss such matters?'

'That would be for you to ask Brother Boso,' the abbot replied gravely.

'He told you about this council?' Werferth queried.

Abbot Brecán gave a gentle smile. 'He did. It is felt that such a council will have a detrimental effect on the position of the Hibernian religious in these kingdoms. Hence my challenge to you.'

Werferth stirred uncomfortably. 'It depends on the final decisions that are made,' he replied.

'But you said it was not a matter of concern for your visit.'

'It might be interlinked with other important matters,' Eadulf replied. 'Brother Boso needs to be questioned about the murder of the *gerefa* at Seaxmund's Ham. He also needs to answer questions about some Northumbrian mercenaries who were said to be coming in this direction.'

'They were apparently led by the thane of the island of Mede Ham Stede,' Werferth added.

'That's north-west of the Gyrwas, the Fen country,' Abbot Brecán mused. 'Why should he and Northumbrian mercenaries come here?'

'Because we believe that they were trying to track down Princess Athelthryth,' spoke up Brother Ator. 'Perhaps they thought that you might have given her sanctuary.'

The abbot and his steward exchanged incredulous glances.

'Are we accused of giving sanctuary to this princess? Would this not bring down the might of Northumbrian warriors upon us?' He waved his hand as if to encompass the community. 'We would be insane to do so. We have heard some of the story of her escape from the northern abbey where Ecgfrith of Northumbria had confined her. But if she escaped and came here for sanctuary, we would have set about finding her a safer place to hide. Sanctuary here, as you see from the poverty of our cabins, is not an option. Not even sanctuary for us if the rumour is true, and King Ealdwulf decides to obey Rome. The Greek Theodoros wants to expel all those who do not follow the Roman rituals. For us, that means expulsion from this kingdom, or worse.'

Werferth stirred uncomfortably. 'So far as I know, no such decisions have been made,' he repeated. 'The council at The Stag's Ford continues and the final decision is not yet made. It is not why we are here.'

It was Brother Siadhal who finally asked: 'To clarify your arrival here, were you following Northumbrian mercenaries whom you thought were coming here or is it Brother Boso that you seek? Perhaps the lady Fidelma should answer.'

'We were following Brother Boso, but then learnt that these Northumbrians might also be heading to this place,' Fidelma clarified.

'How many of these warriors were supposed to descend upon us?' asked the steward.

'There were only three of them on horseback,' Werferth pointed out.

'Only three men? Are we in danger?' Brother Siadhal seemed amused. Then he shook his head. 'We have had no visitors of that description. I am sure someone might have observed three strange warriors if they came here. This countryside is such that there are few places of concealment.'

'I understand,' Fidelma said. 'However, they were not dressed as warriors, but took on the robes of the religious and were once mistaken for Hibernians.'

'But they have not been observed in this vicinity?' Werferth pressed, seeing the growing disapproval on the abbot's face.

During this exchange, Fidelma had noticed that Brother Ator was showing signs of impatience. Finally, the young man stood up.

'Would you object if I went to see if Brother Boso can join us now? I am anxious to see my mentor to ensure he is well.'

'He did say that he wanted time to be spent in contemplation for the rest of this day,' Brother Siadhal pointed out. *'Vincit qui patitur.'*

'Indeed, my boy,' intervened the abbot. 'He prevails who is patient. Sit and let us continue our discourse. Brother Boso was exhausted when he arrived here but I am sure he will join us when he is able.'

Brother Ator had a resentful expression when he sat down again, but the abbot did not appear to notice and turned back to Werferth.

'I am confused. There appear to be three main reports you are placing before me and I wish to be clear. You suggested that these Northumbrian raiders might be involved in the murder of the law-giver in Seaxmund's Ham, or that this has something to do with a pursuit of Princess Athelthryth. You also draw our attention to what we have already heard: that the council at Heortes Ford, The Stag's Ford, might make decisions that will be detrimental to our community. And you say these raiders were heading towards this place?'

'That is what we have heard,' Brother Ator replied before anyone else could speak. 'Of course, these raiders could be coming here simply because this is a convenient place on their route to return to their own territories. It would be easy for them to find a boat along the banks of the Eár, the gravel river, which connects to the heart of the Gyrwas.'

'Can we accept that these Northumbrian raiders have passed here?' Eadulf asked.

'We have had only a few visitors recently and, as for strangers such as you describe, we have had only one stranger, who arrived last evening and did not stay the night. What was his name?'

Brother Siadhal smiled broadly. 'He was an Angle, but he said he followed the teachings of Iona and adopted a name to go with his Faith. It was a strange one for an Angle. It was Brother Clúain.'

Fidelma stared at the steward. 'He gave his name as Brother Clúain?'

Brother Siadhal was about to answer but then he realised the point she was making.

Fidelma glanced to Werferth, who was puzzled.

'Clúain means "meadow" in the tongue of the Hibernians, but in the language of the Saxons it can be "mede",' she explained.

Abbot Brecán's reaction was one of disbelief. 'You don't mean that this Thane of Mede Ham Stede was playing on the name? Can someone describe this man you call Mede?'

When Fidelma described him, the steward and abbot immediately declared he must be the same man.

'He did not raise any suspicions?'

'None,' the abbot replied. 'He had a meal, refused other hospitality for the night and moved on.'

'So what did he want?' Eadulf demanded, trying to hide his excitement.

'Only some hospitality in the form of food and a drink,' Brother Siadhal replied. 'Also he sought news; an exchange of rumour and scandal, as most travellers like to spend time on.'

'I suppose the gossip was about Princess Athelthryth?' Werferth asked heavily.

To their surprise the abbot gave a short laugh.

'I regret to disappoint you. It was not the main subject, although we hear that most people are concerned with that in this kingdom. However, he knew many folk in this kingdom were praying that she has reached the Island of Eels safely.'

'Did he meet with Brother Boso?'

'Only briefly at the evening meal,' Brother Siadhal replied. 'Like us, he was more concerned with the news of this council at The Stag's Ford. The conversation with Brother Boso was brief. Boso retired to the guest hut as he declared he wanted a full night's rest, and then to spend today in contemplation.'

'Did Brother Boso ever mention the murders at Seaxmund's Ham?' Eadulf spoke sharply. 'I am from Seaxmund's Ham. He performed the burial services for my uncle a few days ago. I was told he was a friend of my uncle. That is why we have followed him – to see if we could ask him some questions about the attack.'

Abbot Brecán was shocked. 'He made no mention of this when he arrived. Do you know Brother Boso well?'

'I have been mainly in Hibernia with Fidelma these last seven years,' admitted Eadulf. 'I have only just arrived back to be greeted by the news of my uncle's death and also of the disappearance of my sister, with whom he lived. When we went to ask Brother Boso for information, we were told he had left first for Domnoc-wic. Once there, we were told he had set out for Cnobheres Burg. That is why it is important we speak with him.'

'You shall see him shortly,' Abbot Brecán agreed. 'As I said, he declared he wanted to rest a night and spend a day in contemplation for he had many matters to consider. But he should be joining us shortly.'

'Forgive me, lord Abbot,' Brother Siadhal suddenly interrupted. 'I have just had an idea while we were talking.'

They turned to him.

'Let me send one of our brethren across to the jetty by the Eár and make enquiries among the folk. It's where boats usually moor when collecting goods and passengers, especially when they are heading upriver to Deor Ham and beyond.'

'Why there?' Fidelma asked.

'The Eár is a big river and tidal to quite a way inland,' explained the steward. 'Strong boats, coastal boats, can go upriver as far as Deor Ham, the Enclosure of Deer. In fact, another daughter of King Anna founded a community there. From there it is not far to the Fenlands of the Gyrwas. I do not know the country but I am told that the river rises beyond Deor Ham in a place where snipes nest . . . Snipa's Ham they called it. I am not sure one can get as far as that, but the river can connect anyone heading that way with the country of the Gyrwas, which would bring them to Eel's Island.'

Abbot Brecán turned to his steward. 'Send Brother Indulf to question the locals about boats and if this man we called Clúain took passage westward.'

The steward rose and left them.

'I do not know whether there is any connection,' the abbot told them. 'If this Mede, or Clúain, is simply concerned with the pursuit of the princess, then I presume he would not be involved in the murder at Seaxmund's Ham.'

'I think you are all missing one point,' Brother Ator said suddenly, and they all turned to look at him inquisitively. 'If this river provides an easy passage to the country of the Gyrwas and to the Island of Eels, then a short journey to the north-west across the marshes is the island of Mede Ham Stede, of which you say this Mede is thane. To the south stands The Stag's Ford on the northern bank of what we call The Great Water, or the River Ouse.'

'You say this because . . .?' queried the abbot.

'Because I was born there. I told Fidelma that my parents raised me in the settlement of Saegham, the village by the lake. In fact, from there, westward across the marshland, you can see the Island of Eels.'

'So Clúain, or Mede, might be heading there for several purposes,' Eadulf said. 'Pursuit of Athelthryth, or to return to his island or . . .'

'Or to this council?' Fidelma added.

Abbot Brecán was looking troubled.

'Don't underestimate the power of certain kings and bishops of these kingdoms. After Oswy's decisions following the council at Streoneshalh, many Hibernians, with their Saxon converts, took flight back to the Five Kingdoms. If this Theodoros has his way, those that have remained will be made to follow unless they accept the philosophy and ways of Rome.'

'I share those thoughts,' Fidelma agreed. 'I do think it is very serious. The influence of the missionaries and teachers from Hibernia appears to have diminished considerably.'

Brother Siadhal appeared in the door.

'I have sent Brother Indulf to inquire if this Clúain or any other strangers have been seen seeking passage along the river.'

Abbot Brecán acknowledged him before turning back to Fidelma.

'It is true that many of our missionaries and teachers are being rejected. They are replaced by those claiming obedience to Rome. Franks, Gauls, and Greeks are advanced into positions of power in the western Churches. There is not only Theodoros here but there is also a Berber named Adrianus. He is just as arrogant as the Greek. It is said the Berber was offered the position of chief bishop of Cantwara before the Greek, but he turned it down.'

'I think his name has been mentioned,' Fidelma frowned.

'He had to be satisfied with being abbot of the community near the principal township of the Cantwara,' Brother Siadhal explained. 'It seems that any friend of the Bishop Vitalian of Rome is favoured.'

Abbot Brecán sighed. 'I initially thought that uniting the Angles and Saxons in the New Faith was a task not achievable. Their teachers are already divided while still claiming, after Streoneshalh, allegiance to Rome. Some call themselves Arians, some Apollinaris, others Nestorians or Psilanthropians. They follow different philosophies and I think they will never be truly united.'

'Doubtless what the abbot says has to be taken into consideration,' Brother Siadhal said gloomily. 'It is also true what you said, Fidelma of Cashel. You have a depth of thought that has been proved many times, lady, as your reputation as a *dálaigh* has shown. However, there is this Bishop Wilfrid of Northumbria, who has crossed your path at Streoneshalh. If anyone can unite the Angles and Saxons, it is he.'

'I heard that Ecgfrith of Northumbria has expelled him,' Eadulf pointed out, 'even though he won the debate at Streoneshalh.'

'Theodoros has already demanded that Ecgfrith reinstate him as Bishop of Northumbria,' Brother Siadhal pointed out.

Fidelma thought that the steward was extremely well informed.

There was a silence and Eadulf realised they were getting away from the main point.

'It is growing late for the evening meal. Is it not time that

Brother Boso made an appearance so that we can expand our knowledge on these subjects?'

At once Brother Ator was on his feet again. 'I can go and seek him out, to save time.'

Brother Siadhal looked to the abbot, who made an approving gesture of his hand and the steward took the young man to the door and gave him directions to the guests' huts.

'I am afraid, if the decisions of the council runs against us, the days of our makeshift community at Cnobheres Burg will not exist much longer,' Abbot Brecán confessed.

'You mean that earnestly?' Fidelma asked. 'You feel that you and your community will be expelled from this kingdom?'

'You know that many have either returned to Iona or gone back to the Five Kingdoms. Some have stayed, in spite of restrictions. But even some of the Saxons have not changed their allegiance yet. The Blessed Hilda remains at Streoneshalh, in her abbey of the White House. As Oswy's sister, she is relatively safe and able to continue to follow the ways of our Faith, to which she was converted by Aidan. Cuthbert is still prior of Lindisfarne, but now has to live in isolation on the Lesser Farne Island, hoping the storm will pass. Many of our Saxon converts remain loyal, but they will soon have to make the decision to seek a less persecuted existence, either in Hibernia or in other lands.'

'Have you plans if this happens?' Fidelma asked.

'I fear that we will have to abandon this community. It was founded nearly a quarter of a century ago. We have survived attacks by pagans and by the decisions at Streoneshalh, but now . . . it seems these old Roman-built walls must be abandoned once again.'

'Where will you go?' pressed Fidelma sympathetically.

'My mind yearns for the Múscraige Mountains and the gentle waters of the Laois. It is hard being in this flat marshland when one has been raised among the mountains.' The abbot smiled wanly. 'So perhaps it is time to start the journey back to Muman.'

'You don't feel that you are abandoning those poor people that you have converted to the New Faith?' Eadulf asked, slightly accusingly.

The abbot gave a sardonic chuckle. 'Rather the converts are abandoning us for the new interpretations from Rome. Already people are following the Burgundian, Felix, in preference of us. No, there is no abandoning those who have already abandoned what we tried to teach them.'

'When this Clúain, or Mede, met Brother Boso at the meal last night, was this the subject of their conversation?'

'I only witnessed part of it,' the abbot replied. 'Sometimes you can tell if it was an argument or a friendly conversation. It was something serious . . .'

'Serious?' Fidelma pressed.

Brother Siadhal agreed with his abbot. 'It was not light hearted, and Brother Boso simply shook his head a few times. There was no shouting. I presumed the conversation to be general.'

'So you did not hear whether anything was said about the events at Seaxmund's Ham?' Eadulf asked.

'I did not.' Brother Siadhal shook his head. 'After I saw Clúain and Boso in conversation last night, I did not see this Clúain again and I presumed he had left to find a boat.'

The door opened and a young Hibernian religieux entered.

'Did you find out anything, Brother Indulf?' the abbot demanded immediately.

'I spoke to several around the jetties down along the river. I gave them the description of the one called Clúain, whom I had seen for myself last night. Apparently, he met with two others. They were seen along the river on horses earlier. It was said that although they wore religious robes they looked and behaved more like warriors.'

'What happened?'

'They were looking for passage to Deor Ham, upriver. I could not discover the name of the man who gave them passage. There was some negotiation and the deal was done that the horses would be exchanged for the passage on the boat.'

'When was this?' Brother Siadhal asked.

'The boat set off at noon.'

It was at that moment that Brother Ator returned, looking slightly puzzled.

'How was Brother Boso?' Abbot Brecán asked as the boy resumed his seat. 'When will he join us?

'I found the hut, knocked on the door but there was no answer. I tried it but it seemed to be locked.'

'Locked?' Brother Siadhal was surprised. 'We don't lock huts in this community for we are all under the protection of the Almighty.'

'Well, I called and there was no response, so I presume he is still at his contemplations.'

Brother Siadhal turned disapprovingly to Brother Indulf, who was still waiting.

'I suggest you go along to Brother Boso's guest hut and tell him that it is urgent he join us.'

Abbot Brecán watched the door close on Brother Indulf before returning his gaze to the others.

The sound of running footsteps over the flagstones made them all raise their heads with expressions of curiosity. The door burst opened without any preamble. Brother Indulf stood on the threshold, his shoulders heaving in his exertions.

'You must come quickly,' he gasped.

'What is it?' Abbot Brecán demanded, rising.

'Brother Boso. He is dead in his cell.'

CHAPTER THIRTEEN

'There is no use all of us crowding inside the guest hut,' Abbot Brecán told the small group who had gathered. 'As Brother Boso is dead, I suggest that Brother Eadulf, who is reputed for his knowledge, examine the body to confirm the manner of death. I would also suggest that Brother Eadulf be accompanied by Brother Ator, who will give formal identification of the body of his mentor.'

Eadulf realised that the abbot was punctilious in obeying matters of the law.

Eadulf entered the cabin first and stood quietly looking down at the body stretched face upwards on the cot in the light of a lantern. The collection of cabins within the crumbling Roman walls was of simple log construction and the inside of this one was very plain. The contents were a wooden-framed bed, a box for toilet articles and a few icons hanging on pegs along the wall. The body lay in a twisted blanket on the straw mattress. It was that of a man of late middle age. He wore a tonsure of the Roman style rather than the Hibernian. His fleshy features seemed placid and calm, belying the manner of his death, which Eadulf could easily observe had been by stabbing with a dagger. The brown woollen robe he wore was also twisted around him, showing cuts and tears to the cloth, which was damp with blood.

Eadulf stared at the face for a while, ensuring that the person who lay before him was not the same man that he and Fidelma had seen during the confrontation before the cinders of his uncle's house. He did not expect this man to be the same as the surly one who had dismissed them into the hands of Stuf and the mob, but he wanted to make sure, even though Brother Ator had not recognised the description they had given him. Having made his examination, he stood aside to let Brother Ator move forward.

'It is Brother Boso,' the young man said tightly, then turned swiftly and left the cell.

After Ator had left, Eadulf straightened the body and examined the two obvious stab wounds. He noted one to the throat, which would have prevented the victim crying out. Then he changed his mind, for the second had been a thrust into the back, up between the ribs and into the heart. It would have ensured death was immediate. The other cut, then, seemed to have been made in anger. There was no doubt the stabbings were done by someone who knew what they were doing, most probably someone skilled in arms.

Eadulf stood back, viewing the body, and noticed the fatty paunch, which would not be unusual in a man of Boso's years. He had been taught that body temperature was sometimes an indicator as to when death had occurred, for it began to change towards the ambient temperature of the surroundings and he realised the cell was cold but not ice cold. There was the fact that the body before him was not thin and he knew a thin person's body temperature would cool more quickly. He wished he could remember more of those studies at Tuam Drecain, where learned scholars had discussed such matters.

Eadulf finally rejoined the others outside.

'Brother Boso was stabbed to death, as best as I can tell, not so long ago,' he told them.

'A short time ago?' Abbot Brecán asked puzzled.

'I can only estimate for I have no knowledge of how to make a precise conclusion. It might have been after he retired last night or even early this morning. When was he last seen?'

'When he retired last night,' Brother Siadhal replied. 'As I told you, I last saw him in conversation with the man calling himself Clúain. Before that he said he wanted to spend the day alone in his cell in contemplation, so he was not disturbed today.'

'So that places Clúain, who could be this man Mede, as the primary suspect?' Brother Ator pointed out angrily.

'As Eadulf said, one cannot be specific as to when this happened,' Fidelma said thoughtfully. 'But certainly, he saw Brother Boso late last night. From what I see, this old fortress stands open to many wanderers. Anyone can enter it without challenge. Your community has simply put up a few wooden huts and a chapel in a corner of the place out of the wind. But there are no surrounding walls nor fences and gates. You do not appear to even have a watchman. Your community is not built for security.'

'Neither should we have had need for any security. We are here as missionaries and teachers,' the abbot replied.

'But a lot of newly built communities have gates and watchers on the gate,' Eadulf replied.

Abbot Brecán became morose.

'We were not allowed to build further, nor did we have the facility to command the locals, even if they were our converts, to do any substantial building for a proper community. We were just tucked into this south-west corner away from the winds. I believe this was due to the decision at Streoneshalh, which had influence in many kingdoms aside from Northumbria. Had it not been for that, then we would have been able to start to build more substantially. At the time, this site was all that was given to us, and we also had to recover from its destruction by the pagan Penda. Now we don't know how long we will be able to stay here.'

Brother Siadhal echoed his abbot's point. 'It was clear that this was the worst possible place to maintain a community, even as a temporary shelter. The community, even though they sheltered within these walls, thinking they were protected, found no real protection here. Many were slaughtered by the unbelievers led by Penda. But Penda's son has now embraced the Faith and we thought there was no more to fear.'

Fidelma was sceptical. 'It was foolishness to imagine so.'

'Perhaps Sigeberht, in giving you this place as a base for your community, simply thought you would rebuild it or re-create it as a fortress, as it once was?' Werferth remarked defensively, indicating the great flint walls.

'We are becoming slightly distracted from the question of who killed Brother Boso,' Fidelma pointed out.

'If the attack on Brother Boso was done after dark, then the killer must have known his way to the spot. The obvious person is this Clúain or Mede, whatever he is called,' Brother Ator said again.

'A point to consider is that the killer came here without arousing your guard dogs,' Fidelma added. 'You do have guard dogs, don't you? This place is so open that any wild animal could enter.'

'We don't have guard dogs as such,' Abbot Brecán confessed after an uneasy pause. 'Usually one of the community ensures fires are kept going at either end of the row of huts we use as quarters around the chapel.' He indicated them with a sweep of one hand.

'We have a murder on our hands,' Brother Siadhal reminded them, having caught Fidelma's earlier remark about diverting from the subject. 'So what do we do next?'

'Pardon, Father Abbot.' It was Brother Indulf who interrupted. 'Are people overlooking the fact that I reported that the man Clúain was seen with his two comrades at the jetty selling their horses for passage on a boat going upriver on the Éar? They took passage for Deor Ham and beyond.'

'And so?' Abbot Brecán asked in a heavy voice.

'If Mede his comrades did not leave until this morning, then they must have been here overnight,' Brother Ator replied triumphantly. 'And if Brother Boso was last seen outside this hut . . .'

'Clúain and two companions left this morning by river and he is identified by you as this warrior Mede?' The abbot glanced to the guest hut but did not finish articulating the thought.

Eadulf looked quickly at Fidelma. His expression was serious.

'Without Brother Boso, our investigation into my uncle's murder terminates here. It is obvious my sister was not abducted by these Northumbrians. We are not even sure these men were at Seaxmund's Ham. The purpose of our visit was to ask questions of Brother Boso about his relationship with my uncle. He might have been able to indicate a motive for Athelnoth's murder and the disappearance of my sister. But with Brother Boso's murder there is an end to that possible information. We have already questioned Brother Ator. Even though he was disciple to Brother Boso, he can provide no information that helps us progress matters. So we have come to an end.'

'Is that it?' Brother Ator cried in disbelief. 'You don't intend to investigate these raiders and the murder of my mentor?'

'From what I have gathered – even if we conclude that Clúain is that same person as the warrior named Mede – we do not know whether Brother Boso knew anything at all that related to my uncle's death. We are not even sure about this pursuit of Princess Athelthryth as the Northumbrians' objective. Are we to pursue them in some unending search of the Fen country? With Brother Boso dead, we do not know whether the raiders were connected with Athelnoth's murders, aside from a crazy old woman thinking that she saw them, and something of a similarity in the method of killing, which may be just coincidence. Suspicion but not proof. We do not have the luxury of unending time.'

Fidelma silently agreed with Eadulf, although not entirely. In her mind, the time might be spent more fruitfully than chasing suspects into the strange marshlands of the Gyrwas. Without any other positive information, the murder of Brother Boso seemed unrelated to the murder of the *gerefa* and disappearance of his niece. She was also thinking that the sooner the matter ended, the sooner she could think of the journey back to Cashel.

'I suppose that you have a connection with a local *gerefa*, who will advise you?' Eadulf asked the abbot.

'I hear in your tone that you do not see profit in chasing after this Clúain for your inquiry?' Abbot Brecán replied grimly. 'I understand that Clúain, or Mede, as you say, is only a suspect for Brother Boso's death. At this point your intention is not to pursue the matter further? Well, I have my community to consider and will have to deal with this. I will make contact with the local thane and his lawgiver.' He glanced meaningfully at Werferth. 'It is not my choice at this time, for I would rather not bring my community to anyone's attention when the future of our people in this kingdom is being considered at The Stag's Ford.'

Werferth stirred uneasily. 'You can use my name as witness,' he finally offered.

Brother Ator was clearly angry at Eadulf.

'As no one wants to pursue who killed my mentor, Brother Boso, it will be up to me to undertake that investigation.' He looked around belligerently. 'I was his disciple. He has been murdered. I cannot abandon him by not pursuing his murderer. There is no doubt in my mind it was this Mede who did this. Mede or Clúain, it is the same name.'

Eadulf looked at the young man, slightly surprised at the inflexibility of his tone.

'I thought your motivation was to find Wulfrun. You say that you are in love with her.'

Brother Ator faced him, his features showing even more anger.

'I *am* in love with her. I believe that these mercenaries, who killed my mentor, know what has happened to her. The answer does not lie elsewhere. That is why I shall follow them to the land of the Gyrwas and I shall find them, whatever you decide.'

'Don't you consider it would be a waste of your time and effort to pursue these men to the country of the Gyrwas?' Abbot Brecán asked.

Eadulf looked to Fidelma and tried to read her thoughts.

'So far as the investigation goes into my uncle's murder, I do not think the pursuit of suspects into the territory of the Gyrwas will help,' he announced flatly. 'They have clearly not abducted my sister otherwise she would have been seen with them. The answers lie back at Seaxmund's Ham.'

Brother Ator straightened himself as if in physical challenge to Eadulf.

'Whatever you say, I am determined to take on this task alone,' he said. 'I owe Brother Boso much. I also love Wulfrun. That is no secret, and I am sure the mystery of her whereabouts is with Brother Boso's killers. However, I understand that you Hibernians are not enthusiastic about reporting this and so will be less enthusiastic about providing help because you feel it might bring danger to your community.'

Abbot Brecán flushed and replied before Eadulf could intervene.

'An illegal death should be everyone's concern. We are only twelve souls in this community now. If the Greek has his way, any day we may have to choose to take ship and abandon this place. But we will send a message to the Thane of Coaster and report all we know of this matter. Coaster is the nearest populated township. It is on an island further downriver from here. He should have a lawgiver who is able to help us. I will say that Werferth was a witness to these events. But if you are suggesting we send someone to be a companion with you, at this time we need to keep all our community safe.'

'I shall go to find a boat and undertake the task myself of tracking these raiders eastwards,' Brother Ator declared. 'I will follow them even into the territory of the Gyrwas.'

Eadulf turned nervously to Fidelma. 'Do you believe that I am making the right decision, given the circumstances?' he asked quietly.

Fidelma had already made up her mind but she was surprised at his sudden hesitation and that he should now ask for her approval. It was his decision and she felt that he should make it for himself.

'Do you want to return to Seaxmund's Ham and begin the investigation again by questioning the witnesses to see if anything was overlooked the first time?' she asked.

'Do you object?' he pressed.

'Is there any reason why I should object?' she asked, hoping she did not sound too uncaring. 'You are in charge, for I have no power here.'

When Eadulf seemed confused by her response she decided to continue for emphasis. 'I have no legal authority in your country. You know that. I have no legal position and, from the rumours we have heard about the summons of the kings and bishops of these kingdoms, I may shortly have no status at all.'

'But you are a *dálaigh* and my wife,' Eadulf protested.

'You have always told me that you were a hereditary *gerefa* of this land. It was your uncle that was murdered. Your sister has disappeared. That gives you the status to pursue whatever inquiry you need,' she said.

Werferth interrupted with a noisy cough.

'In case you have forgotten my position in this matter,' he pointed out, 'I am content to let Eadulf continue with whatever decision he wants to make. However, I must shortly return to the king's business for I am answerable to him. As you can guess, my duties will take me to The Stag's Ford. If the raiders are chasing Princess Athelthryth and this killing of Brother Boso has something to do with it, then they will doubtless be heading in that direction. It is not far from the Island of Eels, but neither is it far from Mede Ham Stede. Both bring me close to The Stag's Ford. So I have decided that I shall accompany Brother Ator. My presence will give him some authority in his mission to seek out these raiders, who appear to be serving the Northumbrian king.'

Brother Ator made a gesture of thanks to Werferth, but his face displayed a curious expression of reluctance.

'We shall be sorry to lose your company, Werferth,' Eadulf replied. 'But we return to Seaxmund's Ham.'

'Do you really think that the kings and bishops of all the other kingdoms will be at this council at The Stag's Ford?' Fidelma asked lightly.

'It is the authority of Archbishop Theodoros that they will have to deny. The kings and their bishops of the kingdoms will have to make a decision soon,' returned the warrior. 'I believe it will happen.'

'That is, if the bishops of the various kingdoms agree in recognising Theodoros' authority,' Fidelma pointed out softly.

Werferth shrugged, looking apologetically at Eadulf. 'I dislike abandoning you and the lady Fidelma. You may well be right to return. I shall need to rejoin my king at The Stag's Ford.'

Eadulf seemed hesitant again, looking to Fidelma. For years he had grown used to Fidelma leading a decision or, at least taking a stronger part in decision making. Now he was being asked to decide entirely by himself while Fidelma remained neutral. He did not like the feeling it gave him, nor the fact that he had been aware of a growing antipathy and distance between Fidelma and himself. He did not understand it and knew he must raise the matter with her, yet he felt fearful and timid about doing so. However, he knew he had to decide on their immediate course of action.

'I believe the answer no longer lies with these Northumbrians, as I said,' he reiterated. 'Now I can no longer question Brother Boso, I must return to Seaxmund's Ham. I will more likely find answers there about my sister's disappearance and who killed my uncle. We will return there to discover if there is anything that I have missed. I am determined to find answers.'

Werferth clapped him on the shoulder. 'Then be assured that Beornwulf is a good man. He has my trust and also that of Sigeric, steward of the king's Witan. If you need help do not hesitate to seek it from him.'

Abbot Brecán turned to his steward. 'Brother Siadhal, arrange with Brother Indulf to take my felicitations to the Thane of Coaster at first light and explain what has transpired here and see whether he desires to send a lawgiver to assess matters. At the same time, send someone else to see what are the prospects of finding a boat to take Werferth and Brother Ator upriver to Deor Ham. There is not much we can do before first light tomorrow, now the sun is already descending in the western sky.'

Brother Siadhal bowed his head. 'We must also prepare for the obsequies of Brother Boso.'

'That shall be done tonight at midnight, as is custom. But, with due respect for the lost soul, for the welfare of the community and our guests, we should arrange the last meal of the day immediately.'

Eadulf could not help a confirming glance at the darkened sky.

'Better you start your journey in daylight and finish in daylight.' The abbot seemed to read his thoughts.

'A more important factor is that our ponies could do with a rest and fodder and be refreshed for the journey back, as we should also,' Fidelma pointed out.

'I agree.' Werferth was actually smiling as if in satisfaction at something he was keeping to himself. 'As Brother Ator and I must follow those suspects by boat, and being unable to take our ponies, perhaps I can crave a favour of you both?'

'A favour?' queried Eadulf.

'Take Brother Ator's pony and leave it at Ceol's Halh with Mother Notgide. It was her husband's property anyway. My own warhorse can be left with my good friend Thane Beornwulf for me to collect when I return there.'

'It is an easy thing to do,' Fidelma confirmed when Eadulf hesitated.

Abbot Brecán massaged his hands as if he were washing them of dirty items. It was clear he was not happy with the developments, but he smiled hesitantly at Fidelma.

'We adhere to our customs here, lady. There will be water warmed for a bath before the last meal of the day. Alas, we cannot provide any newly laundered clothing.'

Fidelma had almost forgotten the cleansing rituals of her own people since she had landed at Domnoc-wic. She smiled gravely at the abbot.

'It is hard to follow customs when one is in this strange country,' she remarked.

Brother Siadhal looked reproofed. *'Noli oblivisci tuam in lacrimis tuis.'*

'Indeed, even in the country of the barbarians, do not neglect custom. Well, when the facilities are available, I will follow the advice assiduously.'

'When we bury Brother Boso tonight, perhaps Brother Ator will be so good as to lead the rituals for the repose of the soul of the departed. I shall instruct members of our community to prepare Brother Boso's body for rituals of the grave.'

They had returned to the large hut where Abbot Brecán had first greeted them. He turned to his steward.

'I think that before we go further a jug of the *corma* is in order. We still have some from our homeland. In view of the shocking event of the day, I believe that we are all deserving of it.'

'A curious day, indeed,' Fidelma added.

Eadulf grimaced sourly. 'And who knows what curiosities tomorrow will provide us with?'

'You believe the answers still remain at Seaxmund's Ham?' Werferth asked.

'It is nothing but a feeling,' Eadulf replied. 'I may be proved wrong but I cannot help feeling that we neglected to consider some aspects that we had been told.'

'Such as?' Brother Ator queried belligerently.

Eadulf was about to reply when Fidelma interrupted cynically.

'There was a wise judge who often said no speculation without information.'

Eadulf's cheeks reddened a little, for it was what he had been about to reply.

'We know enough of the facts about what happened at Seaxmund's Ham,' Brother Ator dismissed. 'I still say the answer will be found with those who killed Brother Boso.'

'Why are you so convinced?' Eadulf demanded.

'This man, thought to be Mede, mentioned neither Seaxmund's Ham nor the murder of the *gerefa*,' replied the young man sharply. 'It was clear that he was hiding it; hiding the news because he had a guilty conscience.'

'There could be many answers to that,' pointed out Fidelma. 'But now, I believe, we have worked our minds on this subject. Isn't it time we prepared for the evening meal and then got some rest for our respective journeys tomorrow?'

CHAPTER FOURTEEN

Fidelma had a strange feeling that she could not exactly identify as she and Eadulf rode into Domnoc-wic with the sun just past its zenith. It was Eadulf who suggested that they halt there for midday refreshment when she reminded him they should make sure their ponies were watered and foddered now that they had four to take care of. No one took a second glance at two mounted people leading two other horses as they entered the town with the market a continual event, full of horses and other livestock.

'Shall we head for that tavern where we stayed before?' Eadulf suggested as he tried to negotiate his way through the crowded square.

'One place is as good as another,' Fidelma replied shortly.

The journey had been made mostly in silence, starting as they rode south alongside the Wahenhe. She remembered they had to ford it twice because of the way it twisted and turned. Even as they passed Braggi's hut on the hilltop, and then the turn-off into the wooded marshes they had come to know as the Monk's Enclosure, neither of them suggested they pause. Each was lost in his or her own thoughts.

There was no difficulty finding the tavern run by the elderly Thuri and his wife Mildrith. At the stables they arranged for water and feed to be provided while they went inside the tavern. The place was fairly crowded and busier than when they had first been there. Thuri was bearing jugs of mead to his customers while Mildrith was taking platters of food to others. They hesitated and peered round to find a space.

'By nine sacred prognostications of Wyrd! Long may the goddess of Fate look kindly on us and guide us to the appropriate nine worlds of the Tree of Life.' A thunderous voice from a corner momentarily silenced the hubbub of the tavern.

'Greetings to you, Mul of Frig's Tun,' Eadulf responded solemnly as he caught sight of the one who made the salutation.

With a bit of pushing, Mul made room for them on the corner bench. Although the farmer seemed pleased to see them again his expression was a little serious.

'I heard about your uncle Athelnoth,' he said to Eadulf. 'A merchant came here yesterday and told us the story. Is that why you have concluded your visit so soon?'

Eadulf responded with a negative gesture and added: 'The visit is not concluded, Mul. We are on our way back to Seaxmund's Ham, having followed leads as far north as Cnobheres Burg. We were even at the abbey there a few days ago. It is only because we knew this place, thanks to you, that we decided to break our journey here on the way back and refresh ourselves and your horses that you so charitably lent us.'

'Have you discovered who killed Athelnoth and why?' Mul asked immediately. 'You know he was well liked in the territory.'

'We have not . . .' Eadulf paused as the elderly Thuri came across to greet them and took their orders. They asked for fish, and cider to drink, and while Thuri hurried off to fulfil their wishes, Eadulf turned seriously to Mul.

'As I said, we have not been able to discover anything that gives us even a clue to the identity of the perpetrator,' he confessed.

Observing that Mul was bursting with questions, Eadulf decided to quickly recount what had happened since their last meeting.

'Not a nice homecoming,' Mul finally commented.

'It was certainly unexpected,' Eadulf agreed, a sour tone in his voice. 'Especially unexpected was not being recognised in my own place of birth.'

Thuri was back with the drinks to inform them the food would come shortly.

'My stableman says that you have given him the two ponies to fodder, together with another pony and a black warhorse. I just wanted to make certain they were yours for I thought it unusual that you would be escorting a black warhorse.'

Mul was looking surprised, but Eadulf confirmed it.

'Yes, we have been given charge of these horses by friends to escort and leave at Ceol's Halh and Seaxmund's Ham. We will be returning there after our meal.'

'The meal will not be long,' Thuri assured him.

'A black warhorse?' Mul asked immediately after the innkeeper had left. 'What warrior did you defeat to gain such a prize?'

'I didn't have to defeat him,' Eadulf replied gravely. 'It belongs to our old friend Werferth. You remember him? He asked us to take it back to Seaxmund's Ham. The other pony belongs to Brother Ator at Ceol's Halh.'

Mul was conciliatory about how they had been treated at his uncle's house.

'I could have warned you about Stuf.'

'You know him?' Eadulf queried in surprise.

'Stuf? He's just a step above a *theow*. He has to work for the local thane, but the days are restricted to a set number. Outside of this, his time is his own. He is an opportunist, a thief but mainly a poacher.'

'That much was shown to us,' Fidelma observed softly, speaking for the first time.

'He is not to be trusted for he would turn his hand to anything and use anybody whom he can profit by. From what you tell me, what he tried to do to you does not surprise me. He thought he might benefit from some reward. But, thank the Fates, Werferth and Crída were there to stand by you. All I can say is that Stuf is one that you should never turn your back to.'

'He is unlikely to try anything more now,' Fidelma assured Mul.

'Be attentive still. He is the least trustworthy kind, especially when he harbours a grudge.'

'The most pressing matter,' Eadulf summed up, 'is the fact that my young sister also disappeared on the same night as my uncle's murder.'

'I was hoping to hear you had good news in that quarter,' Mul agreed. 'She was a beautiful girl. Was she not due to get married soon?'

'That is so,' Eadulf confirmed bitterly. 'It is why I am determined to discover what happened at Athelnoth's house that night.'

'There was talk that some conflict had occurred about her marriage,' Mul continued to muse.

'A conflict?' Fidelma questioned immediately.

'A conflict between whether she would marry a young religieux or whether she would marry the *druhting* of Thane Beornwulf.'

'We knew that Brother Ator of Ceol's Halh was in love with her and that they were planning to marry,' Eadulf agreed. 'That was why Brother Ator was so determined to accompany us when we were following some suspects.'

'The *druhting* of Beornwulf is Crída?' Fidelma sought clarification. Thinking back, she remembered Crída's antagonism when the subject of Ator and Wulfrun had been raised.

'Thane Beornwulf's chief retainer,' Mul confirmed.

'Are you saying he might still be in love with my sister?' Eadulf asked.

'It was well known that Athelnoth favoured neither Crída nor the young religieux,' Mul replied. 'But now you tell me that Brother Boso has been murdered by Northumbrian raiders. You say this Brother Ator was Boso's disciple, and that Werferth and Brother Ator are chasing them? So Ator thinks the Northumbrians took young Wulfrun?'

'It is what he thinks.'

'But you do not share that thought?'

'I think the answer still remains at Seaxmund's Ham,' Eadulf replied. 'We saw nothing of Wulfrun on our pursuit of the Northumbrians. It would be pointless chasing them.'

'Let us hope so,' Mul replied shortly. 'I just wondered who Abbot Aecci will send to Ceol's Halh in Brother Boso's place to serve the area for the New Faith?'

'You think it would not be Brother Ator?' Fidelma asked quickly. 'Wouldn't that succession be natural?'

Mul shrugged. 'I don't think he would be Abbot Aecci's choice.'

'Why not?' Fidelma wondered.

'There was always talk of conflicts between master and disciple,' Mul replied. 'In truth, I don't think Brother Boso liked his young disciple much.'

Fidelma was now puzzled. 'That is not the impression we were given. In fact, the impression Brother Ator gave was the opposite. He claimed that he almost hero-worshipped Brother Boso.'

'It is not what local gossip will tell you.' Mul shook his head. 'But then no one likes him much . . . no one likes Brother Ator, I mean. He is a conceited young man; arrogant in his personality.'

'He is certainly knowledgeable and likes to boast of it,' Fidelma agreed.

'With a fearsome temper, they say. Was he not said to be of the

Gyrwas? I heard that he was from Saegham, the township by the marsh lake. His family disowned him. As a young man they say he finally found his way to Domnoc-wic.'

'He said that he had studied here, but did not seem to be known among the brethren,' Fidelma reflected.

'He is known for telling people what they want to hear,' Mul reflected. 'But he is certainly knowledgeable. But don't trust me. When I am not tending my farmstead, I am merely travelling this quarter of the country picking up stories and passing them on.'

'You say, no one likes him much,' Fidelma commented. 'We observed that Crída must be one of those who dislikes him.'

Mul chuckled softly. 'Crída? Stories have it that they even fought over Wulfrun. I mean fought physically, but the conflict was put a stop to by Athelnoth himself.'

'When was that?' Eadulf demanded in surprise.

'Not so long ago. I think most folk were in favour of Crída marrying Wulfrun. Except your uncle, who was, of course, her guardian. But being a lawgiver, he had his own ideas of whom his niece should marry. Wulfrun was believed to express her own opinion in favour of Crída . . . or was it Ator? I forget.'

Fidelma was looking troubled. 'What were Athelnoth's ideas then?' she asked, realising she was about to hear a different story from what she had been told.

'Not for me to say,' Mul replied. 'But he wanted the family to be elevated, especially after he could boast that Eadulf had married a princess, albeit an Hibernian one, begging your pardon, lady.'

'So what is your opinion of Thane Beornwulf?' she asked, ignoring the comment.

Mul looked surprised at the question. 'You don't suspect a noble thane would have anything to do with this matter, do you?'

'In my years since I left Brehon Morann's law school and

practised as a *dálaigh*, I've learnt that no one is above the law. Eadulf knows that full well.'

'Well, lady, in our culture, we are taught to respect our nobles and those of higher rank than we are. We don't challenge them.'

'Bishops or kings, they are people like yourself, Mul. Rank should not prevent you considering them as people. I suspect it is not a matter of what your thoughts are, but of being forbidden to express them. Therefore just pretend that you are thinking aloud.'

Mul thought about this, head to one side, for a moment or two. 'Thane Beornwulf? I have heard nothing bad against him. You have met him. He is a young man, a warrior, who, until now, has been well advised by the late *gerefa*. That death will be a sad loss to him. He is said to be chivalrous and fair and, of course, he serves on the king's Witan. He is well respected. I have heard no scandal or dislike pass anyone's lips.'

Fidelma smiled approvingly. 'It was not hard for you to make your opinion known, was it? It is always good to know what is in the minds of local people in these circumstances.' She glanced to Eadulf meaningfully. 'I suspect, as time is passing, we should be back on the road for Ceol's Halh and return the first of our steeds to its owner on behalf of Brother Ator.' She hesitated and looked to Mul. 'That is, I am presuming Eadulf and I can keep the two ponies you lent us until this matter has been resolved?'

'It goes without saying,' Mul replied. 'I gave my word the first time. Until you have finished the investigation, or leave this territory, they are yours.'

'Once again we are in your debt, Mul.' She paused and grinned. 'One day I am sure we will return to find that you have transformed into an *ealdorman* of your people.'

Mul roared with laughter.

'If I keep in company with you and Eadulf, lady, I do not doubt that I will be declared the *atheling* of my people! In these uncertain times, there is need for a few strong princes.'

GRAVE OF THE LAWGIVER

A short time later, when they were on the road south-westward out of the busy port, Eadulf turned to Fidelma.

'I would not make such jokes about princes with Mul,' he rebuked.

Fidelma was surprised. 'Is humour something else in your culture that one has to suppress?' she asked cynically.

'Not suppress, but we have a sense of the rigidity of ranks and the manners applied to those ranks. One cannot treat a *geburas* with the same propriety as a *ceorl*, or a *gerefa* with the same deference as a *thegn*. We have a saying: the calf belongs to the owner of the cow.'

'It is a wonder how you have survived for so long in my country, Eadulf,' Fidelma replied bitterly. 'People have different roles and rights, but you can still stand in front of a High King and challenge him. We say: the son of a king is not nobler than his food.'

'Only if you're a bard and can frame your criticism by way of satire,' he snapped back. 'I know your law is protective of poets.'

For a moment she hesitated and then grimaced sadly.

'Well, you did learn something while you were among us,' she replied quietly. She was about to amplify her thought, but fell silent. Once again she wanted Eadulf to raise the problem confronting them; wanted him to awaken to the realisation that it needed to be raised and talked through.

Eadulf looked nervously back but Fidelma was examining the ground. Once again he felt the courage ebb out of him to confront her with what he was thinking. Once more she set herself to concentrate on observing the flat wetlands along Mennesmer, through which they were travelling. Once more they were riding along the sluggish river, and once again she was thinking it was a strange country that had neither mountains nor prominent barriers to the great, cold seas that surrounded it. Indeed, she kept hearing that the wetlands had increased so much to the east that it was just a series of islands in the marshlands.

If the truth were known, she would prefer to be on some ocean-going vessel, on a *ler-longa*, a sea-going vessel, and heading home. She felt little desire to ask about the sightings of strange birds or what creatures would be scurrying through the marshlands at the side of the track they were following. So she was quiet.

Ahead she could see the meeting of the rivers at the Oxen Ford, where the small river, the Frome, ran south to make its way through Seaxmund's Ham to join the Alde. It was amazing that only a few days ago they had ridden north thinking that they would find answers from Brother Boso. Now they had not only Brother Ator's pony to return to Ceol's Halh but also to bring the news of the murder of Brother Boso to the community.

The skies were darkening. Clouds were thickening across the eastern sky as the early evening approached by the time Fidelma and Eadulf crossed the shallows of the Frome to enter the small group of homesteads that was called Ceol's Halh.

It was apparent their coming had been observed. As they neared the central chapel among the surrounding huts of the community, a sharp voice challenged them. Emerging from the shadows of the huts and outbuildings were several men. The light of lanterns, hanging from various buildings, glinted on wooden axes and the metal of spades.

'It is Eadulf of Seaxmund's Ham,' Eadulf responded immediately. 'We were here just a few days ago.'

A familiar figure came forward. It was the woman called Mother Notgide, who seemed to be in charge of the settlement. A small man seemed dwarfed beside her.

'I recognise you,' the woman acknowledged. 'But why are there only two of you? Where are Brother Ator and the warrior? You lead their horses but they are not with you?'

Eadulf and Fidelma dismounted.

'We have come to return the horse that Brother Ator borrowed from you,' Eadulf responded.

'Is he dead?' the woman asked. Her voice sounded almost excited.

'Not dead. He and Werferth, the warrior, are continuing their journey, heading to the Fenland by boat along the Éar. As we were returning here, Brother Ator asked us to return his horse to you. At the same time, we are taking Werferth's stallion to Thane Beornwulf from whom Werferth can collect it later.'

'Oh? So Brother Ator is expected to return?'

'You sound disappointed,' Fidelma observed.

Mother Notgide, perhaps recalling that the Hibernian woman had had Thane Beornwulf's support and respect the last time, hesitated in answering her, then said, 'Brother Ator's time here was not a happy one . . . for us.'

You did not like Brother Ator?' Fidelma asked, thinking of what Mul had said.

Mother Notgide hesitated again in response, then turned to the little man at her side. 'My husband Scead will take charge of the pony.' She motioned him forward to take it. Then she looked back to Fidelma. 'We found Ator too conceited and Brother Boso frequently had to remind him of his attitudes. I suspect Brother Boso told you so when you caught up with him at Domnoc-wic.'

'We have bad news for this community.' Fidelma paused. 'We did not catch up with Brother Boso at Domnoc-wic. When we did encounter him we found he had been killed. It was suspected that Northumbrian raiders had done it. The same Northumbrians who had been seen near here the night when Athelnoth was killed. That is why Werferth and Brother Ator are travelling to the lands of the Gyrwas – to pursue them.'

The elderly woman gave a strange, stifled cry and the homesteaders around fell deathly silent.

Mother Notgide sat down abruptly on a stool before her cabin. Her husband Scead had turned to one of the men and instructed him to take care of the horses. Then he beckoned Eadulf and Fidelma to be seated on a bench in front of the hut facing his wife.

'Your news comes as a shock to all of us. I will get cider and ask you to tell us the details of this event.'

Eadulf was about to refuse but Fidelma had more intuition on such matters and accepted for both of them.

'Brother Boso is dead?' Scead asked when he returned with the drinks. His tone was slow and measured. Mother Notgide seemed to pull herself together and took her cider almost in one long swallow.

'He is dead,' Eadulf confirmed. 'Werferth, as commander of the king's bodyguard, felt it his duty to accompany Brother Ator to follow the three Northumbrians because they felt they were suspects,' Eadulf explained. 'I am more concerned with the death of my uncle Athelnoth and the disappearance of my sister Wulfrun. That is why I insisted on returning here. So far as we could tell, the Northumbrians were raiders who, we think, were trying to track down Princess Athelthryth.'

'Had you a chance to talk to Brother Boso?' Mother Notgide asked.

'We followed Brother Boso to Dumnoc-wic, missed him there and then went on after to some place on the Wahenhe River, where we realised the Northumbrians were following him.' He purposely did not mention the Hibernian community.

'What then?' Mother Notgide pressed.

Eadulf shrugged. 'We only mean to leave Brother Ator's horse with you and proceed on to Beornwulf's Hall with Werferth's stallion. I feel I must pursue the matter of my uncle's murder here. By the way, my young sister was not with the Northumbrian raiders.'

'We will return tomorrow as there may be further questions

we will have to ask relating to Athelnoth's murder,' Fidelma added.

'Perhaps more importantly is the question of who killed Brother Boso?' Mother Notgide asked in a voice of suppressed emotion.

'It is suspected that it was the raiders,' Eadulf replied.

'You say Brother Ator and lord Werferth are now chasing the raiders?' Scead asked. 'What was their purpose?'

'It was felt that they were pursuing Princess Athelthryth,' Eadulf repeated.

'We were told that their leader was a Northumbrian thane named Mede,' Fidelma confirmed.

Mother Notgide exhaled sharply. 'Mede, Thane of Mede Ham Stede?'

'How do you know?' Fidelma was surprised again.

Mother Notgide spread her arms. 'I was told that name twice.'

'By whom?'

'It was Stuf who told me the name on the day before Athelnoth's house was burnt.'

'Stuf mentioned Mede's name before my uncle was killed?' Eadulf asked with emphasis.

'Stuf passed through here and said he had seen three men up at the Oxen Ford and one of them was Mede, a thane of an island in the Gyrwas, on the side that comes under the rule of Ecgfrith of Northumbria.'

'How did Stuf know this man Mede?'

'That you will have to ask Stuf,' Mother Notgide replied. 'The story of Princess Athelthryth, who but recently escaped from the captivity of Northumbria, is well known here, she being a princess of our people.'

'The story is well told from place to place,' Eadulf agreed. 'We understand that Northumbrian raiders have been pursuing her with plans to abduct her and return her to King Ecgfrith.'

'Mede's island would also be near the Isle of Eels where the princess built her abbey?' Fidelma queried.

'Fairly close by,' Scead answered. 'It is also near where Brother Ator comes from.'

Eadulf glanced at Fidelma, wondering if he had made a mistake in not following Werferth and Brother Ator. 'If this Mede was here, in this area, then he must have believed that the princess was hiding here.'

'If she was hiding here, she would have been welcome,' Mother Notgide intervened firmly.

'If she was not, why was this Mede seeking to ask questions of Brother Boso?' Fidelma asked thoughtfully. Then she said: 'You mentioned that his name, Mede, was told to you twice. Who was the second person who identified him to you?'

'That was Wiglaf the farmer. He farms some barley crops just to the north of here and looks after a deer herd.'

'We remember Wiglaf. So how did he recognise Mede?'

'He first saw him leading his men in the last Northumbrian raid. Wiglaf was called upon to fight by Cynehelm, who was our thane at that time. It's likely that he told Stuf. He saw these three men near Oxen Ford and was able to identify him.'

'So is that how Stuf knew his name?'

'Perhaps,' Mother Notgide replied after some thought. 'With Stuf you never know what is truth or not.'

'Did Brother Boso make any mention of Athelnoth in this connection? Had my uncle been questioned by Mede? I am told Athelnoth and Brother Boso were friends. Did they share any information?'

'Mede came here the day after Athelnoth was killed. Brother Boso had performed the funeral ritual, came back here and then left for Domnoc-wic. It was not long after he left that Mede came and that's when I spoke to him.'

'The chronology is confusing.' Fidelma was slightly perplexed.

'Stuf was passing through and mentioned he had seen Mede at the Oxen Ford. The next night, Athelnoth's house was burnt down. Brother Boso went to conduct the funeral rituals at noon the next day but returned here immediately. He then left for Domnoc-wic and, just after he'd gone, Mede came asking for him, as I told you earlier. When he was told Brother Boso had left for Domnoc-wic he, too, left.' Scead finished with a shrug.

'Later the same day, you came with Thane Beornwulf,' Mother Notgide added.

'Wasn't it at this Oxen Ford that we saw those mounted men in religious garb?' Fidelma reminded Eadulf.

'The very morning following the burning of Athelnoth's house,' confirmed Eadulf.

'That means that Stuf had seen them at Oxen Ford the day of the evening of the attack and murder,' Fidelma said. She turned to Mother Notgide. 'You say Stuf is not to be trusted?'

'Who does trust him?' she replied. 'And when he is seen one must ensure that nothing goes missing as he passes by.'

'We have had some of his hospitality,' Eadulf said. 'I am surprised he is allowed as much freedom to wander as he has.'

'Well, he is allowed time for his own pursuits. On some days, he is not constricted to certain areas of the thane's domain.'

'I know this,' Eadulf replied shortly. 'But what interests me is that he saw Mede at the Oxen Ford and could even recognise Mede as the Thane of Mede Ham Stede. How did he recognise him?'

'I have told you – you will have to ask Stuf from whom he received his knowledge,' Mother Notgide replied. 'I am no reader of minds.'

'I am beginning to think that I made the wrong decision in returning here.' Eadulf's words of regret were doubtless meant for Fidelma. 'It seems that Brother Ator might have been right in pursuing Mede. I saw no real connection between Mede and my uncle, but hearing that Stuf had also recognised these Northumbrians around the time the burning took place, and knowing what we now do of them, opens up a whole new line of questions.'

'Which we can better discuss later.' Fidelma spoke sharply, as she rose. 'It is certainly not the place and time to continue to talk about things. We need to take Werferth's horse to Beornwulf's Hall. But we will return.'

CHAPTER FIFTEEN

Eadulf and Fidelma were negotiating their way along the path leading beside the fast-flowing waters of the Frome River, running down into the township. Eadulf felt some moments of awkwardness as memories assailed him when he glanced to where the Gull's Stream – the little stream that ran in front of what had been his uncle's house – entered the Frome. It was not far into the centre of the township. With dusk now falling and mixing with the belching smoke of a hundred wood fires and brand torches from the homesteads, they rode carefully to where the Hall of Thane Beornwulf dominated all the other buildings.

They crossed the main square and came to the tall wooden gates. The flames of two hanging iron braziers lit the entrance and Fidelma now particularly noticed the white bleached skeletal wolf's skulls stuck on the gateposts; one to the left and the other to the right. She had not realised their meaning before, having been distracted when she and Eadulf had been propelled through the gates by Stuf and his riotous companions. Now, giving the emblems some thought, she realised the kings and nobles of the East Angles claimed their descent from Wuffa, a noble descendant of their god Woden, and the name meant 'little wolf'. This might mean Beornwulf thought of himself as a Wuffingas, of noble origin. The term 'wolf' seemed to predominate in so many names. Even Eadulf's name meant 'old wolf', which was exactly the same as Ealdwulf, the king.

A hail of challenge greeted them as they neared the gates. When Eadulf replied, it was Crída who swung open the gates for them to pass through.

'Is all well?' was his first question. 'You have come back with Werferth's warhorse but without him in the saddle. What's happened?'

'Have no concern,' Eadulf replied. 'Werferth asked us to leave his horse here with Beornwulf. He and Brother Ator have taken a boat along the River Eár, chasing the three Northumbrian raiders into the territory of the Gyrwas.'

Crída looked surprised. He was about to demand further information when Ardith came to the door of the main building. Recognising them, she called a greeting and demanded they leave their horses with Crída to look after and come inside.

'I will let Beornwulf know you have returned,' she exclaimed brightly. 'I will ask you nothing more as you can explain your news to him when we are all gathered. You have also arrived in time to participate in the evening meal.'

The next moment they were being ushered into the familiar main chamber. It seemed to both Fidelma and Eadulf that little time had elapsed since they had left here to ride to the ruins of Athelnoth's house in search of answers to the mystery of his murder.

The big, bearded thane was at the door of the inner chamber with hands on hips, waiting to greet them. Although it was difficult to see beyond his beard, he was clearly smiling a welcome.

Once seated, with Crída summoned so that the news did not have to be repeated, and with Ardith on hand to ensure servants brought tankards of mead and cider, Eadulf launched into the story of their adventures and the death of Brother Boso.

'This is not good,' Beornwulf said in worried understatement when Eadulf had finished. 'In a matter of days I have had my lawgiver murdered along with his servant Osric, your sister has disappeared, and now, you tell me, Brother Boso, who served this community as the main celebrant of the New Faith, is also dead. Who has done this and why?'

'There are logical suspicions but no proof,' Eadulf confessed grimly. 'This is why I have returned. With Brother Boso dead, I felt the answer now lies here.'

Crída did not seem enthusiastic. 'I agree that suspicion is one thing,' he muttered. 'Proof is another. If this Mede and his men thought Princess Athelthryth was hiding here, or even that Athelnoth or Brother Boso knew her whereabouts, I cannot believe there is any foundation to it. Would Athelnoth be hiding her? That is illogically and socially impossible.'

'That is a good point,' Eadulf declared. 'Logically, if she sought sanctuary with anyone in this town, it would be Beornwulf.'

Beornwulf looked surprised but it was Ardith who replied.

'Why so?' she demanded defensively.

'Because Beornwulf is a Wuffingas, as his symbols proclaim. If a Wuffingas princess was here and needed help, he would know it. Surely you would protect one of your family if they were in the area and in danger?'

There was a pause and then Beornwulf shrugged.

'A point, but I am not of her royal family. But perhaps she is here but not in danger. Does your theorising take that into account? Does it also take into account that these potential abductors suspected she was hiding in the vicinity and merely pursued Athelnoth and Brother Boso for what they did not know? Or was it for what they thought they knew?'

Beornwulf stretched back and seemed to relax.

'If you want a speculation, I would say Princess Athelthryth has more protection among the Fen people than she would have here,' he said. 'Remember, her late husband was a prince of the

Gyrwas. As for myself, I can take oath that I have never been sought to involve myself in hiding or helping her.'

Crída's brows were drawn in thought as he regarded Eadulf and Fidelma. 'If you have left Werferth and Brother Ator to chase those Northumbrian raiders, as you call them, what do you think there is to gain by returning here?'

The challenging tone of the question surprised Fidelma and Eadulf.

'There is still a matter to be cleared up,' Eadulf said. 'Even if my uncle was killed by these Northumbrians – and that was a speculation without proof – there is the matter of my missing sister. She was not with them. I presume no further word has been heard of her in our absence?'

There was an embarrassed silence and Eadulf half nodded towards the Thane. 'Is that strange person Stuf still working out his punishment on your estate?'

Crída glanced to Beornwulf before responding. 'He is.'

'That is good.' Eadulf was grim. 'We need to question him further. Indeed, I want to question everyone again as I am sure I missed some clue before. Now darkness has descended, so we will have to delay the questions until tomorrow. We need to find a place to stay for a few nights and to cleanse ourselves from our journey.'

Beornwulf looked surprised and glanced at Ardith.

'You realise it would be an insult to me if you refused my hospitality,' the thane declared, but with humour. 'The roof of my Hall is yours for as long as you need its shelter.'

Ardith rose. 'I shall give instructions to the servants to prepare the same sleeping quarters that you used before. The evening meal should be ready before too long. Oh, if I remember your customs correctly, you would like water for a wash before your meal. I regret we don't use hot water in a tub in the evening.'

Fidelma, having become used to the difference in custom, politely said a bowl of water would suffice.

As they prepared to disperse, Crída announced his apologies for not joining them.

'I have to be out watching some livestock.' He gave them a ghost of a smile. 'It is part of the joys of managing my lord's estate. Your horses are being well taken care of and if you need help about the township in the morning I shall be at your service.'

'Did the stable boy bring our bags from the horses?' Fidelma asked.

Crída made an affirmative gesture. 'They have been given to one of the *huscarls* to bring in,' he replied. There seemed an embarrassing moment before he left with a 'good night'.

'I was surprised that Brother Ator was so adamant to chase these Northumbrians to exact justice for old Brother Boso,' Ardith remarked as the table was being prepared.

'Surprised?' Fidelma echoed. 'He admired the man very much and seemed almost to hero-worship him. It would seem natural to seek to track down his killers.'

She had decided to ignore what Mul and Mother Notgide had said and merely repeated the claim by Brother Ator himself.

Ardith's eyebrows rose slightly in inquiry. 'Where did you hear that Brother Ator was so admiring of Brother Boso?'

'Why, from Brother Ator himself,' Fidelma answered.

Ardith chuckled cynically. 'That is not how poor Brother Boso saw things.'

'Can you explain?' Fidelma prompted. She felt she should discover what Ardith knew.

'Brother Boso had almost grown to hate that young man for his arrogance and the lies that seemed to fall naturally from his lips. Indeed, even the *gerefa* once asked Brother Boso to report the boy to Abbot Aecci.'

Fidelma was now not surprised after what she had previously heard.

'You say that Athelnoth knew of Ator's arrogance and lies?

Why would he have given permission for Brother Ator to marry Wulfrun?'

Ardith's eyes widened. 'Where did you learn that story?'

'From . . .' began Fidelma and stopped. Then she realised who had told her. 'Are you saying . . .?'

'Athelnoth would have no more given permission for Wulfrun to marry Brother Ator than he would have given permission for her to marry Stuf.' Ardith's tone was one of amusement.

'I noticed that Crída seemed jealous of Ator,' Fidelma said thoughtfully. 'I thought that was jealousy because Athelnoth had looked favourably on Brother Ator. But you tell me that Athelnoth had not favoured Brother Ator?'

'You have come up with quaint notions,' Ardith grimaced. 'I have heard that the earth shook when Athelnoth met Brother Ator's request to wed his niece. He favoured neither Ator nor Crída. Athelnoth wanted better things for Wulfrun.'

'What of Wulfrun's own opinion?' Eadulf asked quietly.

'Your sister was a girl with her own strong set opinions,' Ardith replied after a moment of thought. 'As her brother, you should know that. She would not have been dictated to by anyone.'

'Did she resent her uncle's rejection of her suitors?' Eadulf asked. 'Could she have preferred Brother Ator over Crída and resented her uncle for not agreeing?'

'My understanding is that she wanted neither of them. She had other ideas for her life.'

'Yet why would Brother Ator say—' Eadulf began.

'As I said, Brother Ator was not averse to embellishing his ideas as reality. You have forgotten some of the meaning of names in your own tongue, Eadulf,' Ardith commented. 'He had been given an appropriate one.'

'Names?' Eadulf frowned.

'The root of his name means "venom". His tongue was not to be trusted any more than the tongue of a viper.'

'Venomous?' Fidelma frowned as a memory occurred. 'Someone said Wulfrun had gone to dance with snakes.'

'I don't think that was the meaning implied,' Eadulf commented. 'But Brother Ator appears to have been a venomous liar if the things he told us were fantasies. I was thinking about the stories that he told us about Brother Boso.'

'Then if we accept what you say, we must accept what Mother Notgide told us about the conflict between Ator and Boso,' Fidelma pointed out. 'That makes Brother Ator, and not just Mede, a suspect in the slaying of Boso. He had the opportunity when he left us to go to find Boso. He said Boso would not open the door. We surely have to re-examine things in this light.'

'Maybe we were too hasty in returning here,' Eadulf said heavily, repeating his fear.

'Yet one area that we have not explored is that concerning your sister, Eadulf,' Fidelma said.

'What do you mean?'

'Ardith here has raised some points that might prove interesting. We are told Wulfrun personally rejected the love suits of both Crída and Ator. Wulfrun had her own ideas, which did not include marriage. If so, surely, she would have been supportive and thankful for her uncle's rejection of them?'

'Not according to Athelnoth.' The unexpected comment came from Beornwulf. They turned to him expectantly.

'As my lawgiver, I knew Athelnoth well. As well as I knew Brother Boso. They both came here for the feasting now and again. Both expressed concern about young Wulfrun.'

'Remember you speak of my sister,' Eadulf declared uncomfortably.

'A sister you have not seen in years, since she was a child,' Ardith pointed out quietly. 'It was nothing bad, nothing you would not expect in a young, rebellious and intelligent girl. She simply said that she had no time for romances and marriage. She wanted other things in life.'

'But you said she did not like Athelnoth's rejecting the suitors?' Eadulf pointed out.

'She did not like her uncle being involved in making decisions for her. She felt those decisions should be her own to make. Her ambition was for the pursuit of education and thus to go to study as soon as she able to leave the township.'

'Where did she intend to go?'

'It was Athelnoth who told me and he disapproved strongly of her choice . . . which was to join the abbey on the shore of the Alde.'

'You mean the abbey of Aldred?'

'It could be that she has gone there already. Has anyone thought of verifying that?'

'There was no need, as she was seen on the day of Athelnoth's murder by both Brother Ator and Mother Notgide,' Fidelma reminded him.

'Brother Ator said he saw her at Ceol's Halh on the evening of the fire, and she went back to her uncle's house because she had to do another job for him,' Beornwulf reminded them.

'We know Stuf's story, or some of it, at least. We must question Wiglaf again,' Eadulf decided.

'Wulfrun was at, or near, Athelnoth's house when it was attacked? If she were free at that time she would have surely been among those trying to douse the flames,' Fidelma mused. 'But, of course, she could have left for this abbey soon afterwards.'

'If she left, she would have been seen on the road, or on a boat down to where the Frome joins the Alde,' pointed out Ardith.

'So you think she was abducted, as we thought, around the time of the fire?' Beornwulf queried.

'It is a distinct possibility,' Eadulf said. 'More so than her going to join an abbey just after Athelnoth was murdered.'

GRAVE OF THE LAWGIVER

'So the likely culprits were the raiders?' Beornwulf didn't sound convinced.

'There was no sign of her being with them,' admitted Eadulf.

'I think we still have many questions to put and get answers to before we can even confirm all the suspects,' Fidelma observed. She turned to Beornwulf. 'Athelnoth was your *gerefa* – advised you, as a thane, I understand – but how far did Athelnoth's authority extend? I understand from Eadulf that he was a local lawgiver and would not be of the rank that bore influence with Princess Athelthryth. There's no reason to suppose he even knew her. He was not a member of the king's Witan nor consulted by anyone who would offer sanctuary and protection after the princess fled from Northumbria.'

'You are right, Fidelma. I still say it curious that those warriors would be searching in this area for the princess.'

'I think we have spoken enough for now,' Ardith suddenly said firmly. 'It is time you should have your wash and return for the evening meal.'

Much later, after they had eaten and retired for the night, Eadulf stood by the small rectangular aperture in the wall of the chamber. At the moment, the woven cloth that usually covered it was drawn aside. He gazed with head slightly to one side into the bright moonlit night beyond. Fidelma was inexplicably irritated.

'Can you draw the blind?' she demanded caustically. 'I want to get some sleep and I don't want to wake up being bitten by bugs and flying insects.'

Eadulf did not react immediately. Then he said slowly: 'I was just listening to the night songs of the birds. I haven't heard their songs for a while.'

'I don't recall you taking such interest in birdsong when we were in Cashel,' she observed.

'I was listening to the ones we don't hear in Cashel.' Was there a touch of irony in his voice?

She sniffed in a deprecating way. 'That high, tuneful warble you hear is the red breast, and you can hear that throughout the year. A pleasant little bird. It is quite sweet, but when you hear its penetrating "tic toc", then it is uttering a warning.'

'It is not that sound that I was listening to. I was listening to one I have not heard in many a year. If you listen carefully you will hear slightly harsher sounds.'

'That awful jarring noise?' Fidelma put her head to one side and listened. 'To me that sounds almost like someone sharpening a knife on a grindstone. Not a birdsong that I'd like to fall asleep with in my ears. Anyway, I don't think I have ever heard such an unmelodious noise from birds in Cashel.'

Eadulf sighed and drew the curtain across.

'Neither will you, because it is a bird found only in the territory around here. The Romans called it *caprimulgus*.'

Fidelma was shocked by the name.

'Goatsuckers?' she echoed in disgust. 'You mean they attack goats?'

'No, they are not big enough for that. The ancient belief is that they sustained themselves by sucking the milk from goats. They are really insect eaters and often catch moths and such bugs while on the wing towards dusk. You only hear their night song in this area. It is truly a long time since I have heard them.'

'You miss a great deal about this place, don't you, Eadulf,' Fidelma observed quietly.

'It is only natural,' he replied. 'This was where I was born and grew up.'

'As you say, it is natural,' she admitted. 'But of recent times I have gathered the impression that you yearn for this place more than you do for your life with me and our son Alchú in Cashel?'

'That is not so,' Eadulf immediately protested.

'I thought it not so at first,' went on Fidelma. 'I thought that it was a sense of alienation, of different culture and attitudes. But there are many of the people of these kingdoms who have made their homes in the land of the goddess Éire. Look how many fled to settle in Ireland after the decision by Oswy to follow Roman ritual? Look at those who fled to Maigh Eo – Saxons who did not want to follow Rome. Now they call it Maigh Eo of the Saxons.'

'What are you saying?' Eadulf was puzzled.

'Just that I am aware of how many of your countrymen have settled in the Five Kingdoms and married and raised families. Yet recently I have the impression that you have grown to feel such a new longing for this land of yours that you wish to put everything else aside. It was not just a sense of alienation in a different culture. We have encountered too many different cultures in our travels that you were indifferent to. I begin to think the alienation is more internal.'

'It is true that there have been difficult times,' Eadulf acknowledged. 'But I do not understand what you are implying.'

'Difficult times?' Fidelma sighed. 'Times whose difficulty has been demonstrated over these years even from when we took vows with one another?'

Eadulf started in surprise and opened his mouth to reject her words. Then memories fought their way into his mind and he was hesitant.

'I sometimes felt alien, and some folk were not slow to point out the differences.'

'I had hoped that my brother had resolved that problem by adopting you into the Eóghanacht family as a "kinsman by summoning". That gave you rights equivalent to a prince of the family. Now no one could ever call you, as you have complained of in the past, an *ambuae*, one without cows, which meant that under the law of marriage you were not of equal rights and property; that you were, in fact, a man supported by the position of his wife and her property. As a prince of the Muman, no one would dare question your authority or position. You surely have everything that you want and none may raise a hand against you. You cannot think that we ignored your feelings, Eadulf?'

Eadulf's expression was bleak.

'I understand what you did. I am indebted to your brother Colgú for raising my status among your people but . . .'

'But . . . but that was not enough in your eyes?' she finished the sentence for him. 'There is still a problem that is deep within you. Very well. That must mean it was nothing to do with place and culture. It was to do with what we have together, the feelings we have for each other.'

Eadulf began to open his mouth in protest but Fidelma made a cutting motion with her hands.

'I promised you that I would accompany you when you said you wanted to visit your birthplace,' she went on, her voice slow and cold. 'I have fulfilled my promise. When we found out what had happened to your uncle and that your sister was missing I understood your need to find out the truth, although you had never even told me that you had a sister. I further said I would not think of departing back to Cashel, back to our son, whom I love very much, until some resolution of your family problem was made. I will keep that promise. But my home is in Cashel with my son and I will return.'

Eadulf was subdued and did not try to speak.

'I hope before I leave that you are able to articulate what is in your thoughts, Eadulf.'

She waited a while for a response but it seemed he was sunk in thought.

'You do not have to say anything now. Do not speak as a reaction, but think deeply and long about your true emotions. I will just put one more thought into this matter for consideration. For me, nothing has changed since that day at the Abbey of Fearna when we declared the love we shared. When little Alchú was born, it produced a whirlpool of emotions within me and which you, Eadulf, helped me resolve. With advice, that was a period of depression and you were ready to save me from it. It was the time of "the Badger's Moon" and I remember it well. I recognised reality then and I have not changed. Now I have stood ready to help you. I do not want to be pushed away. But some curious world has grown within you, Eadulf, from which you exclude me. That is the situation. Think on these things and I will be here to talk until this mystery is resolved or until I feel the time has come for me to return to my home with or without you.'

In the silence that descended between them there was only one distracting sound that disturbed the night: the grating almost jarring sounds of the bird called the 'goatsucker'. The bleak thought came into Fidelma's mind as she tried to fall asleep. Eadulf said it was a bird that was only native to this territory. Was that symbolic?

CHAPTER SIXTEEN

The next morning, after Fidelma and Eadulf had washed and eaten their first meal, they went for a walk in the thane's grounds. Their earlier greetings had been stiff and a little false as they tried to appear natural and hide their tensions before Ardith and Beornwulf. No mention was made to each other of their midnight exchange. Beornwulf, who was showing them the grounds, excused himself to speak with Crída about the condition of the stables while Eadulf and Fidelma wandered towards the pig sheds. Just beyond the sheds, the goats were kept in a small, fenced area. The odours were enough to guide them. They had gone only a few steps when they saw the familiar figure that they had come to seek. He was bent over a spade, clearing the excrement.

'Greetings, Stuf,' Eadulf called as they approached.

The thin man turned and a look of sheer hatred registered on his wolfish face. Then he clearly struggled to control his features and try for a more benign expression. But the mask of malignant suspicion remained. He stood erect, the spade held against his side.

'You are just the person we wanted to see,' Eadulf said.

The itinerant worker blinked. 'I am not allowed to pause in my work,' he muttered.

'That's all right. We have the authority of your thane to speak with you,' Eadulf returned easily.

Stuf's jaw clenched.

'It was a mistake,' he said defensively but with bitterness. 'I meant no evil to you.'

'Intention and results can be different things,' Fidelma pointed out in a neutral tone. 'Tell us why you felt your behaviour was justified.'

'I was not alone among the people who suspected that you were part of the foreigners who were seen when Athelnoth's house was set ablaze and he and his servant Osric were killed.'

'You were aware that you had no rights, as a *geburas*, to step forward and take command or even to be part of that mob?'

'It was a mistake, I say. Had I been right and captured those who had killed Athelnoth the lawgiver, I would have been praised and probably been raised from my status to be a *ceorl* with full rights and freedom.'

'The reality was that you acted wrongly. Hence your punishment decreed by your lord Beornwulf,' Eadulf replied.

The man glowered at them.

'You might find some redemption from Beornwulf if you can tell us what thoughts made you believe foreigners had set Athelnoth's house afire,' Fidelma suggested, ignoring his expression. 'I do not think it was just poor Widow Eadgifu's declining memory that inspired the thoughts, nor the fact that the mob was so frightened that they handed control to you rather than make their own judgements.'

'I believed you were involved when that religieux did not support you and allowed me to escort you to the thane's Hall. Had I not been right, he would have told me.'

Eadulf was nonplussed for a moment.

'You mean the religieux who appeared after Brother Boso had conducted the funeral services and returned to Ceol's Halh? Are you saying that you knew him?'

Stuf hesitated and shrugged. 'He was a religieux. He claimed that Brother Boso had sent him to take a few more details that he had forgotten. What more was there to know?'

'As it was, he turned out to be a fake. He was one of the Northumbrian raiders that you told Mother Notgide about. Those whose leader you actually named.'

Stuf's reaction was shock and guilt. He seemed tongue-tied.

'So why would you take notice of him?' Fidelma demanded.

Stuf begun to stutter. 'I-I did not know him. I-I did not really r-recognise him.'

'How did you name the leader of these Northumbrians?' Eadulf insisted.

'The day after the murders, the morning after the bodies were found, I went back to Ceol's Halh and, afterwards, saw the group by the Oxen Ford. Then I saw you both riding and stopping to exchange greetings with Mede and two others.'

'What?' Eadulf almost shouted. 'We did not arrive at my uncle's place until that very day. The day after the burning of Athelnoth's place. Where did you see us exchanging greetings?'

'It was in the woods near the Oxen Ford, just north of Ceol's Halh. Three horsemen waiting. They were on the west bank, talking with one another. Then you both came riding south down the track on the east bank. I saw you exchange greeting with them, after which you and the other horsemen continued different ways.'

Fidelma's eyes widened as she realised what Stuf was describing.

'We saw a group of religieux and we greeted them as is normal when strangers pass in an isolated place,' she reminded Eadulf. 'We did not know them. When they did not return our greeting, we rode on to Seaxmund's Ham.'

'You say that the religieux that came to the ruins of Athelnoth's incinerated house was one of the three who had gathered at the Oxen Ford?'

'He was.'

'How is it, if you thought we were connected, that he did not come to our aid, which would have been easy for him to do?'

It was a point that had escaped Stuf's mind.

'You insisted he was at the Oxen Ford. After you saw him there, you came straight to Seaxmund's Ham?'

'I had business at Ceol's Halh and paused there before I reached Athelnoth's house. He was there.'

'Why didn't you detain the religieux and report this to Crída if you thought that we were in league with the destruction of the *gerefa*'s house?' demanded Eadulf. 'By the way, why did you not tell us that you had seen this religieux before you tried to effect our capture? We subsequently had to go to Ceol's Halh and find out for ourselves that he was a fake.'

Stuf shrugged eloquently. 'Why should I help you after you let Beornwulf punish me for a mistake?'

'But why didn't you accuse the religieux as being in league with us rather than thinking we were in league with him?' Fidelma quietly emphasised. 'In fact, accepting he was a religieux, you used that as an authority to take charge.'

'The mob was trying to do you harm and, as I say, I thought you were both of the Hibernians, especially as the woman is clearly so. It was my duty to secure you rather than trying to accuse the strange religieux.'

'But you did not raise it afterwards when Werferth and Beornwulf identified us?' Eadulf pointed out.

'I had forgotten,' Stuf replied stubbornly.

'You have an answer to most things, Stuf,' Fidelma commented dryly.

'You have forgotten that when you passed through Ceol's Halh, you told Mother Notgide there about the strangers you saw and actually named their leader. Now I am wondering how you could recognise the leader and name him.'

There was no disguising the confusion on Stuf's face.

'Are you calling Mother Notgide a liar?' Eadulf prompted. 'Is it true or untrue? Or do you say that she made that up? It will be easy to take you back to Ceol's Halh and allow her to confront you with it.'

It was clear from his face that the man was desperately trying to find an excuse.

'I was told the name by someone else,' he finally said.

'Is it in your nature to boast knowledge when you only acquire it from someone else? So you boasted knowledge to Mother Notgide that was not yours. This other person told you that this leader was Mede?'

'Yes . . . yes, I was told that.'

'So, you were told his name was . . .?' Fidelma prompted.

'Mede, Thane of Mede Ham Stede in the eastern Gyrwas, the Fen country . . . who is in service to Ecgfrith, king of Northumbria?' asked Eadulf.

'That was what I was told,' Stuf declared.

'By whom?'

Stuf stood silent.

'You say you were told by someone. Who told you?' Eadulf repeated. His voice held a threatening tone.

Stuf was frowning as if trying to conjure a name. He looked again at Eadulf and saw the dangerous look in his eyes.

'Brother Ator told me,' he finally declared.

The answer surprised both Eadulf and Fidelma.

'Brother Ator told you that he knew the leader of the men was Thane Mede in the service of Ecgfrith?' Eadulf asked sceptically.

'I swear by the nine worlds of Éormensgyll. May I die of the coughing sickness if I lie in this.' The man positively cringed before them.

'You don't have to swear by anything,' Fidelma sighed. 'Just tell us why Brother Ator told you this?'

'I had seen the three men at the Oxen Ford, as I told you. I saw you greet them. That was the day after Athelnoth's house was burnt down. When I returned to Ceol's Halh I went to get my boat, which I kept by Brother Ator's cabin. My intention was to go to Seaxmund's Ham and moor for the night before heading down to the Alde to go fishing. It was the plan I had had to cancel when Athelnoth's murder prevented it. I saw Brother Ator and told him that I had seen the three strangers at the Oxen Ford. It was then he told me they were Northumbrians, and the name of their leader. I swear it. May I be torn into pieces by the giants of Éttenhám, if I lie, lord Eadulf.'

Eadulf and Fidelma were confused at the introduction of Brother Ator as the source of the identity of the leader of the Northumbrians.

Fidelma finally gave a long, low sigh and started to turn in the direction of the stables. 'Let us rejoin Beornwulf,' she said to Eadulf.

His expression was hesitant, but then he told Stuf to carry on digging.

When they reached the corner of the livestock sheds Fidelma halted and glanced over her shoulder.

'He's either a consummate liar or . . .'

'I would settle for him being a liar of any description,' Eadulf replied. 'But of all the lies to bring forward, that one is ridiculous.'

'Sometimes truth is hidden in the most outrageous of fantasies.' Fidelma frowned. 'Either Stuf is a liar or . . . think of the alternative . . . that Brother Ator knew all along whom we were chasing. How could he have kept up such pretence for so long? He would have known of the intentions of Mede from the start. He knew him when we arrived at Sledda's homestead but did not show recognition by even the flicker of an eye.'

'By "intentions" you must mean that Ator knew Mede and his

raiders were chasing Princess Athelthryth? He knew they intended to abduct her and take her back to Ecgfrith? That means Athelnoth was somehow involved in this matter.' Eadulf was not happy.

'If Brother Ator knew all this during the time that he was with us, then what an actor he must be,' Fidelma observed softly.

Eadulf shook his head. 'I doubt if anyone could reach such control of emotions to achieve the performance that he did.'

'It can happen,' Fidelma replied, 'but I cannot believe he had that talent.'

'The question is . . . what do we do with this information?'

'Easy. We said we would visit Mother Notgide again. But, first, I think we should have a word with the woman who said she saw the Northumbrians, which she confused with Hibernians, on the night of the fire.'

'We will have to find out how Stuf or Brother Ator knew about Mede. One thing we must make sure of is that Stuf is not allowed to disappear from here until we have finished our investigation.'

They soon found Beornwulf talking with Crída by the stables.

'I want to visit my uncle's hall first,' Eadulf announced as they joined them.

'I thought you might.' The thane smiled thinly. 'I shall come with you. I have the horses ready.' He turned to Crída and gave him some instructions about attending a barley crop, and Eadulf added that he should keep a close eye on Stuf. Crída was more than willing to do so.

Once mounted, Beornwulf led the way with Eadulf and Fidelma behind him. There were few people in the main street of the township. Most of the men were apparently in the fields following their work, or in other occupations. The doors of some huts were open and women sat on stools, busy at their needlework, while others were spinning yarn. Most were intent on their tasks, but those who did look up bowed their heads deferentially to their thane, and some had courage enough to cast curious glances at his companions. A couple of men at the corner of the main street were engaged in a rapid whispered conversation but fell silent as they passed.

The lane up to the Gull's Stream was short and soon they were outside the blackened grounds, which had once been Eadulf's uncle's house.

'What do you expect to see this time?' Beornwulf asked as Eadulf halted his horse to stare at the ruins.

'Probably nothing,' Eadulf said in a tone of fatigue. 'Possibly it was just to search for memories.'

'Would that help solve the problems of the present?' the thane asked.

'Perhaps.'

'We will want to go on to Ceol's Halh,' Fidelma reminded them.

'We seem no closer to answering the question of who did this; why they did it and what happened to the young girl Wulfrun,' Beornwulf said. 'Nothing leaps up at me from this pile of blackness.'

Eadulf sighed. 'You are right, Beornwulf. I was indulging in memories of my childhood. I was remembering how I used to play with the senior retainer of your estate when we were boys.'

'We should try to find those local folk who helped put out the flames of the fire and who might have some useful memories of that night,' Beornwulf suggested.

Eadulf pulled away reluctantly from his contemplation of the ruins and glanced along the track to the other houses nearby. He saw a familiar figure seated outside one of the huts and immediately slid off his house and began to stride towards her.

Fidelma and Beornwulf dismounted to follow him.

'A good morning, Widow Eadgifu,' Eadulf called as he drew nearer.

The old woman glared at him in disapproval.

'I know you,' she said softly.

'I should hope you know me now and remember that I used to live there,' he pointed to the ruins, 'and was always playing around here when I was a youth. Crída and I used to play here.'

She held her head to one side, her bright eyes still on him.

'Boys playing? They were good days. No one plays here these days.'

'That is because we have all grown up. Crída has grown up, as have I. I am Eadulf – Eadulf son of Wulfric. I have grown. I suppose even Wulfrun my little sister has grown.'

The old woman closed her eyes and rocked back and forth for a moment.

'She grew in spite of warnings,' she replied conversationally. 'But children cannot avoid growing. You say that you've grown. Do I know you? I forget.'

'She grew? Who do you mean? You still don't recognise me?' Eadulf paused and sighed. 'Ah well, I suppose you still recognise Crída when he comes by?'

'Crída?' Her voice became sharp. 'He was supposed to grow up but has remained a boy. He is a bad little boy. But she remained but did not continue to play. Children playing? Good days. She preferred to go dancing; dancing with snakes, while he turned his back on the gods. That made her angry for she played with the gods. And the great Wyrm-Haelsere must be fed.'

Eadulf's eyes narrowed, confused.

'What do you mean, Widow Eadgifu? I have no understanding of what you say,' he pressed, trying to keep his tone reasonable.

She blinked and looked at him with her penetrating ice-like eyes. It seemed that she was staring at him without really seeing him, but as if looking through him.

'Did you play here as a boy? No; I do not recognise you. You did not play with Wulfrun. No, she played with other boys. They were the good days.'

'She is my younger sister,' Eadulf attempted to explain. 'Of course, I did not play with my sister. Last time I saw her she was about nine years old. That was seven years ago. What has happened to her?'

'What happened?' Widow Eadgifu seemed bemused. 'She was lured away. Lured to the good times. Dancing with boys. Dancing around the viper trees with the serpents.'

Beornwulf gave an exasperated exhalation of his breath. 'You can see that you can't get much sense here,' he said. 'If you want to talk to the other neighbours, we should do so before going to Ceol's Halh.'

Reluctantly Eadulf stood back and gave a parting smile to the old woman.

'A pity,' he commented. 'I can almost believe she recognises me from when I was a lad. Anyway, there was that farmer, Wiglaf, who was there when we had the problem with the mob stirred up by Stuf, and Stuf seems to have been spreading a few stories about him. I'd particularly like to see Wiglaf.'

He looked directly at Fidelma, who had not really spoken since they had left the thane's Hall.

'It would be logical step,' she replied shortly.

He turned to Beornwulf. 'Would you know this Wiglaf's hut or where he worked?'

Beornwulf chuckled. 'I would be an inadequate Thane of Seaxmund's Ham if I did not. Unless I know all those who owe me allegiance, I would be a poor man from the loss of their tribute. His hut is not far away, but if he is not there, he works the barley fields near Ceol's Halh.'

Eadulf gave a final sad glance to old Widow Eadgifu.

'I'll leave you with your good memories, Widow Eadgifu,' he said with a sad smile. 'Good memories of the young ones dancing.'

The old woman actually smiled a gap-toothed grimace. 'Good days. Two boys dancing at the viper's tree. Beware, boys, for vipers can turn in malignant spite and strike at you.'

Eadulf hesitated for a moment, wondering if it made sense, but the woman's eyes remained staring through him as if addressing someone behind him. He shrugged and turned after his companions. As he did so, another woman approached and shouted at them.

'What are you doing?' Her voice was strident. 'Are you bothering poor Widow Eadgifu again? Have you no respect?'

Beornwulf, who had moved on, swung back and recognised the woman.

'Greetings, Elfrida. Have no concern. My friends are not causing upset to the Widow Eadgifu. We are seeking a clarification to answers. It is with my full authority.'

The woman was startled for the moment. She had been so concerned with Eadulf that she had not even noticed the presence of the thane. She halted and bowed her head in respect to him.

'My lord, you must know the old one's mind goes in and out of this world. You will get little sense from her by keeping questioning her.'

'I understand. The problem is that she was a witness to what happened at Athelnoth's house. Or at least to strangers riding away. We have to try to assemble the scattered thoughts and make them coherent. I have to abide by the expert knowledge of the *gerefa* present, and Eadulf son of Wulfric is to be trusted.'

'I hear that my sister Wulfrun sometimes argued with her uncle,' Eadulf began. 'Did she do this often?'

Mother Elfrida turned her scowl on Eadulf. 'I do not delve into the affairs of others,' she replied.

'Could it be that to spite her uncle for turning down Brother Ator, that Wulfrun herself said she would run away with Brother Ator if he would help her find a place in a religious community to escape her uncle's wish for her to remain with him?'

'I never heard of such a thing,' Mother Elfrida replied sourly.

GRAVE OF THE LAWGIVER

'Daughters do not disobey their father's wishes. You have picked up strange ideas in this land of Hibernia.'

'But did they argue?' Eadulf pressed.

The woman shrugged.

'When did this argument take place?' Eadulf pressed. In fact, Beornwulf himself had been surprised by the question and answer. It was the presence of the thane that seemed to persuade her to respond more clearly.

'Not so long ago.'

'Do you know when Brother Ator went to speak to Athelnoth about his proposal to wed Wulfrun?'

'I did not know that he had, until you told me.' She was obviously reluctant to answer.

'So you know nothing of Brother Ator asking permission of Athelnoth to marry Wulfrun?'

'It's news to me.' Then she glanced to Beornwulf before returning to Eadulf. 'Anyway, shouldn't you be out looking for Wulfrun instead of bothering old Widow Eadgifu? The gossip was that you had all gone north, chasing the men who were seen about here on the night of the fire.'

'Ah, yes,' Eadulf reflected. 'Widow Eadgifu thought she saw men dressed as Hibernians riding away from Athelnoth's house on the night of the fire and of his murder. Such men had been seen in the vicinity. We chased after them but now we are back.'

'They were apparently Northumbrian raiders,' interposed Beornwulf.

Mother Elfrida's expression did not change. She simply shrugged again.

'We have all heard the gossip about Princess Athelthryth. We certainly heard it from the wandering storytellers who visit us. So we heard how she escaped the clutches of the king of Northumbria, who then sent his agents to capture her and take her back to . . .'

'So you think this was connected?' Eadulf asked immediately. Mother Elfrida simply shrugged once more.

'Very well,' imposed Beornwulf. 'What if these men disguised as Hibernians were, in fact, agents of Northumbria searching for the princess and meant to abduct her? Would you have any idea as to why they would be here and why Athelnoth would be targeted by them?'

'I don't understand,' Mother Elfrida replied. 'Athelnoth would have no business with such people. We are all loyal to the Wuffingas. The Northumbrians have long tried to absorb our kingdoms and we have tried to keep from becoming their vassals. You should see Wiglaf about that. He will tell you all the stories about Northumbrians.'

'Wiglaf the farmer?' Eadulf asked, surprised that she was naming the very person he wanted to see.

'There is only one Wiglaf, as best I recall,' she replied sarcastically.

Eadulf sighed. 'Then we should go and see this Wiglaf. He did not seem to want any involvement when he allowed Stuf to take over matters, which Stuf had no legal right to do so.'

'Where do we find Wiglaf?' Fidelma asked.

'He is in the north barley field above Ceol's Halh,' Mother Elfrida replied, speaking more to Beornwulf than to Eadulf. He and Fidelma turned back to their horses, leaving it to Beornwulf to thank the woman.

As they rode into the centre of Ceol's Halh, Mother Notgide immediately appeared to greet them with special deference to the thane.

Beornwulf let Eadulf speak first to her.

'It is an important point I want to clear up. When we were here yesterday you mentioned that Stuf actually identified the leader of the Northumbrian warriors who were seen in this vicinity?'

GRAVE OF THE LAWGIVER

'That is so,' the woman agreed. 'Stuf said the leader was Mede, the Thane of Mede Ham Stede. I think I told you it is an island in the north-west of the Gyrwas country.'

'So you did,' Eadulf agreed. 'But you said that you did not know how Stuf knew this and you told us to ask him if we wanted to know.'

'I did,' affirmed the woman.

'So we asked him. He has said that he was told by someone else here in Ceol's Halh.'

The woman frowned, puzzled for a moment. 'Who among us poor *ceorls* would recognise a Northumbrian warlord?'

'Stuf claimed he only told you to impress,' Fidelma decided to point out.

Mother Notgide stared back at Fidelma for a moment and then shook her head with an angry expression.

'Sometimes Stuf exaggerates the truth to get out of situations he feels threatened by.'

'Furthermore, he named the person who, he says, told him.'

'I will be interested to hear the name of this person for, as I say, I have no memory of it.'

'He says it was Brother Ator.'

There was no doubting from her expression that Mother Notgide was surprised. Then she began to smile and shake her head.

'I would be happy if it was so and that conceited youth could get into trouble for it. Stuf did go to collect his boat, which was tied up near Brother Ator's cabin before he came and spoke with me. It does not surprise. For Stuf, a lie can be sweet at times but it only runs a short course.'

'Is there anyone else in the township who could have told Brother Ator? How else would Brother Ator have been able to recognise this Thane Mede?' Fidelma interposed. She was thinking how Brother Ator had acted in front of Mede. She found it impossible that anyone could act so well if they knew the person and were in some collusion.

'As you can plainly see, there are few men in the township and all are related to me in some way or other,' Mother Notgide replied. 'None would have an opportunity to know a Northumbrian thane. The only two people from our village who might have been in a position to know such brutes, and who have travelled more widely than most, are Brother Boso and, I admit, Brother Ator.'

There was a movement behind them and a strong male voice said: 'You neglect me. I was the one who recognised Thane Mede and told Brother Ator, who stupidly told Stuf.'

CHAPTER SEVENTEEN

They turned to find the stockily built, dark-haired figure of the farmer standing behind them. Wiglaf had approached them unnoticed.

'So when Stuf claimed it was Brother Ator who identified Mede, he was lying?' Eadulf asked, not showing any surprise.

The farmer shrugged. 'It would not be for the first time that Stuf has exaggerated the truth, as Mother Notgide knows. I did speak to Brother Ator on the morning that Brother Boso left for Dumnoc-wic and I told him what I had seen at the Oxen Ford. That was then I saw you greet the three Northumbrians the day after Athelnoth's murder. Later, I saw Stuf heading for Ceol's Halh and told him about that.'

'Then you knew they were Northumbrians and knew the name of their leader?' frowned Fidelma. 'How so?'

'I recognised Mede, which is different from actually knowing him,' Wiglaf replied. Abruptly he rolled up the right sleeve of his shirt. They saw what must have been a deep scar caused by a gash along the arm, which had long healed.

'That's a sword cut.' Beornwulf stated the obvious.

'I was not always just a farmer,' Wiglaf explained. 'Cynehelm, who was previously Thane of Seaxmund's Ham, had to raise a battle host to fight a strong Northumbrian raid. It was my duty as a *ceorl* to answer that call. We marched under the wolf's head standard to meet them. Cynehelm, as you should know, was killed in that battle. I was wounded and left for dead. I have other scars.'

'Are you saying that it was Mede who did this to you?'

Wiglaf shook his head. 'Not Mede in person; only one of his warriors. In the opening of that attack, I was close to him and recognised him as a commander of the warriors that came against us. His image was impressed on my memory on that day as I fell wounded. A comrade had told me who he was. He and his men slaughtered many of our people near a place called Gyrwenigas. The Northumbrians were driven back into their own land. Because of that, I did not die and my comrades carried me back here, where I was nursed and eventually recovered; at least, I could still work my land as a *ceorl*. But I remember the image of Mede very well.'

'How did you come across Mede and his men and so recognise him?' Eadulf asked.

Wiglaf suppressed a sigh. 'I had been to the Oxen Ford to barter for a goat from a farmer there. I was walking down to Ceol's Halh by the river. I suddenly had an inclination to check on the *leldra* to see if they were edible and . . .'

'The what?' Fidelma asked.

'Elderberries,' explained Eadulf shortly in her own language.

'They grow well in marshland,' Wiglaf explained. 'They thrive in most wetlands, and we are soon approaching fruiting times, so I keep my eye on the shrubs of which there are a cluster not far into the swamp woodlands from that route. My wife keeps up a family tradition of making jam if the crop is good and often produces a wine from them.'

Beornwulf smiled. 'The old folk say elderberries are feared by the evil ones, and they often hang branches of *leldra* around their doors to keep evil ones at bay.'

'So you left the river path, you are saying, and went into the woods in search of these ... these elderberries. What then?' Fidelma demanded impatiently.

'The goddess of good luck was on my side. I had not gone far before I heard some horses coming along the path on which, had I stayed on it, they would have encountered me. In fact, it was about where I had turned off that they halted because one of them had called to the lead rider, asking how much further it was to go. The man turned back and I was stunned. It was none other than the Northumbrian warrior that had been identified to me as Mede, the Thane of Mede Ham Stede.'

'So what were he and his comrades doing? Did you hear any further speech?' Beornwulf demanded. 'Why was I not alerted of this intrusion into my territory?'

'I mentioned it to Crída,' Wiglaf replied. 'However, you were attending the Witan at Suth Tun Hoo then.'

'Did they say anything important?' Fidelma insisted.

'Nothing I could hear of significance. Oh, I should add that two of his companions were dressed in brown religious robes with hoods they could pull up over their heads. They did not wear the Roman cut of Blessed Peter, but one of them had the tonsure the Hibernians and Britons favour, which they call the tonsure of the Blessed John. They were seated on their horses when one of them muttered something and they looked across the river. That was when I saw you both riding on the other side and you greeted the three.'

'We certainly saw them and called a greeting to which they did not reply, and so we rode on. What then?' asked Fidelma.

'The three rode off northwards on a track through the forest wetlands.'

'Are we saying they were involved in the burning and murder?' Beornwulf asked, aghast.

'Let us finish the story,' Fidelma sighed. 'Tell us exactly when you told Stuf about Mede. I am confused as to the sequence.'

'I filled my basket with elderberries and walked home. My way lay through Ceol's Halh, and it was there I saw Stuf. He told me that he had seen these same riders taking the path north. He said one looked like a warrior. I told him that the warrior was Mede, the Thane of Mede Ham Stede. I think it was then that he went to tell Mother Notgide. I suppose he took the credit. Anyway, I went to see Brother Ator and that was when I mentioned it to him. It was afternoon and I continued to my cabin, which is near Athelnoth's house, which had been burnt down the previous night. That was when I found Stuf had already reached there and was inciting the crowd against you. As I had seen you greeting the three men, I felt I should not be defensive of you until I knew more.'

There was some moment of quiet while they digested this story.

'So Stuf claimed the entire story you told him as his own. When we challenged him, he said it was Brother Ator who had told him. The man is a positive menace,' Fidelma said.

'Let us go back a day, back to the night of the fire,' Eadulf pressed after a moment.

Wiglaf shrugged. 'It was night, certainly before first light, that I was roused by my wife. She was awakened by noises from the dogs. She had gone out and saw Athelnoth's house in flames. She immediately woke me and alerted some neighbours. Several of us grabbed buckets and other implements to convene on the flames. We did our best but the old hall consisted mainly of very dry wood. It was beyond our capabilities to extinguish the fire. I went to raise the alarm with Crída, your *druhting*, my lord. I thought, as Thane, you should know.'

Beornwulf nodded. 'I remember that. Crída found me when I was breakfasting early.'

'At the time, did you consider that this fire was the result of any action by Mede and the others you saw?' Eadulf asked.

'It wasn't until the next morning. I saw Mede by the Oxen

GRAVE OF THE LAWGIVER

Ford. Widow Eadgifu had told you, my lord, about the riders in Hibernian dress riding away from the scene on the night of the fire.'

'But the next day, you associated us with Mede and that was why you did so little to stop Stuf inciting the crowd,' Fidelma said sharply.

'You know why it was so,' affirmed the ploughman patiently. 'I did not want to get mixed up in the matter.'

'If Mede and his men had slain Athelnoth and his servant and burnt down his hall, what reason could have prompted it?' Beornwulf asked.

Wiglaf shrugged. 'I am just a ploughman, my lord,' he said to Beornwulf. 'I know nothing of why people do such things.'

'You have heard of Princess Athelthryth?' the thane asked.

'Oh, that gossip! I have no time for such stories that are told by women for women. Brides running away from their husbands. Princesses escaping from imprisonment and kings sending after them to have them punished. What has that to do with whether a crop will grow enough to feed a family or whether a goat will give enough milk? I have better things to do to ensure my family's survival than listen to such stories.'

Even Beornwulf looked disappointed with the reply. 'You must answer for allowing a non-freeman to take on a position he had no right to do. We will speak of this later.'

They decided that they were not going to get any further information. With Brother Ator no longer available to question, they decided they should return to Thane Beornwulf's Hall to discuss matters and put more questions to Stuf.

As they approached the gates of the Hall, a woman was guiding a mule cart out of the enclosure. The smell of fish was nearly overpowering. Beornwulf obviously knew the woman and raised his hand with a smile.

'Give you good-day, Mother Afenid.'

'May Eostre of the spring rebirth bring you good fortune, my lord,' the old woman replied.

They waited until she had negotiated the gate and turned into the township.

'That is Afenid, the wife of a fisherman, who brings me tribute out of her husband's catch,' the thane explained. 'We shall feast well this evening.'

When they entered the grounds to Beornwulf's Hall, they found Crída was waiting for them. They dismounted as a stable lad came to take their horses.

'Have Stuf sent to me immediately,' the thane ordered Crída as he led the way into the main room of the Hall and flung himself in his chair. Fidelma and Eadulf also sat.

Ardith came forward with offers of drinks.

'I hope Stuf has a more logical tale to tell than previously,' Eadulf muttered morosely. 'It is stupid for him to lie when he should have realised that, even with Brother Ator away, that story he told could so easily be checked.'

'I am afraid that Stuf does not appear to be one who thinks deeply,' Ardith observed, handing round the cold refreshments.

'We saw Mother Afenid leaving,' Beornwulf smiled. 'I presume that bodes well for the evening meal.'

'We have a delicacy for that,' Ardith agreed. 'Afenid delivered a basket of crab to the kitchen.'

'Ardith here is a wonder at preparing the dish,' the thane smiled. The smile that passed between them gave Fidelma, not for the first time, to suspect there was something more intimate in their relationship than usual between a thane and his house stewardess.

It was moments after Ardith left to see to the fish preparations that Crída entered. He looked concerned.

'Stuf is not where he was supposed to be working. He was supposed to be digging parsnips for lady Ardith. There is no sign of him,' he reported. 'I've ordered a search, my lord.'

'Didn't I say before we left that he was to be watched closely?' Eadulf muttered critically.

'I thought he was,' Crída protested, sourly. 'I had checked on him only a short time ago and told him to hurry up as I wanted him for another job.'

'I suppose we should have expected this,' Beornwulf said wearily.

'Have no worries.' Crída sounded confident. 'I have just let loose the tracker hounds and they will find him.'

'We want him found unhurt in order to question him, and not savaged by animals!' Fidelma could not help but exclaim.

'These are good tracker hounds, lady,' Beornwulf explained. 'They won't attack him. Once he's found they will merely keep him in the one place and raise the alarm by barking.'

Almost as if it were meant, they heard the distant sound of barking.

'The dogs are making a noise in the southern barley pasture by the river, lord.' Crída commented, turning for the door.

Beornwulf sprang to his feet.

'Let's go to see what our friend has to say while he is still unnerved by the dogs.' He had a grim smile. 'Let us give him no time to invent any more stories.'

Fidelma and Eadulf joined him as he followed Crída through the various sheds and fenced enclosures towards the southern part of the estate, which stretched along the side of the river that crossed through the township. It was easy to find where the dogs were from the noise of their excitement and, in fact, two of the thane's workers were already trying to haul the dogs away.

They saw Stuf's body in a corner under a hedge. There was no need to ask if he were dead. The handle of a knife protruded from his back. Much blood had been shed around the wound.

Eadulf immediately turned to the two dog handlers.

'Was this how you found him?' he demanded harshly.

'Yes, lord, we have touched nothing,' one replied nervously. 'We were up yonder when Crída ordered the hounds to be loosed. So we were just at the top of this pasture when the hounds went leaping across down to this spot and started barking. We ran across the field to get the hounds off and then you came. The knife is not ours. We did not harm him.'

'Keep the hounds off while I take a closer look,' Eadulf told them.

The men hauled the dogs away and Crída instructed them to return the animals to their kennels. Once clear, Eadulf went forward and crouched by the body, inspecting it without touching it. Then, shaking his head, he motioned to Crída to help him turn the body on its side as he did not want to extract the knife, which he would have to do to allow the man to lie flat on his back. Even at the awkward angle, he could examine the front of Stuf's body. The eyes and mouth were still partially opened as if the victim had been caught mid-scream.

Eadulf took some time and, finally, he pushed himself away and stood up to face Fidelma and Beornwulf.

'You can probably see as much as I can. He was an emaciated scarecrow of a man. The blow was very sharp. It took one blow and the person knew where to deliver the point. The thrust was aimed upwards into the heart; straight under the shoulder blade. It would not even have needed much strength.'

He was toying with the knife, which he had decided to extract, but suddenly he stopped and held it up. 'I seem to have seen this type of knife before. More a domestic knife used at table. It even has a carved handle. A fish symbol.'

'Obviously a person who liked eating fish,' Beornwulf muttered. 'It brings back memories. Crída, you said that you had kept watch on him and that he was not out of your sight, or anyone's sight, for a short period.'

'That is true,' Crída responded. 'When you returned, it was

only a short time before that I had checked him. It looks as though he was trying to escape.'

'Why do you think that?' Beornwulf asked Crída.

Fidelma was looking at Eadulf and he knew the question she would be asking.

'The interesting thing is that he was killed in a small but open pasture . . .'

'It is, as you see, a barley field,' Crída intervened.

'But with little concealment,' observed Fidelma. 'We have a small open pasture with just this small hedge here and the river running on the other side.'

'This might be where the attacker came from,' Crída said.

'He was killed by what appears to be a single blow from a sharp knife from behind,' Beornwulf said. 'Anything curious in that, Eadulf?'

Eadulf did not need time to consider. 'The curious thing is that Stuf must have known his killer and appeared to trust him.'

'How do you come to that conclusion so quickly?' Beornwulf asked.

'Discounting the idea that the killer was some Otherworld denizen who was able to move about under a cloak of invisibility, the killer had either crossed with Stuf to this place, or had to come through this hedge. Either way, Stuf would have had warning of their approach. If so, it did not bother him. When the blow was struck, Stuf had his back to him. So the conclusion is that Stuf knew him. He knew the killer well enough to turn his back without fear of being attacked.'

Crída grimaced sceptically. 'Even so, Stuf was a timid man and so apprehensive – even of me – that he would not have allowed anyone that he was not totally sure of to come up behind him with a knife.'

'Although,' Beornwulf pursed his lips in a thoughtful expression, 'he was not so timid that he did not leave his boat in the river when he saw Athelnoth's house ablaze and help to try to extinguish the dangerous fire. Although he was not the first to do so, he did join them. Then he showed some courage in thinking he would apprehend the killers, even though he was wrong. He had courage for that.'

'The way people's minds dictate their actions is often not logical,' Fidelma said thoughtfully. 'It is a good point but not conclusive. There has been many a case where the killer has placed themselves in a position when it appears they had been trying to save the person they killed and thus claim innocence. I gather that none of your men would see anyone entering the estate?'

Crída shook his head. 'There were workers about the whole time and no one saw anyone suspicious pass through the gates. The last person through was Mother Afenid with her fish.'

'This river,' Fidelma indicated with her head the river on the other side of the hedge. 'The murderer could have used that as an access to Stuf?'

'They might, but there are points where such a person could easily be seen. Anyone crossing the bridge in the township would have a view of this spot.'

'A view from that bridge?' queried Eadulf. 'I know it.' An idea suddenly came to him. 'Let us have a word with this Afenid. She was the only one who came here before we found Stuf. She would have been crossing the bridge moments later.'

'That's a very long chance,' Fidelma observed, not enthusiastic. 'Where would we find her?'

Eadulf turned to Beornwulf and Crída. 'I seem to remember her and her husband from when I was a boy. Don't they live a little way out on a rise overlooking the sea?'

'Your memory is good,' Crída replied. 'Once over the bridge, you take a track directly east. You go to the seashore and there are a few buildings on the hills that overlook it. It's called Fyrs-dun, the furze-covered hill.'

'I have a feeling it will not lead us to anywhere,' Fidelma admitted, 'but it is better than sitting about in frustration.'

'Often one finds information that, on the surface, looks as if it is without value but can eventually fill in a gap that completes a picture that would have remained blank,' Eadulf said with a cynical smile. 'I was once told that by a learned investigator.'

'At least I can get some sea air,' Fidelma replied.

It was not very long after that Fidelma and Eadulf halted their ponies on the hills overlooking the vast grey expanse of the sea. They had left Beornwulf as he had other chores to attend to with Crída, mainly the arrangements for the burial of Stuf. It did not seem a priority for them to be an escort. Eadulf decided that he and Fidelma could cover the investigation into his death alone.

The gusting winds and bracing scent of the sea, with the salt tang, hit them as they crossed the hill. The wind eventually brought them the shrill sounds of large gulls, which were circling round the huts. Their whiteness and black wing tips were distinctive: dangerous birds that would sometimes pursue and rob smaller birds, and often attack small mammals for their food, and were not put off by the hard shells of mussels, which they would take to smash against rocks.

'Look! That hut down there, just before the nets hanging on the lines, by those boats drawn upon the shingle beach,' Eadulf cried, pointing down the hill. 'That must be the place. There's a horse and cart at the back of the hut, too.'

Fidelma carefully led the way, zigzagging a little for firmer ground, down the furze-covered slope towards the back of the fisherman's hut. She was slightly annoyed now that she saw the positioning of the hut because, had she taken the correct route, she would have been able to reach the hut on a more level track instead of having to climb up and over the hill. Now she could see how the elderly woman could load her cart and guide it without difficulty into the township to sell her fish.

The woman was standing, hands on hips and feet apart, before the door as they came up.

Eadulf came forward and dismounted.

'Greetings, Mother Afenid. Do you remember me?'

The woman examined him and frowned.

'You were with Thane Beornwulf when we passed each other a short while ago,' she replied. Then she hesitated. 'You cannot be the young man who was son of Wulfric?' she asked, after examining him carefully. 'You left the township many years ago to follow the new religion.' Suddenly her hands went to her mouth. 'Athelnoth was your uncle. Oh, by Bealdor's holy light! You have surely heard of the fate of Athelnoth?'

'I have. We are staying at the Hall of Beornwulf, as you saw.'

The woman tucked back some grey hair that was blowing across her weather-beaten face and nodded slowly.

'Is there news of who killed Athelnoth and what has happened to young Wulfrun?'

'I am pursuing the matter and would like some words with you.' Eadulf hesitated, then indicated Fidelma and added: 'This is my wife Fidelma.'

Afenid smiled a greeting. 'Then you must enter for a mug of mead. My man has gone along the coast to pull the crab baskets. We had unloaded the morning's catch and I had just been to the township to sell it. Unfortunately the smell of the catch brings the gulls deafening us with their cries and . . .'

Eadulf smiling held up his hand. 'It is because you called to take your catch to Beornwulf that we have come to see you,' he interrupted.

'There is nothing wrong, is there? The catch was good. Ardith approved of it and she is usually a good judge.'

'I am sure that she is a perfect judge,' Fidelma assured her. 'We will take you up on your offer of a drink. Maybe inside we can shut out the noise of the circling birds.'

The woman turned, grinning and nodding, and ushering the way forward into the dim interior. The smell of fish inside the hut was as powerful as it was outside. The continued *kee-owk, kee-owk, kee-owk, kee-owk* of the shrieking gulls was only marginally muted. She went to pour the drinks from a large jug.

'What we wanted to ask,' Eadulf began, 'was, when you approached or when you left Beornwulf's estate, you came over the bridge. Did you see anything suspicious?'

Mother Afenid pursued her lips and then shook her head.

'Suspicious? No, I barely climbed down from my cart. I had no time to look round.'

'We meant, when you drove up, you obviously saw Beornwulf's *druhting*?'

'Crída? He opened the gate for me to drive in. I drove up to the house where Ardith was waiting and she made a choice of the fish. Then I left.'

'You had noticed no one else apart from Crída and Ardith?'

'Not really. I saw a couple of the thane's workers. I passed Beornwulf and yourselves at the gate. Oh, there was the stable lad and the one I usually see looking after the goats. But,' she shrugged, 'what would be suspicious?'

'Beornwulf has a barley field that runs along the river that goes through the township,' Fidelma prompted. 'The field is separated from the river by a hedge.'

'That is the River Frome,' Afenid replied, happy to answer within her knowledge. 'That means "the brisk water". It is getting less brisk these days.'

'That's it. Part of Beornwulf's estate lies alongside it. When you were returning, coming over the bridge, did you glance along it? Did you happen to see any boats on it?'

'Ah, now you mention that, lady, I could see that rapscallion Stuf rowing his boat southward along it.'

'But, Stuf—' began Eadulf, only to be silenced by Fidelma's interjection.

'Describe what you saw.'

'I recognised Stuf's boat as he often fishes along the Alde and, to get to it, you have to navigate down the Frome. I saw him going past Beornwulf's place as I crossed.'

'You recognised the boat. Did you recognise Stuf?'

The woman smiled. 'Who would be in Stuf's boat but Stuf? Anyway, he had his back to me, and wore a cloak and hood. He was rowing downriver.'

'So it was but a moment that you saw him? You did not stop on the bridge or shout to him?'

'Why should I shout to him, of all people? I can't say I like him. If I left my cart alone in his vicinity, I would guarantee that I would probably find fish missing after he had passed by. No, I did not stop but rode on. After all, I had finished delivering to those who wanted the fish.'

'So you were sure that the person in the boat with his back to you was Stuf and he was rowing south, which would bring him alongside the pastureland of Beornwulf?' demanded Eadulf.

'Haven't I said that?'

'For which we thank you. And now we must be returning. We will mention your kindness and hospitality to lord Beornwulf.'

After they had gone a short distance from the fisherman's hut, Fidelma turned to Eadulf with a grim expression.

'So we know how the assassin managed to get up close behind Stuf without anyone on the estate spotting them. They used the river.'

'But who was it?' Eadulf demanded. 'We know it was not Stuf. Who would use Stuf's own boat? And it was someone who looked like him from the back.'

'That it was the murderer is in no doubt. Exactly so: a person who, from the back, looked like a thin male figure wearing a robe

GRAVE OF THE LAWGIVER

by which they could pass as Stuf, and was known to Stuf and of whom he was not afraid. They rowed to the pasture where Stuf was, climbed out, stabbed him and then departed downriver or upriver.'

Had not Eadulf been holding the reins of his horse, he would have spread his arms eloquently in despair.

In the distance there came the sound of a hunting horn, which made Fidelma raise her head.

'What's that?' she wondered. 'Too late for hunting, surely?'

Eadulf listened a moment. He turned a worried gaze to Fidelma.

'We best get back to Beornwulf's Hall. Those are no notes from a hunting horn. That's a warning blast on a war horn.'

CHAPTER EIGHTEEN

They had just ridden through the gates of Beornwulf's Hall when they saw the thane and Crída standing before the door of the main building, both seeming exhilarated.

'What is it?' Eadulf demanded as they dismounted and let the stable master take their mounts.

'It is Werferth,' the thane explained. 'Werferth has been seen approaching the township with a couple of his warriors as escort.'

They had barely absorbed this unexpected news when a group of horsemen came into the central square and their leader turned and came to the still-open gates. Werferth almost leapt from his horse and came running to greet them.

Beornwulf was busy disengaging the enthusiastic embrace of the commander of the king's bodyguard, and then Werferth was equally demonstrably enthusiastic as he turned to greet Eadulf and Fidelma.

'I have half a dozen of my warriors with me,' Werfeth explained. 'I've told them to take their horses to the tavern and stay there until I give further orders.'

The mention of a 'tavern' surprised Fidelma. She had overlooked the fact that there might be a tavern in the township. But, of course, it was logical. She found Beornwulf and Ardith were ushering them all inside. Werferth moved directly to a chair and collapsed into it as Ardith came forward with a tankard of mead.

Werferth drank the whole lot, wiped his mouth, removing the flecks of the beer froth from his beard, and then looked almost apologetically at Eadulf and Fidelma.

'I needed that,' he grimaced. 'I have ridden directly here from The Stag's Ford instead of following King Ealdwulf to Suth Tun Hoo. I came to tell you the decisions of the council and thus ensure the lady Fidelma was safe and had made plans to return to Hibernia.'

Eadulf looked puzzled. 'Safe? Why should she not be safe?'

'The decisions that we have all been waiting for have been agreed.' Werferth's tone was serious. 'It will not be comfortable now for anyone who does not accept the rulings of the council.'

'I want to resolve the problem relating to my family before we do anything,' Eadulf declared. 'First, I want to know what happened to you and Brother Ator after we left Cnobheres Burg.'

'But you will leave for Hibernia shortly?' Werferth pressed, ignoring the look that passed between Eadulf and Fidelma.

'I have my son awaiting me in Cashel, where my brother is king,' Fidelma replied simply. 'That is my home and, therefore, I shall leave as soon as possible. I presume the decisions at The Stag's Ford have not been favourable for any Hibernian missionaries or teachers here?'

'My priority is to find out who was responsible for Athelnoth's death and the whereabouts of my missing sister,' Eadulf interrupted sharply.

'So nothing was resolved by your returning here?' Werferth frowned.

'What did you and Brother Ator do after we left you at Cnobheres Burg?' repeated Eadulf, raising his voice.

Werferth reacted with a surprised look.

'Brother Ator? Has he not told you?'

His question was not answered immediately, due to their bewilderment.

Then Fidelma asked, 'How would he tell us anything? He went with you following Mede and the Northumbrians. Why would he be here?'

'But he did not come with me,' Werferth answered slowly.

'You had better explain that,' Eadulf prompted.

'We did get on the boat, but travelled together for only a short distance up the river Eár. Then the boat had to stop to pick someone up. Brother Ator said he had forgotten an important matter to tell you, and before I could stop him, he went ashore and disappeared.'

'He has not returned to Ceol's Halh,' Eadulf said suspiciously. 'We have been there and would have been informed.'

'So he has disappeared also,' Fidelma observed quietly. 'It seems he is lost to our investigation.'

'You'd better tell us, what did you do when you left us?' Eadulf prompted in a more reasonable tone.

'After Brother Ator left the boat saying his intention was to rejoin you, I went by river to Deor Ham, as was my intention. From there, I took smaller craft to Snipa's Ham and then into the country of the Gyrwas. It was easy to track Mede and his two companions. Having learnt in what direction Mede intended to go, I had determined to joined King Ealdwulf and reassume command of his bodyguard at The Stag's Ford.'

'So you do not know where Brother Ator went?' Fidelma asked again.

'I thought he was determined to follow you. It would not have taken him long to cross the Eár and the Wahenhe to catch up with you.'

'Provided he could get another horse,' Eadulf muttered. 'We delivered his pony at Ceol's Halh and brought your horse here.'

'It is in my stable,' confirmed Beornwulf.

'For which I thank you,' Werferth replied. 'But it is strange to hear Brother Ator did not follow you.'

'Let us hear what happened when you continued to follow Mede and his men,' Fidelma suggested. 'Did you find out anything about his purpose here?'

'Mede was heading into the Gyrwas country?' Eadulf prompted.

'Realising Mede was undoubtedly heading across the marshes to his own island in the eastern Gyrwas, my goal became The Stag's Ford, in the south of the Gyrwas country. I continued south until I reached a place called Saegham. It was where the Burgundian, Felix, died and is buried. He taught in an abbey he built there. It is not far from The Stag's Ford. I suppose it was because of the impressive abbey at The Stag's Ford that it was agreed to hold the council there and it is right on the border between our kingdom and Mercia.'

'You were following Mede and his Northumbrians until then?' Eadulf tried to hide his impatience at this digression. 'So you abandoned that and went to The Stag's Ford?'

'Not exactly,' Werfeth replied. 'At Saegham there was no need to follow them. Ironically, you can see the Island of Eels across the marshes from that place. It is a short trip by a good flat-bottom Fen boat . . . provided it has Fen men to guide it. The important news is that I heard that Princess Athelthryth is already there and has resumed her role as abbess.'

'So did Mede attempt to abduct her from the Isle of Eels?' Beornwulf asked.

'If it were in his thoughts, it was a foolish idea.'

'Meaning?' Beornwulf prompted.

'I arrived at Saegham the next morning after they had been there. I heard the story. Mede and his men attempted to steal a boat from one of the locals. There was no doubt that they planned to use it to get across the marshes to either to the Isle of Eels or beyond it to the north-west, to his own fortress on Mede Ham

Stede, Mede's island. It is not that far from the Island of Eels. They were discovered trying to take the boat and the local people objected . . . violently. In the affray the three Northumbrians were killed. I did not ask for further details, accepting that the Gyrwas are not renowned for hospitality, patience or forgiveness.'

'It seems a convenient resolution,' Beornwulf remarked grimly.

'But does not answer the question as to what they were doing in Seaxmund's Ham and if they were involved with the death of Athelnoth,' Eadulf said dismally.

'Nor does it explain the disappearance of Brother Ator,' Fidelma added, coming back to the main point. 'He did not appear to follow us, after he left you on the river.'

Werferth shook his head. 'You are sure that he has not returned here?'

'We have not seen him since we left him getting on the boat with you,' Eadulf confirmed. 'We have been among the people in Ceol's Halh and no one has seen a sign of him.'

'We are back to the old questions,' Fidelma sighed. 'I am not convinced he was in league with the Northumbrian raiders. He would have betrayed it when we were in Brother Wermund's hermitage and saw Mede. No one has seen him here, or in Ceol's Halh, or close by.'

Seeing Werferth was confused, she allowed Eadulf to tell him of recent events.

'We discussed whether he could be a good actor,' Fidelma explained. 'However, we found out that we had been misled by some lies of Stuf. A short while ago we found Stuf murdered on this very estate.'

Werferth was astonished. 'Stuf was killed? By whom?'

Fidelma shrugged. 'We have no idea. All of which goes to demonstrate that we are still some way from resolving the mystery.'

'Well, I suggest you concentrate on your own safety now. I am sure the decisions at The Stag's Ford will produce some fanatics, which will lead to complications.'

Fidelma spoke before Eadulf could reply.

'I will stay with Eadulf for a few more days,' she announced. 'I would not like to leave while there is a chance of resolving this.'

'You really want to remain here, trying to find some resolution?' Beornwulf asked in surprise.

'I want to return home to my son as soon as possible. But I have made a vow to Eadulf that I will not leave while there is a possibility that this mystery can be solved,' Fidelma replied stubbornly. 'If this means, Beornwulf, that you feel unable to continue your hospitality under whatever the decisions at The Stag's Ford conference stipulate, and you feel you must comply with, then so be it.'

They were startled when Ardith was the one who reacted vehemently.

'Of course, he doesn't mean that,' she announced firmly. 'He is a man of his word. You are welcome to the hospitality of this house as long as you wish.'

'Even so, lady,' Werferth glanced nervously at her, 'the situation is not going to be easy, for either Hibernians or anyone who does not acknowledge Rome as the ultimate authority of the New Faith. I have not explained the decisions made at the council at The Stag's Ford. I think it is wise to consider your safety now, lady.'

'Then it is time that we should hear the decisions of this council.' Fidelma's voice was taut.

'I rode for this place as soon as Theodoros closed the council,' Werferth confirmed. 'But the news will not be long in spreading.'

'Theodoros? I thought Bishop Bisi was supposed to be presiding alongside our king,' Beornwulf said, surprised.

'That was a farce,' Werferth admitted. 'It had already been

decided that Bishop Bisi would be removed as chief bishop of the kingdom, and that Abbot Aecci would replace him after the council. That was my message to Abbot Aecci when we went to Domnoc-wic. Throughout the council Theodoros sat next to Bisi and, while pretending this was an equal council of the bishops of the Angles and the Saxons, he kept intervening and making sure that all adhered to his own interpretation. They had to accept the recognition of the Bishop of Rome as the first bishop of the Roman Christian world. Oh, there were a few arguments and it was pointed out that there were heads of the eastern and African Churches who contended they had more rights than Rome to be considered leaders of the Faith. But Theodoros achieved his way.'

'But Theodoros is Greek?' Ardith pointed out.

'A Greek who owes his powers to Rome and obeys the Bishop of Rome in all things. Theodoros made clear that Rome would support all who sided with him, but the decision was for the leaders of the Angles and Saxons. He spoke very glibly.'

'So Bishop Bisi and King Ealdwulf had little influence in the council?' Beornwulf seemed resigned.

'There was little opposition from anyone,' Werferth said. 'Each territory has its own strategies and had not engaged in seeking a unity to oppose Theodoros. So there was a curious unity in their diversity.'

'So the council basically endorsed the ruling of Oswy of Northumbria at the council of Streoneshalh?' Fidelma exhaled in a sigh of resignation. 'So why should I, or any Hibernian, be afraid of this now? It did not threaten us then. Why now?'

'Because this council goes further. Although Bishop Wilfrid was not attending, he was represented by official deputies. Theodoros has demanded of King Ecgfrith of Northumbria that he reinstates Wilfrid as his chief bishop and also forgets the matter of Princess Athelthryth. It is now Wilfrid's policies, which are pro-Roman, that are accepted.'

'So how did our allies of Mercia vote?' Beornwulf demanded.

'Their bishop, Bishop Winfrith, voted for Theodoros' Roman stance, and their king Wulfhere had to support him.'

'No one objected?'

'Putta, Bishop of the Cantwara, naturally supported Theodoros and was supported by Eorcenberht, their king,' Werferth shrugged. 'Sebbi, of the East Saxons, and the newly converted Athelwealth, of the South Saxons, gave their endorsement to their bishops. So, my friends, it seems that all the Churches of these kingdoms are uniting in recognition of Rome as the centre of the New Faith and the Archbishop of the Cantwara as the leader among these kingdoms.'

'In practical terms, what does this mean for you?' Fidelma asked Beornwulf.

The thane looked to Werferth for an answer.

'Apparently, the chief scribe Titill has written down the ten canons, which, if disobeyed, will result in punishment, Theodoros has warned.'

'Punishment?' Fidelma's eyes widened. 'I thought the council was a debate on theological ideas and not decisions on temporal law?'

'I repeat, these were the decisions of the council,' Werferth replied.

'And the decisions, disobedience to which are punishable?' Ardith asked.

'One was to confirm keeping to the Roman calculation of Easter made at Streoneshalh. Another, that no bishop, except the Archbishop of the Cantwara, has authority in the territory of another bishop. No bishop has authority in communities governed by abbots except when they are allowed to cast their vote for the abbey, nor are they allowed to seize the properties of abbeys. Religious missionaries are not allowed to wander from place to place unless under special permission from their abbot.

No religious is to perform any rites of the New Faith without the permission of the local approved bishop. Oh, and wandering religious, if they have permission to travel into another bishop's territory, cannot demand hospitality as a right, but must accept what they are offered in charity.'

Eadulf shook his head in surprise.

'There is to be a council of all the bishops of the kingdoms twice a year,' Werferth continued, 'to monitor the ideas so that there is some unity and cohesion between the kingdoms on a religious level.'

'Anything else?' Fidelma pressed cynically.

'No bishop is to claim seniority over another through any means other than the date of their order of consecration.'

'So everyone agreed that the bishop of the Cantwara is now the archbishop of all the bishops of all the kingdoms of the Angles and the Saxons?' Fidelma asked.

'That was the decision,' Werferth agreed. 'The council did discuss that more bishops should be appointed because the numbers of those converting to Christianity were expected to rise, but no decision was made about it. Oh, the last thing they agreed on was no marriage would be recognised as valid unless it was enacted under Christian auspices.'

Beornwulf and Ardith exchanged nervous glances.

'The rules obviously negate any recognition to the Columban and Hibernian religious, as it was meant to do after Streoneshalh,' Eadulf muttered.

'This really enforces the decisions of Streoneshalh,' Werferth agreed. 'Now there are centralised rules among the kingdoms, which all must obey. That is why I suggest that you think of returning to Hibernia, lady.'

Fidelma was looking perturbed, perhaps for the first time in her life.

'I presume that when the areas and kingdoms of the Britons,

who still fight, are conquered and occupied, they will have to surrender their religion as well as their territory? The Britons' way of Christianity has the same philosophies and rituals of the New Faith as those in Ireland, as well as in many parts of Gaul. We know the Angles and Saxons look to the west for their future expansion. That will mean, if ever the rest of the kingdoms of the Britons fall, then the next step is the Irish Churches and kingdoms.'

She avoided looking at Eadulf.

'That day will be a long time coming,' Eadulf dismissed. 'Currently, it is Mercia and Northumbria who contest for the title "Bretwalda" to add to the titles of their kings. Until one of the kings can truly claim to be "lord of the Britons" there will be no fear of them being strong enough to launch an invasion of Hibernia.'

'Can you really see such a threat in this, lady?' Ardith asked.

'I fear it. Truly, I do fear it,' Fidelma sighed.

'Were those all the decisions at this council?' Eadulf asked.

'There was one other decision, as I recall,' Werferth added after further thought. 'It was discussed in depth, and accepted, that all the Churches would assent to teach the philosophy of Monothelitism.'

Beornwulf was bewildered, as was Ardith.

It was Fidelma who found herself explaining.

'This is a philosophy about the personality of Christ.'

'Personality? But he was a god,' Beornwulf exclaimed. 'A god is a god. How can anyone question a god's personality or his will and desires?'

'But this god lived as a human and allowed himself to be killed by humans, after which he rose from the dead. So while he lived and taught, was he human or divine? The orthodox view was that Christ had two natures – one human and one divine. Thus he had two wills. Then it was decided among philosophers of the New

Faith that, although he had two natures, he could only have one divine will. They call that Monothelitism.'

'Are you now saying the Churches of the Angles and Saxons have to enforce this idea?' Eadulf asked.

'They would not be alone,' Fidelma pointed out. 'The Coptic, Orthodox, Syriac, Armenian and Maronite Churches all accept it.'

There was a silence.

'So, in brief, the Churches of the kingdoms of the Angles and Saxons have become united and look to Rome as their centre?' Eadulf finally summed up.

'That is about the sum of it,' Werferth agreed. He suddenly looked awkward. 'When the news is completely proclaimed, as I have said, it might be wise for all Hibernian missionaries and teachers here to leave these kingdoms.'

'Abbot Brecán in Cnobheres Burg and his community certainly saw this event coming,' Fidelma reminded them.

'I should imagine that he and his community have already left, either to Iona or back to Hibernia,' Eadulf grimaced.

'So there were rumours that this would happen?' Ardith asked, still surprised.

'Theodoros has grown to hate Hibernians. He declared that, even among the Cantwara, he was hemmed in by a mass of Hibernian students. He said they were like savage, wild boars that would have to be checked by a pack of hounds.'

'I wish I had attended this council,' Fidelma muttered.

'No Hibernian was allowed to attend, nor any Briton,' Werferth told her.

'It would seem this is a pivotal point in the advancement of the New Faith,' Ardith said softly. 'It is a point where we stand at the crossing of the roads as to how the Faith will progress. Are all the kingdoms expected to expel all the British and Hibernian teachers of the New Faith?'

'It seems that we are expected to obey what Theodoros has

decided. Perhaps Ecgfrith and Wulfhere will continue their war to claim the title of "Bretwalda" so that one or other will dominate over all the kingdoms.'

'Not if there is a Wuffingas alive!' Werferth exclaimed, clapping a hand to his sword. 'The descendants of Wuffa should remember that he was spawned of the mighty Woden and the Wuffingas will not take second place to anyone.'

Fidelma glanced at Eadulf and almost shrugged.

'It certainly does not resolve our problem, and this we must concentrate on for a few more days,' she sighed. 'I have to leave the future to whatever direction the warring sons of Woden think it lies in. It sounds as though it will be a bloody one, for the Britons will continue to fight for their territory, as will the northern kingdoms of the Rheged, Dál Riada and the Cruithne.'

Werferth pressed his lips together in a thin line. 'Well, at least Ecgfrith of Northumbria did not take all the spoils. The Princess Athelthryth is now safely back in her abbey on the Island of Eels and is guarded by men of her late husband's bodyguard. I was assured she is safe enough.'

'Does that not displease the Northumbrian king?' Beornwulf asked.

'He has been persuaded by Bishop Wilfrid to accept his marriage to her is null and void,' Werferth said. 'I think he now has eyes on a princess of the Cantwara – Eormenburgh. Ecgfrith is already boasting that, now Theodoros is supporting him, he intends to lead his warriors against the Britons of the Rheged kingdom and drive them from the land, establishing settlements for his people there. There is no doubt that he is determined to make the title of "Bretwalda" a reality. Lord over the Britons as well as all the Angles and the Saxons.'

'It will not be long before the dark years will encompass our missionaries and teachers,' Fidelma sighed. 'I understand why you come to warn me, Werferth. Hibernian missionaries and teachers were so highly regarded until the fateful day at Streoneshalh. Even young princes were sent to my country for their education. They fled to our teaching abbeys and colleges. Even the son of Oswy, Aldfrith, settled among us to become one of our best-known poets. Much learning and knowledge will be lost. Streoneshalh is happening again.'

'I did not know it would become so serious,' Eadulf said unhappily. 'There are already many separate divisions even in the communities that claim allegiance to Rome.'

Fidelma smiled sadly. 'My people treated all who came from here with hospitality. They gladly fed them, provided them with books to read and instruction, without even asking for payment. It is sad that the friendly relations we had with your people are now changing into antagonism. It is becoming a dark age.'

It was Ardith who suggested it was time that they retired for a wash and prepared for the evening feast.

Later, when Fidelma and Eadulf had retired to their room to sleep, Eadulf gave a long, bewildered sigh.

'I don't see how what Werferth told us relates to the death of my uncle and disappearance of Wulfrun. I can see that there are serious issues that arise from the antagonism, but I cannot see how they affect this investigation.'

'Perhaps there can be no absolute solution,' Fidelma replied. 'In many cases one is left with suspicion. Perhaps we have to accept what is called circumstantial evidence. I was hoping to clear up this matter satisfactorily without resorting to conjecture. I don't know what your courts would accept in comparison with the Brehons.'

Eadulf pursed his lips moodily. 'I suppose the best thing to do is present the evidence to Thane Beornwulf for his judgement. Werferth is here to stand as a witness, being a member of the king's Witan.' He hesitated and added, 'I presume you will go through your conclusions with me beforehand . . .?'

'Have I not always discussed each case with you?' she responded. 'In this matter, above all matters, you are more part of it than I am. Of course, we shall discuss everything.'

'So when shall I tell Beornwulf that you will be ready to discuss it?'

'I have one place to visit tomorrow morning, if I can persuade Crída to guide us. Then I can be ready in the afternoon, if Beornwulf is willing to allow me to make my report before leaving.'

'You really think you have the answer to the mystery then?' Eadulf was unconvinced.

'I believe so,' she replied with quiet firmness.

Eadulf grimaced doubtfully. 'I see only the one likely solution, but we will discuss it when you are ready.'

'I am finally beginning to see a solution to this mystery, but you won't like it,' she told him.

Eadulf, startled, regarded her for a moment.

'Surely it doesn't matter what I like or not, so long as it is a logical conclusion. Since we were first together that is the one thing that I have learnt about you and respected, Fidelma: that you have a logical and analytical mind. You come to your judgements without embellishment or bias.'

'Thank you for that, Eadulf,' she replied quietly. 'In these legal matters, I acknowledge you have been a full partner in resolving many of them. But tell me, either you or Crída once said you played on a place in the marshland that you called an island.'

'A long time ago. I couldn't remember the name. We built a tree house there. I have long forgotten the detail of those childhood games. Why do you bring that up?'

'Call it curiosity. However, that is where we shall go tomorrow.'

'Then what?'

'Then I shall say what I think has happened.'

'Then you intend to return to Cashel. I would like to discuss the matter that you raised in conversation the other night.'

Fidelma tried to keep her features mobile.

'I intended that discussion once this matter has been sorted,' she replied. 'I have already given you my thoughts and intentions. I shall be ready to hear your thoughts about it.'

'As soon as you have given your thoughts to Beornwulf, I shall try to respond with my feelings on it.'

She was about to speak further but a strange sound interrupted her. It sounded like the cry of a lost soul in torment. It was a curious, frightening noise: a boom followed by a screeching cry of anguished distress. She rose and went to the window where the last glow of light was fading towards the west. She heard Eadulf stirring behind her but did not turn.

'What in the name of your gods is that?'

Eadulf roused himself from the supine position he had just adopted and, supporting himself on one elbow, listened to the intermittent sound. Then he sighed.

'That is a bird. I have not heard that one in a long time. It does not dwell in other lands. It is a marsh dweller and rarely takes to the air. We call it a bittern.'

'Another curious species of your land,' Fidelma accepted almost sadly. 'That, and the strange creature that exists here, which you told me about the other night, are certainly enough not to encourage people to dwell in this countryside.'

Eadulf turned over to sleep and did not respond.

CHAPTER NINETEEN

The first meal of the day was served when Ardith looked around at those at the table and frowned as if perplexed.

'You are all looking miserable,' she observed. 'I thought, Fidelma, that you were going to declare the possible solution to Athelnoth's murder today? Isn't that a reason for an expression of satisfaction or some positive feelings among you?'

Fidelma returned Ardith's sad smile.

'Satisfaction is something when one is feeling positive and the arguments are watertight. Like the fisherman who rows out on a stormy sea and knows there is no weakness in their vessel; that the planking won't spring apart and waves will not suddenly rush in and engulf them.'

'You fear that?' Ardith was slightly surprised. 'Then you do not intend to go ahead with your judgement?'

'I will express an opinion, but supposition is never a good base on which to form a judgement. Without hard evidence, you may believe a man stole a goat but until you have someone who saw the man stealing the goat, or the goat is found in the man's hut without good and logical reason why the goat should be there, belief is not fact. No one should be condemned without indisputable facts. Here there is suspicion and belief and circumstantial evidence. I can argue that, but it is not good to declare guilt. Even if accepted, in law, it leaves a bad feeling because there will always remain doubt.'

'Are you saying that you really want more positive evidence to feel satisfied, but you do feel that the circumstances point to the guilt of one person?' Werferth asked.

'That is exactly what I am saying. I will have to argue what I know and what I presume from the knowledge. Then it must be left to the judgement of others.'

'We have no lawgiver,' Ardith pointed out. 'To whom are you appealing?'

'I will appeal to the logic of your husband, Ardith,' Fidelma replied automatically.

The woman started in surprise. Even Beornwulf gasped as he stared at her in surprise.

'How do you—' Ardith began.

'Do not be concerned,' Fidelma replied at once. 'I regret I spoke without consideration. Yet it is true, isn't it? You can disguise many matters with words but the language of bodies is very precise.'

Beornwulf was looking embarrassed. 'Since we came to Seaxmund's Ham, we have kept our marriage secret. We have not accepted the New Faith, and that would prevent me from sitting in the king's Witan.'

'Tell me how you knew that we were married?' Ardith was serious.

'Beornwulf is your husband but not under the Christian rites,' Fidelma replied calmly. 'Your *Asatru,* or wedding, was before you came here as thane. That was in Beoderic's Worth. Among what you call the *weofodthegn*, the witnesses, was Mother Elfrida, who came from that same township. I suspect Werferth might also have been one of those witnesses or, at least, he knew the situation. I presume that you fought the Northumbrians together at one point.'

GRAVe Of The LAWGIVeR

'How do you know this?' gasped Werferth. Even Eadulf seemed askance at Fidelma's words.

'I heard others mention the word *weofodthegn*, and Eadulf told me that it meant the witnesses to the pagan ceremony to ensure the groom provided a symbolic dowry of an ancestral sword, shield, a bridle, horse and cattle. They were the *brydgifu* blessed by your goddess Fríg.'

Werferth cut in, scarcely keeping back his tone of admiration. 'It was two days after that ceremony that Beoderic's Worth was almost wiped out in the Northumbrian raid. At that time most of the witnesses, as you say, were killed as well. Beornwulf and I fought together. In the same raid my friend, Beornwulf's cousin Cynehelm, then Thane of Seaxmund's Ham, was killed. Beornwulf then agreed to become thane in his place.'

'Thankfully my wife Ardith and the woman Elfrida were among those who survived the raid,' Beornwulf added. 'When we came here, we knew that this township had just been converted to the New Faith. We were told that Sigeric, the high steward to the king, would not allow King Ealdwulf to have any of the Old Faith in his Witan or council. When Redwald became our first king to convert to the New Faith fifty years ago, within a short time he resumed the Old Faith. After that a succession of short-lived kings remained pagan until Sigebert, and with the accession of Anna, whose brother Ealdwulf now rules, it was ordered that the kingdom become Christian. No one in the Witan is of the Old Faith.'

Fidelma smiled sadly at Ardith. 'So when Beornwulf was chosen as Thane of Seaxmund's Ham he was given a seat on the king's Witan. You realised then that he should be of the New Faith in order to be approved of by the king. But old beliefs do not vanish overnight. You had married under the Old Faith.'

'That is why I pretended to be just the stewardess, the keeper of Beornwulf's house,' Ardith admitted reluctantly. 'Only two people knew the truth. One was Elfrida the Wise. She was, as you rightly heard, a witness. She makes no apology for maintaining her original beliefs. The other witness was our good friend Werferth.'

'But, as commander of King Ealdwulf's bodyguard and a member of the Witan, you must be Christian?' Eadulf demanded.

'I am. But does that stop me supporting my friend and comrade?' Werferth replied.

'What do you intend to do with this knowledge?' Beornwulf asked, cutting the explanation short.

'Nothing,' replied Fidelma. 'Your relationship with one another was obvious, but it does not concern me. It is of no relevance except you should be careful in the days ahead when the influences of the Greek, Archbishop Theodoros, are felt. They *will* be felt, and not only among the teachers and missionaries from my land and, of course, the poor Britons as their kingdoms get conquered and absorbed. These new decisions will also be felt by those who hold on to the earlier Faith and other Christian philosophies. My advice, therefore, is that you find someone to give you a blessing with a Christian ritual before the effects of this Stag's Ford council start to spread.'

There was silence for a while before Ardith asked: 'Can you do that blessing, Fidelma?'

'I left the religious some time back,' she replied. 'Moreover, I am a Hibernian and uphold the Faith as it was given to my people. My word counts for nothing under the decisions of this council.'

There was a pause and then Eadulf cleared his throat.

'Although I was converted by the Blessed Fursa and his brothers, and went to study in Tuam Drecain in Hibernia, I continued my studies in Rome. I was ordained as a wandering monk in Rome and was sent to Streoneshalh to be an advocate for the Roman rituals in the great debate there. That was when I first met

Fidelma. She was an advocate for the Columban Churches. I argued with Wilfrid for Rome. My views have mellowed but I am, technically, still empowered to perform and bless rituals. My name, as an advocate of Rome at Streoneshalh, will be known to Bishop Wilfrid.'

'And you are suggesting . . .?' Beornwulf pressed.

'I can perform the ritual and blessing, and then write a parchment attesting to the same, which I, Werferth and perhaps Crída can witness. To do this, of course, you have to accept the physical and spiritual protection of Christ in place of Fríg.'

'We will accept,' Beornwulf declared after a glance at Ardith, who gave a brief nod.

'Then we will make the *handa sellen*, the official handshake to agree, and I will write the parchment as proof after I have heard your vows exchanged in due form. That will be enough for any pro-Roman bishop to accept, especially Bishop Wilfrid, who is now a friend of Archbishop Theodoros.'

It was midday, when they were toasting the event with strong cider, that there was a noise of raised voices outside. They heard a servant answering the main door. A female voice, which seemed familiar, was raised in a mournful tone. A moment later, the servant was standing respectfully at the inner door.

'My lord, Mother Notgide is demanding to see you. She is very distraught.'

'Mother Notgide from Ceol's Halh?' Beornwulf repeated in surprise. 'Can't Crída deal with it?'

'Crída left a short time ago to attend to delivering two calves promised to a farmer downriver.'

Beornwulf had forgotten the *druhting* had left just after he had been a witness to Eadulf's ritual. Reluctantly, the thane gestured for the woman to be brought inside.

Mother Notgide was clearly agitated as she was shown in. She found some difficulty observing the courtesy of bowing to her thane. It was Ardith who, seeing her condition, moved forward and gave the woman water to drink. Mother Notgide took several swallows before turning breathlessly to Beornwulf.

'My lord, we came downriver to give you news . . .'

'We?' queried the thane.

'My husband Scead took the oars. He remains in the boat.'

'Scead? A good protection.' The thane tried to joke to alleviate the woman's clear anxiety. Eadulf wondered whether Fidelma would appreciate that the name Scead actually meant a 'protector'. The woman from Ceol's Halh obviously ignored the attempt at humour.

'So come now,' Beornwulf encouraged, 'what brings you downriver in such a state?'

'Earlier, we heard some rumour that Stuf had been murdered by someone using his boat, which he usually moors on the river at Ceol's Halh.'

'I know this,' the thane frowned.

'A short time ago, we noticed his boat, almost hidden near the hut used by Brother Ator.'

'Stuf was killed in these very grounds,' pointed out Beornwulf. 'He didn't need his boat.'

'I went to look at his boat . . .' continued the woman, then paused dramatically. 'There was a body in it.'

'A body?' prompted Beornwulf.

'It was Brother Ator.'

There was a surprised silence.

'So he did return to Ceol's Halh?' Werferth finally said with satisfaction, not fully appreciating the implication. 'Did he say anything to you when you saw him?'

Mother Notgide looked at him almost in pity.

'I said it was a body. There was blood all over him. He was lying on his face in Stuf's boat.'

Her words were again greeted by astonishment.

'Covered in blood? You mean he was murdered?' Fidelma asked quietly, although she had already guessed.

'He was stabbed in the back, lady.'

Eadulf exhaled sharply. 'When was this boat last seen at Ceol's Halh?'

'It had been moored in the area by Brother Ator's cabin after it was decreed that Stuf had to stay here and do work here, my lord.'

'Are you saying that Stuf had not used it since he came to do the compensation service for lord Beornwulf?' Eadulf asked. He turned to Fidelma without waiting for an answer. 'If that is so, then Afenid was right. The boat was used when Stuf was killed and it was Brother Ator who was the killer of Stuf, just as the fisherman's wife described?'

'The fisherman's wife thought she saw Stuf rowing down-river to that point,' Fidelma explained to the others. 'Sadly, the rower had his back towards her and she assumed it was Stuf. Now we know that Stuf's killer could have been Brother Ator. But that supposes an even bigger problem. If he killed Stuf and managed to get back upriver unseen to Ceol's Halh, who killed him?'

There was total confusion among them and, since no one answered, Fidelma said: 'We have to examine this body.'

'Then I suggest Werferth accompany us and let Mother Notgide take us to the body,' Eadulf said.

'Better yet,' Beornwulf interposed, 'it would delay us by getting the poor woman's husband rowing back upriver to Ceol's Halh. I will let one of my men take the boat back while we ride to Ceol's Halh. I will take Mother Notgide behind me on my horse while Werferth can take Scead. As thane, I need to be a witness to this.'

They reached Ceol's Halh fairly quickly. Leaving their horses at the cabin of Mother Notgide and Scead, they followed the woman to the river bank. Stuf's boat was apparently where Mother

Notgide and her husband had left it, with a local man standing guard by it. It was just outside Brother Ator's cabin.

'Just to be clear, the boat was not here when you found it?' Fidelma asked.

'No,' replied Mother Notgide, pointing to an overgrown area of the river bank. 'It was hidden among those reeds and rushes. We only noticed it around midday.'

The young religieux's body was still lying face down in it. Mother Notgide assured them that nothing had been moved. Fidelma stood back and motioned Eadulf to enter the boat and examine the cadaver. A moment later he stepped back on to the bank with a grimace.

'It is the same technique that I have seen with the corpse of Stuf. A thin blade inserted from behind and at an angle that goes through the ribs upwards and must penetrate the heart. A slight twist before removing it and the victim is dead within moments.'

'So it is the same hand that killed Stuf?' Beornwulf queried in bewilderment.

'I would not go so far as that; but I say it is the same technique. Certainly it was done by a similar weapon in a similar manner.'

'I don't suppose you can estimate when this happened?' Fidelma asked Mother Notgide.

'It must have been some time during the night or early this morning,' she replied. 'We had no idea that Brother Ator was even here. We thought he had gone north with the lord Werferth. We only found him after we noticed Stuf's boat at midday. Then we came straight downriver to report it to Thane Beornwulf.'

'No one saw Brother Ator arrive here? Did they see the boat missing yesterday?'

'Not that I know of,' Mother Notgide affirmed. 'You would not see the boat unless you came to the river and looked among the reeds and growths along here. There were not too many boats up or down the river yesterday.'

'Brother Ator must have been alive to row downriver in this craft to have killed Stuf in the way he did,' Eadulf mused. 'Therefore Brother Ator must have rowed back upriver to be killed after he reached here.' He turned to Mother Notgide and Scead. 'You claim that no one in the hamlet saw anything until you found him this morning? It is all very suspicious.'

'What are you implying?' demanded Mother Notgide, seeing the scepticism on his face.

'One moment,' Fidelma interrupted, sensing a useless antagonism. 'We presume that it was Brother Ator in this boat going downriver. We presume he landed at Beornwulf's pasture, climbed through the hedge, surprised Stuf and killed him. Then we have to presume he was able to row back upriver.'

'Of course,' Eadulf agreed. 'I can claim further evidence. Remember when we were up in Cnobheres Burg and found Brother Boso stabbed to death? It was done by the exact technique as this. We blamed it on Mede, as a means to stop our pursuit. But, remember, it was Brother Ator who left us for a short time to go to inform Brother Boso that we were with the abbot. He returned to say Brother Boso had not opened the door. It was soon afterwards we found his corpse. The same technique was used to kill both Boso and Stuf.'

'And, from what I was told, to kill Athelnoth and Osric,' added Beornwulf, frowning.

'The same technique?' Fidelma frowned.

'That means the mystery is solved,' Beornwulf declared triumphantly. 'The same type of knife that slew Athelnoth, Osric, Boso and Stuf was held in the hand of Brother Ator.'

'My uncle was killed by Brother Ator and his house burnt because Athelnoth refused to accept Brother Ator's request to marry my sister Wulfrun.' Eadulf was summing up, turning to Fidelma for agreement. 'What was it your favourite Latin lawyer used to say – we have proved the proposition we set out to demonstrate? *Quod erat demonstrandum?*'

'I am afraid I have to amend that to *deficit in demonstrandum* – it fails to be demonstrated.' Fidelma shook her head. 'It fails by the simple question – who killed Brother Ator? I agree that the knife used was held and inserted with the same technique. However, it was not held by the same hand.'

'How can that be?' Beornwulf demanded wonderingly.

'We have talked about presumptions. What if our presumption was that Brother Ator was not the person in the boat who went downriver to get into the pasture and stab Stuf? I don't think Stuf was so friendly with Brother Ator that he would have turned his back in such a way to lay himself open to attack. What if Brother Ator was already dead and in this boat and this is not Stuf's boat? Because a boat belongs to someone it does not mean the person using it was the person who owned it.'

It was Scead who moved forward a pace.

'I can confirm whose boat it is. I did Stuf a favour once. I repaired a splintered piece of wood in return for a crab.'

Fidelma indicated the boat. 'Show us.'

Scead climbed down and looked along some of the planking.

'My repair is here, so this is Stuf's boat,' he said.

'I am confused, Fidelma,' Beornwulf declared. 'Do you say that Brother Ator was not the killer, in spite of Eadulf's clear accusation?'

'I said the technique was the same, but not the hand holding the blade. Because, even if he killed Stuf, you are overlooking the main thing. I repeat: who killed Brother Ator?'

They stood in silence.

'I was going to suggest suicide,' Werferth proposed.

'How does a person commit suicide by stabbing himself in the back through the ribs in such a manner to ensure it pierces the heart?' Fidelma mused sarcastically. 'I suggest that the body of Brother Ator was here while the killer used another boat to go downriver to Beornwulf's Hall. By the way,' she turned to

Beornwulf, 'Crída handed you the knife that he found plunged in Athelnoth's back on the night of the fire. Do you still have it?'

The thane thought for a moment and nodded. 'I think I do. It is in my box of weapons.'

'Good. I shall want to look at it when we return to your Hall. By the way, how long will Crída be gone on this errand for you?'

'He should be back by this evening.'

'What do we do now?' Eadulf asked in exasperation. 'We don't have any other leads to pursue.'

'The finding of Brother Ator's body now has confirmed my suspicions,' Fidelma replied. 'It is a step forward to confirming the explanation that I had been considering.'

'I don't understand,' Eadulf muttered. 'Why can't you tell us now?'

'As I said before, I want to make one journey before I explain. However, it must wait for Crída's return, for a lot will depend on what he tells me.'

'You say Crída is the answer to this conundrum?' Beornwulf demanded.

'He has an answer that I need,' Fidelma said firmly. 'After I have seen what I want to see, then I will deliver my conclusions before you as if I were delivering them to a Brehon in my own country. But you will probably have to wait until tomorrow morning unless Crída comes back early.'

It was after the first meal of the day that Fidelma rose and went outside to stretch herself, breathing deeply of the fresh morning air. She saw Crída, who had not returned until midnight the previous evening, on his way to the stables. She called him and he paused and turned towards her.

'I heard about Brother Ator when I came back late last night, lady. I was surprised that he returned from Cnobheres Burg. Is there something I can do?'

'You once mentioned a special place where you and Eadulf played as boys. Do you remember where it was?'

Crída was amused.

'A place in the marshes where we once built a tree house? Childhood memories are sometimes long lasting.'

'Eadulf has forgotten the name and its location.'

'Eadulf's memory can be very selective,' Crída replied with a shake of his head.

'But you remember?'

'I haven't been there for many a year, but my childhood memories are sharp. It was an island in the marshland which we called Snaca-aeg. So why would you want to know that?'

'Snaca-aeg? Do you think you could find it now?'

'I am sure of it.'

'So will you conduct us there?' she insisted.

'Will this have Beornwulf's approval?'

'Naturally. He and Werferth should accompany us to the spot.'

'It's not an easy route. It is a treacherous marsh, just west of Ceol's Halh. There's a narrow path through the marshes, and one misstep and you will be up to your neck in the mire.'

'Once we are in the marsh, is it a long journey?'

'Not long, as I recall from my childhood memories, but it has to be undertaken on foot. When would you want to go there?'

Fidelma glanced up at the sky. 'As soon as we can be ready.'

'In that case,' Crída said, 'I shall go and arrange the horses, for we should ride them north to Ceol's Halh and go on foot from there.'

'I understand,' Fidelma assured him.

'Just let me know when you are all ready to leave.'

It was mid-morning before they left the thane's Hall. Crída led the way on one of the Beornwulf's ponies, with the thane riding next with Werferth, and Eadulf and Fidelma following. They rode through the township, up the rise to the Gull's Stream. The people once more showed their respect to their thane, whether they were standing at their cabins or walking along the roadways, by bowing their heads, although the women, seated at their spinning wheels and occasional looms, mostly had their heads bent to their tasks. Ironically, as they rode, Fidelma remembered that Eadulf had told her that Seaxmund, who had named the township, bore the name which meant 'knife protector'.

It was a warm day. The sun had risen bright in a cloudless sky. They passed the blackened cinders of what had been Athelnoth's house, the building where Eadulf had been born and grown up, and where Eadulf's father Wulfric had once been the *gerefa* of the area.

As they passed by, Crída pointed to a wooden cabin some distance away and called over his shoulder: 'That's my family's home. My sister and her man live there now. I grew up there and that's why Eadulf and I were friends as boys – we lived so close together.'

No one spoke as they rode on, joining the track along the River Frome. Even Fidelma fell deep into thought. It occurred to her that the advocates from the Roman Christian world were achieving what the legions of the Roman Empire had not achieved when they had annexed the Britons and their kingdoms five centuries before. The new, conquering Angle and Saxon settlers had arrived here scarcely two centuries before, and she wondered how long memories would last.

She had grown up when her own people were in the midst of a flowering literacy and what was to be called a 'Golden Age' of learning. A wave of sadness overcame her as she looked about and wondered how much longer Eadulf's people would be remembered by their descendants, or whether they would vanish from memory like the Britons that once lived here before them. At least the Romans had left records and histories, like those written by Tacitus, whom she had been able to read. She knew from his writings the names of the Britons who had inhabited these very lands a few centuries before the Angles had arrived. The Iceni and the Trinovantes were once famous peoples but had now vanished. Kingdoms came and disappeared; empires certainly came and disappeared. That seemed the way of the world. Everything was so impermanent.

It was not long before they reached Ceol's Halh. Mother Notgide and her husband came out to meet them. Crída quickly explained what was wanted and, moments later, with their horses left in the charge of Mother Notgide and her husband, he was leading the way westward towards the darkness of the swampy forest with its curious rotting atmosphere and almost suffocating odours.

'Is this where you used to play?' Fidelma asked Crída in a disapproving tone.

'Not there yet.' Crída indicated eastward into the dark forest area. He glanced at Eadulf, who was quiet, his brow furrowed. 'I'm sure you recognise it now, Eadulf. Do you remember, the track into the forest marshlands? Do you remember our island in the marsh?'

The look on Eadulf's features indicated that he was struggling with his memories.

Fidelma recognised that a number of the trees along the way were those that thrived in damper and watery areas, such as alder and grey willows, even a few birches, and she also caught sight of clusters of ancient oaks. She could recognise much of the surrounding growth: wood sorrel, reeds and even rushes, which clustered into marshland areas.

'Do we need to go in there?' Beornwulf asked, speaking for the first time for a while. It was clear that the thane did not like the idea. 'What has a children's play area to do with this?'

Fidelma regarded him determinedly.

'It is why I suggested coming here,' she replied, unable to hide her irony.

'The wetlands, even among the marsh-loving trees, are not a pleasant environment,' the thane replied.

'Are there wild animals that I should be warned against?' Fidelma asked Crída. 'What was the name of this island that you told me about?'

Crída replied, 'I told you Snaca-aeg. Snake's Island. So long as they are not threatened, those reptiles do not attack. It is a responsive action. Water voles, mice, shrews and even otters prefer to keep themselves to themselves. The creatures you have to be wary of are the flying creatures: the insects that bite, even those that crawl can dig into your skin and leave infections. Often we would have to come out here and leap into the river. You remember that, don't you, Eadulf?'

Eadulf expression showed he would have preferred not to engage in these memories of his childhood.

'I also warn you, lady,' Crída shrugged, 'to ignore flowers and pretty flowering growths like frog orchid. Even water parsnips are tempting to bend down to touch, but that can result in being bitten by inhabiting insects.'

'Are you sure this visit to the marsh is essential to resolving these murders, Fidelma?' Werferth asked, seeming to back up Beornwulf. 'It's not a place to go wandering in.'

'We have a guide and I think Eadulf's memory will come back once we start in. We are looking for the mound on which Eadulf and Crída played as boys.'

Beornwulf shook his head in bewilderment. 'I don't see it. What do you expect to find there?'

'An answer,' she replied, exasperated by their prevarications.

'It is many years since I have wandered this path,' Eadulf confessed. 'My memory might not be as good as it once was but . . .'

'But I remember we used to mark certain trees by cutting into them,' Crída said.

'With the passing of the years I would imagine that the weather will have eliminated signs of childhood.'

'A possibility,' Crída agreed light heartedly. 'But we won't know until we set off.'

Fidelma remembered how Brother Ator had led them into Toft Monachorum.

'I understand,' she said. 'How shall we proceed through the swamp?'

'I suggest that I go first,' Crída replied. 'Beornwulf should follow. Then you, lady, Eadulf, and finally the lord Werferth.'

'So we are looking for some hill?' Werferth queried.

'It is more of a large mound, rising dryly from the marsh. There are a few oaks growing on it.'

'This place you called Snaca-aeg?' Fidelma asked.

'Snake's Island?' Beornwulf muttered. 'That does not sound inviting.'

'That is why I have my stick, my lord, and will walk in front,' Crída agreed with a thin smile. 'Those creatures, as you know, are shy of man's footfall and will slither off into the marshes or into high grass. If we don't bother them, they will avoid us. That is why I will lead the way to herald our passage. Are we ready?'

Fidelma noticed that Werferth and Beornwulf both eased the swords in their sheaths before they indicated they were prepared.

'We will enter here.' Crída pointed and began to move into the darkened woodland. For Fidelma, it was as if they had passed through a door from the bright, warm sunlight into a dark, gloomy cavern as the trees seemed to shut out sunlight and warmth. What she was unprepared for was the stagnant smell of the marshes whose odours were so foul that she felt nauseous within moments. Every time she took a breath it was as if she were inhaling a cold, foul wetness that created a coarse, rotten taste in her mouth. She was aware of buzzing insects hitting against her face like little pellets and after a few futile gestures she realised it was impossible to drive them away by merely waving her hands.

'It's worse than I recall when I was a boy,' Eadulf muttered loudly.

'So you are beginning to remember?' Crída called. 'You've been away a long time. Your skin has probably been softened in calm foreign climes so that you are going to feel the ticks, mites and bugs of this place.'

'Do not worry, lady,' Beornwulf called to Fidelma, who was also looking uncomfortable. 'Mother Notgide is one brought up with the healing balms. She mixes extraordinary unguents and salves from thyme, mint and honey, which will calm these bites. When we leave, which I hope will be presently, we will see that you are well treated. In fact, we could all do with the treatments.'

Fidelma muttered her thanks and began to regret that she had insisted on this expedition. Perhaps she should have waited outside the forest wetlands and let the others go in and examine the land. But in an investigation she could not delegate to anyone what she was not prepared to undertake herself. She set her jaw tight with tightened lips to proceed onwards into the fetid gloom.

She thought she had been careful in preparing herself, by putting on strong leather boots that she had had made for her by the best shoemaker in Cashel; boots of brown tanned leather called *cuaran*, which had seven folds or layers of hide to protect the feet. However, she could already feel the squelching mud of the swamp seeping in through the joints; cold and discomforting to the feet. She thought she was well acquainted with the bog lands of her own country but this was different. The entire area was without significant hills and certainly no mountains. It seemed to be a place that had just risen from the seabed or that was about to vanish into it.

It occurred to her again that this was not her country and it could never be a place where she could settle. She wondered why so many of her people, converted to the New Faith, had left their land to come to this strange flat country, giving up the luxuriant green meadows, the tall mountains and protective granite barriers that kept the sea at bay. It was not logical. Now, it seemed, the fanaticism of the dictates from Rome were more against them than in the days when they were of the Old Faith. She wondered how they would survive.

She hesitated and then her mind adjusted back to the realities of being in the dark swamplike forest, following her guides in the putrid murkiness. She realised how much she longed to be in her brother's secure fortress in the land of her own people. In doing so she was surprised to realise she had begun to feel an understanding and sympathy for Eadulf and, at the same time, to hope that somehow she was making a mistake. In spite of her logical mind, she was hoping that she was wrong in her deduction.

The path twisted and turned, and she realised that it was not the distance that took such a time but the way the path meandered back and forth. It was something like the river that had misled them on the way to Cnobheres Burg. What was it called? The Wahenhe, weaving and looping, so that she had not realised that they had crossed it twice until she had been told.

She could not resist calling out, 'Are we on the right track?'

'I think so,' Eadulf replied. 'I have spotted one or two marks on the trunk of trees, obscure now but clear enough. I remember making such marks to find my way when I was a lad.'

'True,' Crída confirmed at the front. 'We are near the place now.'

In front of them the overgrowth seemed less clustered and there was more light. The trees and undergrowth were thinning.

'The ground of this path seems firmer,' Werferth muttered.

To Fidelma, with her wet, mud-encased boots, it still felt soft and squelchy. However, she did detect a slight rise in the path.

Then Crída gave a shout of triumph. 'There ahead! A clearing!'

GRAVE OF THE LAWGIVER

Through the trees Fidelma could see there was a large opening of light as if the trees were making a large circle. Then she could see a mound rising until it became clear that it was a small oval hillock. It rose up above the flat marshlands, almost devoid of growth other than flat grass. She knew that probably rabbits or other creatures kept the verdure low and level. Yet on it, not exactly on the summit of the mound but to one side, were two leaning oak trees, looking ancient and gnarled, and twisting and entwining one another like anxious lovers. There the branches spread in a curious fork and on this they could see the strange shape of a shelter.

Crída gave a cry of elation. 'See it, Eadulf?'

Eadulf uttered a long, soft exhalation of breath. 'I see it,' he replied. 'Our tree house! It still stands after all these years. A miracle!'

Crída moved forward rapidly.

'Indeed, our old tree house where we used to come and play and pretend there was no one else in the world. It still stands and . . .' He suddenly halted and beat the ground before him with his stick, not as if he were aiming at anything but as if to make a vibration on the earth.

'Be careful,' he called. 'It's midday, the hill is warm and that's perfect to entice certain friends out to bask in the sunlight. So watch out.'

Beornwulf, in front of Fidelma, was looking on the ground.

'Careful where you step, lady. Crída means that there might be snakes about.'

'They usually vanish when they sense the presence of people,' Werferth assured her. 'That's why Crída thumps on the ground with his stick. Snakes sense the vibration and slither off. But you need to watch where you tread, just in case.'

Behind her Eadulf muttered apologetically, 'This is why we called it Snake's Island. Snaca-aeg. But according to the Old

Faith, snakes are our protectors. They were said to be the children of Eormenwyrm, the Great Worm, whose breath was poison and bite was venomous to those who dared attack the creators of the Nine Worlds. So as long as we did not harm them, they would protect us. Thus, we were never harmed.'

She became aware that Crída had suddenly halted and was staring across the mound to the oaks. She followed his gaze. Something was hanging from one of the lower branches. It was a rope ladder attached to a branch above, no more than the height of two tall men, where the dark shape of the tree house was balanced. She realised there was a bundle of clothes at the foot of the rope ladder, No; not clothes. With a growing coldness she realised it was a body, hanging upside down. One foot seemed to be caught in one of the rungs, the foot suspended a distance above the ground, above the bundle of clothes. So the body hung head downwards on the ground.

Crída moved forward to what was now seen to be a corpse with a profanity that was stifled in his throat.

Fidelma saw Eadulf tense and then move forward and go to his knees beside the body. Then he let out a gasping sob. She moved forward to him. She already guessed who it was lying lifeless on the ground.

It was Crída who breathed the name.

'Wulfrun!'

CHAPTER TWENTY

Fidelma reached forward and touched Eadulf's shoulder. 'Is this your young sister?' It was an unnecessary question but she felt, in her legal mind, confirmation was necessary.

'I have not seen her in more than seven years.' Eadulf was staring at the body as if in denial. 'I hardly recognise her.'

'Eadulf,' she spoke quietly, 'my heart is with you at this time. However, there is something you must do, for only you, in this company, can do it. I have called upon you as my partner for all these years, for your ability and knowledge of medical things. Will you use your skills and tell me how she came by her death?'

Eadulf looked up at her. His eyes were dry but the muscles around his mouth and jaw were trembling.

They all stood back as Eadulf bent forward to the corpse. It seemed to free the tightened muscles in his neck and shoulders to relax as he formed a new concentration.

'There is redness and bruising on the head and arms, some on the leg on the ground,' he began in a hollow voice. 'There is swelling; lumps are prominent. I can see some discoloration and swelling of the lips, which are open, and I can see the gums and tongue, which are also swollen. On the cheek I perceive bite marks.'

'Bite marks caused by what?' prompted Fidelma.

It was Crída who answered her. 'She has been bitten, not only once but several times, by vipers.'

Fidelma turned her gaze back to Eadulf. 'Is this the work of the one poisonous snake you told me that your country has?'

'It is the work of a viper or several vipers,' he replied in a taut voice.

'Several? How could this be? Was she not a strong, healthy woman?'

'I remember she was always a sickly child. That was because of her birth. My mother was ill and died bearing her. Perhaps there was something inherited. I have not been cursed with that problem but I remember my mother always had illness and fever when she was stung by a bee. There was swelling and redness, then she passed into a fever. It could be the same reaction that brought illness and death to her just after she gave birth.'

Crída was shaking his head. 'But we all knew that snakes avoided us when we were children. We knew that they did not attack without provocation. So we did not provoke them. How could it be that Wulfrun was attacked, and not by one but at least two or even three vipers? There are bites on the face, bites on the arm and on the leg. This does not make any sense.'

Beornwulf was staring down at the corpse reflectively.

'I think I see how,' he offered, turning to Eadulf. 'Did your sister know about this place?'

It was Crída who again replied.

'I showed it to her once, just after I had finished my argument with Athelnoth when he dismissed my proposal to marry. And we both agreed it was an excellent hideout, if she ever needed it. She had fierce arguments with her uncle even when she was small.'

Beornwulf glanced to where the foot of the dead girl was still caught in the rope ladder. He turned to Fidelma.

'Therefore the girl knew this place and knew, with the right precautions, she could hide here, up in that tree house. She must have slipped, climbing down . . .'

'I am afraid this was an accident,' Fidelma agreed. 'I had begun to suspect that Wulfrun had been hiding somewhere after the night that Athelnoth and his servant Osric were killed and the house set ablaze. We will discuss all that later. I think this morning, she was descending by the rope ladder and somehow caught her foot, lost her balance and fell down. With evil luck, she fell on a poisonous snake, which struck out at her in defence from a perceived attack. It bit her on the cheek. She threshed about in pain, which caused other serpents to bite her arm and leg. With her foot caught, she could not free nor defend herself. Eadulf has said, the result of a sickly condition being exposed to so much venom caused a reaction to which she succumbed and she died. The heart was poisoned or some other toxic issue took the life from her. Would that not be your diagnosis, Eadulf?'

Eadulf slowly rose to his feet and looked down at the corpse of his young sister. His eyes were still dry but grief etched his features. He exhaled in a long, anguished breath.

'Your reason seems to be logical,' he muttered.

'If you will unloose her foot,' Fidelma instructed, 'my duty as a *dálaigh* is for me to climb up the rope ladder and check our supposition that she has been hiding here for some time. Oh, and please maintain a watch for any more of these venomous slithering creatures. We will have to carry her body out of here.'

While Eadulf and Crída joined in freeing and laying out the body, Beornwulf and Werferth stamped about the mound, making sure the vipers knew of their presence and could resort into their natural wary, retiring states.

Meanwhile Fidelma, probably to the surprise of those that did not know of her physical dexterity, grabbed hold of the rope ladder and swung quickly up to the makeshift tree house. It was immediately clear her supposition was correct and, from the items she saw, the girl must have spent some time hiding there. Fidelma noticed the construction had been renovated over a period. There were blankets, a lantern, jugs for water, some discarded clothing, and straw baskets in which were some remains of food. There were even a few texts in Latin and a carved emblem of a fish nailed to the tree. Below it, on a makeshift shelf, was a slim-bladed knife. It had been sharpened recently. The handle was a simple one of wood with the image of a fish carved delicately on it. Fidelma took this and managed to push it into the leather sheath with her own knife at her belt. She glanced around and shook her head sadly. The word 'misguided' formed on her lips.

She looked down and called to Eadulf.

'You should come up to be a witness to this. Stay there and hold the ladder steady while I come down. Then I shall do the same for you when you climb up.'

After Eadulf had climbed up, he did not stay long. His look was just cursory and then he rejoined her on the ground.

Fidelma turned to the others.

'As Eadulf will witness, the girl had been in the tree house for some time, presumably since the night of the fire and deaths at her uncle's house. I think she might have been using it for longer and that someone helped her keep the construction in good order.' She looked at Crída.

'Not I,' he said immediately. 'I showed her this when she was a young girl but have not been here since.'

Fidelma produced the knife she had taken. 'I removed only this. A knife with a fish engraved on it. That is a Christian symbol. We will compare it with the knife Beornwulf has kept that was used to kill Athelnoth.'

'The same symbol is carved on a piece of wood nailed to the tree,' Eadulf added.

'We will take the body back to the township,' Fidelma continued. 'This afternoon, as I have promised before, I will attempt

GRAVE OF THE LAWGIVER

to explain what has happened here. We need Crída to guide us back while perhaps Beornwulf and Werferth will carry the body. I will follow them with Eadulf. Hopefully, we shall be protected front and back from these poisonous creatures. Does that meet with approval?'

There were no objections.

It seemed to Fidelma that their exit from the wetland forest was much quicker than their entrance, even carrying the body. It seemed hardly any time before they burst out of the gloomy forest into the bright sunlight of midday.

As they were emerging beyond the tree line, Fidelma remembered what Crída had said about the desire to jump into the river to cleanse their bodies when they emerged. She felt that overwhelming desire now.

Then she saw the old woman.

The Widow Eadgifu was hobbling along by the aid of a carved oak stick, with a basket slung over her shoulder. She stopped abruptly and looked from one to another, examining their faces, and then her eyes fell on the body. Not by a flicker did her expression change.

'She does not need your food now, Widow Eadgifu,' Fidelma told her in a sad tone.

The old woman exhaled with a long tremulous sigh, her shoulders sinking.

'So she has finished her snake dance?' she asked.

'The snake dance is over,' Fidelma replied solemnly. 'For her, at any rate. But for some of us that dance must go on until we understand its purpose. Only when we realise its meaning can we step aside from the dance.'

Widow Eadgifu looked at her with narrowed eyes.

'Are you of the adept, Hibernian?' she whispered.

'I am proficient in what I do,' Fidelma returned, 'but if you mean am I one skilled in the mysteries of the mind, I have glimpses as when a curtain is drawn aside. Usually, it is like trying to view and describe a person's countenance through a piece of sacking pressed closely to the eye. It can never be perfect and sometimes the truth is never known. I shall send someone to bring you to the thane's Hall this afternoon when I shall try to remove some of that curtain to reveal the darkness beyond.'

'But at least she has had her short time dancing with the snakes. Inevitably, those who dance with the snakes are consumed by them. I shall be waiting for my journey to Éormensyll to be welcomed to the care of Wena, Fríg and Neorde. My time in this world of *Hélham* will soon be over.'

With that the old woman turned and began to limp back down the road towards Seaxmund's Ham.

They spent a little time at Ceol's Halh, where the body of the girl was placed in a boat, which Crída and Werferth had volunteered to transport down to Seaxmund's Ham. Before that, they all bathed in the soothing cold waters of the river before Mother Notgide treated their skins with some of the balm she had prepared to soothe and heal the various bites and discomfiture caused by the midges. Beornwulf decided to ride back ahead of them so that he could make preparations. This left Fidelma and Eadulf to ride back together.

'I presume that your sister will be interred at midnight tonight, as is the custom?' Fidelma asked to open the conversation.

'It is not always a custom followed,' Eadulf replied solemnly. 'But I know Beornwulf will do what is for the best.'

'Then I have to tell you that early tomorrow, Eadulf, I shall be heading to the sea port, Domnoc-wic. I will try to find a ship to get back to my home.'

Eadulf looked at her blankly. 'So soon?' he asked in a tone bereft of emotion.

'This afternoon, when I give my report to Beornwulf, as thane, it will be your prerogative to disagree with me. But I am sure logic will prevail. I have said, as soon as this matter is resolved, I cannot wait to get back to my . . . to our home and our son. I will ask Werferth if he will escort me to that port, partly as protection and partly to help me negotiate a passage. Even in different circumstances, I see no future in this country after the people obey the results of this council at The Stag's Ford. Of course, it depends how the decisions are implemented.'

'So soon?' muttered Eadulf again with a shake of his head.

'I think I have given you enough time to consider my thoughts. For myself I have no wish to stay. The choice is yours. If you desire to remain here, it is your decision. I will regret it, for I feel that you have become a part of me and my family. I thought you might have felt the same, irrespective of the child we share. But something happened – I don't know what. You started to reject our way of life, my family, and were drawn here.'

Eadulf did not respond for a short while. Then he shrugged.

'You are right, Fidelma. I started to feel a strange emotional stirring some time ago – feelings for the place I grew up, the culture that shaped my thoughts, the family I believed that I had . . .' He paused. 'I felt things as if they were like sirens that seemed to be calling me until I knew that I had to come here. You see, I always felt a foreigner in your land – not just in your land, but wherever we travelled. When your brother legally adopted me, under your Brehon laws, it stopped many people making the inevitable comment. But I believe they still regarded me as a foreigner in spite of your laws. So much I wanted to strike out and say: I am as good as you; my family is as good as yours . . . I have my pride, traditions and culture, too.'

'I am sure that I never gave you reason to think otherwise—'

'Not you, not you,' he interrupted. 'In fact, it was no one specifically, just a feeling of being an alien in a strange place. Perhaps I made too much of it. Now I have come to my home and realise a sharp reality. I have become an alien here. I now have to deal with it. I will deal with it later on this afternoon. I suspect I know what you are going to say in your summation and I also suspect I will agree with all you say. I will wait until you say it.'

'You don't feel like considering our relationship before that or whether there is a future for us?'

'Our judgement is an important one, Fidelma. So let us wait until the pronouncement you make before I can clear my mind. A clear mind is essential to such decisions.'

'Is the mind ever clear?' she mused. 'A mind is always filled with thoughts that one accepts or rejects, depending on judgement of emotion and time. For my part, I cannot envision the future without you.'

Eadulf glanced at her quickly and his jaw tightened for a moment.

'I do not make this situation out of self-delusion, Fidelma. It seems some demons have gripped my soul and twisted it this way and that. Am I responsible for my parents' deaths and now my sister's death as well? I just don't understand how these events have been put into place.'

'You think that you are responsible by having chosen to follow the teachings of Fursa and his brothers when you were young, when they came to preach the New Faith here? That is talking "ifs", and you can comfort your mind by inserting an "if" in anything you want. An "if" is the most deceptive word in any language.'

'I shall listen to your summing up. I know it is going to be hard for me to accept it. Perhaps this is what the Wyrd, the Fates, have meant for me all along.'

Fidelma frowned. 'I thought that we both shared a belief in the philosophies of Pelagius? Did he not teach that nothing was preordained and that we are responsible for all our actions? Whether we go to heaven or hell, the decision lies with us. The decision might be for good or evil, but it is our decision alone. We can change our destiny, Eadulf. Your thoughts may have been shaken for some reasons, but remember: whatever you decide you are the master of the stream of your life.'

It was mid-afternoon by the time they had all gathered in the main room of Beornwulf's Hall. Fidelma had suggested to Ardith how the seating should be laid out so that it was comfortable enough to remind her of being in a traditional Brehon's court. Beornwulf and Werferth would sit as if judges, being the only officials of the community. Fidelma sat to their right alongside Eadulf so that he could be called on for interpretation or advice if needed. Opposite was Ardith, who sat with quill and vellum like a scribe. Fidelma was surprised that she had learnt the art of writing. In what would have been the well of the court were Crída, Wiglaf the farmer, Widow Eadgifu and Mother Elfrida. Mother Notgide and her husband Scead sat close by. There was no one else who could play an intimate role in the proceedings, for neither had a replacement for the office of *gerefa* been proposed, nor had Abbot Aecci yet appointed any successor to Brother Boso or Brother Ator to represent the Faith.

'This is an unusual proceeding,' Beornwulf said, turning his gaze to Fidelma, when he saw all was ready. Fidelma was certainly not concerned about the legality of the matter according to the laws of the Angles. Her concern was just presenting the facts as she had deduced them.

'Eadulf assured me that you have the powers to assess the evidence as thane of this town.'

'Because of this, I need to record a few words, and to do this I have asked my wife Ardith to act as what the Latins called a *tabellio* – a recorder of matters in writing, which art has been adopted by the Witan to whom this report will be taken by Werferth. If there is an objection, say so.'

There was none. Beornwulf continued.

'Eadulf is of a family of a hereditary *gerefa* or lawgiver of this township and is the only one among us who can guide us on the law of our people. However, Eadulf has relinquished that role for this hearing because of his involvement. The lady Fidelma will present the case, being a qualified lawyer of her own culture. If she does not act totally contrary to our laws, we will accept her summation of the events and rule on guilt or innocence. To that end we acknowledge that she is a senior lawyer in her own country where I am told she is famous, alongside Eadulf, for her ability to resolve mysteries and make riddles appear simple. Kings accept her solutions to conundrums. So today, she will give us her solution and views. I, as your thane, will consider whether this matter must be taken further. Do I hear any protest?'

For the second time there was none.

Beornwulf motioned with his hand for Fidelma to commence. She rose from her seat and inclined her head to Beornwulf as a matter of respect as if she were in a normal Brehon court.

'This matter started on the day before Eadulf and I arrived at Seaxmund's Ham to visit his family. His family being his uncle Athelnoth and his younger sister Wulfrun. We had just arrived at the sea port of Domnoc-wic. There is no need to remind you of those facts. I would merely add that Athelnoth and his servant had been stabbed to death using a small dagger on whose handle was a symbol of a fish. Beornwulf took that in evidence and I have compared it with a similar one found this morning.'

She paused briefly. There was silence except for the scratching of Ardith's quill pen.

'Eadulf's younger sister Wulfrun had been placed in the care of her uncle Athelnoth until she was of age. That night she disappeared and time was spent trying to find her, as it was initially thought that she had been kidnapped. We found her this morning.'

Once more, she paused and glanced round to ensure everyone was following her. Her gaze finally rested on Eadulf, who sat, head low, tragedy moulding his features.

'As you will know, when we found her, she was newly dead. Her death was an accident. She had fallen while descending from a tree and fell among several reptiles you call vipers, venomous creatures that, thankfully, you do not find in my country. Reacting to a perceived attack, they bit her several times. Being of a frail disposition, she was dead in a short time.

'Eadulf has told me that her mother and thus Wulfrun were susceptible to serious illness from bee stings and, therefore, we might conclude, snake bites. The mother died of a bee sting. It is one of those ironic turns of fate that Wulfrun met her death in a similar way, and just before we found her.'

Of those sitting before her, Fidelma saw it was only Widow Eadgifu who registered no bewilderment at her assertion.

'Let me sum up in simple terms. Wulfrun killed her uncle, perhaps stabbing him before she stabbed his servant, who had been witness to her attack. She was not so far into her rage that she overlooked to eliminate all witnesses. It was Wulfrun who stabbed Athelnoth with a short knife bearing a carved religious emblem of a fish. As I say, this Beornwulf has. In her hideaway was its companion – a weapon exactly the same.'

She turned to Beornwulf with a prearranged silent instruction. He leant to the table and removed a piece of cloth revealing two similar thin-bladed knives.

Fidelma turned to Mother Notgide. 'I think you can tell us something about these.'

'It was Brother Boso who showed me the four knives,' she replied. 'He said they were very ancient and he had been given them by someone religious who had returned from Rome. He told me that he was going to give them as a gift to Athelnoth.'

Beornwulf was puzzled. 'Why such a gift?'

'The symbol of the fish is an early Christian symbol. It is a secret sign first used by Christians for identification with one another when they were being persecuted in the Roman times.'

'But fish symbols make no sense to me. I thought the symbol of the Christians was a cross, symbolising how the Romans executed those they judged as criminals.'

'Let me explain it this way,' Fidelma said. 'The dominant language of the first Christian communities was Greek. Who was their central godhead?'

'Jesus Christ,' Beornwulf responded.

'The early Christians were persecuted by the Romans. So how does "Jesus Christ, Son of God and Saviour" translate into Greek? How would these Christians disguise their religion and keep a secret way of identifying one another?'

'We are not all scholars,' protested Crída.

'They took the first letters of that title and formed the acronym ICHTHYS . . . and this also spells the Greek word for . . .?'

No one seemed to have knowledge.

'Fish!' Fidelma declared firmly. 'So when you saw a fish carved somewhere you would know that it identified Christians. So Mother Notgide witnessed Brother Boso saying he would give those knives to Athelnoth, perhaps persuading him to be tolerant of the New Faith for the sake of his niece.'

'You are saying that Brother Boso's gift to Athelnoth was used to kill him and his servant?' Beornwulf asked.

'One of them was. Another was given to Brother Ator and that was used to kill Brother Boso. Another he used to kill Stuf. The fourth one was found in Wulfrun's hideaway.'

Beornwulf cleared his throat.

'Are you placing all these knives in the hands of Wulfrun? Are you suggesting—'

'What of the murder of Brother Boso?' Crída interrupted. 'That clearly must have been done by Brother Ator. We have Ator returning here and, for some reason, he killed Stuf? The wound could have been made with the self-same knife.'

'Brother Ator did kill Boso because he was persuaded to,' Fidelma replied calmly. 'But Brother Ator was already dead by the time Stuf was killed . . . killed by the hand that killed Athelnoth.'

'But you said Brother Ator killed Brother Boso,' Werferth said. 'He returned to Seaxmund's Ham and was himself killed. So who are you now claiming was responsible for the deaths?'

'I will explain as simply as I can. Crída first set me on the course with his outward animosity towards Brother Ator. Crída thought he was in love with Wulfrun and he went to see Athelnoth, who refused his proposal. Wulfrun was uninterested in him except as a friend. She had another ambition than to marry, and encouraged someone – Brother Ator – she could use to further her idea of joining a religious community.'

'She did not love Ator!' Crída protested immediately.

'She did not want to be confined in this township,' Fidelma went on, ignoring him. 'She wanted to join a religious community and become an abbess with power. It was power she wanted and not to serve religion. From her birth status she could not obtain power in any other way. She thought she might use Brother Ator as a path to her objective. She fell for all the lies that Brother Ator was telling her because they bolstered her vanity and self-importance. Thus encouraged, Brother Ator went to Athelnoth, but Athelnoth also refused him. Wulfrun was more than upset.

'We had heard from Widow Eadgifu, Mother Elfrida and many others that Wulfrun, as young as she was, was of a fiery temperament, given to unusual bursts of anger. Her uncle had successfully thwarted her plans. That night, returning from hearing the news, from Brother Ator at Ceol's Halh, that Athelnoth had rejected him, and therefore her ambition, she saw her uncle had thwarted her. Their disagreement turned into an argument. The argument developed and Wulfrun lost control. Some of you know that loss of control could be dangerous. Crída certainly witnessed her rage. In her anger she grabbed one of the knives Brother Boso had presented to Athelnoth and stabbed him. The servant who witnessed this was stabbed just to keep his silence. Then she set fire to Athelnoth's house, hoping that would destroy any evidence and provide a false lead.

'Two things happened – Mede and one his men had called to question Athelnoth, as lawgiver, about their task of trying to track down Princess Athelthryth. Mede's presence there led to a false trail. The king of Northumbria's search for the escaped Princess Athelthryth added another layer to the mystery. This is now resolved. I learnt that Athelnoth and Brother Boso engaged in messages written in an old form of your language understandable to learned Franks, Jutes, Angles and Saxons. It is called *futhorc*. Werferth knew it, but the point was that Athelnoth and Boso corresponded in it. Moreover, Athelnoth corresponded with someone else in Northumbria who knew it and I am guessing that this was Aebbe, the abbess of Coludi, who gave sanctuary to Athelthryth to escape King Ecgfrith. Perhaps messages were sent in this archaic writing to Athelnoth and Brother Boso in order to help to get the princess back to the Isle of Eels. Mede tracked this correspondence and came to see the *gerefa* too late to question him because Wulfrun had just killed him. Mede then turned his attention to following Brother Boso, whom he saw at Cnobheres Burg. He extracted from him the information that the princess was on her way back to the Isle of Eels. But he did not kill him. It was Brother Ator who killed Brother Boso, using one of the knives that Wulfrun had given him. He thought that Boso knew or suspected the truth behind the killing. Brother Boso knew the temper that Wulfrun could exhibit and had mentioned it.'

There was a curious silence in the room.

'We know from Werferth the fate of Mede and his men,' she

continued. 'They were killed at Saegham while trying to get to the Isle of Eels.'

'Why did Wulfrun go into this extreme of hiding?' Beornwulf demanded.

'There are some possibilities. It could be that Mede had seen her setting the fire, for he and a companion were witnessed riding away from the direction of Athelnoth's house at the time of the blaze. Mede probably told Boso when they met at the Oxen Ford the next morning. There was the possibility he told Brother Ator. It was when Brother Ator realised that Brother Boso had recognised the knife that killed Athelnoth and was linking it to the knives that he had given him, and these might incriminate Wulfrun, that he decided to join us in following Brother Boso. His intention was to kill Boso to stop him identifying the knives, or silence him if Mede had identified Wulfrun to Boso. Brother Ator learnt from us about the meeting at the Oxen Ford. He meant to kill Boso and then return to join Wulfrun. I am inclined to think that he feared that Brother Boso knew far more than he did.'

She paused to regard the silent figure of Widow Eadgifu.

'Widow Eadgifu was one of those who alerted me to Wulfrun's character. She had known Wulfrun had displayed behaviour that was selfish and not with a normal perception of reality. Her ambition was dominant to the point where she was insensitive of everyone else. Yet Widow Eadgifu tried to be supportive to her. After all, her mother had died in childbirth; her elder brother had converted to the New Faith and left to study in Hibernia, and not long after that her father had died. Her uncle Athelnoth was of the same, dominant personality. That only increased Wulfrun's own inclination to self-absorption and vanity.

'Widow Eadgifu was always supportive and kindly to her, and even with her confusion brought on by age, Widow Eadgifu remained supportive. She said as much, but in ancient symbols that I did not readily understand. Right from the start she had said that Wulfrun had gone dancing with snakes.'

'What of Crída's role?' Werferth demanded. 'He was the one, not Eadulf, who led us to her hiding place.'

Fidelma held up a hand before Crída could return an outraged protest.

'That very fact showed he was not party to this. It was Brother Ator who knew the truth, and Wulfrun used him to protect her until she was ready to escape from this neighbourhood to somewhere she could fulfil her ambitions. When Brother Ator returned, it threw her plan awry. He had to be eliminated. Going back to the night of the fire when Wulfrun was visiting Brother Ator at Ceol's Halh, she knew that Stuf knew about Mede, Mede meeting Boso, and that Ator knew of it. Maybe she thought Stuf was waiting to use it to some advantage to himself. Now, she thought, here was an opportunity to get rid of two problems; two problems in her eyes.

'When she learned Brother Ator was back, she went to his cabin in the dead of night and killed him, leaving him to be found in his boat. Her madness was overwhelming now. We are told of hallucinations, of persecution by her uncle and other matters that who knows where it would have stopped? Anyway, she used Stuf's boat to go downriver and kill Stuf. How she managed to escape after that I am not sure as I do not know your rivers, marshes and waterways. I am sure she used them.'

'Are you saying that she was mad?' Beornwulf asked.

'She had been developing her curious views of the world since she was very young. We are not dealing with a normal logic. She had absolutely no compassion nor feeling. It is as if she had shed the fact that she was human. I would say that it was an illness. After killing Brother Ator and Stuf, she returned to hide. Widow Eadgifu was to let her know when we had departed. Then she would have left and searched for a place where she was not known. Her plan was probably to make it to some community where she thought she could build some powerbase as she believed was her due. She had once suggested Aldred's abbey.'

Fidelma looked at Eadulf, still sitting with hunched shoulders as if in a defensive mood at what he was hearing.

'Do you have any further comments? Is there anything you disagree with?'

'I am afraid there is nothing I can disagree with,' he said slowly, as if he had trouble finding the words. It seemed as if all emotions had been drained out of him.

'Do you agree with what Fidelma has said?' Beornwulf demanded.

'I am afraid I have to accept my young sister was a disturbed person,' Eadulf replied softly, forming his words carefully. 'I share some of the responsibility. She might have been different if I had not left my home years ago to follow the New Faith, which guided me to Hibernia. I know our mother died just after Wulfrun was born. I know it is now claimed that my father died, probably of grief, when I left. I put a lot of stress on his life for he wanted me to follow his path and became a *gerefa*, just as Athelnoth wanted Wulfrun to follow him. Maybe my father and then my uncle became too strict in her upbringing. I don't know. I know there are a lot of "ifs" in my thoughts. Fidelma said "if" is the most damaging and negative word in any language. Yet I am left with it as my inheritance and must try to make sense of it.'

Fidelma turned back to Beornwulf. 'That is the explanation I put forward, my lord. It is up to you to accept or reject it. If rejected, I can do no more. If accepted, it would judge you to have the ability to do the best for your community. Is there anyone who disagrees with this?'

Widow Eadgifu was stirring and raised her head to Fidelma. 'It is the truth as I know it; it is the truth as you say it.'

epilogue

In Fidelma's culture, it was usual to bury a corpse at midnight on the same day or the next day. It was a custom borne of the need for hygiene and cleanliness, but she had to remind herself that here the customs were usually different. However, Beowulf, with Eadulf giving the religious blessings, gave approval for the burial service to go ahead before midnight. It was decided that Wulfrun would be buried alongside her uncle Athelnoth, the law-giver. It occurred to Fidelma that it was a curious circumstance that the victim would have his murderer placed alongside him. There was even a sadder irony that Eadulf, as the relative of both victim and murderer, was the only ordained religious in the township who could conduct the ritual of the ceremony.

As the body of Wulfrun was interred, Fidelma realised it was the first time she had stood in the graveyard where Eadulf's family were buried. Rows of graves were aligned with the sunrise and sunset. As Werferth told her, it had been with the arrival of new settlers of Angles that the burial traditions in the area had changed. While the ancient tradition of the people had been inhumation, the Angles favoured the cremation of bodies whereby the ashes were deposited in clay urns and placed in rows. Only sometimes nowadays were bodies buried.

It was what happened after the funeral that concerned Fidelma.

GRAVE OF THE LAWGIVER

She had decided that as soon as it was dawn, it would be time for her to leave. She would ride to Domnoc-wic, find a boat, hopefully a *lers-longa*, as she knew them – a vessel designed for the high seas – to take her back to her own country. She had made her intention plain to Eadulf and left the decision to him as to whether he would accompany her or not. These last hours he had submerged himself in a deep melancholia that she found difficult to penetrate and so the brief exchanges were simply monosyllabic and one sided.

It was Werferth, who noticed the tension between them, to whom Fidelma turned in desperation for communication. She told him about the problems that had arisen between them and asked for an escort to the sea port. The warrior was sympathetic and agreed that, if nothing improved, he would be happy to take her.

'Life is never simple,' she reflected, when he asked for details. 'I can see some of what passes in his mind. For a long time he has built up an idea of his family and his home. It took such a shape that it grew out of proportion. He seemed to change, to build up an image of the importance of his own family, and he would regard this image with boastfulness. He was always trying to juxtapose it with my family, even when my brother, the king, tried to absorb him officially into the Eóghanacht, my family. It seemed that Eadulf preferred to cling to the image that he created of his own family. He took an excessive interest in the importance and abilities of his own people.'

Werferth understood immediately.

'So what happened here must have been devastating for him. I have known such people, who grow to love their own self-image. Some even try to overshadow others by their excess of self-importance and, what is more, they try to dominate others into believing in this image. But you say that this has only been a recent thing with Eadulf. I do not remember him being like this when you were here seven years ago.'

Fidelma agreed. 'It is something that came about only recently.'

'Perhaps it is but a passing phase in life?' Werferth suggested. 'Eadulf was young when he first left this township. First his mother died, and from something as mundane as a bee sting. Then his father, left with a young baby girl to raise, died too. We have learnt his father died of disappointment when Eadulf left to follow the new religion. His young sister was given to the care of Athelnoth. So was Eadulf suppressing his guilt? Maybe this grew from the need for self-justification.'

Fidelma stared at the warrior in surprise. Werferth read her look and gave a humorous grimace.

'Warriors are not all mindless killing folk, lady,' he remarked.

'I know you are the commander of your king's bodyguard, Werferth,' Fidelma acknowledged. 'Yet you have a way with words.'

'I am a member of the king's Witan, as well, and an adviser to the king must have some intelligence.' Werferth gave a subdued chuckle. 'I fear our Witan will be needing more wisdom in the coming months, lady.'

'Oh, you mean when the effects of Archbishop Theodoros' new rules and ideas about the New Faith take hold here?'

'Exactly so. Then much reliance will be placed on the Witan's advice,' Werferth confirmed.

'How exactly does this council function then?'

'The king is the ultimate power and that is the same for all the kings of Angles and Saxons. The king appoints and summons his own leading advisers, who sit on the Witan, his council of the wise. These wise men are the most powerful thanes and ealdormen of the kingdom. Recently, with the new religion, bishops are deemed to have a right to do so. As bishops are always from the noble classes, it does not change the situation.'

'Will there be war over that title, "Bretwalda"?' she asked.

'It is a war that will probably be fought out between Northumbria and Mercia. They are the strongest kingdoms now. The title is claimed when one of the kings becomes able to exert power over the whole island and is able to conquer all the kingdoms – the Angles and Saxons as well as the Britons. The title itself means "overlord of the Britons".'

Fidelma grimaced sourly. 'So war is inevitable, as you explained before?'

'The quest for land to conquer and settle is the driving force that brought us, the Jutes, the Angles and the Saxons, across the sea from our former territories. All of us came seeking land to conquer and settle, and so it will continue. It seems it is something we must do.'

'I hope that I'll find a ship in Domnoc-wic,' Fidelma suddenly remarked sadly, changing the subject.

'I am sure you will. I will be there to help you find it. There are plenty of merchant ships trading between here and the Frankish kingdoms, and even parts of Gaul that the Franks have not conquered. The further south you go, the more ships trade with your own land. I know, for I've spent many times in the great harbour of Gipeswic, as well as in Domnoc-wic, talking to the captains of these crafts.' He paused and smiled. 'I can make sure you can find the right ship and then I can take your pony back to Mul the trader.'

'That would be excellent.'

So it was that at first light, having said a farewell to all, except, sadly, to Eadulf, who, Fidelma was told, had been out walking most of the night and was nowhere to be found, she and Werferth set off with two bodyguards as escorts. It was cloudy and cold as she and Werferth passed by the Ceol's Halh and then the Oxen Ford, where they turned eastwards along the Mennesmer towards the sea. It had been a sombre period after they had left the farewell gathering. It was hard to dismiss morose goodbyes from those who came to see her and Werferth take the northern roadway, while nods were exchanged with Widow Eadgifu, Mother Elfrida, Wiglaf and even Mother Notgide.

She was shocked and disappointed that Eadulf had not even come to say goodbye. But she had said to him all that could be said. The rest was now up to him and it seemed he had made a decision. She submerged her sorrow and feeling of abandonment and set off with Werferth, trying to concentrate on reaching the deep-water port.

She tried not to think about how she had landed not that long ago with suffocating feelings of trepidation. Now her apprehensions had become a reality. But she must try to think positively. Soon, she hoped, she would be seeing her son Alchú with old Muirgen the nurse. There would be her brother Colgú and his new wife Gelgéis to give her comfort. Soon she would be home again. Soon she would be riding through the oak gates of her brother's fortress. Perhaps her anxieties would all evaporate at that time.

Werferth seemed to know what thoughts were in her mind for he maintained a companionable silence as they rode along the river path. Fidelma was oblivious now to the vast flat spaces of the copious wetlands; the sedges, rushes and mosses that spread under the big sky. As they proceeded eastward to the great sea, she didn't notice the placid deer standing under the watchful eyes of the antlered stags. The dominant movements in the skies were marsh harriers, never far from their breeding grounds, but neither they, nor even the curious cries of the distant gulls, racing up and down the shoreline in search of prey, disturbed her thoughts.

Her mind kept coming back to a central thought – how much was she to blame for this situation. Should she have taken more notice of her initial thoughts after she and Eadulf had met at the debate at Streoneshalh? It had been two years after they had first met that they had even agreed to enter the traditional trial marriage of a year and a day customary of her people. After that Fidelma had agreed to formally marry. Nothing had been rushed into and there had been much questioning on both sides. Alchú had been conceived during their trial period but they had never let that become a reason for their final decisions. Maybe she should have held out from making her own final decision for much longer. Maybe the enthusiasm and pressure for the marriage had all been from Eadulf and maybe his desperation to be married had come, not from feelings for her, but from his insecurity, which she was now witnessing.

Could that be possible? Was Eadulf's motivation to get married and settle not due to anything other than a desire to be settled somewhere? Just to belong? That was not the right reason to settle in any relationship.

She was plunging back into the dark bitterness of her thoughts when she looked about her and realised they were on the long straight road across the flat marshlands with only the sea in front. Soon they would have to turn slightly north towards the deep-water port of Domnoc-wic. It was at that moment when Werferth glanced over his shoulder.

'Rider coming up fast,' he called. He hesitated a moment staring. 'Why . . . it's Eadulf!'

Fidelma turned to look back at once. It was clearly Eadulf on the second dappled-grey pony. She tried to retain her composure but her heart began to beat wildly. She and Werferth reined in and waited as Eadulf came up, slowing and halting before them. He edged his mount nearer to Fidelma. He had a curious emotional expression on his pale face and was breathing stertoriously as if he, and not his horse, had been in pursuit.

'There is nothing for me here,' he finally said between breaths.

Fidelma tried to maintain a stony composure.

'And so?'

'I finally realise I want to go home to our son Alchú.' He paused a moment and added: 'To go home with you.'

'Home?' she asked, trying to suppress the emotion in her voice.

'Home,' he repeated emphatically. 'Home to Cashel.'